KT-195-920

Gill Sims

WHY MUMMY SWEARS

She's not angry.
She's just disappointed.

C334346881

HarperCollins*Publishers*
1 London Bridge Street
London SE1 9GF

www.harpercollins.co.uk

First published by HarperCollins*Publishers* 2018
This edition 2019

5 7 9 10 8 6 4

© Gill Sims 2018

Gill Sims asserts the moral right to be
identified as the author of this work

A catalogue record of this book is
available from the British Library

ISBN 978-0-00-828422-0

Printed and bound in Great Britain by
CPI Group (UK) Ltd, Croydon

All rights reserved. No part of this publication may be
reproduced, stored in a retrieval system, or transmitted,
in any form or by any means, electronic, mechanical,
photocopying, recording or otherwise, without the
prior written permission of the publishers.

MIX
Paper from
responsible sources
FSC™ C007454

This book is produced from independently certified FSC paper
to ensure responsible forest management.

For more information visit: www.harpercollins.co.uk/green

To AE and AT

CONTENTS

JULY

Monday, 18 July

I have one week till the summer holidays begin. I can't help but feel awfully jealous of the Famous Five's parents – not only did Julian, Dick and Anne's mama and papa simply bung them off on Aunt Fanny and Uncle Quentin at the slightest excuse, but Aunt Fanny was always sending them off to islands and moors and coves FULL OF CRIMINALS AND WRECKERS AND SMUGGLERS so that Uncle Quentin could work in peace at his inventing. I have frequently wondered if I could do similar, as I *did* once invent a very fabulous app that made splendid amounts of money for a little while, even if the app world is fickle and today's hit is forgotten tomorrow and no one buys it anymore. I'm sure I could probably do the same again if only I could just send the children to live outdoors and go feral for the summer (and stop faffing about and eating biscuits). As I recall, Uncle Quentin's inventions never even made any money, which was why he and Aunt Fanny were poor and had to look after the beastly cousins, which makes it doubly unfair that it is now so frowned upon to hand your children a bicycle and a packet of sandwiches on the first day of the holidays, and tell them not to come home till it's time to go back to school. Jane is eleven now, you see, and more than of an age for Famous Fiving. I did once wistfully suggest this to her, when we were in the middle of one of our frequent rows about why she is not allowed an Instagram account yet, and she pointed out the many illegalities with this plan and threatened to call Childline if I ever broached it again.

I am feeling particularly bitter about the expenditure the summer holidays necessitate, because I have been reading the Famous Five books with Peter, though somewhat against his will, as he informs me each night that he would much rather watch DanTDM than endure another chapter of marvellous Blyton-y japes, frolics and foiling of beastly common-criminal types. Jane has obviously point-blank refused to take part in any such babyish activity as being read to in the evening, and so we compromised with her promising to read something herself instead, which I felt was a perfectly reasonable offer, until after two chapters she announced that *Anne of Green Gables* was stupid and boring and why was Anne always wittering on about imagination and I shouted that Jane had no soul and was clearly a changeling as no child of mine would speak thus of Anne Shirley. Now I pretend not to know that she is watching YouTube make-up tutorials instead of wandering the enchanted lanes of Avonlea with Gilbert Blythe (who I still *totally* would, incidentally).

Peter, however, has not quite succeeded in breaking my spirit to the same extent as Jane, and so I am still forcing him to sit with me and roam Kirrin Island. I think he is going for a chemical-warfare option to get out of our reading sessions, though, as I swear he farts far more when he is supposed to be sitting and reading with me than he does normally, and that is saying something for a child who once proudly announced he had made his teacher feel sick with his flatulence. The chapter has had to be cut short once or twice due to my eyes watering.

In theory, this summer should be less fraught for me than previous ones, due to my possibly dubious decision to take voluntary redundancy three months ago. I'd had grand plans to become a top games and app designer, on the strength of creating an app, which I called *Why Mummy Drinks*, two years ago. Taking the redundancy seemed like a brilliant opportunity to have a bit of a financial cushion until I came up with the latest hit game. When I quit the old job, I had a plethora of brilliant ideas that I was quite sure I only needed time to make into something splendidly lucrative. But when I actually try to translate them into a game or an app, they're just a bit ... well, shit. Also, the fact that I am really, really rubbish at working from home and managing my time properly might have something to do with my lack of productivity, and after years of dreaming about escaping from the office it's actually quite lonely working at home by yourself with no one to talk to. I even find myself missing Jean from Shipping, who used to tell long and involved stories about the state of her gall bladder. Also, when you are at home all day by yourself, you eat a startling quantity of chocolate biscuits. So not only am I failing to achieve Great Things, and feeling lonely, I have gained a stone and am now alarmed by the size of my own arse every time I accidently catch sight of it in a mirror. I feel like one of those cardboard children's books *That's Not My Arse, It's Far Too Enormous* ...

Anyway, with the summer looming, I have been booking sports camps and childminder slots, and making complex childcare deals with friends so that we can all have some semblance of having our children looked after during the holidays AND be able to try to get some work done without spending vast sums of money. Obviously we will all end up spending vast sums of money anyway, as the children will require entertaining for the summer, as well as being fed at alarmingly close intervals, leaving me wondering how they cope when they are at school and can't constantly squawk for food, like starving baby starlings, beaks agape, begging for snacks.

Friday, 22 July

And they are done for the summer! All week the children have come tottering out of school, buckling under piles of tattered exercise books and dog-eared artwork, all of which is liberally sprinkled with glitter, now gently dusted over my house, and all of which apparently must be kept for posterity, because according to Jane, 'When I'm a famous social media influencer, Mummy, this could all be worth a fortune!' I am struggling to see how Jane's indifferent copy of Van Gogh's *Sunflowers*, which looks identical to every other child's in her class, is someday going to be of any value to anyone but me, but it seems that I will be trampling their dreams and casting their childhood aside if I bin any of it. Obviously, I am discreetly removing several pieces every night and chucking them in the outside bin, while lovingly claiming that everything is carefully stored in the attic.

Peter has also brought home his holiday homework – a small plant that must be kept alive during the holidays, and indeed nurtured over the coming year. Marvellous. I have a poor track record with plants. Even cacti shrivel and die at the touch of my black thumbs. I asked Peter if he knew what sort of plant it was, so I could purchase an emergency replacement if need be. Peter helpfully replied, 'A green plant, Mummy.' I'm not sure how much help that will be as I scour the garden centres of the land with a desiccated twig for reference. Perhaps it's my come-uppance for letting the class hamster make a break for freedom when I was allowed it home for the weekend when *I* was nine, and forcing my mother to tour every pet shop in town until she found a suitable replacement, as Hannibal was never seen again. Mum swore she could hear him scampering around at night for years afterwards, but I think that was only to stop me crying after I discovered Alphonso, her vicious Siamese cat, licking what looked like hamster fur off his chops and looking more pleased with himself than ever.

Monday, 25 July

The first day of the holidays. I suppose it could've been worse. I had a book called *The First Day of the Holidays* when I was little, about delinquent penguins who stole a motorbike and went joyriding and crashed it (no idea why penguins were stealing motorbikes), and there were at least no auto thefts or joyriding animals today. What there was, was a lot of moaning.

I had taken today off, thinking it would be nice for the children for us all to do something together on the first day. Jane demanded the cinema, Peter demanded Laser Quest, I declined both, insisting we were going to do something wholesome and fun. I had the children's best friends Sophie and Toby for the day too, as part of the complex childcare arrangements with my friend Sam (as a single father, Sam's childcare issues are possibly the most complicated of all my friends), and I brightly announced that perhaps it might be a lovely idea to go to a stately home and learn about some history.

'Booooorrrrring!' moaned my children, while Sophie and Toby clearly thought the same but at least were well enough brought up not to say so.

'Why do we have to do this? This is so crap,' huffed Jane.

'Mummy, can we take our iPads?' whimpered Peter.

'IT WILL BE FUN!' I bellowed. 'IT WILL BE INTERESTING AND EDUCATIONAL AND THE STUFF THAT HAPPY MEMORIES ARE MADE OF! And also it will go some way to me getting my money's worth from my very middle-class National Trust membership that your father keeps moaning on that I don't use enough.'

Of course, as soon as we got there I remembered why I don't use the flipping National Trust membership – because National Trust properties are full of very precious and breakable items, and very precious and breakable items don't really mix with children, especially not small boys. Where I had envisaged childish faces glowing with wonder as they took in the treasures of our nation's illustrious past, we instead had me shouting, 'Don't touch, DON'T TOUCH! FFS, DON'T TOUCH! I SAID DON'T TOUCH, DON'T CROSS THAT ROPE, DON'T SIT ON THAT, OH, JESUS CHRIST, OH, FML,' while stoutly shod pensioners tutted disapprovingly and drafted angry letters to the *Daily Mail* in their heads. Maybe I could design an app that you put on children's phones or iPods that can detect when they are in the vicinity of something expensive and breakable so it starts vibrating and sounds an alarm and squawks, 'DON'T TOUCH THAT!' to save parents the trouble. It would be useful in many situations, not just in National Trust houses – the china department of John Lewis, for example. Though if you are foolish enough to take children into a china department, then you probably deserve the inevitable carnage that will be left in your wake …

Because the children had managed to eat the lovingly packed picnic on the way there, as they were obviously 'starving' within three minutes of us leaving the house, I was forced to take them to the café for lunch. A self-service café with four children in tow is not an experience to be recommended. In theory, at eleven and nine the children should have been relatively self-sufficient, but in practice, complex tasks like standing in a queue, holding a tray or choosing what flavour of juice they wanted proved quite beyond them, so that by the time we sat down I think the entire county hated us. The pasta bake Jane had maintained she had to have and would definitely eat was immediately declared inedible, as she thought she saw a bit of red pepper and I *knew* she didn't like red pepper; Sophie burnt her mouth on her soup, despite me telling her to wait for it to cool down; Peter and Toby inhaled the contents of the children's lunchboxes that they had insisted they wanted in one mouthful and looked around expectantly for more, while I poured cold water down Sophie and scraped the mayonnaise off *my* sandwich for Jane and hissed, 'No, *no one* is having Coke,' promised crisps when we got home and resisted the urge to simply walk out of the café and bang my head repeatedly against the picturesque brick wall outside. Though I would probably have been told off for damaging National Trust property.

I provoked further shocked looks when I rallied the children to go by shouting, 'Right, come on then, you monstrous hell fiends.' I am still not sure whether the shock was due to me referring to the precious moppets as monstrous hell fiends, or the fact that they responded to the name.

How many more days of the holidays are there?

AUGUST

Thursday, 4 August

The children have been at Sports Camp this week. Sports Camps are a very good idea thought up by some sadistic bastard somewhere under the guise of providing fun for children and affordable childcare for parents in the holidays. If your idea of 'affordable' is approximately eleventy fucking billion pounds. And your idea of 'fun' is providing five different changes of clothes a day for all the different activities, including swimming kit that has to be rescued from their bags each night and washed and dried or else they will just leave it there to moulder and keep stuffing clean towels on top, because they are rancid beasts.

Every time I sign the children up to something like this I have secret hopes that they will discover their hidden talent and turn out to be a tennis/football/gymnastics virtuoso. So far this has not happened, as they seem to spend most of their time eating crisps before pleading for money for the vending machines afterwards, so that my darling poppets, who in theory should be worn out by a day of vigorous activity, are instead smacked off their tits on the energy drinks that they bought even as I howled, 'Just get Hula Hoops, sweetie, nothing else, I said Hula Hoops, no, don't open that can, DON'T OPEN THAT. Oh FML!'

Simon is in Madrid, doing whatever it is he does on his important business trips, which I suspect are not nearly as much hard work as he claims, given he gets to stay in a nice hotel (how I appreciated his text informing me he had been upgraded to a suite) and go out for nice dinners in actual restaurants, some of which don't even serve chips, and where he doesn't have to issue strict instructions to the staff about how there must be no sauce whatsoever allowed anywhere in the vicinity of the children's food because obviously terrible things will happen if their burgers are contaminated with anything as awful as mayonnaise or relish, although they will immediately douse them in a vat of ketchup, so they wouldn't taste the offending sauces anyway. I dream of hotels. I never got to go on fancy trips in the old job, but I had some vague idea that my new career as an app designer might involve me getting to go to conferences and possibly even conventions. Las Vegas seems to have a lot of those sorts of things, and I had visions of myself sending casual texts to Simon from there about what a good time I was having, probably in an upgraded suite, eating food with sauce. Instead, it is just me. And the biscuits. Staring hopelessly at a blank screen and wondering what the fuck I am going to do, and trying not to think about how almost all the redundancy money has now gone. A lot of it spent on biscuits.

I had, obviously, planned that the children being at Sports Camp would be an excellent chance to get some work done, but it hasn't really worked out. Does anyone actually ever get any work done when they are working from home, or is it just me? I mostly just stared out the window, and perused the *Daily Mail* website to see who is 'stepping out' (going to the shops), 'flaunting their curves' (also going to the shops, but in a slightly tighter top than just 'stepping out') or 'slamming' a fellow Z-lister in a 'feud' (putting something vague and attention-seeking on

Twitter before deleting it an hour later when the *Daily Mail* has taken notice). I also played a lot of solitaire before sending a flurry of emails at 2.45 p.m., just before I had to leave to go and pick the children up. Foolishly, one of the emails I sent was to Simon, ever the supportive and beloved husband, who replied to my email questioning the lack of work I had achieved today by saying that yes, it is just me, and he does not procrastinate ever. This is a massive lie, as I have seen his version of working from home, and it involves just as much *Daily Mail* as mine, and also a lot of browsing *Autocar* looking at sports cars he can't afford, then staring pathetically into cupboards FULL OF FOOD (apart from biscuits, because I've eaten them all), feebly enquiring why there is never anything to eat in this house.

I think it is safe to say that my virtuous resolution not to drink on week nights is not going well.

Aunt Fanny never had these problems.

After two glasses of wine, and an unpleasant foray into online banking that confirmed my fears about the state of my account, and no adult interaction all day apart from the perky 'coach' at the Sports Camp getting me to sign the accident book again, due to Peter's decision to headbutt the floor for reasons known only to him, I decided that something needed to change, and I signed up for a recruitment agency. Maybe just a little part-time job, to make some money, but that leaves me with plenty of time to come up with my brilliant app idea. And that also will involve lovely business trips to exotic places (there wasn't actually an option for that, but there really should be).

Friday, 5 August

Oh dear. Oh dear, oh dear, oh dear. I fear I have done a foolish thing. I am at Guide Camp with Jane. I signed up as a parent volunteer at a meeting about the camp a couple of months ago, feeling it was a good and worthy thing to do that would give me a chance to spend some time with Jane like a nice caring mummy, and also – on some level – I would be proving my old Brown Owl wrong for drumming me out of the Brownies for insubordination. (I can't even remember what I did. I have a vague recollection of objecting to excessive knot-tying and taking the piss while singing 'Ging Gang Goolie', but whatever it was, apparently I was Not the Right Sort). But Guide Camp! Guide Camp would make up for it all. A verdant green field, with stout white canvas tents and smoky camp fires to make cocoa on. We would probably get the milk for the cocoa from a local farmer. There may even be ruffianly sorts lurking, just waiting for me to rally the girls and solve a mystery. Oh, yes! I was going to be *marvellous* at Guide Camp! I eagerly thrust my hand in the air, practically bursting with enthusiasm, when Melanie the Guide Leader asked for volunteers. Too late, I realised I needn't have been quite so keen, as every other parent had breathed a sigh of relief once they saw that some other poor fool was willing to do it and get them off the hook. Melanie, meanwhile, did not look entirely entranced at my selfless gesture.

'Ellen!' she said weakly. 'How kind of you! Err, are you sure this is your sort of thing?'

I assured Melanie that *of course* it was my sort of thing.

'Only, you know, you'll be in charge of some of the girls. *By yourself.* Are you quite sure you would be able to cope with that?' said Melanie anxiously.

I feared Melanie was thinking back to the unfortunate evening a few weeks ago when I had been the parent on duty at Guides and she had been called away to deal with a nosebleed. A nice policeman had come along that evening to give a talk about self-defence, and Melanie had thought it quite safe to leave the rest of the girls in the care of PC Briggs and myself. It was most unfortunate that PC Briggs was quite a young and naïve police officer. It was equally unfortunate that Amelia Watkins had chosen the moment when Melanie was out of the room to ask to see PC Briggs's handcuffs, claiming she was considering a career in the police force. No sooner had the poor young chap handed them over for Amelia's inspection, than she swiftly handcuffed him to a chair, and the rest of the girls, sensing weakness as only the under-twelves can, descended mob-handed and relieved him of his baton and walkie-talkie too, before going full-on *Lord of the Flies*. They danced around him, mocking his pleas to be released, while Tabitha MacKenzie radioed menacing ransom messages back to base and Tilly Everett tried to break Milly Johnson's arm with the baton and I made ineffectual pleas for them all to settle down.

This all happened within the three minutes that Melanie was absent from the hall. By the time she returned, PC Briggs was on the verge of tears, his radio was crackling ominously with threats of 'back-up' being dispatched and Milly had Tilly in a headlock trying to disarm her (Milly at least had been paying attention in the self-defence demonstration).

One shrill blast of Melanie's whistle restored order, PC Briggs departed hastily, his radio now crackling with hysterical laughter about Girl Guides, and I was sent to sort out the boxes of felt-tip pens, being deemed too irresponsible to even be allowed near the PVA glue.

Nonetheless, as no other parent was now willing to come forth, since a Volunteer had been found, Melanie was stuck with me.

'Do you know much about camping, Ellen?' she enquired, without much hope for my answer.

'Oh, yes!' I informed her brightly. 'I went to Glastonbury once. It was marvellous. I'm sure Guide Camp will be much the same. It'll be fun!' I assured her. Melanie looked unconvinced.

And now here I am. In a field. Quite a muddy field. There are many, many Girl Guides here, for apparently it is a County Camp, and they have come from far and wide and Melanie wishes to make a good impression. I fear Melanie had not factored in my bright pink Hunter wellies when she was planning her Good Impression. I also fear that she may be slightly judging my jaunty ensemble of denim shorts and a Barbour, which was not dissimilar to my Glastonbury outfit twenty years earlier when I was hoping to channel the likes of Kate Moss and Jo Whiley, but too late I realised that in fact Kate Moss and Jo Whiley are the only women in Britain over the age of twenty-five who can successfully pull off wearing shorts and I looked not so much festival chic as Worzel Gummidge on acid chic. On the plus side, the fake tan I applied to my legs has gone such a lurid shade of orange that they probably glow in the dark, so I will be easy to find if I get lost in the field at night.

If Melanie was disappointed in me, I was equally disappointed to discover that instead of the proper white canvas bell tents I had envisaged, we were accommodated in nasty nylon monstrosities in a fetching shade of puce green. These were, Melanie informed me, far more practical and hi-tech that an old-fashioned tent, and I would be both warmer and more comfortable.

'But the other ones are so beautiful!' I sighed, as an increasingly exasperated Melanie tried to direct fifteen over-excited girls and me to put the tents up, and I gazed longingly across the field to a row of Proper Tents. 'How could they be less comfortable than these horrors? Why, the beautiful tents are just crying out for bunting and cushions and strings of fairy lights!'

'For Christ's sake, Ellen!' snapped Melanie. 'You're at County Camp, not a Cath Kidston convention. Where is your Baden-Powell Spirit?'

Where was my Baden-Powell Spirit indeed? It was becoming increasingly clear that I seemed to be sorely lacking Baden-Powell Spirit, which was possibly the real reason I had been so ignominiously thrown out of the Brownies all those years ago. I couldn't help but think mutinous thoughts that if there were mysteries to be solved and criminal sorts to be thwarted, the thwarting would almost certainly fall to those lucky souls in the charmingly rustic, vintage tents.

Saturday, 6 August

I have decided I do not like camping. Camping is basically sleeping in a field. Sleeping in a field is fine when you are twenty-two and off your tits on fifteen pints of cider and some dubious illegal substances after dancing like a loon to splendid nineties rock and pop, but other than that, why would anyone want to go and sleep in a field for fun when they have a perfectly good house and bed? Moreover, why would they sleep in a field *when they were stone cold sober*? It is not right. There is nowhere to plug in my hair straighteners. But then again, there is nowhere to wash my hair either, so at least the grease is weighing down the frizz, so you know, swings and roundabouts. I think a beetle got in my hair last night too. I am sure I could feel something moving. Melanie wasn't very impressed when I woke her up after I tried to get the beetle out of my hair. She asked me to go back to sleep as there are no poisonous beetles in Britain. She was unsympathetic when I whimpered that what if I was *allergic* to the beetle and didn't know on account of having never had a beetle in my hair before. I think Melanie is regretting letting me come, which is fair enough, as I am very much regretting coming myself. It is not at all like Glastonbury, and nor is it anything like my Famous Five fantasies. I think we have the wrong kind of mud here.

There is no adorably smoky wood fire to cook sausages on. Instead there is a terrifying gas stove that could take my eyebrows off when I light it. It is even worse than lighting the Bunsen burners in the chemistry lab at school. I didn't say this to Melanie, though, as between Beetlegate and her having to get up multiple times in the night to settle homesick girls/break up midnight feasts/minister to tummy aches brought on by excessive consumption of Revels at 3 a.m., she did not look like concern for my eyebrows was top of her list. Nonetheless, I am quite admiring of Melanie, even if a part of me suspects that she made me light the gas stove in the hope that I would manage to set myself on fire and she would be relieved of my ineptitude. She just gets on with it all, and even when the Guides are being really annoying, she doesn't lose her rag with them and tell them to just fuck off, like I probably would if I was in charge. Nor does she resort to mainlining gin, which would probably be my other coping strategy if I was her. I think it must take someone really quite special to do something like this – perhaps that is where the Baden-Powell Spirit comes in.

I always thought that I would have been quite splendid in the Blitz – that I was a trooper and would have been some sort of inspirational figure, leading rousing sing-songs and fashioning ingenious things out of clothes pegs, but it is becoming apparent that I would probably have spent the Blitz being useless and flapping around while the Melanies of the 1940s built bomb shelters with their bare hands.

There are no signs of coiners or smugglers to thwart, which is probably just as well, as all the girls seem more interested in going to the toilet *en masse* and stuffing their faces with more contraband sweeties than they do in Solving Mysteries. There was an archery session, where Jane came over all William Tell and had to be restrained from trying to shoot a Granny Smith off Tilly Morrison's head, and an orienteering activity during which the girls were unimpressed with maps and compasses and pointed out that Google Maps existed.

'Ah,' I said. 'But what if there was no Google Maps?'

'Why would there be no Google Maps, though?' said Amelia Benson.

'Well, you could have no signal, or your battery could be dead,' I pointed out, but the girls looked unconvinced.

'Or you could have lost your phone,' I added.

'So, we've lost our phone, but we just *happen* to have a map and a compass?' objected Olivia Brown. 'It's not very likely, is it, Ellen?'

'Well,' I said, starting to get irritated, 'maybe there has been a nuclear apocalypse and Google Maps no longer exists because civilisation has been wiped out along with most of the human race, and you are one of the lone survivors and all you have to help you get to safety before you starve to death is a map and a bloody compass, and if you are unable to navigate by them then you will die by the roadside like the rest of the population of the planet!'

Mia Robinson burst into tears. 'I don't want to be the only one left alive!' she sobbed. 'What about my hamster? Can hamsters survive nuclear apocalypses?'

'No,' said Jane. Mia sobbed harder, and proved quite inconsolable. Melanie had to be summonsed to comfort her and assure her that there was no chance of a nuclear holocaust any time soon, and the orienteering was just a bit of fun, and her hamster would be *fine*, yes and her mum and dad too.

While Melanie was doing this, her own orienteering group managed to wander off and get lost somewhere in the woods and a search party had to be launched. The other Guide leaders were quite judgemental of Melanie for losing her Guides, and I fear she blames me for all this. We were summonsed to a singalong this evening and we had to sing some complicated clapping song where you also had to clap the hand of the person next to you, and I'm pretty sure that Melanie didn't need to slap my hand nearly as hard as she did. Hopefully there will be no beetles tonight, as I think she might do more than slap me if I have to wake her up. I'm sure there were no beetles at Glastonbury – it's probably the wrong kind of mud here that attracts them. I wonder if I am too old to go to Glastonbury again? Do they let in fortysomethings? Could I even hack the pace, or would I just die? I mean, obviously one could no longer dabble in illegal substances, because one is middle-aged and respectable, and all the cider would make me need to pee all the time because I've had two children and my bladder is not what it was, and I'm not sure I could cope with festival toilets anymore. Maybe I would have to go to one of the Old People's Festivals, like Rewind or something? I wonder if they have better toilets? But they are often billed as being 'family friendly', and if I have escaped my own cherubs to get pissed up and behave badly for the weekend, the last thing I want is Other People's Children roaming around. Oh God, I am a terrible person. Melanie can probably tell, and that's why she hates me. As well as the whole traumatising one of her Guides and making her lose six others thing, obviously.

Sunday, 7 August

I am home! I am washed! Eventually. Oh, the bliss. Sort of.

This morning, after Dicing with Death with the Stove of Doom and dispensing frankly revolting eggy bread to the girls, who didn't seem to care, we took the tents down. Melanie was relieved to find that I am not *totally* useless, and could at least work out that to take the tent down, you simply reverse the putting-up procedure, and it all went relatively smoothly, despite the Guides' best efforts to get trapped in the middle of collapsing tents. We didn't lose any more girls, and I managed not to upset any more of them, which was just as well, as Melanie was up several times in the night with Mia having nightmares. Hopefully she won't tell Mia's parents that it was me who has caused her fears of the Nuclear Winter. Something has bitten me in an unspeakable place, though. I suspect the killer beetle.

On arriving home with a grubby and sleep-deprived Jane, I was hopeful that Simon and Peter might have kept the home fires burning in my absence. I may lack Baden-Powell Spirit, but sometimes I am an incurable optimist. Sadly, my optimism was misplaced, as the house was a pit of fucking hell. I would go so far as to say squalid. I am not going to be an optimist anymore, I have decided, I am going to be a pessimist. It seems a much better idea. A pessimist will only ever either be proved right or pleasantly surprised – there is no disappointment lurking for pessimists the way there is for optimists.

Simon was the picture of injured innocence as I shouted about why were there pants strewn in places that pants ought not to be, and no one had emptied the bin or flushed the bog, let alone removed the skidmarks or wiped the counters, and instead of putting away the clean dishes in the dishwasher to make room for the dirty ones, they had simply taken to piling the dirty dishes on the worktop above the dishwasher, waiting hopefully for the Magical Bastarding Dishwasher Fairy to wave her wand and furnish them with clean bowls.

'What exactly have you done while I have been gone?' I ranted. 'And DON'T say "Looked after Peter". He is hardly a baby that needs constant tending.'

'Actually, darling,' said Simon with irritating smugness, 'I have cleaned out the fridge and sorted through the cupboards and thrown out everything that was out of date.'

I went cold. 'You have done what?' I said in horror.

I flung open the cupboards. All the spices – gone!

'Some of them were two years out of date,' said Simon indignantly.

I whimpered.

The cupboard full of posh rice and pasta and the token bag of quinoa, because middle-class – empty.

'FOUR years!' Simon informed me. 'The quinoa was four years out of date! It hadn't even been opened! And the risotto rice expired last month, and the red carmargue rice was two months out of date, and there was a packet of funny shaped pasta that went off six months ago. And there was a tin of spaghetti hoops that was SIX years out of date!'

'These things don't go off,' I said furiously. 'Spices are MEANT to be out of date! Nobody has in-date spices, the people who say you should throw them out after six months are just trying to trick you. When they start tasting like dust is when they are getting GOOD. And pasta and rice are clearly edible for months after the arbitrary date on the packet and now I will have to waste money buying more quinoa for no one to eat, because if we have no quinoa in the cupboard are we even middle-class? And tinned stuff NEVER goes bad. NEVER! That is why people hoard tins for after the nuclear apocalypse. If there is a nuclear apocalypse tonight, we needn't bother trying to survive, because we will all starve anyway because YOU THREW OUT MY EMERGENCY SPAGHETTI HOOPS!'

'I think you're over-reacting again, darling.' smirked Simon. 'Look in the fridge.'

I opened the fridge. No jam. No ketchup. No mayonnaise. Not a single vegetable. The three tubs of antiquated houmous that were looking increasingly menacing and I was actually quite scared to touch had also vanished, which was something.

'All out of date,' beamed Simon.

'The potatoes?'

'Out of date yesterday.'

'Carrots, onions, garlic?'

'Gone, gone, gone!'

'But there was nothing wrong with them. Unless they are actually sprouting, going green or decomposing, they are absolutely fine.'

'Out of date! Out of date!' insisted Simon. 'They had to go.'

'FML,' I muttered. 'Well, I suppose we're getting a takeaway for dinner, then. And where is the ham? That wasn't out of date.'

'No, but it said eat within two days of opening and it had been open for more than two days, so out it went.'

'FFS!' I said. 'Literally NO ONE pays any attention to that. NO ONE! I am going to have a shower and scrape off field residue, and you can go to Sainsbury's and BUY SOME FUCKING FOOD.'

'But I've been busy sorting all this out and looking after Peter all weekend! Even though, really, sorting out the fridge and cupboards should be your job, now you're not working, but I did it *for you* anyway.' protested Simon. 'Can't you pop to the shop?'

'Firstly, I AM working, I am trying to build myself a new career, I'm hardly sitting around reading magazines and eating bonbons all day like a lady of leisure,' (this might be a slight lie, obviously) 'so I don't know where you get the idea that everything in the house is now my responsibility. Secondly, I HAVE BEEN SLEEPING IN A FUCKING FIELD AND BEEN TORMENTED BY BEETLES AND RISKED MY LIFE WITH A VERY DANGEROUS GAS STOVE IN ORDER TO CREATE WONDERFUL CHILDHOOD MEMORIES FOR *YOUR* DAUGHTER, WHILE YOU THREW OUT VAST QUANTITIES OF PERFECTLY GOOD FOOD!' I roared. 'YOU go to the bastarding shop!'

Simon went to the shop. He came home chuntering in outrage at the iniquitous price of food, which frankly serves him right for throwing everything out. How marvellous it is to be home. I have several weeks more of such fun to look forward to.

Wednesday, 10 August

Today, lacking any other inspiration for something to do with my darling children, we went to the park. I hate the park. The park is where mummies go when their precious moppets have driven them so fucking mad that they now need to be in the presence of witnesses to stop them doing something they regret. Sometimes I wonder about trying to tot up all the hours I have spent in cold, draughty parks since the children were born, but frankly it is too depressing. Also, everyone witters on at you about the dangers of getting piles in pregnancy, but no one, not one single fucker, ever tells you that actually you are more likely to get piles from the hours upon hours upon hours you will now spend sitting on a chilly, damp park bench. Still, at least it is summer, so the risk of piles and chilblains is slightly diminished.

I cannot enter the hallowed portals of the actual play park because I brought the dog with me, so we lurk outside while toddlers' mummies glare at us in case we make a break for the gate so Judgy can do a shit in the sandpit and I can rub it in their cherub's eye and BLIND THEM FOR EVER! Obviously, I know dog poo can be very dangerous, and of course I don't condone people who let their dogs crap in children's play parks. I just resent the hisses of horror from the mummies whenever a dog ventures within a hundred feet of the gate. Luckily, Peter and Jane are now old enough that they don't need close supervision in the park anymore. Peter is perfectly capable of trying to break a limb on the monkey bars all by himself, and Jane is more interested in taking selfies with Sophie on the old iPhone she cajoled out of me and now insists on taking everywhere with her despite me pointing out that she doesn't actually need a phone at the park.

While the children played, I had a quick look through my emails, where there was nothing of much interest – another Nigerian general just needed my bank account details to transfer his millions (I wonder if I could invent an app that somehow spams back the spammers?), Gap had another sale (when does Gap not have a sale? Does anyone ever buy anything full price in Gap? Maybe I could make an app for Gap, for all their sales. Oh, they already have one. Bugger), and one more email from the recruitment company I had signed up for. I almost deleted the recruitment company's email, as despite carefully filling in the forms telling them my qualifications, my interests, the fields I wished to work in and the salary I was looking for, so far they had sent a steady stream of jobs that were nothing to do with my expertise, were located five hundred miles away and paid approximately a third of what I previously earned. However, mainly so I could look like I was doing something important – and thus avoid catching the eye of any of the other parents and having to engage in conversation – I opened it, and lo and behold, IT WAS ONLY MY DREAM FUCKING JOB!

It was perfect. I'd be working for one of the hottest new tech start-up companies of the last five years, who occupied a sexy, shiny, modern, glass office block, instead of a grey building on a grey industrial estate, yet was only about twenty minutes' drive from my house.

I have often passed the office building and metaphorically pressed my nose against the glossy mirrored-glass windows. Apparently, it's just as cool inside (yes, I might have googled it. Repeatedly), with light and space and acres of white desks and Beautiful People. OK, maybe I am imagining the Beautiful People, but I am pretty sure everyone who works there is super-cool and trendy and probably wears hipster glasses and ethical trousers. They probably have Whatsapp groups to discuss things instead of insisting on pointless two-hour meetings to resolve something that could have been sorted with one email, and if they *do* have meetings they sit on … oooh … I dunno, beanbags or something. Actually, do I want to work somewhere with beanbags? I'm almost forty-two. Could I manage to get up off a beanbag with dignity? They probably don't have beanbags, it'll be fine.

And I'd actually be doing something quite stimulating and challenging and interesting, unlike the old job where the best thing I got to do was tell Dodgy Ed in Accounts that actually, no, it wasn't possible to eradicate all traces of the hardcore porn that he had 'accidentally downloaded' from his laptop (in a fit of malice I also claimed that, in fact, the internet tracks everything you do and so even if he bought a new laptop and threw that one in a river, the internet *would know about the porn* and so his wife would still be able to see what he had been watching).

The pay is really good, too. Which would be awfully nice, as the redundancy money has almost run out, and I hate the idea of not having my own money. I know it all goes into the joint account anyway, but I've always contributed to that, and the idea of being 'dependent' on Simon sticks somewhat in my throat. The only downside is that it would be a full-time position.

I suppose I should really have discussed the whole full-time thing with Simon first, but I was so excited about my perfect job coming up pretty much right on my doorstep (and mentally I had also spent most of my lovely new salary already) that I just went ahead and told the agency to put me forward for it. Oh, what bliss it would be if I got it! And now the children are at school most of the time, the extra money would easily cover any increased childcare costs, and then some. I am crossing my fingers and toes and legs and ... what else can one cross, apart from eyes? Maybe I am still a bit of an optimist.

Saturday, 20 August

I am rested, recharged and raring to go after my wonderful, relaxing family holiday with my darling children and beloved husband. Oh, what a splendid time we had! Oh, how we frolicked! And the japes. The japes! One day the children will look back on those golden sun-drenched days, and they will smile fondly at the #happymemories created as they laughed and ran along those sandy Cornish beaches in tasteful knitwear, the wind in their hair and their youth before them. Or at least they will if they look at my Instagram account, which reports on the holiday I would like to have had, as opposed to the holiday I actually had, which mainly consisted of doing laundry, attempting to play an ancient game of Mousetrap that was missing half the pieces, trying to cook in an unfamiliar kitchen and swearing because every damn knife in the place was blunt. Incidentally, why are knives in holiday houses ALWAYS so blunt? Is it because they are concerned that under the pressure to have a marvellous time and keep those #happymemories coming that someone might crack and try to murder their family if they have to listen to one more whine about how everyone else goes to Center Parcs and why do we have to go to Cornwall (because we are middle-class, darling, and also slightly pretentious), and can we go to Center Parcs next year? (No, sweetie, because your father hates People.) Then there's the moaning about why is there no wifi (because we're here to talk to each other, poppet, and have a lovely time, not stare at our tablets, and yes, I did go outside to get a 4G signal, but I needed to upload my photographs to Instagram because how else will anyone know we are having a lovely time? We ARE having a lovely time. YES, WE ARE! WE ARE HAVING A LOVELY TIME BECAUSE I FUCKING WELL SAY WE ARE HAVING A LOVELY TIME! No, you can't borrow my phone to play Pokémon Go. Because there aren't any Pokémon in Cornwall. No, of course I'm not lying to you, why would I lie to you?).

Were it not for the fact that I am just as adept as the next person at lying on social media, I would be convinced that every other child in the country spends the entire summer holidays in some sort of sun-drenched, golden Enid Blyton world, laughing and frolicking on beaches, skipping through wildflower meadows, flying kites and building sandcastles with their loving parents, but according to Facebook and Instagram, with a little help from a few filters, my children had done exactly the same all summer long.

Anyway, we are home now, everyone is exhausted after the long and hideous drive, we appear to have brought most of Cornwall's beaches back with us in the car and the suitcases, and there are vast mounds of laundry to be done, and frankly, I don't actually know why we bother going on holiday, when you need another holiday to get over going on holiday. But anyway, I do at least have some lovely photos, even if the children did keep complaining that I took too many photos of them and whining about why did I need so many photos and I snarled that I needed the photographs for my dotage, when I was old and grey and they had grown up and left me and all I had to remember their childhood was these photos. I even got a nice photo of Simon, which is miraculous as usually he just pulls stupid faces when I point a camera at him. I suppose at least I know where the children get it from!

BUT, on the way back, I got a phone call to say that the Dream Job want to see me for an interview! Simon was somewhat dismissive, pointing out that an interview is very different to being offered the job, sighing deeply and telling me not to get my hopes up, but fuck him. It's a step in the right direction, even if Simon is insisting on pissing on my chips as ever. Just for once, it would be nice if he could be positive about something I do and encourage me, instead of always seeing the dark side and predicting dire results. Just a little bloody faith, that's all! Is that too much to ask? Anyway, *much* more important than Simon Misery Pants FartFace, is the question of what I am going to wear?

Astonishingly, Peter's plant is still alive, despite being abandoned for a week.

Friday, 26 August

How many weeks has it been? It feels like forever. Will they ever go back to school? I am starting to lose hope the holidays will ever end. The only bright spot at the moment is the upcoming interview, and the potential to become a high-powered, corporate Proper Person, instead of a dispenser of snacks and referee-er of fights. I suggested today that building a den in the garden might be a fun way to pass the time. The children looked at me as if I had proposed that they should shit in their hands and then clap. Instead, since it was sunny, they demanded to have a water fight instead. Much against my better judgement, as I am firmly convinced that water fights are nothing more than a fast track to A&E with a broken limb, or at the very least some blood and nasty bruising, but lacking the strength any more to argue, I agreed.

For at least ten minutes they were outside hurling water and screaming before they decided they were bored and cold and instead it would be far more fun to tramp mud and water and grass through the kitchen, use an unfeasible number of clean towels, get dressed in a whole new set of clothes to the ones they were wearing earlier, and then, just as I had mopped up the swamp from the kitchen floor, request to play on the Slip'N Slide.

I denied them the Slip'N Slide, as we had been fortunate enough to get through the water fight without anyone being maimed, so I was not tempting fate by getting out the plastic Mat of Doom that should really be renamed the Slip'N BreakYourNeck. I pointed out the many wholesome activities available to them in the garden: they could jump on the yellow and blue monstrosity that has destroyed any tasteful Zen vibes in my garden, they could play with the swingball, they could read a book underneath a motherfucking tree, but they were not coming inside on a glorious summer's day to stare at a screen and nor was I taking them anywhere or spending a single penny on their entertainment that day. They were playing in the garden – and that was final.

With that, I retreated inside to stare at a screen under the guise of work. Well, I told them I was 'working'. In actual fact I was googling 'cool interview outfits' (all of which seemed to involve alarming high heels and very thin people in amazing jackets that I don't think I could get my tits into) in an effort to present myself as ruthlessly professional but also Down With the Youth at my interview. I was also fretting because all the women in the photos were carrying takeaway cups of coffee – is this now a required accessory? Might they not take me seriously if I *don't* turn up clutching a cardboard cup of a grande soy latte? Is that even the order the words go in? Also, I thought all the big coffee chains were frowned upon as unethical tax dodgers. Maybe if I bring the wrong sort of coffee I'll be off the shortlist before I've even opened my mouth. Perhaps I should just take the free coffee from Waitrose. Is Waitrose considered ethical? I DON'T KNOW! I only know it is middle-class! All these, and other worries, were swirling around in my head when after half an hour or so, I realised I could hear something terrifying. Silence. There is never silence from my precious moppets unless Something Bad is happening. I flung open the back door to find a disconsolate Jane trying to disentangle a yoyo string.

'Where's Peter?' I demanded.

Jane shrugged. 'I dunno.'

'Well, isn't he out here with you? Didn't you notice him going somewhere?'

Jane shrugged again, and mumbled he was probably inside and that wasn't fair, if he was on his iPad then, she, Jane, who had not defied my instructions, deserved EXTRA iPad time to make up for Peter's getting time just now and also even more extra time to reflect her obedience. I cut short Jane's lengthy argument about her screen time and dashed inside to look for Peter. I bellowed and shouted, to no response. He wasn't in his bedroom, he wasn't in the sitting room, he wasn't in the loo, he wasn't even in Jane's bedroom stealing things to annoy her.

'JANE!' I shouted. 'Are you SURE you didn't see where he went?'

Jane insisted she had not, adding a hasty disclaimer that whatever fate may have befallen Peter, it was definitely not her fault.

That icy dread started to grip me. My rational brain was churning out statistics, reminding me that the chances of him being absolutely fine were really very high, while the rest of me was screaming silently inside because my baby boy was missing, and I didn't even know what he was wearing to give a description to the police because he had changed clothes so many times today already due to bloody water fights.

WHY hadn't I just let him play on the Slip'N Slide? Better an afternoon at A&E with a mildly mangled limb than the scenarios now playing out through my head – the treacherous ponds; the unmarked vans screeching to halt and speeding off again, unseen by anyone; the boy racer, flying down a suburban street slightly too fast to stop for the small figure darting out to chase a ball. For a fleeting second, I wondered whether there were any disused mine shafts around that he could have fallen down. Would Judgy Dog be able to track him? Probably not. He hates Peter with a vengeance, and the feeling is mutual.

By the time all those thoughts had run through my mind I was out on the street, yelling Peter's name at the top of my voice and trying not to sound too hysterical. He could only have been missing for fifteen minutes at the very most – it was too soon to call the police, I told myself. Hearing me shouting, my neighbour and kindred spirit Katie appeared from across the street, and I gabbled out what had happened.

'Oh God!' she said. 'I'll help you look. Let me grab my girls, then I'll go down that way and you go down the other way, and if he doesn't hear us shouting, we'll start knocking on doors. We'll find him, Ellen, don't worry.'

I nodded, too afraid I would cry if I had to actually speak, and set off, bellowing for Peter, Jane trailing behind (I could not let her out of my sight. It was bad enough I had mislaid one child; to lose another would doubtless cause Lady Bracknell-esque pronouncements upon my parenting).

I got to the end of the street, still shouting, and was working my way back up, my voice now hoarse and the fear held at bay by the thinnest of threads, when Karen Davison at number 47 opened her door, looking surprised.

'Peter's here!' she said. 'Didn't you know?'

'No!' I choked. 'I thought he was in the garden and then he was gone.'

'He's here, playing on that bloody Slip'N Slide with my grandsons,' said Karen. 'He was playing in your front garden when we came past on the way home from the shop and the boys asked him if he wanted to come over. I told him he had to check with you first, and he went inside and came out with his swimming trunks and said it was fine, so I assumed he had told you.'

I was too relieved at finding Peter alive and intact and not trapped down a collapsing mine shaft to even be angry at him for buggering off without telling me. I grabbed him and hugged him tightly (a bad move in hindsight, as he was soaking wet), and then rather embarrassingly burst into tears and sobbed, 'Don't you EVER, EVER do that again. I was so worried!'

'I'm sorry, Mummy,' said Peter. 'I thought it would be OK because I wasn't going very far. I didn't mean to scare you.'

'I was only scared because I love you,' I wept.

'I love you too, Mummy. I won't scare you like that again, I promise.'

Oh God, I nearly lost my son because I was too busy worrying about what sort of coffee to take to an interview! What sort of mother am I? Maybe I should give up all thoughts of going back to work full-time and just become an earth Mother, and do crafts with them – even though I hate crafts – and devote every moment of my existence to them to make up for my previous abject failings, in the hope that they are not too scarred by my selfishness. I mean, they *seem* unscarred – the only person who seemed to be traumatised by this afternoon is me, but maybe the damage is deeper and will only be revealed in their thirties when they enter therapy and realise that *everything* that is wrong with their life can be traced back to my dubious parenting?

Both Jane and Judgy Dog were unimpressed by Peter's safe return.

SEPTEMBER

Monday, 5 September

Argh! The job interview is THIS FRIDAY! I still have nothing to wear, but I think I need to stop worrying about that and start thinking about what I'm actually going to SAY. I haven't been to a job interview in years. What do I tell them? Oh God, I'll have to pretend to have hobbies and be a proper person and try not to gabble at length and fall back on my favourite conversational gambit of telling people about the interesting fact that otters have opposable thumbs. I'm pretty sure the only reason one could have to legitimately discuss otters in a job interview is if one was applying for a job as an otter wrangler or something. (Actually, that really would be my dream job. I love otters and have frequently expressed a desire to keep one in the bath. Simon does not even dignify this suggestion with a response, but I have seen *Ring of Bright Water* many times and think keeping an otter in the bath would be perfectly feasible – I could get reduced red label salmon from the supermarket for it to eat. And tangents like this are exactly why I get so nervous about interviews.)

I also always come out of an interview with absolutely no idea what I might have said in response to the questions and all I can do is hope that when asked, 'Why do you think you would be the right person for this job?' is that I replied something about my skills, qualifications and interests, and threw in something about being a team player and didn't actually answer, 'Because my lord and master the Dread Cthulhu thinks it would suit me. I slaughtered a black cockerel and inspected the entrails for portents and signs, and he spoke to me thus.' But I am never sure. It's a bit like when voting in important elections and despite carefully making sure my cross is in the right place, as soon as I pop my ballot paper into the box I am gripped with dread that I voted for the wrong one, and what if the election comes down to the wire and every vote counts and I voted wrong and now Western Civilisation will collapse and it will ALL BE MY FAULT?

I tried discussing my fears and concerns with Simon, but he is still not entirely sold on the idea of me going back to work full-time. 'I just don't see why you need to be full-time,' he said. 'Doesn't it fit in much better with the children if you are part-time, and you can be there to help with homework and make dinner and stuff? I'm not entirely sure I like the idea of them being latchkey children.'

'They will hardly be latchkey children. I only worked part-time when they were tiny because it meant we didn't have to spend such prodigious sums on childcare, and yes, we thought it was better if one of us could be at home with them at least some of the time. But they're both at school full-time now, and there's breakfast clubs and after-school clubs and in another year, Jane won't even be at primary school. They're not babies anymore, they don't need me as much as they used to, and as time goes on they will need me less and less, but I might not get another opportunity like this, so I'd quite like to give it a shot.'

'But why now? Why can't you wait until they're older to go full-time, and just get another part-time job? I don't think you are really thinking about what's best for the children here, darling.'

'Because I want THIS job! I don't WANT another part-time, stop-gap job. It was only ever meant to be a temporary fix, to keep the wolf from the door while the kids were little. The only vaguely interesting thing I have done to earn any money in the last eleven years was designing that *Why Mummy Drinks* app, which, if you may recall, did rather well. And now the children are really not that little anymore, if you haven't noticed, so I'd quite like to do something that is a bit more stimulating, a bit more challenging, instead of babysitting the computer illiterate and explaining to Jean from Shipping for the eleventy billionth time why her computer does not "hate her" and does not "eat things". Why is it so wrong that I want to do something for ME? What about MY hopes and ambitions? Do YOU think of what's best for the children every time you make a career decision, or do you think about what YOU want?'

'Well, you did literally just tell me your main ambition in life was to keep an otter in the bath,' pointed out Simon. 'So forgive me if I don't try to facilitate all your dreams. And of *course* I think about what's best for the children,' he lied. 'I just don't think that that's having two full-time working parents, that's all.'

'Well, darling,' I said. 'If you are so very concerned about the children's welfare, there is a very simple solution, you know.'

'What?'

'Well, if I get this job, I'll be earning as much as you. So if you are really worried about it all being a bit much with us both working full-time, you could always go part-time instead and take on responsibility for the house and the childcare?'

Simon paled. 'Err, no, no, I'm fine, I'm sure we can make it work. If this is what you want to do, I'll support you. No need for me to go part-time. I'm sure the children will be OK.'

'Thank you, my love,' I said sweetly.

Tuesday, 6 September

Ha, ha. I am READY! Bring. It. On.

The uniforms have been bought, at vast and painful expense.

Hours upon hours have been spent queuing in Clarks, desperately clutching our little ticket and glaring menacingly at any parents who look like they might be trying to queue-jump, and more appalling sums of money have been handed over for shiny new school shoes that will shortly be battered and scuffed and caked in mud, leading me to wonder why I spent eleventy billion pounds on properly fitted shoes so my precious moppets' tiny, youthful feet will not be squashed and can develop into suitably middle-class trotters, when they couldn't care less and will trash them within the first week. And I could have saved myself the money and effort and bought them a pair from Asda for a tenner.

Trainers and gym shoes and PE kit have been purchased. School bags and pencil cases and water bottles and what appears to be the entire bastarding contents of Smiggle are now grasped in my darlings' sweaty paws, while they continue to whine about the unspeakable injustice of my refusal to pay £5.99 for a SINGLE RUBBER!

My hands are calloused and bleeding from sewing name tapes on to all this cornucopia of capitalist consumerism. This is due to my starry-eyed naivety when Jane started school, which led to me ordering them five hundred fucking name tapes EACH from the kind people at Mr Cash's label emporium, thinking fondly as I did of how smart their uniforms would look with the pretty labels sewn in (green for Jane and blue for Peter, with a little motif of a dinosaur for Jane and a choo-choo train for Peter), but completely overlooking the fact that I can't sew, that I hate anything to do with sewing, and that I invariably end up throwing any project that requires sewing across the room and swearing furiously. Also, do you have any idea how many name tapes there are in a bag of FIVE HUNDRED? Approximately eleventy fucking billion, that's how many! There will be enough to see them off to university, and actually, the website recommended the name tapes for nursing homes, too, and I wouldn't be surprised if those bloody bags of name tapes were still going strong by the time Peter and Jane are ready to enter Shady Pines themselves.

Next year I am buying one of those clever stamper things for labelling their stuff. Admittedly I say this every year and forget to order one until there is no time left, so I end up swearing and bleeding on the new white shirts as I wrestle with the sew-in ones, but maybe next year will be the year I remember. Actually, the really clever thing to do would be to order one NOW, so I have it to hand, but that seems wanton and profligate when I still have SO MANY BLOODY NAME TAPES and have just spent so much time sewing them in.

Anyway, it is done now. Well, most of it is done. Well, OK, I sewed in three labels, looked at the mountains of stuff that still needed labelling and went, 'Life's too short', had a glass of wine and got a Sharpie and wrote their names in the rest. It's possible that this happens every year, which is why the supply of name tapes never actually diminishes much.

But the alarm is set, bright and early for tomorrow morning, and another school year shall commence. Hopefully, this will be the year when my darling children finally reveal their hidden talents and turn out to excel at something, so I can be the proud, smugger-than-smug mummy in the playground, boasting shamelessly about their achievements, but given I am now struggling to come to terms with the fact that I am almost forty-two (FORTY-TWO! Withered cronedom is approaching at an alarming rate, despite the obscenely expensive creams I slather on my face) and I still haven't discovered my own hidden talents, I think it is unlikely.

When I check on the children before bed I will just have one more peek at their drawers filled with their lovely clean new uniform, as it will be the last time it looks like that this school year. Within a week they will have transformed those bright white polo shirts into grubby, paint-stained rags, and when given clean laundry to put away will either dump everything on their bedroom floor willy-nilly or cram it all anyhow into the drawers, completely ignoring the time I spent carefully folding it for them. At least I have the wit not to iron their uniforms, though I eased my guilt at my slatternly ways by buying the 'non-iron' uniforms.

Wednesday, 7 September

Well, today went well. Peter and Jane have blithely spent the entire summer holidays getting up at 6 a.m. for no apparent reason other than to annoy me by galumphing down the stairs like a herd of elephants and then loudly fighting over who gets which iPad (as it is UNFAIR if one of them has to use the slightly older iPad, despite the fact that it makes NO SODDING DIFFERENCE to their horrible cartoons on Netflix), but this morning, when they had to get up and get ready for school so that we would actually start this academic year as we meant to go on – well, of course, this was the morning that they chose to sleep in!

I had to drag them out of bed, both of them snarling like angry weasels and complaining bitterly that they were still tired, while I spat back that they were probably still tired because they had not gone to bloody sleep when they were told last night. Instead, they had spent two hours after bedtime getting up for drinks of water and trips to the loo and come downstairs and tell me about how they couldn't sleep until I became incensed with rage after tucking them back in for the sixth time and shouted that OF COURSE they couldn't sleep, because they were up wandering around the house, and I wouldn't be able to sleep either and maybe if they tried actually staying in their actual beds they might be able to get some actual sleep. And, more importantly, I could watch *Game of Thrones* without them walking in at every single inopportune moment just when someone had got their tits out! Apparently this was mean of me, and I was told once again how EVERYBODY ELSE in their class gets to choose their own bedtime and go to bed whenever they want, and also THEIR mummies let them watch 18-rated films and play *Call of Duty*. So all in all, I was distinctly lacking in sympathy for my darlings' protestations of weariness and exhaustion this morning.

I did, however, manage to feed and wash and dress the cherubs (well, I didn't actually wash or dress them, obviously, at nine and eleven they are – allegedly – perfectly capable of doing that themselves; I just hurtled into their rooms and shouted at them to PUT THEIR CLOTHES ON, while Peter fannied about with his Lego and Jane complained that she only had the 'wrong kind' of socks), and we were all ready(ish), with plenty of time to take the obligatory First Day Photo.

The First Day Photo, as every parent knows, involves finding the corner of your house that looks least like a shithole and hustling your offspring into it, while shouting, 'SMILE, darlings, JUST FUCKING SMILE. I need one nice photo of you today, just one, so I can send it to your grandparents and show them what adorable poppets you are. And put it on Facebook, so people know I love you! Oh FFS, please, it's not that hard. You both just have to SMILE and LOOK AT MY PHONE at the same time. No, you BOTH have to look at the phone. Together. No, with your eyes open. Because you're not fucking looking at the phone if you've got your eyes shut, ARE YOU? And SMILE! For the love of God, SMILE!'

Some parents actually have special signs made for their children to hold, with the class the children are going into and jaunty little 'Back to School' phrases, the better to smugly remind us all via social media that they are #soblessed and just love #makingmemories, before lamenting that the holidays are just too short and their #mamahearts will be missing their #babies who are #growinguptoofast. I am not one of those mothers. I fear I do not even have a #mamaheart, as sadness is NOT the emotion I feel when my beloved munchkins are returned to the glorious bosom of education after six long bastarding weeks of us #makingmemories that mainly consist of everyone crying into ice-creams after being thwarted once again by the British weather.

It was especially important that I got a suitable photo of the First Day of Term this year, because a) I forgot last year and had to fake it the next day and bribe the children not to tell their grandparents that it was in fact a 'second day of term' photo that I sent them (with the inevitably scuffed shoes cropped out) and b) quite astonishingly, it is Jane's last year at primary school. I can't quite believe it. Everyone says, 'Oh, they grow up so fast,' and I always wanted to snarl, 'Do they? Really? Because I am not convinced they will grow up at all, ever. I think that my life will now consist of trying to stop this small wrecking ball destroying my house and picking half-chewed organic rice cakes out of my hair, and that is ALL THERE IS NOW!' but it really doesn't seem that long ago that I was counting down the days until she could start playgroup, and now she is *finishing* primary school and next year will be at BIG SCHOOL!

I finally got some approximation of the photo I wanted, but not before I had ended up with an entire camera roll filled with photos of the children gurning and sulking, which I will feel guilty about deleting because #firstdayofterm, and, after yet another argument with Jane about why she is not allowed her own Instagram account ('Because you have to be thirteen! Are you thirteen? No, no, you are not, so you are not having your own account! I don't CARE if the rest of your class has their own account! It is not happening!'), we were ready for the off, for even I can manage not to be late on the first day of term.

Simon, obviously, wasn't able to come with us for the first day of term because he had to go to work and be very busy and important. It never fails to astonish me how Simon's busy and importantness always seems to coincide with school events, so I have to go myself. I used to make a point of talking about 'MY HUSBAND' in a loud voice on such occasions, but since my husband never actually materialised I have stopped doing that, as I am afraid that all the teachers think I am a mad fantasist who has invented a husband for some reason and only wears a wedding ring to affect some strange 1950s notion of 'respectability'.

Anyway, the children were at least dispatched without further ado – Peter's teacher is a rather sweet young probationer, but judging by her rather tight and low-cut sweater, there might be a sudden influx of daddies in that class volunteering to take part in school events, and Jane has a new teacher as well – an actual man is teaching in the primary school. Well, I say a man. In truth he is more of a boy – when I saw him in the playground I actually thought he was only slightly taller than an average Year 6.

I suppose this will start happening to me more and more now. First I think the teachers look terribly young, next thing I will be complaining how youthful the policemen are and then insisting I want to see a 'proper doctor' as I don't believe the whipper-snapper before me can possibly be properly qualified. Actually, this has almost happened already – the last time I took Judgy to the vet I was unconvinced they had given me a real vet, such was the youth of the Man Child before me. I realised, of course, that clearly he WAS a proper vet, and a highly knowledgeable and skilled one when he exclaimed, 'Well, that's a fine wee terrier you've got there!' Anyone who can recognise my dog's superiority *clearly* knows his stuff.

Thursday, 8 September

Oh, fuckety fuckety doodah. The interview is tomorrow. TOMORROW. I am not ready for this – what was I *thinking*? Why would some cool, futuristic, space-age company employ ME? They do not want someone like me who is already complaining that the teachers and doctors and policemen are very young, they want those very young people who should clearly still be at school. At least after much browsing I have found something to wear. I had to go for the stupidly high heels, because I tried a slightly-cropped-trousers-with-ankle-boots look in the hope it would make me look like a millennial, but it just made me look like I'd got dressed in the dark and couldn't find my socks or any trousers that fitted. The girls on Pinterest didn't look like that. Christ, I can't even pull off *dressing* as a millennial, so how on earth am I going to pull this off?

I have researched all about the company, and rehearsed my HR-friendly answers, but who knows what people even ask in interviews anymore. Maybe they don't want to know about my strengths and weaknesses. (I'm a team player, obviously, but sometimes I'm too much of a perfectionist – ha ha! No one tells the truth about their strengths and weaknesses in interviews do they? 'My biggest strength is actually my ability to sleep at my desk with my eyes open, thus making it appear that I am present and productive, while actually napping, and my main weakness is probably an inability to use the toilet when there is anyone else in there because I am afraid I might inadvertently fart and someone will hear and they will call me FartGirl forever more, so sometimes I end up wasting a lot of time in the loo waiting for there to be no one else in there even when I only need a wee.') But is that what they want to know now? Maybe they've gone all 'blue-sky thinking' and 'outside the box' (Ooooh, another strength – 'I was the reigning office champion at Buzzword Bingo in my previous job for three years running'), and will ask you 'zany' questions about 'What sort of tree would you be, if you were a tree?' and 'Squirrel or raccoon?' that reveal some hidden psychological depths about you.

Katie across the road came over for a coffee before school pick-up, as her oldest, Lily, has just started school.

'It feels so strange, Lily being at school,' said Katie. 'Just me and Ruby in the house. I don't know why, because it's been just Ruby and me while Lily was at nursery, but somehow it feels different. I can't believe she's at school. She looked so grown-up going in!'

'Ha!' I said. 'I know. The thing is, you will have thought she looked grown-up now on her first day, but in a couple of years you'll be looking at the tinies going in and thinking how little they are and are they really big enough for school.'

'They grow up so fast,' sighed Katie, before shrieking, 'RUBY! RUBY! LEAVE THE DOG! I SAID LEAVE JUDGY ALONE!

DO NOT PULL JUDGY'S WILLY! FFS, what is WRONG WITH YOU! Oh, Christ, scrap what I said. They don't grow up fast enough. RUBY! Do NOT pour your juice over Judgy. I said NO! Oh God, why don't they grow up faster?'

'Do you think I could pass for a millennial, Katie?' I asked hopefully.

'Well, millennial is quite a *broad* term, isn't it?' said Katie kindly.

Friday, 9 September

The Big Day dawned. The day on which it all hinged. I escaped the house without getting anything sticky on me, which frankly was a miracle.

I had carefully factored in time to stop at a suitably artisanal and ethical coffee shop on my way, so I could swish in brandishing my soy chai organic latte, thus demonstrating my hipness and also how caring I am.

I sashayed over to the receptionist and gave my name, and was bidden to stare into a camera and issued with a lanyard with my hastily printed photo on it, which made me look like a serial killer and also made me wonder what the fuck had happened to my hair on the way in from the car park.

A Youth in too-short trousers binged out of a shiny lift to collect me and shook his head in disappointment at my extortionately expensive virtuous coffee. (What is it with the too-short trousers, especially on men? And no one seems to wear socks with them either. I wonder if this trend has caused a downturn in the sock industry?)

'Oh!' he said in surprise. 'Did you forget your own cup? I didn't even know they still *did* takeaway cups.'

'It's biodegradable,' I bleated hopefully. 'Non-chlorinated cardboard. Recycled.'

'Mmmm, but do you know how much energy it takes to recycle it?' he reproved me. '*Much* more than just washing a reuseable cup, you know.'

Fuckety fuckety doodah. I had fallen at the first hurdle. I had been convinced that as long as something could be recycled it would be approved as suitably sustainable and twenty-first-century, but obviously I was wrong. I discreetly abandoned the cup on a window ledge as the Youth whisked me along shiny glass corridors, before depositing me in a white room with artificial grass on the floor.

'This is our Thinking Space,' he informed me. 'We brainstorm and throw concepts around in here. The walls are designed to be wipe-clean, so we can just throw ideas up on them to run past everyone else. I'll just go and tell Ed and Gabrielle and the others that you're here.'

I nodded solemnly as the Youth gestured round the extraordinary room, and tried not to notice that the only thing currently drawn on the walls was a large cock and balls. I wondered if I should wipe it off before the interviewers arrived, in case they thought I had done it? But what if they arrived while I was in the process of wiping it off, and then they *really* thought I had done it? Or what if it was a test, to see how broadminded one was, and wiping it off would reveal one as repressed and bourgeois? But on the other hand, what if it was a test of initiative, to see if one would have the wit to whip the cock and balls off the wall before the officialdom came in? Literally all I could think about now was the cock and balls.

As I stared gloomily at the genitalia on the wall, which seemed to be getting bigger before my eyes, the door opened and four people came in.

'Hi, Ellen, sorry to keep you waiting,' said one of the women, who was totally pulling off the cropped trouser and ankle boot look, without a hint of having got dressed in the darkness. 'I'm Gabrielle from HR. This is Ed, who would be your line manager.' She gestured to a morose but otherwise perfectly normal-looking man, who more importantly was not young and perky, but rather looked in his late forties, which gave me hope that they might be open to employing someone who was old enough to remember Rick Astley for something other than rickrolling. 'And these are Tony and Gail, who'll be sitting in too, if that's OK.'

I beamed, and mumbled something that hopefully sounded like a greeting.

'We keep it very informal here,' said Gabrielle. 'We don't like the traditional panel approach of you facing us across a table, so we'll all just pull up a seat and have a chat.' She gestured around at the 'eclectic' mix of furniture, which I was sorry to see did include the dreaded beanbags, and various squashy-looking cubes and foam shapes that I presumed we were to perch on. As she waved at the 'seating' she noticed the drawing on the wall.

'Oh, for God's sake, what is THAT doing there?' she exploded.

'It wasn't me, it was there when I came in!' I put in quickly.

Gabrielle looked at me slightly oddly. 'I didn't think it was you,' she said. 'I mean, why would you …? Anyway, never mind. Tony, find out who had this room last and have a word, will you? That's really not acceptable. Anyway, let's take a seat and get on.'

Cunningly, I grabbed one of the squashy cubes to perch on rather than a beanbag, which I definitely wouldn't have been able to manoeuvre out of with dignity as my new trousers were a bit tight, and I was worried they might split if I had to heave myself up from a beanbag. It didn't seem the sort of place where flashing your fanny in the interview would secure you the position. Unfortunately, that meant that Ed, who would be my boss, should I get the job, was relegated to a beanbag. He didn't look impressed and muttered something that sounded distinctly like 'FFS' as he gingerly lowered himself down. I fear that was possibly not a good first impression to make.

The rest of the interview was all-rightish, I think. I don't know. Ed asked various questions about my skills and experience, which I answered perfectly well, but he just sort of grunted after each reply and frowned more, so I don't know if he had already decided he hated me and couldn't work with me because I had made him sit on a beanbag.

Gabrielle asked the usual HR questions, which I never know how to answer – do you go for bland and generic and try to appear normal, or do you attempt to be quirky and unique to try to stand out from the other candidates? Also, I am never sure which questions are genuine questions about yourself, and which are trick questions designed to tell if you are a psychopath. Tony and Gail didn't say much at all, but kept making notes during certain questions, which made me suspect that they were the ones doing the psycho-assessing.

No one asked me what sort of tree I would be if I were a tree. I had already decided on a silver birch, as they are shiny and stand out from the crowd, but also birch is a very multipurpose and useful tree. Maybe it was just as well no one cared what sort of tree I would be.

I have blisters from the new shoes, and also there was an unlucky moment when Ed was asking me a complicated question when I realised I had toast crumbs in my bra and they were chafing my nipple. I didn't even dare try and wriggle discreetly to dislodge them in case Tony and Gail thought I was twitching in a psychopathic way.

I suppose I will find out in due course how it went. It wasn't completely awful, like an interview someone I was at university with had, where they accidentally set the interviewer's desk on fire, but it definitely could have gone better. I still suspect the cock and balls was some sort of psychometric test, and I have almost certainly failed it.

Saturday, 10 September

Tonight was the now-traditional pop to the pub for the first week of term debrief with Hannah and Sam. I hoped they might reassure me that it didn't sound like the interview had gone that badly, but Simon just shook his head and said, 'Why on earth did you feel the need to tell them you hadn't drawn on the walls? What had you done that would make them think you *had*?'

Katie, alas, was unable to join us and listen to our grumbles about homework and packed sodding lunches. (I can't work out why I hate packed lunches so much, and find them such an utter chore – they take literally five minutes to make, yet they loom over my mornings like doom-laden black clouds of horror. Maybe it's the tedious inevitability of having to make them *every single term-time morning*, or maybe it's just because my precious moppets refuse to deviate from ham sandwiches for Peter and cheese sandwiches for Jane, with sausage rolls as a 'treat' on the odd Friday when I have lost the will to even make sandwiches, or maybe it's just that I am a really, really terrible mother?)

Simon seemed to be on top of things, and didn't annoy me by asking hopeless questions while I was trying to get ready, so I was a good and kind wife and did not ply the children with

Haribos before I ran out the door and left him to deal with the fallout (oh, the petty revenges we stoop to when you have been married as long as us), but my calm and serene poise was shattered nonetheless when I popped into the sitting room to say a loving farewell to my handsome husband and adorable children and found Simon and Jane playing on Jane's phone.

'What are you doing, darlings?' I said fondly, as I gave them each a kiss.

'Nothing!' snapped Jane, looking shifty. 'Nothing. Daddy's just helping me with something. You'll be late, Mummy, you'd better go.'

Jane has never given a toss about me being late in her life before. In fact, she usually goes out of her way to fanny about, annoy me, delay me and generally do everything she can to MAKE me late. Her favourite is to wait until I am literally going out the door with my coat on and then suddenly remember some incredibly important story she has to tell me, question she has to ask me or letter she has to show me *right now*. So my suspicions were immediately roused.

'Simon, what are you doing?' I demanded.

'Don't worry, sweetie, I'm just setting up an Instagram account for Jane. She said you said it was OK, but you didn't have time to do it for her, and she needs an email address for it, so she's using mine.'

'JANE! You LYING TOAD!' I bellowed. 'I have told you until I am blue in the face that you are NOT having an Instagram account BECAUSE YOU ARE NOT THIRTEEN! How DARE you lie to your father about this?'

Jane looked mutinous and shouted back yet again about HOW UNFAIR I am, because EVERYBODY ELSE had one, and I was ruining her life, and DADDY had said it was OK, so why was I so mean.

'SIMON!' I yelled. 'Why the actual fuck did you agree to this?'

'I DIDN'T!' said Simon indignantly. 'I said if you had said it was all right, then I didn't have any objection, and Jane said you had said she could have an account.'

'I SAID SHE COULD HAVE AN ACCOUNT WHEN SHE IS THIRTEEN!' I howled. 'I'm so angry with you, Jane. We have been over and over this, and yet you thought you could get one over on me by lying to your father. Did you think I wouldn't find out? I don't know what makes me crosser, the blatant disregard for my rules or the lying to your father. Don't you agree she has behaved very badly, Simon?'

'Er,' muttered Simon, 'I suppose it's not ideal …'

'Simon, FFS! Not ideal? Is that all you have to say?'

'Well, it's not the end of the world, is it? I think you might be overreacting a tiny bit. It was just a misunderstanding.'

I took a very deep breath and calmly said, 'Jane, could you please go to your room, while I discuss this with your father?'

Jane slouched out, still muttering her favourite mantra about everything being so unfair, and then despite the several additional deep breaths I had taken while she was making her leisurely exit from the room, I could no longer speak calmly, as I shrieked, 'Simon. It was NOT a misunderstanding; it was a deliberate manipulation of us by Jane. She knows perfectly well I have said she is not to have an account yet. She just thought you were a soft touch and she would get round you while I was out, and I would be none the wiser. And WHY can't you just bloody back me up with the children? Why the fuck do I always have to be the bad cop, and you get to be the good cop, while I rant and rave and you just refuse to take anything seriously? You ALWAYS DO THIS, and it's NOT FAIR!'

'You do realise that you now sound like your eleven-year-old daughter, claiming things aren't fair?' said Simon, in his special

'I'm going to sound annoyingly rational because I think you are hysterical' voice.

'But it's NOT fair!' I howled. 'You never punish them, you always leave it up to me, so when they grow up and write their memoirs I will be the Mommie Dearest figure and you will be some sort of fucking saint. Joan Crawford probably wasn't even that bad a mother. She probably just had a husband who DIDN'T BACK HER UP!'

'I think she was quite a bad mother ...' remarked Simon.

'Don't change the subject,' I snapped.

'I do back you up though. I backed you up over Peter's screen ban last week.'

'Well, apart from the two of you downloading and watching *Guardians of the Galaxy* while I was at the supermarket. And letting him play *Fortnite*! Apart from that, you totally backed me up,' I said with what was supposed to be a hollow laugh, but sadly came out more as a strangulated snarl.

'Oh, for fuck's sake! I DO back you up, you just overreact ALL THE TIME. My God, are you hormonal or something? Is this the start of The Change?'

'I am not hormonal,' I said coldly. 'I resent your assumption that every time I express any emotion, it must just be because I am an irrational ... *beachball* ... just swept away on an uncontrollable tide of hormones.'

'What an image!' sniggered Simon, who was fiddling with his phone. 'And actually, darling, according to the period tracker app on my phone, you are due on, actually.'

'MY FUCKING CYCLE HAS NOTHING TO DO WITH THE FACT THAT YOU ARE AN INCONSIDERATE PRICK! AND THAT APP IS FUCKING CREEPY AND A TOTAL INVASION OF MY PRIVACY!' I snarled.

'On the contrary, sweetheart, it's a useful reminder for when I need to don my Kevlar vest each month,' sighed Simon.

'I am late,' I responded with as much dignity as I could muster. 'I am going now. We will talk about this tomorrow. In the meantime, do not let Jane have an Instagram account, if that is not too much to ask!'

I swept out of the house on that parting note, pausing only to pop upstairs and throw some tampons in my bag, as I had a horrible feeling he was right about me being due on. I do hate it when he is right.

All in all, therefore, I was not in the best frame of mind when I arrived at the pub to meet Hannah and Sam, and before we even got onto the subject of this year's teachers and class groups I indignantly relayed my tale of woe. Sam's daughter Sophie and Hannah's daughter Emily are the same age as Jane, although Hannah's children are at a different school, due to the vagaries of the catchment system, and they at least shared my outrage and concerns, as I hiccupped about paedophiles and sexting, unlike Simon who had made unhelpful suggestions about privacy settings and parental controls when I had raised these concerns.

Nonetheless, despite her sympathetic noises about this, and about my tales of the short-trousered millennials with their reuseable cups and their meeting rooms that were more like upmarket soft-plays, and did they think that I had said the right thing in answer to that question, I could not help but feel that Hannah was not wholly concentrating on Instagram or my interview, and indeed was squirming in her seat like a newly potty-trained toddler in need of a wee.

'Are you all right, Hannah?' I said. 'You look a bit odd. Have you got a UTI?'

'What?' said Hannah. 'Why would I have a UTI? I *do* have some news, actually, but I'm not supposed to tell you yet!'

'Well, you have to tell us now,' said Sam indignantly. 'You can't just say, "I have news" and then refuse to say what it is!'

'Oh, fuck my life, you're up the duff!' I gasped. 'That's why you're wriggling around and needing a wee – you have pregnancy bladder. Oh my God! But you're forty-two! You will have to go to the special unit for the *geriatric mothers*, with all the other old people who have been shagging. Still, I suppose that's better than all the OAPs who are apparently filling the clap clinics because they are all at it like bunnies and not taking precautions now they're too old to even worry about being a *geriatric mother.*'

'Thank you, Ellen, for your supportive comments,' said Hannah dryly. 'Firstly, I don't think they call them "geriatric mothers" any more. It's advanced maternal age or something, which isn't much better, but you are classed as one of them at thirty-five, so it's not like I'd be the only dried-up husk of a medical miracle if I *was* knocked up, which I'm not, because as you may have noticed, I'm the best part of the way down a bottle of Cab Sauv! Which I'd hardly be doing if I was fucking *pregnant*, would I now, Miss Marple?'

'I suppose not,' I conceded grudgingly. 'So what is it then?'

'Shall we guess? Let's guess!' suggested Sam excitedly. 'We could make a drinking game of it and do shots every time we get it wrong?'

'Or Hannah could just tell us, because I am her best friend and she tells me *everything*, like she promised she would when we were eleven,' I said. 'Maybe she'll just tell me, and not you, Sam, because *I'm* her best friend!'

'Ah,' said Sam. 'But I am her best *gay* friend, which means, according to the laws of cliché, that actually she tells *me* everything.'

'Ha!' I said. 'Yes, but according to the laws of cliché, after a Gay Best Friend is told a secret, they have to go shoe shopping with you and then drink Cosmopolitans, and you hate shoe shopping and Cosmos give you heartburn. I WIN!'

'My God!' said Hannah. 'Do you actually WANT to hear my news, or do you just want to squabble between yourselves until I put you on the naughty step?'

'I know. You've won the lottery! Like millions and squillions and you are going to share it with your *best* friend,' I squawked.

'Will you both shut the fuck up? I'm not preggers and I've not won the lottery, BUT Charlie has proposed. We haven't officially announced it yet, because we haven't told our parents, but I couldn't keep it a secret. Look, look at my ring!' said Hannah smugly, fishing a rather swanky little leather box out of her bag.

'Oh my God! Oh my actual fucking God! You're getting married! To Charlie. It's like a fairy story,' I babbled, only slightly tearfully, because my best friend in the whole wide world was getting married again, and this time to a lovely man, instead of a dickhead goblin troll, like her horrible first husband who had unexpectedly walked out on her three years ago.

'Oh, babe. That's amazeballs!' said Sam, also with suspiciously moist eyes. 'Oh, wait. I'm trying to stop saying "amazeballs". Sophie told me it was the lamest thing she had ever heard and she was embarrassed for me.'

'Ooooh, just look at the rock too!' I squeaked. 'Shiny shiny shiny. Put it on. Oh, blissful bling, it's gorgeous! And can I help you plan the wedding? Please say I can? What about a dress? When is it? Oooh, you should totally have one of those vintage shabby chic weddings in a barn, with hay bales and antique bottles full of wildflowers and wellies under your wedding dress!'

'Ellen, does it ever occur to you that you spend a tiny bit too much time on Pinterest?' enquired Sam.

'No. There is no such thing as spending too much time on Pinterest. And anyway, I am the one who got Hannah and

Charlie together, so I should *totes* be the wedding planner extraordinaire. And the guest of honour. Oh, frabjous day! I can finally buy my dream hat. Oh, I'm so glad you are getting married, Hannah, and I can get a hat.'

'Firstly, Sophie informs me that "totes" is also one of the things only lame, sad old people say, and secondly, some people might say that getting Hannah and Charlie together now was the least you could do, after breaking his poor heart at university and letting poor Hannah pine after him for all those years, so that they ended up marrying unsuitable other people,' said Sam, rather unkindly, I thought.

It is true that Hannah and Charlie and I do go back a very long way, and it is also true that I might have once led him on a tiny bit and then got off with Simon instead, and possibly, yes, if I was a better person then maybe Hannah and Charlie would've got together twenty years ago, but I did do the right thing in the end when I bumped into Charlie a couple of years ago, and so really I think I do deserve all the credit. And the best hat at the wedding.

'We are talking about hats, Sam, not past indiscretions,' I said with dignity, before babbling more at Hannah about my Vision for her elegant, rustic, Pinterest-tastic wedding.

'I don't want to get married in a barn with wellies under my dress, though,' protested Hannah. 'And anyway, we haven't even set a date yet, so put down your phone and stop bidding on vintage bottles on eBay, Ellen!'

'I was just *looking*!' I said indignantly. 'There's no harm in *looking*. Ooooh, just think, we can go dress shopping. And get shitfaced again on the free champagne in the posh dress shops. Oh, just think … A wedding dress. An elegant, tasteful one, not a confection of taffeta monstrousness like last time. Can I be a bridesmaid? Can I still wear a hat if I'm a bridesmaid? Emily and Sophie and Jane could be bridesmaids too!'

'Ellen, I'm forty-two, and we are both getting married for the second time. I'm not having dozens of bridesmaids – this is not the Royal Wedding, you know!'

'It would be nice,' I muttered sulkily.

'I've DONE the big wedding, Ellen. And had no control of it, because my mother arranged most of it, and what *my* mother didn't take over, my bloody ex-monster-in-law did, as she did her best to make the day all about her, right down to the old hag turning up at the church in what looked suspiciously like a wedding dress herself, before trying to claim that it was "tradition" for her to dance the first dance with my new husband. I want this day to be about Charlie and me. And you are my best friend, and so of course I want you to be involved and help me plan it. Just don't get carried away!'

'Can I get carried away with my hat at least?' I demanded.

'Do what you like with your bloody hat!' said Hannah.

Monday, 12 September

Today is my birthday. I am now the grandly depressing age of forty-two. And it is a Monday. There should be a law against having birthdays on Mondays. It is absolutely the worst day of the week to have a birthday on.

My forty-second birthday was not nearly as good as my fortieth. I had been rather in dread of my fortieth, convinced that it was nothing more than the marking of the inexorable slide into cronedom and haghood, that it would be the bringer of sagging and wrinkling and walking into a room only to announce that I couldn't remember what I had gone in there for (actually, that is happening more and more). But in the event, Simon swept me off to Paris for a gloriously romantic weekend (though I do not recommend having sex after you have been eating croissants in bed, the crumbs get *everywhere* and are very hard to remove).

We walked hand in hand by the Seine, and Simon grumbled yet again about why I felt the need to buy old postcards ('Because I just *do*, OK, Simon, it's not my fault that you have *no soul*'), we baulked in horror at the queues for the Eiffel Tower, and Simon was forced to bundle me out the Louvre when I took exception to the crowds of tourists clustered around the *Mona Lisa*, as I was very *hot* and rather over *people* and was remarking loudly that I was not at all impressed and wasn't it rather small and dingy a painting for people to make such a fuss about, and some of the tourists, having travelled halfway across the world to make a dream come true by seeing the *Mona Lisa*, were muttering and taking exception to my views on Great Art. Due to the many people in Paris, I also found it necessary to frequently pop into bijou cafés and have my equilibrium restored with delightful *pichets* of *vin rouge*, which meant that I largely spent the weekend in a splendidly blurry haze.

There was one quite unfortunate moment, though, when Simon left me alone in the very posh hotel, as I wanted a soak in the bath, and he decided to go down to the bar for a drink. The hotel had the most gloriously huge, deep, wide bathtub I had ever seen – not only that, but it was a Jacuzzi bath! Oh the bliss, I thought! How relaxed and reinvigorated I would be after a good old wallow in that!

I tipped the tiny little bottle of 'complimentary' bubble bath into the splendidly deep, hot bath I had run, hopped in and set the Jacuzzi settings to 'high', but instead of lying back and enjoying a tranquil moment with lovely warm jets of water soothing my aching muscles, I found myself being spun around into a vortex. The bath was so large, and the Jacuzzi so powerful, I was sucked into a whirlpool in the middle of the bath, unable to reach the controls on the side and turn the bastarding thing off. In addition, the VERY FUCKING TINY bottle of bubble bath had been whipped into a giant foam mountain, obscuring my vision, disorientating me as to where in the bath I was or where the control panel was, and very shortly spilling over the edge of the bath.

Simon, thank God, had got downstairs to the bar, realised he had forgotten his phone and come back upstairs for it. He opened the door to our room to be greeted by bubbles pouring from under the bathroom door, and me screaming for help. When he finally finished laughing he did at least turn off the bath and rescue me, but it is very difficult to attempt to maintain any illusion of poise when one has had to be fished from a killer bath, looking like a drowned rat.

This was also the evening that I insisted we went to a jazz bar in Montmartre so we could be cool and Parisian and sophisticated. Simon had warned me I wouldn't like it, and sure enough, within about ten minutes I was grumbling that it was just *noise* and there was no proper *tune*. Simon looked smug and pretended he was enjoying it, while calling me a philistine. He wouldn't let us leave till we had finished our drinks, and as I had demanded a Campari and soda, thinking it would make me look very European, as well as being pretty and pink, it took me quite a long time to choke it down. It turned out that Campari and soda actually tastes like very nasty cough syrup and Simon said that he wasn't buying me another drink if I wasted that one, as it had been the princely sum of €15 in the over-priced jazz bar. Sometimes Simon is very cruel.

Anyway, now I am forty-two. Quite irretrievably into the realms of the fortysomethings, which is even worse than when I turned thirty-one and had histrionics because I was now a thirty-something (mainly because I remembered watching *Thirty-*

something in my teens and thinking how terribly old they all were, and now I was a fucking thirtysomethinger myself, and I was afraid of turning into Hope, who always seemed so boring and sanctimonious, even though everyone found her inexplicably fanciable, a bit like Sharon in *EastEnders*). My forty-second birthday was celebrated by hoovering, doing the laundry, shouting at the children that they were not even to look at each other, much less speak to each other since they did not seem able to say a single word to their sibling without winding them up, and eating an indifferent takeaway when I insisted I wasn't cooking on my birthday, as Simon had huffed and puffed about going out because he had an early meeting the next day, and 'It *is* Monday night, darling, and it's not like it's actually a *special* birthday, is it?'

No, no, he's quite right, it's not a *special* birthday, because it's only *my* birthday. Everyone else in this house gets *special* birthdays every year, because I bloody well make *sure* they are special, but no one ever thinks to repay the favour for me.

Tuesday, 13 September

Well, I don't know what the significance of the cock and balls in the interview room was, but whatever it was there for, I passed the test (either that or the other candidates reacted to it even worse than I did – perhaps they added spurting jizz and pubes?). Anyway, the whys are not important. What *is* important is that I got a SECOND INTERVIEW. It's next Monday, which should give me plenty of time to prepare, and even better, it's with their head of development who is in currently in California, so it's a phone interview and I don't have to worry about what to wear! There was a horrible moment when I thought it might be a video call, and I would have to find a non-scabby corner of my house to sit in and look executivey, but they said just an ordinary conference call with the Very Important Man and Morose Ed would be fine, so I don't even have to put make-up on and can fish crumbs out of my bra mid-conversation if need be! Happy belated birthday to me! Maybe my family is indifferent to me, but at least the universe or karma or something is on my side.

Wednesday, 14 September

Oh buggering bollocking arseholing twatbums. Tonight was 'Meet the Teacher Night'. Everyone knows that even if your child has had the same teacher for the last three years, you have to go along to Meet the Teacher Night (although you don't *actually* get to Meet the Teacher – you get to sit on a tiny chair and watch a PowerPoint presentation about the curriculum that will in fact bear no resemblance whatsoever to what your child will really learn about over the coming year), because if you don't you are Judged, both by the Unmet Teacher and by the other parents, who will notice your absence. And of course, despite the fact that most people have more sense than to shell out for a babysitter to enable them both to go to the Meet the Teacher Night, there is always at least one extremely smug and enthusiastic couple there together, who hold up all the proceedings by asking inane questions about how the teacher might deal with completely hypothetical situations. Meanwhile the rest of us attempt not to roll our eyes or face palm because these tits are causing tedious delays until the moment when we can pop home and sink face first into a large gin.

I thought I was being nice by giving Katie a lift to Meet the Teacher Night, so she didn't feel daunted walking into the school by herself, but it turned out that this was a foolish thing to do, because although Katie is very lovely, and also a kindred spirit, which is nice to have living across the road, she is also a much better person than me, as well as still being naive and innocent in matters of playground politics.

Thus it was that when we walked into the school foyer together and found Fiona Montague and Perfect Lucy Atkinson's Perfect Mummy standing there, brandishing clipboards menacingly as they attempted to sign people up for the PTA, instead of sidling past with a feeble excuse and trying not to make eye contact, Katie stopped and said she would LOVE to hear more about the PTA.

'Oh, that sounds marvellous!' said Katie with enthusiasm. 'I mean, who wouldn't want to help raise funds for the school? And I expect it is also a really good way to meet other parents, isn't it?'

Lucy's Mummy and Fiona brightly assured Katie that yes, indeed, it was an excellent way for someone new to the school to meet other parents, probably much the best way there was.

'And what about you, Ellen?' suggested Katie, 'You'll join too, won't you, and keep me on the right track, stop me making any terrible playground-politics faux pas? I don't really know how all this works, but you must be an old hand by now.'

'Errr,' I said desperately. 'Well, the thing is …'

'What's wrong, Ellen? Don't you want to help raise money for the school?' asked Katie with wide-eyed innocence.

'Yes, of *course* I do,' I protested indignantly. 'And I am already on the list of people who have agreed to help at actual events. I'm just not totally sure that I'm really a committee person, that's all!'

'Oh, there's nothing to it!' said Lucy's Mummy.

'It really takes hardly any time at all!' chirped Fiona.

'Think of the children!' begged Katie.

And so somehow, after seven years of cunningly avoiding joining the PTA, I found myself agreeing to go along to the AGM and even to consider a committee role, as long as it wasn't Treasurer, in case I accidently embezzled the money and had to go to prison while the children featured in a Sad Face article in the *Daily Mail*.

Simon laughed like a drain when I told him of this when I got home, and reminded me of how, when Jane first started school, I had been so terrified of being forced to join the PTA that I had had a series of distressing dreams in which I was attending PTA coffee mornings or committee meetings, only to find that I was stark bollock naked. Sometimes I fear that Simon is not as supportive a husband as he could be. I also really hope that there was nothing prophetic about all my naked PTA dreams – no strangers need to see a woman of my age naked, no matter what Trinny and Susannah used to claim as they made those poor unlucky women strip off while they jiggled their boobs. Thinking about it, that was such a weird programme. Who thought going on it would be a good idea? 'I know, I'm not very confident, and I don't like my clothes, so I'll go on national telly and let a pair of poshos grab my tits, before advising me that a nice scarf will be the end to all my woes!' It was probably the thin end of the wedge that led to programmes like *Embarrassing Bodies*, when people who claim they are too ashamed to go to the doctors are quite happy to whip their suppurating cocks out on camera (I once made the mistake of watching a clap special of *Embarrassing Bodies*. On the plus side, I lost three pounds, as it put me off my dinner for days).

Monday, 19 September

Aaaargh! Today is my second interview, by phone, and oh happy days, Simon is sick. Really sick. Not just with a sniffle, or a cold, or a bit of cough. He is terribly, dreadfully debilitated, and it is touch and go whether he will make it. He sits hunched over his laptop, wrapped in his nastiest and most synthetic fleece, googling and googling his symptoms, finding ever more terminal diagnoses and wondering aloud every five minutes whether he should call NHS 24 or an ambulance. In between he groans dramatically, or coughs feebly.

'You have man flu!' I said unsympathetically.

Simon moaned pathetically. 'I think it might be Zika virus,' he whimpered.

'How can you have Zika virus? You haven't *been* anywhere with Zika!' I pointed out briskly.

'I was in London last week. There was a woman on the Tube who kept coughing. That could be where I caught it.'

'No, darling, you did not catch Zika on the Tube, because it is not an airborne virus. It is spread by the special Zika mosquitoes. And anyway, Zika is only serious if you are a pregnant woman, and last time I looked, my love, *you were neither a woman nor pregnant*! So I think perhaps you might be malingering a little and making something of a meal out of the fact that you are suffering from a *common fucking cold*!'

'I'm sure I have a fever,' Simon mewed, still tapping away at Dr Google. 'Can you take my temperature? Ebola is airborne. Maybe I've got Ebola. The first symptoms are a fever, a headache, joint and muscle pain, a sore throat and severe muscle weakness. I have all of them! Oh God, I have Ebola. I'm going to die. Don't you even care? You are so unfeeling. Please take my temperature.'

'If you did have Ebola, why would I want to come anywhere near you?' I said. 'But you don't. You have a severe case of hypo-fucking-chondria, that's all.'

'My poor nose is so sore,' sniffed Simon. 'Why don't we have any of the special Balsam tissues?'

'Because they cost twice as much as ordinary tissues.'

'Why are you so unsympathetic?' he whimpered.

'Because you have a cold. A fucking cold! Man the fuck up!' I snapped brusquely.

'But I feel so ill. It must be more than a cold. Please take my temperature.'

'You know the most reliable way to take a temperature is rectally …' I said evilly.

'What? No! You're not putting it up my bum! Just put it under my arm or something.'

'That gives very inaccurate results …'

'I just want a bit of love and sympathy from my wife. Is that too much to ask for? Just a little bit of nurturing, but instead you are threatening to violate me with a thermometer. Why are you so cruel?'

'I am sympathetic. I made you a cup of tea when I got home from picking up the kids and made no comment whatsoever on the bloody mess you made in the kitchen while I was gone, while apparently being too sick to get off the sofa!'

'I was just trying to keep my strength up,' whispered Simon feebly.

'Well, now you have fortified yourself, you need to look after the children and keep them QUIET, because I have this phone interview at 5.30 p.m. Do you think you can do that?'

'What? Who has a *phone interview* at that time?' scoffed Simon.

'One of them's in America.'

'So?'

'The *time difference*? I can take the call upstairs, if you can just keep the kids down here and out of my hair so I can actually concentrate and hear myself think. Please, Simon, this is important!'

'But I feel *awful*,' groaned Simon. 'What am I supposed to do with them? Can't you just tell them to play quietly or something?'

'NO! Someone needs to be supervising them, because otherwise, the minute I am on the phone their radar pricks up and they immediately start causing havoc and barging in and screaming and bellowing. Don't you remember a couple of years ago when I tried to have a work call at home and we ended up in A&E because Peter managed to get a pea stuck up his nose?'

Simon looked blank. 'Did he?'

I sighed. 'No, of course you don't remember. You weren't here. You were on yet another trip, which was why I was dealing with everything by myself, *yet again*, which is why it would be nice if just for once you could help me out and keep the kids out of the way.'

'I'm just saying, I'm not well,' complained Simon. 'Yet I'm supposed to look after the kids. You know, my mother would never have expected my father to look after us.'

'What the fuck does that have to do with it?' I snapped. 'You are not your father and I am not your mother and this is the twenty-first fucking century, so just get with the programme and LOOK AFTER YOUR CHILDREN because I am going to get ready for my call!'

'But what about dinner?' Simon wailed plaintively after me. 'Am I expected to do that too?'

'I'll make dinner when I've finished,' I shouted over my shoulder. 'Just keep the kids QUIET!'

The call started well. Max, the very important boss man, turned out to be American as well as being in America, so he did that lovely American thing of being very jolly and positive and polite. Ed still did not say much, and mostly was a slightly disturbing heavy-breathing presence on the line while Max and I chatted. After about twenty minutes there was a screech from downstairs. I tensed. Shortly afterwards there were thunder footsteps on the stairs, and I braced myself, while seething with fury. Then the hammering on the door and the bellowing began.

'Is everything OK, Ellen?' asked Max kindly. 'There seems to be kinda a funny noise coming from your end?'

'Yes,' I said desperately. 'It's, err, it's a crossed line, I think.'

'A crossed line?' said Max in confusion. 'Isn't this your cell phone though? I didn't think you could get crossed lines on a cell. Heck, I didn't think you still got crossed lines at all!'

'It's, um, it's a British thing,' I improvised as the screaming increased, and I thanked my lucky stars that at least the bedroom door had a lock so the little fuckers couldn't get in. 'We still get them because our networks … errr … the war … you know?'

Ed made what could have been a snort of derision, or possibly just a snore because he had fallen asleep, having not said anything for the last fifteen minutes, and Max said, 'The war? Um, OK, I didn't know that, that's interesting.'

I tried desperately to concentrate and sound calm and professional for the brief remnants of the rest of the conversation, but I think the damage was done by my frantic babblings about the war. Everyone knows you Don't Mention the War. I know almost every episode of *Fawlty Towers* off by heart, so why the FUCK would I mention the war instead of just apologising and explaining that it was my delinquent hell-fiend children?

I stormed downstairs afterwards to find Simon sauntering out of the loo with a self-satisfied expression on his face.

'What the fuck do you think you were doing?' I yelled. 'You just had to keep the kids quiet for a bit. That was all. Where were you?'

'I had to go for a shit,' said Simon indignantly. 'I TOLD you I wasn't well. I'm all out of sorts. Usually I only shit in the mornings – I'm very regular – but clearly the Ebola has affected my digestion.'

'And you couldn't wait? You couldn't hang on till I was off the phone, so I could actually have what is possibly the most important call of my life in peace without the children fighting outside the door because apparently Peter has taken some fucking keyring of Jane's and so her honour was impugned and she had to scream the house down about it, despite neither of them having a key to put on it? You couldn't have just left it for a FEW BASTARDING MINUTES?'

'When you have to shit, you have to shit!' said Simon. 'So, what's for dinner?'

'Oh, go fuck yourself!' I snarled.

Thursday, 22 September

Well, I went to the PTA AGM. I dragged Sam with me too, on the basis that if I was going down, I was taking as many people as I could with me. He objected strenuously to this, pointing out that I should really have known better than to have succumbed to the pressure of Perfect Lucy Atkinson's Perfect Mummy and Fiona Montague, even though everyone knows how hard it is to resist them, especially when they are holding their Very Important Official-Looking Clipboards. He tried to wriggle out of it by sighing that sadly, as he was a single parent, he had no childcare. But I was prepared for that and had already told Simon that he would be looking after Sophie and Toby, as well

as his own darling poppets, and so, finding himself outmanoeu-
vred, poor Sam had little choice but to accompany Katie and me
to the school hall, down the corridors scented with an eternity
of school dinners – that heady whiff of cabbage and stale chip fat
– to find Lucy Atkinson's Mummy and Fiona Montague presid-
ing over a hall containing a grand total of eleven people, out of
the approximately seven hundred parents at the school. I felt
very bad about never coming along before – I had always
assumed these meetings were brimming over with enthusiastic
voluntary-type people who had filofaxes and liked organising
things and knew how to use glue guns. I had never realised how
poorly attended they were, which certainly shed some light on
why Lucy's Mummy and Fiona could be slightly militant when
trying to drum up PTA support.

Lucy Atkinson's Mummy kicked off proceedings by tendering
her resignation as Chair and inviting someone to come forward
to take her place. A deafening silence met her words.

Cara Cartwright was sitting beside me and whispered, 'Don't
worry. She resigns every year, and no one has yet dared try and
replace her. She just likes to feel needed.'

Lucy's Mummy, however, shouted, 'Come ON! Someone
must be willing to replace me. I DON'T WANT TO DO THIS
ANYMORE. If no one will step up and replace me, there will
be no PTA. There will be no Halloween disco, no Christmas
Fayre, no Summer Fete, AND NO FUCKING MONEY FOR
SCHOOL TRIPS, NEW WHITEBOARDS OR ANY OTHER
BASTARDING THING! This is my daughter's last year at
primary school and all I really want to do is spend ONE school
event with her. Actually WITH her, not throwing another pound
coin at her to go and have a few more shots on the tombola
because I'm too busy running the event to do anything with her.
Is that so much to ask?'

The silence was really quite awkward now.

'RIGHT!' bellowed Lucy's Mummy, slamming her Important Clipboard down on the table. 'FUCK THIS SHIT! I am out of here. Hell mend the lot of you!'

'Me too!' said Fiona Montague.

Ohhhhhh, this was MEGA awkward. I do hate a pregnant pause, and so before I really knew what I was doing, just to end the tense atmosphere, I somehow found myself putting my hand up and mumbling, 'Errrr, I'll do it. If no one else wants to, that is?'

Fuck it, I thought to myself. I clearly had blown all chance of the Dream Job and so I might as well do something useful with my time in between the eating biscuits and inventing abortive apps.

'Will you, Ellen?' said Lucy's Mummy, a slightly manic look in her eye. 'Oh, that's marvellous news! Now we just need a treasurer to replace Fiona, and a secretary.'

'Umm, Sam?' I hissed, nudging him in the ribs. 'And Katie, you got me into this.'

Sam sighed. 'I'll be the treasurer then.'

'And I'll be the secretary!' said Katie.

'Oh *wonderful*!' cried Lucy's Mummy. 'We're FREE. I mean, that's marvellous of you to offer. Technically you should be proposed and seconded, etc, but to be honest it's so hard to get people to volunteer in the first place that we haven't bothered about that in years. Now, would anyone else like to join the committee?'

'Oh, go on then,' said Cara Cartwright. 'In for a penny, in for a pound!'

'I'd like to join as well,' said a new voice from the back of the hall. Everyone craned round to see who it was. A tall woman with immaculate hair and full make-up had walked in, with two very clean children in tow.

'Sorry we're late,' said the new woman. 'I'm Kiki. I was just taking some photos of Lalabelle and Trixierose playing outside. Yes, I would like to join. I think there's a lot of things that could be improved.'

Lucy's Mummy had looked nonplussed for a moment, but she ralled enough to interrupt. 'Errr,' she said, 'I just need to stop you there. The thing is … sorry, was it Coco?'

'Kiki. With two Ks.'

'Right. Kiki. This is the PTA. We only deal with fundraising for the school, not school policies. You want the Parent Council for that.'

'Oh,' said Kiki with two Ks (it's hardly Anne with a bloody E, is it? Also, isn't Kiki a parrot's name?). 'Well, I'm here now, so I might as well stay, as I'm interested to see what the PTA funds are used for. I'm sure there are better ways of spending the money – for example, the playground is very grey. It's really hard to get a decent photo of the girls out there. If some money could be spent on some nice paving, maybe some plants, and obviously a mural wall is a MUST.'

'Why?' asked Lucy's Mummy.

'Because everyone loves a mural wall as an Instagram back-drop!' cried Kiki. 'Instagram is the future. Schools really need to get on board with this.'

Lucy's Mummy turned puce at this, as Fiona Montague nudged her, and I distinctly heard her whisper, 'Let it go. Not our circus, not our monkey anymore! Let's wrap things up quickly and go to the pub. She's Ellen's problem now.'

Kiki ploughed on oblivious. 'While we're on the subject, why isn't the school on Instagram? Maybe I could help with that. I'm actually a social media influencer, with over 300 followers. I'm @kikiloveandlife if anyone wants to follow me – it's about children and lifestyle and travel. People tell me I'm an aspirational inspiration, which is humbling!'

The first icy realisation of what I may have done began to dawn on me.

The rest of the meeting mainly consisted of the outgoing committee handing over to us, the new, slightly daunted committee, with proceedings only minimally held up by Kiki interrupting to tell us her latest Instagram stats, and asking for another pause while she took more photos of her daughters colouring in and then suggested a group selfie, which everyone politely declined, and reminding us again that we all *really* should follow her, as a *lot* of people have told her she is inspirational.

The only saving grace was that Kiki didn't actually seem interested in volunteering for any position within the PTA other than starting an Instagram page, which I am pretty sure the school will veto.

When I got home and 'fessed up to Simon about how I was not only on the PTA committee, but was in fact the new Chair, he looked at me in disbelief.

'So what you are telling me is that Perfect Lucy Atkinson's Perfect Mummy actually gave her resignation by publicly shouting "FUCK THIS SHIT" and that was the point at which you decided it would be a good idea to take on the role that had reduced her to that?'

'Ummm, well, it was such a very *awkward* silence. Someone had to say something. I panicked! I hate silences.'

'Usually you fill any perceived awkward silences by babbling hysterically about how otters have opposable thumbs, not by volunteering for what appears to be the most thankless task in the history of humanity.'

'I did consider my otter soliloquy, but it didn't really seem appropriate. And how bad can it be, when I have Sam and Katie helping me? And Cara, she seems perfectly nice, and normal. It will be *fine*, Simon, I don't know what you are worrying about. We have already agreed that it would be a much better idea to hold our meetings in the pub – I bet that will get lots of people along!'

'Hmmmm,' said Simon doubtfully. 'Well, I will try not to say "I told you so" when it all goes tits up.'

Friday, 30 September

I GOT THE JOB! I don't know HOW, but I got the job. Gabrielle just said that Max had found me very 'creative' (Gabrielle didn't sound totally convinced by this). Maybe being able to make up bullshit on the spot is a positive life skill now, instead of being frowned upon? And because I don't have to hand in my notice anywhere else, they want me to start a week on Monday, which, oh fuck, is just over a week away.

Obviously I am now totally *totally* panicking about everything. Am I up to the job? Can I actually do it? How am I going to manage juggling being the Chair of the PTA with working full-time and everything else? Will my children now be emotionally stunted and traumatised for life? And most importantly, *what if I can't find the toilets in the new office*? I spend a lot of time worrying about toilets; toilets are important to me. If I can't find them it will be distressing. I still recall my first job, where everything was fine for the first six months because I knew where the toilets were, but then they moved me to another department, a department with no obvious toilets, where every-one else was male and I didn't like to ask anyone where the ladies' were, so I spent the *next* six months trailing back and forth to my old department so I could have a wee, until I had the bright idea of following another woman who worked on the same floor as me, and finding the toilets like that. It's not just me who has toilet issues; Hannah once went so far as to turn down a job because she was worried the building was too big and she would never find the loos (I mean, there were other factors too, obviously, but the toilets were definitely a part of it). Also, they are a modern and innovative company, so what if they have gone all *Ally McBeal* and have unisex toilets? I don't want unisex toilets, I don't want to listen to Brian from Marketing grunting as he shits out last night's biryani while I'm trying to change a tampon, and what if they talk about wanking while I'm trying to put my lip gloss on? Do men talk about wanking in the toilets? I have no idea. How would I possibly know what men talk about in the toilets, and that's the way I like it! And if I can't even wee while there are other women in the ladies, how on earth am I going to be able to 'go' if there are *men* in there? (Although I would at least be able to blame the farting on them, should I accidentally let one rip.)

I felt rather nostalgic for the familiar, comforting surroundings of the loos in my old office, the loos I knew the exact location of, where Brenda the cleaning lady would leave the cupboard with the spare loo rolls unlocked for me because she knew I got anxious if we were down to less than half a roll in the holder. You couldn't do that in a unisex loo, with Brian and his biryanis. Everyone knows men would not respect such bog-roll privileges. But then I cheered up. I had got the Dream Job! In the face of everything, including the cock and balls on the wall, Simon's general lack of enthusiasm, the wrong sort of coffee cup, the feral screaming children and the toast crumbs in my bra, I HAD GOT THE FUCKING JOB! Obviously I would need a smart new capsule work wardrobe. Hopefully they wouldn't expect me to wear those stupid heels all the time, and maybe I will finally master how to wear the cropped trousers with funky boots without looking like a fanny.

OCTOBER

Saturday, 1 October

I got an email from my father today, suggesting we all 'get together' for lunch soon, which was quite unexpected as I thought he was still living in Portugal. Apparently he has a 'surprise' for me. I am dubious about this, because although part of me is an eternal optimist and thus immediately thinks perhaps he is coming to tell me that he has decided to transfer a large sum of money to me, or that he has put his house in Portugal into my name now to avoid death duties and because I need it more than my sister, no good ever comes of his 'surprises', as they inevitably take the form of his announcing that he is either getting married again or divorced again.

If one were feeling generous, Daddy could be described as something of an aging roué, with a rather Leslie Phillips vibe going on, but really as he gets older, his habit of getting married and divorced on what seems like an almost annual basis is getting rather embarrassing. We did think that his last wife, Caroline, had finally got him to settle down, and she did stick it out a remarkable seven years, before throwing in the towel when she caught him in bed with her ironing lady, at which point he decamped to Portugal, claiming that it was for the golf, and not, as Mummy waspishly suggested, that he had run out of shags in Sunningdale, since he was reduced to bedding the staff.

My fears over his latest 'surprise' were confirmed with a call from my dear sister Jessica, who had received a similar email, also summonsing her to the meet-up. Jessica, trying as ever to be the condescending elder sister, poo-pooed my concerns that we were about to be introduced to our latest stepmother.

'For heaven's sake, Ellen. He's seventy-five years old. Why on earth would he want to get married again at his age? Surely he's learned by now.'

'Maybe not. Remember Carrie Barker? Her granddad got married three times after his first wife died when *he* was seventy-five!'

'Yes, but his wives kept dying of old age, so he had to get another one because he'd never washed his own pants. That's hardly the same as Daddy. He's spent enough time between wives to be reasonably self-sufficient.'

'Well, what do *you* think he wants then?'

'How should I know? Maybe he's decided to move back to the UK so he can spend more time with his grandchildren.'

'He hates children. He didn't even really like us that much when we were little, and pretty much went out of his way to avoid us. He is immensely proud of the fact that he has never changed a nappy, and still complains about the time Jane vommed on him when she was a newborn. That's been the only saving grace in the revolving door of wives. At least his general dislike of children meant that there were no new brothers and sisters to take a share of our inheritance!'

'He likes Persephone and Gulliver.' said Jessica, with the indignation of a mother's love. 'Everyone likes Persephone and Gulliver – I'm constantly told how charming they are. Maybe it's just your children he doesn't like!'

'He does not like your children!'

'HE DOES!'

'NOT!'

'STOP being so petty!'

'SHAN'T!'

'Ellen, I will hang up if you can't conduct a civilised conversation like a normal adult.'

'Oh, all *right*!' I grumbled. I honestly don't know what it is about Jessica. She is my only sister and I love her, I honestly do, but I don't really like her very much. She always rubs me up the wrong way, usually by being so bloody *superior*, and then I find myself just fighting the urge to kick her in the shins, or push her over in a muddy puddle and laugh at her. Our ability to still squabble like children at the ages of forty-two and forty-five does not give me much hope that the magical day will ever dawn when Peter and Jane will stop fighting and be friends and get on without one or the other trying to brutally murder their sibling. And anyway, Jessica's children are monsters of hot-housed over-achievement and will doubtless be running the country before they are out of their teens, if Jessica has anything to do with it. (I still cringe, though, every time I remember that I have a niece and nephew called Persephone and Gulliver, but Jessica is immensely smug that *nobody* else she knows, not even any of the children of the other NCT mummies from either of her pregnancies, has the same names as her offspring, and in fact since records began neither 'Persephone' nor 'Gulliver' has ever appeared on a list of 'Most Popular' names. She was mildly less smug when after a brief googling I was able to inform her they did both appear on a list of the Most Pretentious Middle-Class Children's Names. That was a very good day …)

However, the mystery of why Daddy wanted to see us all was no closer to being solved, so Jessica announced she would book a table for lunch (hopefully not at a restaurant that doesn't serve chips. I took Peter to a chip-free restaurant once and it ended very badly).

Friday, 7 October

Aaaarrrrgghhhh! It's Fuck It All Friday. I have been trying to get ready for starting my new job next week, including booking childcare and batch-cooking nutritious meals for the freezer so my babies won't have to live on ready meals and get diabetes and scurvy, I have failed to nail the capsule wardrobe, but I have bought a lot of 'quirky' trousers that I am really not at all sure I can pull off, and a very corporate-looking handbag that frankly scares me with its grown-upness, and all I want is a glass of wine in peace, yet the children clamour constantly to be fed. All those baby books, all those parenting manuals with their wise words, and their fucking routines and their 'helpful tips' – do you know what they omit to tell you? That your children will want dinner *every single bastarding night*, even though they don't actually like any food ever, because they are picky little twats.

Oh, I had such high hopes once. *My* children weren't going to be picky eaters! If you had a picky eater, it was simply because you had made a rod for your own back, entirely through your lazy, underachieving ways. My children, I was so smugly sure, would be enthusiastic gourmands, yumming down delicious exotica from the four corners of the earth. Oh, yes.

Jane had other ideas, though. Jane hated everything. Except chocolate. She liked chocolate. I would spend hours lovingly cooking, pureeing and freezing, only for Jane to spit out whatever delightful concoction I had created for her and scream like I was feeding her ground glass. Eventually, regarding my freezer full of special Tupperware trays filled with Annabel Bloody Karmel specials that Jane wouldn't touch, I had a brainwave! Clearly, I could save myself a lot of bother – and wasted food – by finding out what she liked by giving her a selection of bought baby food, and then once we knew what she enjoyed, I could simply cook that for her! Off I went to Sainsbury's and came home with every variety of Ella's Kitchen pouches and Baby Organix jars available (to ease the middle-class guilt at feeding my precious first-born moppet on jars of baby food). Jane liked most things out of jars (she was particularly fond of a revolting-looking 'steak and spinach' concoction that was a sort of green-ish black sludge and looked exactly the same coming out the other end as it did going in). It turned out she just didn't like anything I cooked for her. Jar of vegetable lasagne? 'Yummers!' said Jane (well, she didn't actually, obviously. She couldn't talk). Homemade vegetable lasagne? 'Bleurgh!' said Jane. And so it went on.

I had bought a sodding TRAVEL BLENDER so I could puree tasty things for Jane on the move. A TRAVEL BLENDER? What sort of fuckwit has a travel blender? Jane continued to only want her jars of mush until she was old enough to eat chips and chicken nuggets, at which point she would happily have subsisted on nothing else (with a healthy dose of refined sugar and E numbers, obviously).

I was in despair. I trailed to the health visitor each week to bewail Jane's intractability (and intractable she was – if you could manage to get a spoonful of something into her mouth, she would sit for hours refusing to swallow it. I was highly amused the night Simon came home and found Jane sitting with a mouthful of something green and slimy, and said, 'This is ridiculous, Ellen, I'll get her to swallow it!' and held her nose. I could have warned him what would happen next of course, but it was funnier to see her spray the green goo all over him!), only to be brightly told that she would 'Eat when she was hungry' and 'No child has ever starved themselves to death'.

Maybe not, I thought darkly, BUT WHAT IF SHE WAS THE FIRST?

Peter was not as bad, being basically ravenous from birth (his indignation the one and only time I tried him with a dummy was hilarious – he was outraged that he was expected to go to the effort of sucking on something that would not provide him with food), and he did consent to eat my pots of mush, which was just as well, because I don't think I could have afforded enough jars to spoon into his constantly gaping maw (although there was an unfortunate incident with butternut squash when he filled his nappy just as I drove onto a motorway, and by the time I was able to stop and change him his bum had been stained bright orange – he looked like a baby baboon for days), but again, come toddlerdom, he decided chippies and cakey were sufficient to sustain him.

And now, they just push the food around their plates while loftily informing me that I KNOW they don't like such and such. They could have happily eaten whatever it was every single day of their bloody lives, but I am supposed to telepathically infer their likes and wants on any given night. And then, of course, if one of them likes it, the other won't – Peter loves shepherd's pie, but Jane hates it, and Jane loves macaroni cheese and Peter claims it is toxic, even though he will happily eat pasta with butter and grated cheese and seriously WHAT IS THE FUCKING DIFFERENCE?

Then there is Simon, who turns his nose up at most of the things the children will eat and claims they are 'boring', and sniffs at chicken as also being 'boring', and sighs and says he just fancies something 'tasty', by which he means something out of my nice Ottolenghi cookbook, which is all very well, and the food IS delicious and the recipes very reliable, but Yotam Ottolenghi quite clearly has at least one person, possibly more, to do his washing-up for him, as his recipes tend to call for All the Pots. Simon, being a man, does not understand while I rail so furiously against this, because for him, ALL cooking involves using All the Pots. And All the Knives, All the Spoons, All the Spatulas and All of Anything Else in the Kitchen!

Basically, the only thing anyone can agree on to eat in this house is lasagne. Bastarding lasagne. Which also uses All the Pots. I used to like lasagne. It used to be a lovely treat. When someone else was making it. But now – now the very word strikes Doom and Rage into my soul. I think the thing that makes me crossest about lasagne is the fact that however much I point out that it is actually quite a faff, Simon labours under the impression that it is a simple and easy meal to make. I once even went to the lengths of making him make it himself. I talked him through each step of the process, of course, after I lost the will to live as he bleated for the eleventy billionth time that he couldn't find the chopped tomatoes (on the SAME SHELF in the SAME CUPBOARD as they are always are) and did I think he should add some cumin to the sauce (NO), and for the white sauce, should he use a spoon or a whisk, and what temperature did the oven need to be on at? I suspect he was hoping to annoy me into doing it myself, but I held strong and made him do it, under supervision, only to have him say smugly as we sat down to eat, 'I don't know why you make such a fuss about lasagne, darling. It was a piece of piss! Oh, and you'll clear up the kitchen, won't you? I mean, fair's fair, I cooked.' Sometimes I really think I must be some sort of saint, blessed with a truly extraordinary amount of patience. It is the only explanation for why I haven't yet run amok and killed anyone.

Still, as it is FIAF, at least I can feed the cherubs pizza, claiming that it is a treat for them, and not suffer from a guilty conscience about being a terrible Jeremy Kyle-style mother. Everyone knows that anything goes on FIAF – though I am wondering now why I spent so much time this week on lovingly cooking stews and soups and tagines so the little darlings could enjoy a nutritious and balanced diet even though they were being abandoned by their mother for the evil world of commerce, when I am 99 per cent sure they probably won't eat any of it. Oh well, maybe it will go some way to easing my own maternal guilt at sacrificing the fruit of my loins upon the altar of my career. I wonder if men feel like this about working full-time? I must ask Sam, as I suspect Simon most certainly does not.

Sunday, 9 October

I was RIGHT! Take that, Jessica. I *said* Daddy wanted to introduce us to his latest popsy, and indeed he did. Apart from a mild amount of glee at being righter than Jessica, though, this is a most distressing turn of events.

We arrived at the restaurant (thank God for online menus, so I at least was able to assure Peter in advance that there were chips, and promise him that I wouldn't make him eat any vegetables) to find Daddy already sitting at the table, with a very pretty woman with dark hair. Very pretty, and VERY FUCKING YOUNG! Well, I say 'young', I don't mean *illegally* young, obviously; she was about my age, which is *very fucking young* for my father.

Daddy looked like the cat who'd got the cream as he smugly announced, 'Everyone, I'd like you to meet my wife, Natalia. Natalia, this is my younger daughter Ellen, and her husband

Simon, and my grandchildren, Peter and Jane – Peter, darling, what are you *doing*?'

'I'm dabbing, Grandpa, OBVS!' said Peter scathingly. 'Don't you know what dabbing is?'

'You look like you're having some kind of a fit,' said Daddy in horror. 'Please stop it now and say hello to Natalia.'

Peter dabbed again.

'Hello, Natalia,' I managed to say faintly.

'Hello, Natalia, hello, Ralph!' bellowed Simon, going for the age-old British tradition of covering up social discomfort by being incredibly hearty and ignoring the elephant in the room. Not that Natalia was an elephant. She was annoyingly slim.

'Hello, Ellen, Simon, children! I'm so pleased to meet you,' said Natalia. Oh God, she was foreign. Daddy had finally gone and done it once and for all. His new wife was far younger than him, gorgeous and foreign. He had got himself a mail-order bride! Oh, *Daddy*!

'Sit next to me, Ellen,' said Natalia politely, as I tried to surreptitiously text Jessica with the news.

Jane eyed Natalia beadily. 'I like your eyeliner,' she said. 'Mummy can't do flicky eyeliner like that, you know.'

'Oh,' said Natalia. 'Thank you.'

'You could have a YouTube channel giving make-up tips,' said Jane. 'With eyeliner like that, I bet you'd be really good at it. Are you on Instagram?'

'Errr, yes,' said a somewhat nonplussed Natalia.

'Lucky you,' sighed Jane. 'I would offer to follow you, but I can't because Mummy won't let me have an account. Does that seem fair to you?' she demanded. 'Do you think it's right that I have to wait till I'm thirteen when ALL MY FRIENDS have their own accounts already?'

'I … I don't know.'

'It's not fair!' said Jane firmly. 'It's very unfair.'

'Enough, Jane!' I said. 'We've only just met Natalia. The last thing she wants to hear about is you going on about your lack of a bloody Instagram account!'

'Well!' said Jane indignantly. 'That's not very nice, is it? I mean, Natalia is my step-granny now, so I thought it only right she knows what you make me go through, how UNFAIR you are. Maybe I will go and live with Natalia and Grandpa, and then we'll see how you like that!'

Natalia turned pale.

'Don't worry, don't worry, of course she's not going to come and live with you,' I assured her. 'Do you have children?'

'No!' said Natalia, and I swear she mouthed the words 'Thank fuck' as she looked at Peter, who was now having an argument with Simon about why he needed to order a drink in a plastic bottle so he could demonstrate his prowess at the bottle-flip challenge to his cousins.

'Can I get you a drink, Madam?' asked the waiter.

'A glass of wine,' I gasped. 'A LARGE glass of wine!'

'So, Natalia,' said Jane. 'About your YouTube channel. I could help you present it. I have been practising making vlogs, and I really think I am very good at it.'

'So, Daddy, when did this happen?' I asked, trying to smile brightly and look like I was totally fine about having a new step-mother the *same fucking age as me*!

'Oh, about three weeks ago,' said Daddy airily.

'And you didn't think to invite us?'

'We didn't want to wait. We eloped!' chortled Daddy. Oh holy fuck, I thought. Definitely a mail-order bride! Why? Why does he have to do this? Oh FML, I wonder if he got a pre-nup? What about the remnants of my inheritance? Will it now be squandered on faux leopardskin and hair bleach for Natalia after she shags Daddy (MY DADDY) into an early grave? (In fairness, she had neither bleached hair nor was she wearing leopardskin, but I wasn't about to let that interfere with my preconceived stereotypes about mail-order brides.)

'Where are you from, Natalia?' I enquired.

'Russia,' replied Natalia. Ha! See. Definitely mail-order.

Jessica arrived at that moment, and Peter managed to knock over his lemonade as he leapt up to dab enthusiastically at Persephone and Gulliver, while demanding if either of them had a bottle about their person.

'Dabbing isn't allowed at our school,' sniffed Gulliver primly.

'Auntie Jessica, is that a water bottle in your bag?' demanded Peter.

Jessica, clearly so stunned by the fact that Natalia was younger than her, absent-mindedly passed a half-empty Evian bottle to Peter, as I shouted 'NOOOOOO!'

Peter hurled the bottle at the table, sending cutlery, wine glasses and flowers flying.

Simon and I, accustomed to Peter's attempts at the bottle-flip challenge, had managed to leap clear, but Natalia ended up drenched in my red wine.

'Well,' said Simon. 'Welcome to the family!'

'I have a new job!' I said brightly.

Monday, 10 October

The First Day. The most important thing is obviously that I found the toilets, and they are not unisex, so that is a huge weight off my mind. The second thing to note is that I have the wrong sort of shoes. My ballet flats are far too mumsy and I need quirky trainers, stat.

Ed showed me around and introduced me, and I tried to remember everyone's names. It was all a bit of a blur, but there is definitely an Alan and a James and a Lydia and a Joe, I'm just not sure who is who (well, I know which one is Lydia, obviously), so I will have to work on that over the next few days. There are also some interesting shirts and the aforementioned quirky trainers. I am feeling very let down by Pinterest now, as I was obviously browsing the wrong 'Cool Work Clothes' boards.

There is no hotdesking, which I am slightly disappointed by, as I have always quite fancied hotdesking, even though I am not entirely sure of the point of it, as I wasn't really paying attention in Management WankSpeak 101. I think I am sitting next to Alan. Or it could be James. Ed seems to mainly hide in his office and try to avoid people. I think this is admirable in a boss, and if I am ever important enough to have my own office I will definitely do the same. There are no biscuits in the kitchen, and everyone seems terribly healthy – there was a lot of avocado eaten at lunchtime. The toilets have nice loo roll, though, so I think it could all work out. I can always hide biscuits in my desk, especially if there is no hotdesking for me to forget them and leave them behind.

I am bloody knackered tonight, though, after the scramble to get the kids out the door to breakfast club (and that was with Simon helping. God knows how we'll manage on the mornings when there is only one of us available to do it), and then the dash home to pick them up, hurl dinner down them and do homework, and actually attempt to have a conversation with them before shooing them into bed at a decent hour.

Tuesday, 11 October

FML. So as if the new job and having to spend all day pretending I am a proper person, not hysterically talking about otters to fill lulls in the conversation and hiding my biscuit-eating under my desk (it is definitely Alan I sit next to. He spent some time this morning explaining to me about 'bulletproof coffee' and his clean-eating and cross-fit regime, and sniffed most suspiciously when I rammed in a Mint Club at 11 o'clock. Also, bulletproof coffee sounds like the most disgusting drink I have ever heard of, and that's even taking into account Simon's sister, who used to put her husband's jizz into smoothies), this whole PTA thing is also starting to bite.

Shortly after my Mint Club – while Alan was still complaining he was sure he could smell mint Aeros (fool, Mint Clubs are far superior) – Perfect Lucy Atkinson's Perfect Mummy sent an extremely detailed series of emails. At that point I was sitting at my desk trying to look as though I was concentrating very hard on something very important so no one would talk to me and I wouldn't have to make more polite chit-chat with my face aching from smiling constantly so people think I am friendly and approachable, since I don't have an office to hide in, like Ed, the lucky bastard, who doesn't even pretend to be friendly and has informed me that there is no need to speak to him unless it is unavoidable and that an email will do perfectly well, which suits me fine. The emails covered the dos and don'ts for all the forthcoming PTA events, and other helpful tips, starting with the sodding Halloween Disco:

Hi Ellen,

Halloween Disco

Hall is booked for Friday 28th October 6.30–8.30pm. Parents will complain this is not actually Halloween/why is it on a Friday night/that it starts and finishes too early or too late. Tell them it is so that they can go trick or treating with their darlings, that it's on a Friday so the children aren't tired for school and that they don't have to bastarding come if they don't like the time. Any other complaints, tell them to go fuck themselves.

Parents MUST stay with their children – this is why we run a bar so we can fleece them for overpriced tepid Chardonnay to numb the pain of the disco (I've already got the licence). The teachers used to come and supervise, but refuse to do this now due to issues with parents taking the piss, and not turning up to pick kids up on time. Under no circumstances let unsupervised children in, or there will be carnage. Especially watch out for Oscar Fitzpatrick's mum, who will claim she is just popping to the shop and will be back in a mo, only to vanish for the whole time so Oscar runs amok, and Edie Prescott's mum who will claim she can't stay as she has a feverish child at home who needs her. I fell for this the first two years and then realised I was being scammed.

There is usually a tuckshop, apple bobbing, doughnuts on a string, face painting, tattoos and a slime lucky dip. Poundland is now your friend.

You will need to send at least six emails appealing for volunteers and threaten to call the whole thing off before you get enough people to help.

Have Fun! Xxxx

I am rather warming to Lucy's Mummy. I had no idea she was so sweary, or nurtured a similar hatred for People as I do. Nor, to my shame, did I realise how much work she had put into the PTA, or how utterly thankless it was, as we fled from her brandishing her clipboard and her books of raffle tickets, assuming she only did it to feel important. I fear I misjudged her, but when am I going to send these emails/do all this organising? I only just managed to shut the window with the email before Alan came sniffing behind me, still on the track of the minty chocolate (which suggests that he can whang on about bulletproof coffee and the evils of carbs all he likes. Anyone that obsessed by the smell of chocolate has something missing from their lives), because I don't feel the PTA really fits in with my new image of cool not-quite-a-millennial in my should-probably-eat-fewer-Mint-Clubs-because-they're-still-a-bit-tight trendy trousers.

Thursday, 13 October

I am so bloody tired. I feel like I've spent all week before and after work just running on the spot to catch up. Work actually feels like a break, apart from Lucy's Mummy's emails, which are still pinging in regularly. I sent an email to all the parents at school, suggesting a meeting to discuss planning for the disco, but little to my surprise the silence was deafening, so instead Sam, Cara and Katie came to mine tonight and we fed the cherubs fishfingers while we drank wine and tried to come up with new and exciting ideas for the disco, before deciding that we couldn't be arsed, and we would just do as Lucy's Mummy suggested and go to Poundland and buy a load of tat to flog onto the kids at a suitable mark-up.

'Do you think we should dress up?' said Katie.

'I think it's expected …' I said gloomily.

'We could cause outrage by wearing slutty Halloween costumes,' suggested Cara cheerfully. 'People are always complaining about the lack of dads involved in these events. I'm sure the three of us in some fishnets and PVC would shake them up a bit. And Sam could provide the eye candy for the mums!'

'I'm not some cheap piece of meat!' said Sam with wounded pride.

'Of course you're not!' I comforted him. 'You're totally fillet steak. Well, definitely rib eye, anyway.'

'Oh, go on!' cajoled Cara. 'Be a sport. I'm single, remember, and my opportunities for meeting men are limited – I have to take my chances where I can. It might be fun!'

'There is nothing "fun" about middle-aged women in fishnets!' I responded with as much dignity as I could. Unfortunately, that was the moment that Simon chose to walk into the room.

'Fishnets?' he said in glee. 'I think you should definitely wear fishnets!'

'See?' said Cara.

'I am not wearing fucking fishnets! We are meant to be discussing where to buy the cheap booze to mark up and flog to the parents, not whether or not we should wear fishnets. What if we are mistaken for prostitutes on the way home?'

'Go on!' said Cara.

'Go oooon!' said Simon.

'I will wear fishnets, if Sam will wear fishnets,' I offered.

'I have a position in the community to uphold,' insisted Sam. 'I can't turn up at the school disco dressed as Frank-N-Furter. I am a respectable person.'

The fishnets debate rumbled on for some time, and by the time everyone had to take their children home to bed, no real decisions had been made about the disco (except that I was not wearing fishnets). I fear we are not taking PTAing as seriously as Lucy Atkinson's Perfect Mummy and Fiona Montague did. Maybe I should get a clipboard to brandish menacingly, to keep everybody on track? Or just set an agenda before the meeting. That seems awfully bossy, though. I don't want everyone to hate me because I've turned into Mrs Bossypants.

Friday, 14 October

The telephone call I had been awaiting from Jessica after last Sunday's disastrous lunch with Daddy finally materialised.

Jessica, with her usual dismissive approach to everything I do, obviously decided to call me at work.

'I can't really talk now,' I hissed. 'I'm at work.'

'Oh God, Ellen, it's not like you do anything very important. You just faff around with *computers*,' scoffed Jessica. 'Of course you have time to talk to me.'

'It's a bit more than faffing around with computers,' I responded with dignity. 'I design software interfaces.'

'That's what I said,' insisted Jessica. 'You're hardly saving lives with Médecins Sans Frontières, are you?'

'Well, neither are you. You're a bloody banker. At least my work is useful to some people instead of just being a ... a ... recession causer!'

'Ellen, do you actually have any idea of what I do?'

'I have as much idea as you do about what I do.'

'Anyway,' sighed Jessica, 'I'm at work too, so if I've got time to talk, so do you.'

'No, I don't! And we don't all have the *luxury* of our own office to just call people and chat. I'm hiding in the bloody loo. I only answered in case it was some kind of family emergency, which it clearly isn't if you only want to chat about Natalia a whole week after we met her!'

'Honestly, Ellen, the fact that at forty-three –'

'Forty-two! I'm forty-two!'

'Whatever. That you still have to hide in the loo to take a personal call is hardly my fault, is it?'

'I'm hanging up now, *someone is coming*,' I hissed, as Lydia shot into the bathroom, also hissing furtively into her phone before swiftly clicking it off when she saw me.

'Everything all right?' I asked breezily.

'Yes,' said Lydia quickly. 'Yes, all fine. Such a pain when someone calls when you're on the way to the loo!'

'They must have a sixth sense!' I laughed, as I wondered who Lydia's call was. Probably not a bossy boots sister who thinks everyone has to dance to their tune just because she is the eldest and has a very important job that therefore means she can feel superior.

Saturday, 15 October

Hurrah! SUCH FUN! After what felt like the longest week in the world, tonight was Hannah and Charlie's engagement party. Tired though I was, I was very much looking forward to a night getting drunk with people who I could just be myself with, instead of sucking in my stomach and worrying that my emergency cool trainers purchase was still not 'on fleek' and I would shortly be shunned as old and sad and past it, or worst just a bit weird and inappropriate. I hadn't dared make any jokes all week because I was scared that my new colleagues would not get my sense of humour, and so I have been very serious and just nodded and smiled a lot. I haven't even read a single *Daily Mail* article – I think I might crash their servers if I tried to go on the website, an alarm would probably sound and my ergonomic chair would eject me from the building. I feel strangely liberated by this, but also slightly adrift without my daily diet of Z-list celebrity shit.

Hannah stuck to her guns and refused to let me take over organising the party, no matter how many Pinterest boards I bombarded her with, but even though I still maintain that it could only have been improved by upside-down umbrellas hanging from the ceiling filled with ivy, and some hessian table runners, it was still a very nice evening.

It is quite blissful that after a few years of wedding drought, once all our friends were married, some of them are being kind enough to get divorced and have second marriages, so we have a lovely round of more weddings to look forward to. Simon called me a monster when I remarked on this, and suggested that perhaps our friends were not going through major emotional traumas and life upheavals merely to provide me with an opportunity to browse the Coast sale and get smashed on warm Prosecco. Obviously I knew that. I only meant that I do love a wedding. And a nice silk floral frock …

Hannah looked all glowing and gloriously happy (so glowing, in fact, that had she not been necking the champagne like it was going out of fashion, I would have suspected she was indeed awaiting the patter of tiny feet), and Charlie looked like he was about to burst with pride.

They both made a lovely speech together, the best bit of which was obviously where they mentioned me getting them together and everyone became quite misty-eyed.

'Isn't it lovely?' I said to Simon. 'It almost makes me wish we were getting married again.'

Simon choked. 'Bloody hell, never again! It took long enough to pay off one wedding!'

'We could always renew our vows?' I sighed.

'I thought you once said that every time you heard about a couple renewing their vows, your first thought was always, "Oooh, I wonder which one of them cheated, and is having to prove their commitment with a vow renewal?" And whenever you see celebrities who make a big thing of renewing their vows, they're always divorced shortly afterwards.'

'True,' I lamented. 'Mariah Carey and Thingy she was married to apparently renewed their vows every single year, and that didn't exactly work out terribly well for them, did it? Maybe we should just have a second honeymoon instead.'

'If we're not getting married, surely it's just a nice holiday, not a second honeymoon?' objected Simon.

'Why do you always have to be so fucking *literal* about everything?' I said crossly. 'I was just trying to be romantic, that's all! *You* should try it sometime, you know. It wouldn't fucking kill you!'

'I *am* romantic, darling. I put the toilet seat down, don't I?'

'Yes, and actually, I rather wish you wouldn't, because then Peter comes along and doesn't bother to put it back up and just pisses all over it, and then I come along and sit in it. There is nothing romantic about sitting in someone else's cold urine and then spending the rest of the day sniffing suspiciously at yourself and wondering if you got it on your jeans and if you now smell of wee, and if maybe you should explain to people that you aren't incontinent, your son is just a filthy, lazy, pig troll who pisses on anything that takes his fancy – oh hello, Mrs P! I didn't see you there.'

Hannah's mum had come over to chat to us. I do adore Hannah's mum, but however many times she has instructed me to call her Julia, to me she is forever Mrs P. I think it's actually etched into my DNA now – I couldn't ever call her anything else. I did try to call her Julia once, but I couldn't even get the word out. Hannah's mum virtually adopted me when Hannah and I were teenagers, and I probably spent more time at her house than I did my own. On my wedding day, my own mother straightened my veil, looked at me critically and then said, 'Well,

I suppose *he* knows why he's marrying you. He's a very *patient* man, anyway, I'll give him that!,' whereas Hannah's mum took me aside and said that she only had one piece of advice for me about marriage and grown-up life, and that was not to bother with ironing. She said it had taken her years to realise that it was quite unnecessary and a massive waste of time, and although most things in a marriage needed to be worked out by the two people who were actually in it, the ironing advice would stand me in good stead and save me from wasting as much time as she had. She was right too. I have taken her advice religiously. The advent of the wonder of non-iron shirts has also helped a lot, of course.

'Isn't this LOVELY!' beamed Mrs P. 'Charlie is so much nicer than that prick Dan she married the first time.'

'Isn't it just fabulous?' I beamed back. 'I was just trying to persuade Simon that we should renew our vows, but he isn't keen.'

'Quite right!' said Mrs P. 'Waste of money, if you ask me. I've never really seen the point myself, and everyone will only assume you're doing it because one of you has had an affair. Which you haven't, I presume?'

'Of course not!' I spluttered, while Simon smirked smugly beside me.

'Good,' said Mrs P. 'There does seem to be an awful lot of it about these days. Of course, in my day it was all about the wife-swapping.'

Simon choked.

'Oh no, not *us*,' she went on. 'But apparently there was a lot of it about. We never seemed to be invited to those sorts of parties, of course, but any time we did go to a party, Edward always made me put the car keys right at the bottom of my handbag so we didn't give anyone the wrong idea. Though, seemingly, it was mostly the PTA members who were at it. That's why I never joined the PTA when you girls were at school. Edward wouldn't let me, in case we accidentally ended up at a sex party.'

Disconcerting though it was to hear Mrs P talking about swingers and sex parties, one of the best things about talking to your friends' parents is that however old one might get, to them you will always be a girl. It's nice to be referred to as a girl by someone in a non-ironic way.

'Ellen's just joined the PTA, you know, Julia,' said Simon. 'Do you think she's trying to tell me something?'

'Oh no, I shouldn't think so!' said Mrs P. 'There's the internet now. I expect that's where people go to find sex parties, instead of having to make their own fun through the PTA. You can find anything on the internet, you know. I almost bought a hedgehog the other day, to keep the slugs down in the garden, but then it turned out to be some sort of dwarf African hedgehog that you have to keep indoors, and what good would that be to my hostas, now? Oh look, I think Hannah wants me for something. I'd better go and be a dutiful mother. Lovely to see you, darling, and stay away from the sex parties, won't you?'

Simon was still chortling to himself at the thought of the PTA sex parties as I hissed at him, 'See? I was right to say we shouldn't wear fishnets at the Halloween disco. We would be giving totally the wrong impression, especially now we know what we know about the PTAs in the eighties. In fact, I think I might have to totally rethink my idea of having an eighties disco as a fund-raiser, in case people think it's going to be a sex party. I don't even really know what a sex party *is*, other than they sound unhygienic,' when Sam came over full of indignation.

'Hannah told me she invited some bloke she works with tonight for me to have a gander at,' he complained.

'And?' I asked. 'That was nice of her. You were only complaining the other day how you were going to be alone and unloved forever.'

'Well, *look* at him!' Sam gestured to a fairly innocuous-looking chap, who was now talking to Hannah's dad.

'He looks all right? All his own teeth. Bit beardy for me, and the shirt has definite hipster overtones, but all in all he looks inoffensive.'

'Exactly!' snapped Sam. 'He's inoffensive-looking. He has enough of a beard to show that he *wants* to be a hipster, but not enough courage of his convictions to carry it through. Likewise the shirt is just a bit hipster, but not full-on hipster with braces and going to bars where they serve artisanal fucking cocktails in jam-jars. He has a bike, but not a penny farthing, but he talked for fifteen minutes without a pause about bastarding coffee. He is boring as fuck and a pretentious twat. What did Hannah think I would have in common with him?'

'But Sam, you hate hipsters,' I said, confused. 'You have repeatedly and loudly voiced your intense, bordering on obsessive, dislike of hipsters. Now you are complaining because he's *not* a hipster?'

'I am complaining because he's too boring to even be a proper hipster. It would be less offensive if he *was* a hipster!'

'Would it?'

'Well, no. That would be really fucking annoying too, because then clearly Hannah wouldn't have listened to a single word I'd said, ever. But that's not the point.'

'I'm still not sure what the point is,' I said.

'Neither am I,' said Sam sadly. 'I suppose I just live in eternal hope that one day I will meet The One and when Hannah said she'd invited someone I might like, I thought maybe *he* would be The One, and instead he's this boring little man that even in my

youthful man-whore days I don't think I could've got off my tits
enough to fuck, let alone now, when I'm grown-up and sensible
and don't even know where you would buy poppers should you
want them anymore, and I am unreasonably disappointed. Until
a few months ago I thought I was resigned to being alone, you
know. Me, the kids, the dog. That was all I needed. But now
Sophie's going to high school next year, and it's starting to dawn
on me that the children are going to grow up and leave me, and
then it will just be me and the dog, and he will die, and then it
will just be me. Just me. And I've still got all my life to live, and
I've got all my love to give.'

'Are you quoting Gloria Gaynor at me? And you complain
about gay clichés!'

'I am POURING MY HEART OUT!' said Sam. 'And what if
I never meet anyone else? After Robin left the kids and me, I
didn't want to get my heart broken again, but now I think
maybe that I do want to meet someone else, and what if I don't?
What if I don't, Ellen? And that guy, well, he just brought it
home a bit about how *hard* it is to find someone you want to
spend the rest of your life with, or even go for a fucking coffee
with, without them boring the fuck on about single-estate,
bastarding Arabica, dark-roast twatting COFFEE BEANS and
what sort of coffee maker is best to bring out the flavour. But
what if he's all that's left? What if it's Mr Coffee Faux Hipster
Pants or an eternity of loneliness, Ellen? WHAT THEN? And
Hannah and Charlie are so happy, and I will never, ever find
love again …'

Simon had wandered off somewhere around the complaints
about the inadequate hipsterness of Sam's potential shag,
murmuring something about getting another drink, so the full
force of Sam's existential crisis was left to me to deal with.

'Firstly, darling, have you been on the gin?' I enquired.

'Yes,' mumbled Sam tearfully.

'OK, well that's probably not helping then, is it? You know gin makes us over-emotional and paranoid.'

'Does not!'

'Bloody well does too! Don't you remember last year, when we went to that gin tasting and I spent all the next day crying and looking up dog rescues to put a plan into action for when my darling Judgy died, so I could have a replacement lined up, even though he is only six and in disgustingly rude health?'

'Well, yes,' admitted Sam. 'But just because you're a fucking basket case on the gin, doesn't mean that my concerns for my lonely future aren't valid.'

'No, I'm just saying the gin doesn't help. But don't you also remember that right before Hannah and Charlie got together, we had almost this exact same conversation with her, right down to the children leaving her and her being alone forever. And now look at her! You never know what's around the corner. You could meet the love of your life tomorrow in Sainsbury's, buying milk. He could be out there, right now, waiting for you. He could even be Beardy Coffee Guy, if you gave him a chance.'

'He's not Beardy Coffee Guy,' said Sam firmly. 'Beardy Coffee Guy is a knob. But Ellen, what if I *don't* meet someone, anyone? What then?'

'Well, what about someone I work with? There's lots of gorgeous blokes!'

'Are there?' said Simon, materialising again at exactly the wrong moment.

'Aren't they all hipster wankers too? You have a soft-play room,' grumbled Sam.

'They're not so bad,' I said brightly.

'Oh GOD!' said Sam. 'Are you becoming one of them? You already said they are weirdly obsessed with coffee too, and now they're "not so bad"? WHO ARE YOU AND WHAT HAVE YOU DONE WITH ELLEN?'

'Fuck off, Sam, I'm just saying they're not all bad. Anyway, if all else fails, according to Hannah's mum, in her day the PTAs were notorious for having sex parties, so maybe there's some hope for you there?'

Sam shuddered. 'I cannot think of anything worse than a PTA sex party,' he said. 'At what point do you think the yummy mummies would stop wittering on about how much difference KonMari-ing their drawers has made and boasting about how advanced little Cressida and Barnaby are, and actually get down and dirty with it?'

'Probably never. Can't you just see Tabitha MacKenzie's Mummy still bleating on about how she really thinks that sending Tabitha to that early advanced maths class when she was two has made all the difference as Felix Jenkins's Daddy bends her over Perfect Lucy Atkinson's Perfect Mummy's Perfectly Annie-Sloaned dresser, and then Tabitha MacKenzie's Mummy cries out in ecstasy as she spots the Marie Kondo book on the coffee table?'

'Sometimes, Ellen,' said Sam sternly, 'you take these things too far. However, that horrific image has at least shaken me out of my massive pity party, so I suppose for that at least I must thank you.'

'Oh, pull yourself together and come and dance,' I said. 'And don't even think about suggesting shots!'

Of course, Sam suggested shots, and of course we did them, and astonishingly, even Simon joined in the shots, and we all ended up getting really quite splendidly, if shamefully for our age, rat-arsed. And then Simon remembered that a new architect had started at *his* office last week, and maybe *he* would do for Sam, because he didn't have a beard, and he had never heard him mention coffee other than to say he was making some and did anyone else want any.

'No!' shouted Sam. 'I findsh him myshelf! At Shainsburysh, with the milk! Our eyesh shall meet and boom! Love. True love. I don' want a man who will "do" for me. Love! I'sh gonna find love!'

'Awww!' mumbled Hannah. 'Everybodiesh should all be in love! Like ush, yesh, Charlie? Lovely love!'

'To LOVE!' I bellowed, and promptly missed my mouth and poured an entire shot of flaming sambuca down my cleavage. Luckily Charlie is a doctor, and thus after all those years of excessive drinking as a medical student is still able to keep his wits about him in a crisis, so he managed to hurl a glass of water over me before my bra caught fire, which was lucky, as me setting my tits alight would have been a memorable but unfortunate end to the party.

Saturday, 29 October

Aaaarrrrrghhhhhh! I am GREEN! Not metaphorically. Fucking LITERALLY! My face is a shade that can only be described as a fetching pea green. What the fuck am I going to do?

Last night was the PTA Halloween Disco. All Perfect Lucy Atkinson's Perfect Mummy's predictions came true, in that I had to throw the hissy fit of all hissy fits to actually get people to step up to the mark and volunteer to help; Oscar Fitzpatrick and Edie Prescott's Mummies did indeed try to abandon them; and most of the parents were more interested in propping up the bar and getting smashed than they were in actually keeping an eye on their children who were running amok, smacked off their tits on refined sugar. But hey, they were glugging Herculean quantities of Australian Chardonnay that we had got for £4 a bottle in Asda and were flogging for £4.50 a glass, and after all, it's all about the money!

The hall looked rather fabulous, though, liberally strewn with the entire contents of at least three branches of Poundland, and the happy cries of the precious moppets as they rammed said refined sugar and E numbers down their throat suggested that we had done rather a splendid job. Although of course Kiki (dressed as a slutty witch with her tits out, and selfie-ing like mad) sighed that it wasn't quite what she had had in mind and she wasn't sure it was really 'content worthy', and if the school would only get on Instagram the whole thing could have probably been #sponsored by Party Pieces and maybe even Pippa Middleton would start following Kiki back. Or, at the very least, Binky from *Made in Chelsea*.

With Mrs P's dire warnings about PTA swingers still ringing in my ears, I had taken immense care to dress up as the least-sexy witch in the world – my inspiration was mostly drawn from Grotbags off the *Pink Windmill Show*, complete with painting my face green. I looked, if I did say so myself, rather good, if somewhat terrifying – a few of the reception children were reduced to tears by my outfit.

After the disco, our ears still ringing to the strains of the 'Macarena', most of the volunteers magically melted away, leaving only Sam, Cara, Katie and me to clear up. The volunteers in the bar, it turned out, had been opening bottles at random to pour glasses of wine, instead of finishing one and opening another, so there were quite a lot of opened bottles that would obviously go off, so it would have been rude for us not to start drinking them.

There were too many bottles to finish over the clearing-up, so we took them back to my house to polish off while we counted the lovely money. I do love counting money, even if it isn't mine – there is something very cheering about rustling piles of tenners. I sometimes wonder if I haven't missed my vocation as some sort of cash-based, dodgy, Lovejoy-esque antiques dealer? I would also probably be very good at solving the crimes that would obviously go hand in hand with such a career choice, although not right now as I am a bit conspicuous, being, as I mentioned, BRIGHT FUCKING GREEN.

Anyway, money counted, vino finished, everyone tottered off home and I found myself really rather tired after the very busy night at the disco, and the wine, and so I just sat down on the sofa to have a little rest. Still with my Grotbags face paint on. And now, it's the morning, and I woke up still on the sofa, and although I was quite alarmed by the initial sight of myself, I reassured myself that it was only face paint and would wash off, only it turns out that you are not supposed to leave face paint on for fourteen bastarding hours BECAUSE THE FUCKING STUFF STAINS YOUR SKIN AND SO I AM BRIGHT FUCKING GREEN!

Oh, FML! What am I going to do? I can't go to work like this. I can't even do the school run like this. Things like this never happened to Lucy Atkinson's Mummy. Google suggested olive oil, and I have slathered myself in most of a bottle of extra virgin, but I am STILL FUCKING GREEN, because GOOGLE LIES! Maybe coconut oil? Olive oil is so passé, anyway. Simon and the children keep pointing and laughing, so I am glad my pain is at least amusing to someone. Bastards.

Monday, 31 October

Still green. It is fading slightly, but there is still a definitely green-ish hue. In a flash of inspiration, I remembered that you get green concealer to cover up redness, and so I thought perhaps the reverse would work too, and if I covered my face with blusher under my foundation, it would cancel out the green. It didn't. I was just a livid shade of puce. With a hint of green. I cancelled all my meetings today and tried to just hide at my desk with my hair over my face, like the oldest emo in the world, hoping very much that nobody came over to try and talk to me. Of course, today was the day *everyone* wanted to talk to me, even Ed, who actually left his office for the first time since I started.

'Are you all right?' he asked.

'Yes, I'm fine!' I mumbled, staring at my desk.

'Are you feeling OK?'

'Totally A-OK! Tippety top!'

'You're a funny colour.'

'Am I?'

'Sort of … green?'

'I expect it's the lighting in here. I think Alan has a touch of eau de nil about him?'

'No, it's just you who's green.'

'Oh, did you say GREEN? Yes, yes, I might be a bit green, actually, now you come to mention it.'

'Why?' said Ed.

Oh, fuck. Why? Why was I green? Ed might not say much, but he doesn't seem the sort of person who is very easy to bullshit. I decided to come clean.

'Well, the thing is, I actually was at a Halloween party in fancy dress, and I might have had a bit too much to drink and left my green make-up on for too long, and it has slightly turned me a little bit green,' I admitted.

'Oh. Well. I thought maybe you had something contagious,' said Ed. 'Good. Um, try not to make a habit of being green, though, if you wouldn't mind?'

'I won't,' I said, with as much dignity as possible under the circumstances.

When Ed had hastily retreated to the safe space of his office, where no verdant females lurked, Alan started laughing.

'Rock and ROLL, Ellen!' he chortled. 'I thought you were all about clean living and yoga.' (I may have given the impression I do yoga. Technically it wasn't a lie; I DID do a yoga class once, and I even have a yoga mat I got cheap in TKMaxx.) 'I thought maybe you'd overdone it on the green smoothies and turned yourself green. I did a green-smoothie detox once. I shat algae for a week. Never again!' he shuddered.

'Getting drunk at a party ...' sighed Lydia. 'I remember getting drunk at parties. Before babies. Now I just feel like I have a permanent hangover because I'm up with the toddler most nights. Lucky you, Ellen! I can't even remember the last time I went to a party that didn't serve the food in brightly coloured little Ikea bowls. Or that served anything other than sausage rolls and mini pizzas.'

'Well, it wasn't quite like that ...' I started to say.

'My flatmate did something similar at university,' said James. 'He got it off with Swarfega.'

Swarfega! Aha! Why hadn't I thought of that?

'Oooh, it's lunchtime,' said James. 'I'm going to the deli down the road. Does anyone want anything?'

'Shit, I better go and call the nanny. The baby had the squits when I left this morning,' said Lydia.

'Nothing for me, James. I'm going to the gym,' said Alan.

'It wasn't very rock and roll at all,' I said to the empty office, but everyone had scattered.

NOVEMBER

Friday, 4 November

Join the PTA, they said. Feel all warm and fuzzy that you are doing something nice for the children, they said. It will hardly take up any time at all, they said. Well, they were LIARS! All of them. Big, fat, filthy liars!

No sooner had the Halloween green faded from my face, than another email popped in from Lucy Atkinson's Mummy. I had instructed Simon that he could be the one to rush back from work and pick up the kids and shovel their Friday pizza down them, because I was going out for Friday drinks at a cool bar with my new colleagues. A young people's bar! I would even abandon the car and get a taxi home, so I could be a proper grown-up. I wasn't therefore best thrilled as I chugged down my third Gibson (a cocktail with pickled onions in it. What bliss!) to see her email. I get a cold chill down my spine when I see an email from Perfect Lucy Atkinson's Perfect Fucking Mummy ping into my inbox, as, like with emails from Jessica, there is never any good news to be had there. I really shouldn't have opened it while I was Out Out and half cut, because sure enough – bam!

Hi,

As you know, I usually organise the collection for the teacher's Christmas present, but I wondered if you would consider doing it this year, as I am very busy.

Xxxx

Four kisses. This is an indication of the shit storm into which I have just been landed. When people you don't know very well sign off with kisses, I find the number of kisses is a passive-aggressive indicator of just how much of a ball ache they have just dumped on you – the more kisses, the worse the situation. And the teacher's present is a bastarding minefield! It should be perfectly simple – everybody stick a fiver in an envelope, and give it to the nominated person, who then buys John Lewis or M&S gift vouchers, which is a polite way of saying, 'Dear Lovely Teacher, Thank you for putting up with our monstrous offspring. Please accept this small token of our appreciation, which you can now use to buy booze to numb the pain caused by our devil spawn. Or pants, if you so wish. Lots of love, All The Mummies And Daddies.'

But it is never that simple. I have been copied in on eleventy billion of these email threads, because the people who like to fuck the whole thing up also insist on hitting 'reply all' for every single message BECAUSE THEY ARE UTTER BASTARDS, and I just know the whole thing is going to descend into a giant clusterfuck – especially if I am in charge of it. Lucy's Mummy, annoyingly perfect though she is, with her skinnier-than-skinny jeans and her soy lattes on the way to her yoga class and her hair THAT ALWAYS LOOKS PERFECT EVEN WHEN IT IS WINDY was very good at tactfully talking down the mummies who wanted to adopt a Guatemalan orphan for the teacher or buy them recycled earrings made out of Himalayan goat droppings. I am not tactful. There is an excellent chance I will tell them all to go fuck themselves by the third email.

Oh, and joy of joys, another email:

> Forgot to say – the person who organises the teacher present usually just organises the Mums' Night Out at the same time. Looking forward to it!
>
> Xxxxx

Five kisses! Oh, FML. Organising the Mums' Christmas Night Out. That is a poisoned chalice, if ever there was one (quite literally a poisoned chalice if the Cocktails of Doom on last year's Night Out were anything to go by). Thirty over-excited women (well, twenty-eight and Sam, who is granted Mummy status by dint of being a gay single father, and Julian, who insists on telling every woman he meets how 'sensitive' being a stay-at-home dad has made him, by which he means he'd like to try to get into their knickers. Oddly, Julian's sensitivity does not appear to extend to actually doing anything useful like helping at PTA events, but he is very good at coming on the Christmas Night Out and being lecherous, and also at dumping his offspring on any other unsuspecting parent who shows even the slightest interest in his 'photography' business, as obviously it's 'so hard, being a full-time parent and trying to run a business, so actually, if you could just have Phoebe and Marcus for a couple of hours that would be amazing! I could give you a discount off one of my family portrait sessions as a thank you! Oh, you're a star! I won't be any later than 5 p.m. to pick them up! 6 p.m. at the very latest. Absolutely definitely no later than 7, for sure, as Susan is home by then. Cheers! See you later! Oh, and you don't mind giving them dinner, do you? Just remember that Phoebe is gluten-free and Marcus is lactose-intolerant. Super! Byeeeeee!') crammed in a pub, forced to wear paper crowns against our will while eating over-priced lukewarm turkey and pretending that we have anything in common with each other apart from the fact that we happened to force another human out of our bodies in one or another unspeakable way in the same twelve-month period (apart from Julian and Sam, of course, though Julian has a worrying habit of trying to join in the labour stories by relating Susan's birth experiences, which doesn't really seem appropriate given no one has ever met Susan in the two years that his kids have been at the school. I would start to think that Susan is a figment of Julian's imagination and he just borrowed the children from an unsuspecting friend years ago to try to help him pull the Yummy Mummies, but then I remember that Simon is so rarely seen at the school either that I suspect a lot of people think that I have just made up a husband).

I just wanted ONE night being a grown-up in a nice bar. Just one! Why did all this shit have to land tonight? Along with several whining texts from Simon about when should he put the pizza on?/when would I be back?/did the kids have a whole pizza each or one between them? etc., I was seething quietly about this when Alan brought over a fourth Gibson and winked at me.

'It's plain to see you're single, Ellen,' he grinned.

'What? Why? Why would you say that?' I said. 'Do I look like some sad old desperate tart or something?' Oh God, I've tried too hard, haven't I? I should have stuck with what I know and worn ballet flats and a nice cardigan instead of trying to be edgy. I KNEW getting a fringe cut last week was a bad idea.

'No, it's just that no one would have four cocktails with pickled onion garnishes if they were going home to snog someone, would they?' He winked.

'I might as well have all the pickled onions,' sighed James. 'My wife's either too knackered or too busy with the kids to snog me anyway.'

'Yeah, well, that's what happens when you end up with the old ball and chain,' sniggered Alan. 'You could be footloose and fancy free like Ellen and me!'

I rather liked the sound of being footloose and fancy free. Also, after four Gibsons I wasn't really capable of stringing together a coherent enough sentence to correct Alan, and merely beamed around hazily, hoping I wouldn't fall over when I had to go for a wee.

Monday, 7 November

So, one month into the new job, and I think it's safe to say that some cracks are starting to appear. I say 'cracks'. I mean massive great buggering chasms. In an effort to make sure the household tasks are shared equally between Simon and me, I drew up a careful rota of who does what and when etc., including whose turn it is to make dinner on any given night. I pinned it to the fridge and talked Simon through it. He huffed and he puffed and he sighed and he tutted, but he has been doing his allotted tasks. His allotted tasks and no bloody more, I should add, so if it is his day to drop the kids at school, and they spill Coco Pops all over the floor, he won't hoover them up if it is not his day to hoover, he'll leave them to be crushed into the floor until I get home and hoover them up, because it's 'my turn' for that. I would very much like to implement a similar work-to-rule strategy, but I lack his stubbornness and ability to turn a blind eye to the mess.

I spent Sunday afternoon cooking and freezing various dinners for throughout the week, because we are starting a big project this week, the first really big project I've been involved in since I started, and I was probably going to have to stay late some nights, so I reckoned that at least if there were some back-up dinners in the freezer I could just defrost something and everyone could still have a decent meal.

When I came home tonight to find that instead of cooking anything himself, he had defrosted not only the tagine that I had intended for tomorrow night but also the chicken casserole I had earmarked for Thursday, because apparently 'we couldn't decide what we wanted,' I lost the plot.

'FFS, Simon! I made that for tomorrow. You were supposed to make dinner tonight.'

'I DID make dinner tonight! I heated all that up! What is that if not MAKING DINNER?'

'CHEATING! It's cheating! It's not cooking, it's heating up the stuff I had made for the rest of the week.'

'How is it OK for you to just defrost and heat it up, but not for me?' he demanded.

'Because I MADE IT IN THE FIRST PLACE! Because I spent MY Sunday afternoon making it, while you lay on the sofa in front of *Wheeler* Fucking *Dealers* –'

'I was not watching *Wheeler Dealers*. I haven't watched it on point of principle since Edd China left!' he interrupted.

'Whatever. It doesn't matter. I don't care what you were watching. The point is, you chose to spend Sunday afternoon doing fuck all, while I chose to spend it cooking so I didn't have to think about it for the rest of the week, and now you've gone and CHEATED by using the stuff I made, ALL the stuff I made, and chucking out the leftovers. So you can bloody well cook tomorrow. And the rest of the week.'

'Why? Why do I have to do that? I am *doing* my share. Your children are fed, on my night. Tomorrow is *your* night, YOU bloody well cook!'

'But you haven't cooked. *I* cooked!'

'Well, if you're going to cook ahead for the week, I don't see why you can't cook enough for every night, instead of just your nights,' said Simon nastily.

'Because I shouldn't have to,' I said. 'Because then I'm cooking for every night of the week – and what are you doing? Do you want to do more housework instead?'

'I'M DOING ENOUGH BLOODY HOUSEWORK!' roared Simon. 'Christ, do you have any idea how hard it is trying to hold down a fucking career and having to be a sodding charlady as well?'

'YES!' I yelled back. 'Funnily enough, I DO. I'm only asking you to do your equal bloody share, that's all.'

'And do you think my father would have been as successful as he was if HE'D had to think about the fucking hoovering or the bastarding dinners? NO! He got to concentrate on what HE needed to do, because he had my mother to look after him. And how am I meant to be a success when you are constantly nagging me? My father came home to a proper dinner, not some shit out the freezer, and a clean house, and no one ever fucking whined on at him about childcare or ANY of that crap!'

'What the FUCK does your father have to do with this?' I demanded. 'Things have changed. WOMEN WORK NOW, they don't generally tend to get the option of staying at home, playing the little woman to the big man who goes out into the fucking world and brings home the woolly mammoth to feast on. I CAN BRING HOME MY OWN MAMMOTH, even if your mother couldn't.'

'LEAVE MY MOTHER OUT OF THIS!'

'You started it, going on about your bloody father. And do you think he gives your mother any credit for her part in his success? Can't you see that your mother has spent most of her life bored and frustrated trying to find a way to validate herself?'

'My mother is perfectly happy. She enjoyed looking after us all. It's a shame you don't feel the same.'

'Your mother washed your pants and did every bloody thing for you until you moved in with me. She bought you SIXTY PAIRS OF PANTS when you went to university, so you could go home every couple of months and get your washing done, so you didn't have to do it yourself. Your mother is a big part of why you are such a useless fucker now. And FYI, NO ONE ENJOYS WASHING PANTS, SIMON, NOT EVEN YOUR MOTHER!'

'You're being ridiculous. I can't talk to you when you're like this. All I want is a wife who supports me, and all I get is grief!'

'All I want is a husband who fucking supports me, and all *I* get is complaints because I'm not some sodding Stepford wife. Go fuck yourself!'

'YOU go fuck yourself!'

'I said it first. I win!'

'See? You're impossible and childish.'

We aren't speaking now.

Tuesday, 8 November

The morning started badly. Sometimes I feel like I might as well be invisible as an actual person – my role is to find missing PE kits and water bottles and homework while everyone else faffs around and expects me to facilitate them. The final straw today, which might not sound much, but sometimes it's the little things, was Simon vanishing into the en suite just before I had to leave to drop the kids at breakfast club to go for a lengthy and leisurely shit, meaning I couldn't get in to brush my teeth, despite me loudly announcing that I was going to brush my teeth and then we were leaving immediately after that. Bad enough that he had ignored the chaos around him, focusing only on making and drinking his coffee, while I slapped together sandwiches and filled in permission slips that the children had 'only just found' and tested them on their spellings while trying to put on my make-up so that I looked like a calm and present-able professional person. But to pick the bathroom where my toothbrush was for his morning shit, leaving me the choice of being late, or going with unbrushed teeth, was just selfish! I hammered on the door and broke my vow to never speak to him again, as I bade him hurry up, to which he replied these things *couldn't* be hurried. I hammered again and told him *he* would have to take the children to school, and was informed he couldn't possibly, because he is very Busy and Important, and that would make him late, despite me hammering on the door again and reminding him that *I* had a big meeting this morning and also couldn't be late. Finally, he sauntered out, looking pleased with himself, and I was able to dash in (holding my breath against the stench) and have a very perfunctory scrub, before hurling the children in the car and screeching off down the road, while the children asked what the rush was, and I explained once more about my NEW JOB and IMPORTANT MEETING and they looked bored and uninterested. Neither of them wished me luck, or said well done, or that they hoped my day would go well. As far as my loving family are concerned, my sole reason for existence is to serve them. I do not exist as a person in my own right to them. I am just the packed-lunch maker, the clothes washer, the hooverer, the fishfinger cooker and the pants picker-upper.

I hurtled into the office, only just on time, and slid into the Thinking Space about ten seconds before Alan, who was followed by James looking hollow-eyed and yawning.

'Been out on the piss, James?' said Alan.

'No, my fucking five-year-old had nightmares – he was up half the night. Every bloody time my wife came back to bed, she woke me up and I'm knackered!'

'Doesn't your wife work too?' I said.

'Yeah, apparently she fell asleep on the train this morning and missed her stop or something. She's blaming me for some reason, FFS!'

Lydia shot in shortly after James, jabbering frantically into her phone.

'I know, I know, please, Mum, I'll be back as soon as I can, please just for the morning, OK? I'll try to get Chris to come home if I can't get away.'

'Everything all right, Lydia?' enquired Alan smoothly.

'Yes, fine,' said Lydia shortly.

'Another domestic crisis, is it?' said Alan. 'What is it this time?'

'My nanny's sick,' said Lydia miserably. 'So my mother is standing in for the morning so that I can be here, but she is not coping very well.'

'Jesus Christ!' said Alan. 'Are we the only ones keeping it together this morning, Ellen? James over there with eyes like pissholes in the snow. Lydia – Lydia, you're wearing odd shoes! And Ed and the new client are due in at any moment. And Joe's not here because he's at his girlfriend's first scan, so no doubt he will shortly be joining the ranks of the sleep-deprived zombies too. I bet you're glad you don't have kids, Ellen, looking at the state of these two.'

I opened my mouth, and thought of the rows, the ingratitude, the being taken for granted. Although obviously I loved my family, just at the moment I didn't like them very much. I closed my mouth again, and Ed shuffled in, looking disgruntled at being dislodged from his office, with the VIP client in tow. Lydia hastily shoved her feet under a beanbag.

Wednesday, 9 November

Oh fuckadoodledoo, buggeringratsarses, cockingdogsknobs and twatdiddlingfucksticks. Buoyed up with smug superiority at the wonder of the Halloween Disco I had organised (apart from the green face thing, that was not so good), I had been blithely swanning along, feeling like I had discharged all my PTA duties most splendidly, and could forget all about it now.

Apparently not, because while I was hiding in Pret with James, avoiding Alan, who had given us a long lecture on the evils of gluten and why we should all be eating sashimi for lunch (Alan's 'clean eating', I have noticed, seems to take the form of being a sanctimonious cross-fit fucker Sunday to Thursday and drinking his own body weight in anything vaguely alcoholic Friday and Saturday. Apparently, he assures me, this is totally what the cavemen would have done, had they had cave pubs), in came another email from Lucy Atkinson's Perfect Mummy:

Hi Ellen,

Just realised that I hadn't forwarded you the list of stall holders who have already booked for the Christmas Fayre – here you go. I should probably also remind you that you need to get the posters etc advertising the Fayre up this week, as the hall is booked for Friday 2nd December. There's quite a few stalls already booked, but you will need at least another ten – try and book different things, as no one wants a Fayre that is only selling scarves and cupcakes. You also need to talk to the nursery about their stall, and the school Fairtrade committee about their stall, and make sure you have enough mulled wine and mince pies for the night, and you'll need plenty of volunteers to help set up and clear away, ideally some big strong dads to put all the tables up and down. Oh, and you'll need to get someone to be Santa for the grotto. And you'll need a grotto. Don't worry, it's really nothing a few fairy lights can't do! Oh, and don't

forget to ask for donations for raffle and tombola prizes! A bottle tombola is
always fun, and avoids those donations of 1970s bathsalts!
    Good Luck! Xxxxxx

Fuck My Fucking Life. As well as a full-time job and keeping up
the façade of being childless to my colleagues, because now it
would be officially Awkward to come clean, I have to pull
together a Christmas Fayre (FFS, why is it a Fayre? Why not a
Fair? Is there some bylaw that we have to use a cutesy ye olde
worlde spellinge to make it more Festivitied? I may rebel in my
first significant act as PTA Chair and declare it to simply be a
Christmas Fair), and I have three weeks to do this. I am almost
certainly going to have to use a glue gun to achieve this. Possibly
a staple gun as well. And given the difficulty to get the bastards
to volunteer for the Halloween Disco, possibly a real gun to
dragoon parent volunteers in on pain of death. I will try to look
on the bright side and pretend it is an episode of *Challenge
Anneka*, and I am pulling everything together against the odds
but with less running around manically while wearing a
jumpsuit.

I shall start by sending a Stern Email to all potential helpers.
And then I shall abandon James to his crayfish salad and
passive–aggressive grumbles about his wife, before I tell him to
shut the fuck up and take some responsibility for his kids, and
then go and cheer myself up by buying a pair of impractical and
probably unethical shoes.

Thursday, 10 November

Well. My Stern Email had mixed results. I suggested a quick meeting at teatime with children welcome and me once again providing the fishfingers in the hope that free fishfingers might entice all the parents who complained they couldn't come to meetings because they were too late and they didn't have child-care (my earlier, gloriously optimistic idea of enticing parents in by holding meetings in the pub having fallen at the first hurdle), but unsurprisingly the only people who were able to come were Sam, Katie and Cara Cartwright.

I hurtled in from work, shoved two dozen fishfingers and a bag of frozen chips in the oven, and we cracked on. I agreed if Cara wanted to dress up as a sexy elf, she was welcome to, but on her head be it if people thought we were a sex party PTA, at which point she somewhat lost her enthusiasm for slutty elf costumes. Despite Cara's obsession with fishnet stockings and skimpy get-ups, nonetheless we were powering through organising it nicely, as we are basically all sensible people with the same goal.

Katie was delegated to price up and buy the cheapest mulled wine that could be found that still had a reasonable alcoholic content without actually endangering eyesight, Sam had grudgingly agreed to be Santa, but only if he was allowed to take the Santa suit home and thoroughly boil wash it first, as it did have some very dubious stains and a whiff about it that suggested it hadn't seen a washing machine since Mrs P was avoiding PTA swingers in the eighties.

As I could obviously no longer surreptitiously print the posters at work, I volunteered Simon to do it and whack them up all over the neighbourhood, while I tried to drum up some stalls via the wonder that is the local Facebook groups. I say 'wonder'. Mostly they are a fascinating demonstration of the utter batshit-crazy and thinly veiled racism that lurks within our suburban streets, among the 'urgent' requests for recommendations for 'reliable' tradesmen (why is it always urgent? I get how you could urgently need a plumber or an electrician, but I am always baffled by the people who need a decorator, stat). Some of my favourite crazy posts, apart from the endless debates about dog shit, were the lady who posted for weeks demanding to know who had stolen her budgie, which had flown out the window and not returned, complete with insisting she was going to involve the police, and the man who started a campaign to stop people trimming their hedges, as it was 'torturing plants'. Add to that the veiled threats about 'You know who you are, you, who did that thing, that I'm not going to say what it was, but you know what I am talking about,' followed by heated rows about how it wasn't them what done it and I know what YOU done but I'm not saying here, you slag, and what appears to be the general complete and utter lack of any grasp of spelling or grammar in the local populace – an astonishing number of people have trouble with their TV 'ariels', and if it's not their 'ariels' playing up, it's their 'arials', plus many a 'chester draws' is offered for sale, along with my own personal favourites of a 'knecklace' and a 'Victorian cabinet – stamp says made in 1914', and you can while away a frightening amount of time and judgement. It's actually better than Jeremy Kyle. However, it also appears to be useful for finding stallholders for Christmas Fayres/Fairs, so I shall have to dip my toe into the murky waters instead of merely watching agog.

Cara was to menace tombola donations out of unsuspecting parents and purchase the entire contents of Poundland, and we pretty much had it all sorted when Kiki with two Ks appeared.

'Oh,' she sniffed, 'I see you've started without me. I was trying to get some photos of Lalabelle and Trixierose playing in the autumn leaves, but they kept crying they were cold, which is useless and a total waste of the tasteful knitwear I bought them. You should have said if it was going to start promptly!'

'Sorry, Kiki,' I said. 'I did say we would be starting at 6.15 sharp and it is … 6.43 now. Do your girls want some fishfingers and chips?'

Lalabelle and Trixierose's faces lit up at the sight of the delicious beige freezer goodness that the other children were shovelling in, doused in liberal quantities of tomato sauce. Kiki, however, recoiled.

'GOD, no, Ellen! We are total clean eaters. Don't you have any micro salad leaves, or pomegranate seeds, or manuka honey?'

'There's a token bowl of cherry tomatoes and cucumber on the table for the children to ignore,' I suggested.

Kiki peered at the bowl. 'They don't seem to be multi-coloured heirloom tomatoes?' she complained.

'No,' I said. 'They are bog-standard ones that were on special offer because no fucker is going to eat them. They are only there to salve my conscience and make me feel like I've made a gesture towards nutrition.'

'Mummy, can we have the fishfingers now?' pleaded Lalabelle.

'Darlings, you know we don't eat things like that, do we?' sang Kiki.

'But we do, Mummy,' said Lalabelle in surprise. 'We do it all the time. We had chicken dippers and smiley faces last night!'

'No, darling. Last night we had an avocado and quinoa salad, didn't we? Mummy took a lovely photo of you and Trixierose enjoying it for Instagram, *remember*?'

'Oh,' said Lalabelle in disgust. 'You mean the yucky stuff you made us pretend to eat before we had our proper tea?'

'Ha ha ha!' trilled Kiki. 'Such an imagination you have, Lalabelle, aren't you funny! Oh fine, yes, have the fishfingers.'

'Right,' I said, once Lalabelle and Trixierose had helped themselves (since I had failed to ever ask Kiki the inspiration behind her children's names, she had insisted on telling me anyway – apparently her main goal when naming her children was to find something 'unique' that would be part of her 'brand' and really 'stand out' on social media. I did try not to judge. I failed). 'Let's get on then. I think we've really got everything pretty much sorted now, Kiki, though any help you could offer would be fantastic, of course.'

'Well, I'm very busy with work, so I can't do much,' said Kiki.

'What do you actually *do*?' asked Cara.

Kiki laughed merrily. 'I've *told* you Cara, I'm a social media influencer. None of you have followed me yet, though I keep telling you @kikiloveandlife!'

'And is that an actual job now?' said Cara. 'Do you make money?'

'Well,' said Kiki, 'I mean, I'm still building my brand, of course, but the really big influencers can make millions.'

'Yes, but how do you become one of them?' said Cara, who I suspected was just winding Kiki up now.

'Um, well, you build your brand … you network … um … I like to travel. So I offer a really unique view on how to travel with children and then brands get in touch and offer to partner with you for holidays and the like.'

'So, like free holidays, you mean?'

'Well, not *free*, you are working while you are there, you have to take photos and write reviews. It's harder than it sounds,' insisted Kiki.

'So, what sort of places have you been to then?' enquired Cara silkily (I rather admire Cara's ability to be quite evil under the guise of being caring and concerned. I lack such subtlety and guile).

'Well, we went to the Seychelles, all-inclusive, to a luxury resort last month,' said Kiki smugly.

'Oh,' said Cara, the wind rather taken out of her sails.

'Ugh,' interrupted Lalabelle. 'I hated the stupid Seashells. The food was all funny and it was TOO HOT!'

'Nonsense, darling, you loved it. Mummy has lots of lovely photos of you having a *fabulous time*,' hissed Kiki.

'But what about actual money, to live on?' said Cara.

'Well, sometimes they pay me too,' said Kiki.

'And is that enough?'

'Well, it doesn't really matter. My husband's a hedge-fund manager.'

Cara muttered something unrepeatable. I don't think she will be following Kiki on Instagram anytime soon.

'Right, could we just get back to the Christmas Fair, PLEASE?' I said in a desperate attempt at assertion, much though I had enjoyed Cara interrogating Kiki.

'Hang on!' cried Kiki. 'I'm going to take a photo of all the children round the table, it's perfect for a "family chaos" shot for my blog.'

'Hang on,' objected Katie. 'You can't just take photos of *our* children as well to put online!'

We all chimed in agreeing that Kiki was not using our kids as content fodder, about which she got quite sulky and said we were being very unreasonable. And Jane wonders why I am trying to discourage her from Instagram!

When we FINALLY returned to discussing the fucking Christmas Fair, Kiki said, 'What about décor for the hall?'

'Fuck, yes, good point!' I said.

'I could be in charge of that!' offered Kiki.

'That would be fabulous, thank you,' I said gratefully. 'I think someone said there's a box of decorations somewhere in the PTA cupboard at school – tinsel and stars and bits and pieces – and I'm sure we could all lend some fairy lights for the night too.'

Kiki blinked slowly. 'I was thinking more some sort of Scandi chic theme,' she said. 'I really want to make this stand out – the Halloween disco was a bit tacky, if you don't mind me saying so. We should do something really eyecatching for the Christmas Fair. What is the budget for décor anyway? I reckon I could do it all for about two grand, but obviously if the budget can stretch to more I could really make it pop.'

Once we had all finished laughing, we gently explained to Kiki that there was no budget for decorations. If the entire evening RAISED £2,000 we would consider it a job well done. At best, if the tinsel in the school cupboard was particularly thread-bare and bedraggled, she might be allowed £5 to run amok in Poundland.

Kiki was wide-eyed with horror, until Cara suggested that she should look on it as a challenge, and use it as an chance to write a blog post about Christmas decorations on a shoestring. Kiki still looked unsure, but Cara had said the magic words of 'Instagram opportunity' and so Kiki was unable to refuse. She retreated to a corner to pout into her phone and take some self-ies while her children mainlined ketchup and we tied up the loose ends. Once everyone finally left, I cleared tables, loaded washing machines and stared hopelessly into the fridge for inspiration for something for dinner for Simon and me, while snacking mindlessly on leftover fishfingers until he finally got home, having opted to 'work late' rather than face the PTA hell of a house full of children.

Friday, 11 November

I had little desire to go straight home after work for another evening of resentful silences and angry sighing at each other, so since the children were both on a sleepover at Sam's house, I accepted the invitation to go for Friday drinks with the rest of the team (minus Lydia, who was rushing home so the nanny didn't hand in her notice again, and Ed, who could not come because it would involve speaking to People. I sometimes think I should introduce Ed and Simon – they both seem to have the same fear of People and could sit in a companionable silence, quietly hating everyone around them).

I had the wit to stay off the Gibsons this time, not because of the pickled onions but because they are neat booze, they get you shitfaced in an unseemly short amount of time, and I wasn't entirely sure I was capable of undoing the complicated fastening of my trousers in time if I was hammered, before I weed myself.

I took a deep breath and braced myself before I opened the front door, ready for the horrible atmosphere inside. All was quiet, apart from Judgy Dog, who hurled himself upon me with joy. One always gets at least ten minutes of unadultered adoration from Judgy when you come home – he is happy you are back because he thought you were gone forever, and then he remembers that you left him and so he sulks for the next hour after that. Out of all of us, though, Judgy seems to be the one coping best with my return to full-time work, as he gets picked up by the dog sitter in the morning and gets to spend the day terrorising (terrierising) her other charges, before being returned in the evening. I love the lovely dog sitter.

'At least someone is pleased to see me, hey boy?' I said, scooping him up and burying my face in his fur. People rave about the delicious scent of a newborn baby, but I never really got it. Babies smell of talcum powder and sour milk and Sudocrem and shit. I much prefer the smell of Judgy's fur, which is sort of biscuity, with a hint of mud and a whiff of fresh air. Unless he is wet, of course, in which case he just smells of wet dog, which is not so nice. He did his favourite thing of snuggling into my neck and making a strange groaning sound, while wrapping his paws round my hand so I couldn't let him go.

'Someone loves me anyway, don't they, Mr Woofingtons?' I whispered in his ear. He looked at me indignantly. He doesn't like being called Mr Woofingtons, as he feels it is beneath his dignity.

There was no sign of Simon, who I assumed had either pissed off out since there were no kids at home, or was sulking somewhere, so still holding Judgy I trudged through to the kitchen in search of another glass of wine, and maybe some crisps to act as blotting paper.

I almost dropped the dog when I found Simon in the kitchen, apparently cooking, and through the door into the dining room, which we only use on special occasions, I could see the table was laid for two, with candles lit (and all the crap which is usually piled on the table had also mysteriously vanished. Where was it? Hopefully not thrown out – I had many useful pieces of paper Carefully Filed among the piles of shit).

'Are you expecting someone?' I enquired coldly.

'Only you, darling!' said Simon cheerfully (what did the bastard have to be so cheerful about, I wondered darkly? Throwing out my Important Bits of Paper?).

'I thought I'd make us some dinner!'

'Did you actually make it, or did you defrost something I made?'

'Well, technically I bought it from M&S. Does that count?'

'You may count that as you cooking,' I conceded graciously.

'I thought perhaps we need to spend some time together. Without rushing about and juggling stuff and trying to do eleventy billion other things at the same time, to use your favourite phrase.'

'"Eleventy billion" is not my favourite phrase. "Arsed-faced cockwombles" is my current favourite phrase!' I informed him.

'I quite like that,' he said. 'Anyway, I thought it might help. To have a meal together, to talk instead of shouting, maybe even to try and remember why we married each other ...'

'Is this about sex?' I said suspiciously. 'Are you only doing this because you want a shag?'

'No! I mean, I wouldn't *say* no, but that's not why.'

'And are you going to do the dishes as well?'

'Of course, darling, that's the beauty of kind Mr Marks and Mr Spencer providing dinner; there will be two plates to go in the dishwasher and the rest can be chucked out.'

'That's not very green,' I grumbled. 'They would frown upon such a cavalier attitude to sustainability at work.'

'Well, you're not at work now, are you?' said Simon briskly. 'So why don't you put down that smelly mutt and come and have a glass of wine and something to eat.'

'He smells LOVELY!' I objected. 'Don't listen to him, Judgy, he doesn't know what he is talking about.'

'Hmmm,' said Simon.

Over dinner (beef Wellington, a bit retro, but jolly tasty) he said, 'I'm sorry, I shouldn't have said that about my mother supporting my father. I just feel ... inadequate sometimes, when I look at where my father was at my age, and where I am. Actually I feel like a failure compared to him – we'll never be able to afford a house like theirs, or to send two kids to boarding school. And I suppose I'm jealous, not only of what he achieved but that he never had to worry about picking up kids or cooking or housework. He cut the grass on Sundays and that was it.'

'But no one is where their parents were at their age anymore,' I said. 'Of course you're not a failure, it's just that the world has changed. Most people don't live like they used to, or live like their parents, and women no longer want to just be housekeepers living off their husband's money, even *if* their husband can afford for them not to work. Look at Kiki. Her husband earns a fortune, and she's still trying to make it as a social media influencer –'

'A what?'

'Never mind what it is, darling. The point is that she wants something for herself, achievements of her own, beyond fulfilling her basic biological function. We all do. And if it was all easy and fabulous for your dad, how do you think it was for your mum, always putting him first, thinking of everyone before herself? It must have been quite boring and frustrating for her – she has almost said as much at times.'

'I suppose so. Oh God, Ellen, when did life get so *hard*? It all sounded so easy, didn't it? We got married and we were going to live happily ever after. What happened to us?'

'I suppose we grew up.'

Later he said, 'I miss you. I feel like we're just ships that pass in the night at the moment.'

'That's what my parents used to say when they were both working. We could leave each other notes, like they did.'

'With all due respect, darling, I don't think that's the solution, given your parents went on to have an extremely bitter and acrimonious divorce.'

'No, I suppose not. What is, then?'

'I don't know, darling. We'll think of something.'

Tuesday, 22 November

An email from Jessica today. I suppose at least I should be grateful that she had heeded my instructions not to call me at work
(even though I have noticed they are fairly relaxed about
personal calls, I just don't really want to talk to Jessica because
she will invariably have something she wants to boss me around
about). My heart still sank when I saw her name pop up in my
inbox, for there is never any chance that Jessica is just getting in
touch for a chat, or to impart good news, or to send me an amusing cat meme. She always wants something, or is ordering me to
do something. I am finding it hard to make the transition from
eternal optimist to pragmatic pessimist, though, so I remained
hopeful, despite the subject header being 'Christmas'.

Hi Ellen,

Mum says you haven't answered her yet about whether you are going to her and
Geoffrey for Christmas. She says can you get back to her asap, as she is booking
her Waitrose delivery slot now and she wants to complete the order so she
doesn't have to think about it again, because she's got so much else on.

Neil and I and the children are going, of course, and Geoffrey's daughter
will be there too, so I really think you all should come as well.

Please can you email Mum and let her know your plans, because you know
those Christmas delivery slots get booked up so fast, and she really doesn't want
to miss out?

Best wishes,

Jessica.

Fuck's sake! Mum only emailed me yesterday! YESTERDAY!
And she made no mention of the urgency to reply to her
IMMEDIATELY so she could book her hallowed bastarding

Waitrose delivery slot. None whatsofuckingever! In fact, the whole tone of the email suggested that us coming to her for Christmas was pretty much a fait accompli, as she had decided that was what was happening and so we would do as we were told. And now she has gone off complaining to Jessica the Fucking Golden Child about how her second-best daughter has not even bothered to reply, because clearly cruel and uncaring second-best daughter is not concerned about whether or not she gets a prime delivery slot, because second-best daughter is selfish and rude, which is why she loves Jessica the best. Also, what the actual fuck is Mum so busy doing that she has to put her sodding supermarket Christmas order in in NOVEMBER? Is the tennis club going to crumble if she lets her grip on the committee slip for a second? Will the choir mutiny if Mum takes an hour off to put an online order in, and run amok, making the vicar walk the plank? Will the Horticultural Society go mad without a steady hand on the tiller and repeat the dreadful scene of 2013 when they planted geraniums and begonias in the hanging baskets beside the village shop (Mum still shudders at the memory. Apparently it made the village look terribly common, and just 'awfully *municipal*, darling')?

Perhaps she fears that with her watchful eye distracted in the Festive Season, Geoffrey will take advantage and have an extra sherry before dinner and unleash his inner *Daily Mail* reader, shouting angrily about The Left and The Immigrants and demanding the Return of National Service, instead of just being quietly racist and homophobic in the corner. God only knows. Mummy likes to describe herself as 'keeping busy', but really that means she likes interfering and bossing people about. Especially me. Oh, and the joy of Geoffrey's perfect daughter Sarah, and Piers, her equally perfect husband!

And Geoffrey. Mum was as smug as a smug thing when, having spent fifteen years playing the lead role of Wronged Wife to rave reviews, after she kicked Daddy out when he got caught with his pants down shagging his secretary at the office Christmas party (quite literally, I do hope they disinfected that photocopier afterwards) about thirteen years ago, she managed to bag herself a rich widower ('*So* much more convenient than a divorcee, darling, no tiresome ex-wife to bother with or alimony payments to take into account when working out how much of his pension one will be entitled to') and departed to live in Georgian splendour in Yorkshire, where she takes great delight in playing the Lady of the Manor, and mercilessly organising the rest of the village, whether they want to be organised or not.

But although as far as Mum was concerned, Geoffrey was a catch (all his own teeth, solvent, Tory voter, suitable house – 'I don't know how you *manage* without an Aga, darling, isn't it terribly *difficult*? Well, I do think you're *awfully* brave. Can you even make *anything* from Mary Berry, or do you have to rely on *Delia*, you poor thing. Or do you just use Nigella? I know her father is dear Nigel Lawson, but she's just so terribly *licky* when she's cooking. Like an over-sexed Labrador!' – that handy dead wife, and best of all as far as Mum was concerned, 'At least he's not the sort who *pesters* one for *that*!'), I can't say I have ever really warmed to him. Of course, our relationship probably wasn't helped when he told me his beloved only daughter had been very active in the Young Conservatives, and I laughed and said what a good joke and he said, no, really, she had found it super fun, and I said what, *really*, because I didn't think people actually did things like that unless they were William Hague, and he got a bit huffy. Also, even though I was twenty-nine when they got married, and had in fact been married myself for several years, Geoffrey felt it was his place as my new stepfather to try to

give me paternal advice, such as suggesting that I would probably get pregnant quicker if I gave up my job and stayed at home,
as he had read an article that suggested that sitting in front of a
computer all day would, in fact, speed up my biological clock.
Given that Simon and I weren't even trying for a baby at the
time, I wasn't entirely grateful for this helpful tip.

I am not calling her back yet. I am Very Busy And Important,
and I have better things to do than dance immediately to the
tune played by Jessica and Mum. I wonder if she has only
summonsed us so that Daddy and Natalia can't have Christmas
with us. It wouldn't surprise me. Usually she and Geoffrey spend
Christmas on a cruise, but I could quite see that she would take
a malicious pleasure in knowing that it wouldn't even have
occurred to Daddy to start thinking about Christmas yet, so by
getting in first and summonsing Jessica and me to Yorkshire she
will in effect have thwarted any ideas he might have had about
spending Christmas with his daughters and grandchildren.
Twenty-eight years after divorcing him, I think it's safe to say
that Mum is still harbouring a grudge. Of course, she forgets that
it probably won't have crossed Daddy's mind to spend Christmas
with us, and he has probably booked a cruise himself.

Wednesday, 23 November

Feeling fat and bloated and sluggish after a surfeit of surreptitious
Mint Clubs, I had asked Alan about his gym. He brightly
informed me that they do lunchtime classes that last as little as
twenty minutes. Twenty minutes! 'I can totally do a twenty-
minute class,' I thought to myself. 'In fact, I will probably go and
do more afterwards. A mere twenty-minute class won't be very
taxing.'

So it was that this lunchtime I picked up my brand new shiny gym bag and trotted off after Alan, feeling thinner already, just for purchasing new trainers!

'It's called a HIIT class,' Alan told me. 'It's about high-intensity work followed by rest periods.'

'Rest periods?' I scoffed. 'A twenty-minute class that included *rest* periods?' I was so going to ace this! Back in the day I had often gone to hour-long step classes, with *no* rest periods. Truly, I thought smugly, these millennials are indeed a snowflake generation.

It turned out to be a tiny bit harder than I had anticipated. There were awful things called 'burpees', and also vile things called 'squat jumps' where you squat and then have to jump up. There were jumping jacks, which they literally made us do at school as punishments. It was horrible. And the so-called 'rest periods' were about two seconds long, which was just about enough time to reflect on how much you wanted to just die before the torture began again.

The worst part came at the end. We finally got to lie down and the sadistic bastard instructor shouted that we were going to do pelvic-floor exercises. I brightened at this. I can *do* pelvic-floor exercises. A nice gentle finish would be just the job, though I hadn't realised men could do them too. Perhaps it tightens their prostate or something, I thought.

The bastard man loomed over me. 'DO YOU KNOW HOW TO DO PELVIC FLOOR EXERCISES?' he bellowed.

I haughtily assured him that I *most* certainly did. Then recoiled in horror as he thrust a large weight at me. What the actual fuck? Were we … were we meant to … *insert* it? Surely that could not be safe? Or hygienic? Where would the *men* put it? On second thoughts, I didn't want to know!

It turned out, to my relief, that by 'pelvic-floor exercises' he had meant exercises for one's lower back and core that are performed while lying on the floor. I considered having a stern word with him about misrepresentation, but mostly I wanted a shower and then to lie curled in a foetal position in a darkened room while whimpering. I wasn't entirely sure my legs still worked.

As I staggered out, puce and heaving for breath, and Alan smirked and said, 'Did you enjoy that, Ellen?' and I wished I had the strength remaining to pick up one of the free weights and smack the smug fucker round the head with it, Mum rang.

'Hello,' I gasped.

'Oh my God, what on *earth* is wrong with you?' twittered Mum. 'Oh *Ellen*, you're not having *sex* are you? Have you become one of those women who finds fulfilment in sordid lunchtime trysts in seedy hotels?'

'No, Mum, I'm at the gym!' I protested.

'Oh!' she said. 'Well, I must say you could probably do with it!'

'What do you want, Mum?'

'That's not very nice! I'm *trying* to be considerate and call you at lunchtime after you said I wasn't to call you at work anymore, though I don't see that what you do is so urgent you couldn't talk to me, but anyway. You *still* haven't replied to my email about Christmas. Didn't Jessica speak to you? I need to *know* Ellen, I *need* to get that Waitrose order in *today*! ARE YOU COMING OR NOT?'

Simon had actually been quite cheery about the invitation when I'd told him, as usually we end up having Jessica and Neil and the gruesome twosome (I mean my adorable niece and nephew) here for Christmas, along with whoever else I've happened to see in December while pissed and have decided it would be a good idea to invite, and so Christmas a) ends up costing an arm and a leg because I've invited so many people who need to be fed and watered. (Oh God, the worst year was when Simon's sister Louisa descended on us for Christmas, along with her six unwashed children and her then husband – the appalling Bardo. If I am never grateful for anything else in my life, I will be eternally grateful for Louisa ditching Bardo and pushing off to live in France next door to Simon's poor parents, so I am unlikely to ever have to spend Christmas with her again. It was literally the worst Christmas of my life – Louisa and Bardo and the offspring were gluten-free vegans who lived primarily on lentils and the effect of this on my plumbing was nothing short of disastrous.) And b) means that I end up getting myself into a complete state because I have put a ridiculous amount of pressure on myself and end up screaming at everyone. One unfortunate year I even hurled a tray of mince pies at Simon's head after he suggested I should 'just try to relax a bit'. Simon pointed out that if we go to my mother and Geoffrey's for Christmas we will save a fortune, and also, because my mother doesn't trust me in the kitchen (she still insists on bringing up an unfortunate incident in my teens when I managed to set some spaghetti on fire when I left it hanging over the edge of the pot), I won't be running around like a blue-arsed fly, shouting that ALL I WANT TO DO IS WATCH *IT'S A WONDERFUL FUCKING LIFE*, WHY IS THAT SO MUCH TO ASK? He also remarked I might even manage to watch *It's a Wonderful Life*, which would in itself be a Christmas Miracle. Also, if we go to Mum's I can concentrate on work, not on constant emails from Jessica about gluten-free bastarding stuffing.

So I gritted my teeth and said, yes, Mum, we'd love to come etc., etc., which was when she dropped the bombshell about why they are not going on a cruise this year – Geoffrey's daughter, Sarah the Wünder Child, the blonde, perfect manifestation of purely distilled smugness in human form, the daughter Mum likes even better than Jessica, is With Child.

'*Isn't* it *exciting*!' trilled Mum. 'Our first grandchild! *Such* marvellous news!'

'Errr, Mum, you already have four grandchildren,' I pointed out.

'Oh, do stop being *difficult*, Ellen. You know perfectly well what I mean.'

No, I didn't have a fucking scoobies what she meant, I rarely do. I was propped up against the wall of the gym by now, and in grave danger of actually falling over.

'Anyway, Mum, I have to go now,' I said feebly, while I eyed up the fifty yards I had to totter across to get to the changing rooms.

'Right, darling, me too. Waitrose orders to do!' trilled Mum.

I think my legs might fall off.

Saturday, 26 November

Jane has been vile today. A snarling, snapping, shouting bundle of fury (admittedly that isn't that unusual for Jane – it was pretty much how she came out of the womb), but she took it to a whole new level today. I was torn between fretting that clearly Jane was feeling unloved because she was now an abandoned child who might as well be raised by wolves due to her mother's selfishness, and being utterly terrified that perhaps this was the beginning of the hormonal horrors. I am not ready for Jane to embark on a monthly round of premenstrual rage – she is too young, and I am not strong enough. However, after much spitting, door-slamming, stamping, shouting and screaming, we finally got to the bottom of it, after Peter made an innocent comment about Jack O'Connor in his class and Jane went proper batshit.

'Jack O'Connor is HORRIBLE!' she shouted. 'And his sister Megan is EVEN WORSE! I HATE her, I hate their whole family!'

'WTF?' I thought. The O'Connors had always seemed a perfectly nice family. Oh God, oh God, what if they're not? What if the children are actually vile and are bullying Jane, and I hadn't even noticed because I had just assumed the O'Connors were perfectly pleasant on account of driving an Audi and wearing Boden and so being proper middle-class, but actually the chil-dren are psychopaths and torment Jane, but she didn't feel she could tell anyone, because I am a Bad And Uncaring Working Mother (maybe on some level she knows I am pretending not to have any children at work), and so her innocent, childish psyche has been scarred forever, firstly because I left her with a child-minder when she was six months old so I could work part-time because, you know, we needed money for luxuries, like food and a roof over our heads, and now I am pursuing my career at my children's expense, including letting them drop their lovely middle-class extra-curricular activities when they declare them-selves bored with them, and even worse not signing them up for more, so now they will never be well-rounded people and, OH FML, I am a terrible mother and I have ruined Jane's life and IT IS ALL MY FAULT!

While I was agonising to myself about my many maternal failings, and wondering whether to google how to sensitively and empathetically approach the subject with Jane, Peter cut to the chase and simply said, 'Why don't you like Jack and Megan anymore, Jane? Is it because you're a massive bumhead? Who smells of poo?'

'Peter,' I snapped. 'Don't talk to your sister like that.'

'But she called me Farticus, the Prince of All Farts,' whined Peter.

'I don't care! I don't want to hear either of you speaking to each other like that.' (Oh God, maybe Peter is emotionally traumatised as well. Maybe I am an unfit parent because I didn't carry them around in a sling until they were old enough to buy a round in the pub. I had somewhat been under the impression that Peter's world entirely revolved around food, pooing, Pokémon and insulting his sister, but perhaps he has hidden depths that I had failed to plumb. Admittedly, the last time I panicked about him being emotionally stunted and suggested he could talk to me about his feelings, his response was to remark that he could feel a big poo coming on, but even so.)

'Jane, darling!' I said, putting on my Caring And Concerned Mummy Face. 'Tell me what Jack and Megan have done to you, to make you so upset.'

'I don't want to talk about it,' sniffed Jane. 'And Peter IS Farticus, Prince of All the Farts. Farticus, Farticus!' she chanted at him.

Oh God. She was trying to distract me from her pain. Admittedly, by causing her brother pain, but it still counted. Perhaps I should get a Barbie and tell her to show me on the doll where they had hurt her?

I tried again, still with the Caring Face. 'You can tell me, you know. Mummy will understand. I love you, Jane, and you can talk to me about anything.'

'Ha ha,' said Jane. 'Mummy loves ME, Peter, not you!'

'MUUUUUMMMMMMYYYYYYY!' howled Peter. 'She said you don't love me! That's not fair!!!!'

Jesus fucking Christ. All those bloody articles about communicating with your children, really talking to them, listening to them, encouraging them to open up to you – not one single bastarding article tells you what to do when your children are more interested in winding each other up than having deep and meaningful heart-to-heart with you. All those sodding children in the articles can't WAIT to tell their mummies and daddies all about their hopes and dreams and secrets and fears. THEY don't bloody well think it is more amusing to come up with cruel yet witty nicknames and accuse each other of farting! I don't believe those sensitive, emotionally balanced children even exist. I think it's like the girls in the Judy Blume books who would rush home in excitement to tell their mums the minute they got their periods. Like periods were a *good* thing, and something you wanted to talk about! I mean, who even does that? Especially at a difficult point in your adolescence. I think my friends and I were well into our twenties before we would even admit to each other that we had periods. Certainly the thought of announcing it Loud And Proud when we first came on would NEVER have happened. And I'm pretty sure that the last thing Jane will do when she starts is to dash in the door crying, 'MOTHER, I AM A WOMAN NOW!!' I do hope not, anyway. That would be very embarrassing.

'Of course I love you, Peter,' I said firmly. 'Jane's just being silly.'

'No, I'm not. Mummy doesn't love you because you're not her real child. She found you in a bin,' crowed Jane.

'MUUUUUMMMMMMYYYYYY!' screamed Peter.

'JANE! For FUCK'S SAKE! Shut UP!' I howled.

'I thought you wanted me to TALK to you,' said Jane indignantly. 'You just *said*, "You can talk to me about anything." You LITERALLY just said that RIGHT NOW, and then you told me to shut up. Which is it? You are being very confusing.'

'Arrrgh! Yes, talk to *me*. I want you to talk to *me*. NOT to start tormenting your brother by telling him he was found in a bin. Again!'

'It's not fair. I can't even say *anything*,' huffed Jane.

'But MUUUUMMMMYYYYY!! She said I was found in a bin. It's NOT TRUE, is it, Mummy? Tell her it's not true. I hate her. Why can't we get rid of her, she's horrible,' squawked Peter.

'Of course you weren't found in a bin, darling. Jane was just being silly,' I assured Peter, as Jane shrieked, 'You told me to talk to you and now you are ignoring me and just talking to the BIN BOY!'

Oh, fucking hell. I had a headache now.

'SHE CALLED ME BIN BOY!'

'I WISH YOU HAD NEVER BEEN BORN! I WISH I DIDN'T EVEN HAVE A BROTHER!'

'I WISH I DIDN'T HAVE A SISTER! YOU ARE A BITCH!'

'MUMMY, HE CALLED ME A BITCH!'

'SHUT UP! JUST SHUT UP! BOTH OF YOU JUST SHUT THE FUCK UP AND STOP CALLING EACH OTHER NAMES! I AM GOING MAD!'

'But –'

'But –'

'No buts! NO BUTS!'

'She said, "No butts,"' sniggered Peter

'YOU have no butt!' retorted Jane. 'You have no butt because I unravelled your belly button while you were asleep and it fell off!'

'ENOUGH!'

I finally restored some sort of order, and tried again, because God knows, I DO try to be a good parent, despite the abandonment issues I have probably caused and the fact I appear to be raising feral hell beasts, not human children.

'Right, Jane. What exactly is your issue with the O'Connor children?'

'Nothing,' said Jane sulkily.

Peter opened his mouth.

'No, Peter, I'm talking to Jane right now. You can talk in a minute,' I said, ramming a handful of Jammy Dodgers into his mouth to muffle whatever insult he was about to come out with.

'Come on, Jane. Something has obviously upset you. Just tell me what it is.'

'I had a dream …' mumbled Jane.

'Sorry, what?'

'I *said*, I had a dream. Megan was best friends with Sophie in my dream and she was really mean to me and she took my favourite Smiggle rubber and told Sophie not to talk to me.'

'Ohhhhkaaaay. Just to clarify, this was *all* in your dream? Has Megan actually done anything horrible to you in real life?'

'Well, no,' admitted Jane. 'But I just said, she was *really* mean in my dream. So now I hate her.'

'Oh Jane, darling. You can't hate people for things they do in your dreams. They are not responsible in real life for things you dream them doing when you're asleep,' I said.

I felt a little bit hypocritical as I tried to explain this to Jane, as I have frequently found myself seething at Simon for days for the terrible and iniquitous things that Dream Simon has done (the worst one was when I dreamt that Dream Simon had run off with Dream Hannah – how could they? My husband and my best friend! I was LIVID with the pair of them for the unspeakable betrayal by their dream counterparts).

Peter finally managed to swallow his mouthful of biscuits and burst out with, 'You're BONKERS! You can't be angry with Megan and Jack for something Megan did in your dream. That's just WEIRD!'

'I can so!' spat Jane. 'I heard Mummy telling Daddy that she was really pissed off with him about something that HE'D done in one of her dreams. So why can't I be angry with Megan?'

'Jane, please don't say "pissed off", it's not very nice,' I said sternly, in an attempt at maternal discipline.

'You say MUCH worse!' retorted Jane.

'That's not the point. I'm a grown-up. I'm allowed to.'

'That is so hypocritical of you!' protested Jane.

'Well, tough. Anyway, the point is, you cannot go into school on Monday in a huff with Megan for something she doesn't even know that she didn't do.'

Jane looked unconvinced.

Later, I heard Peter talking to Simon.

'Daddy, are all women just a bit mental?' he asked gloomily.

'Why do you ask, darling?' said Simon.

'Mummy and Jane are mental.'

'You really shouldn't call people "mental", it's not very nice,' said Simon, non-committally.

'But they *are* mental! What should I call them then?'

Simon still did not actually deny that his beloved wife and adored firstborn child were 'mental', instead suggesting that perhaps 'highly strung' might be a better term for Peter to use.

'*Fine*,' said Peter. 'Are all women as "highly strung" as Mummy and Jane?'

'Oh, my son,' said Simon sadly. 'You have no idea of the deep and all-encompassing crazy that the female sex is capable of. And I'm afraid it is going to get an awful lot worse around here before too long.'

'How come you can call them "crazy", but I can't call them "mental" and have to say they are "highly strung"?' demanded Peter. 'And what do you mean it is going to get worse? Do you mean they are going to go even more batshit than they already are?'

'Peter, please don't say "batshit". Where do you even learn words like that?'

'From Mummy. I overheard her saying that Auntie Louisa was a batshit hippy loon. It's quite a good word, isn't it? "Batshit." She also said that you were going to go batshit when you found out she'd scraped the car again. Did you go batshit?'

Thanks for that, Peter. Thanks a fucking bunch. I was waiting for the right moment to tell Simon that I *may* have had a bijou *tête-à-tête* with a small bollard in a car park, but now you've dropped me right in the proverbial, you little toerag!

'Mummy scraped the car again? What the fuck? How? When? When was she planning on telling me?'

'Dunno,' said Peter vaguely, having 'accidentally' volunteered just enough information to cause trouble and now losing interest with the blue touch paper thoroughly lit. 'What did you mean about Mummy and Jane getting worse, though, Daddy? I shouldn't think Jane could get any worse. She is very mean to me. Are you sure we can't get rid of her, Daddy? We could have her adopted. We'd have to lie, of course, and tell them she was a nice person, because no one would want Jane if they knew what she was really like.'

'Peter, that is not a nice way to talk about your sister.'

'But she isn't nice to me. She threatened to bog-wash me, just because I was in her room LOOKING at something. I didn't even take anything, or touch anything. I was only LOOKING!'

'What on earth is bog-washing?' said Simon in confusion.

'It's when you hold someone's head down the toilet and then flush it. That is the sort of person she is.'

'Oh.'

'So you see, *I* don't think she could get any worse, but you said she would, so what did you mean?'

'Errrr, nothing, son. Nothing. We'll cross that bridge when we come to it. With your mother too. But just between us, we will probably be wanting to keep our heads below the parapet for the next few years. And hide any sharp objects. Now if you'll excuse me, I need to find your mother and see how she has managed to wreck the car this time.'

I have no idea what he means either. I hid in the larder till I heard Simon go out to the garage, so successfully avoided the conversation about the car. It really is only a tiny scrape. And just a bit of a dent. You can hardly notice it.

DECEMBER

Friday, 2 December

Firstly – AAAAARRRRGHHHHHH, FML, HOW in the name of everlasting fuck is it December already? I am not ready! December is for decking the halls with boughs of holly and rosy-cheeked carollers and Baileys, so much lovely Baileys, and I am not ready, not in the slightest. Work is frantic, with the Big Project to be finished for early January, I am still going to those awful HIIT classes, though I am not entirely sure why, apart from the fact that I don't want Alan to feel that I am beaten that easily, but I do seem to be wobbling slightly less, and my desire for Mint Clubs has somewhat abated after reading how many burpees I would have to do to burn each one off. My festive spirit is lacking, gone away, hiding under a rock. I dunno. December will undoubtedly herald (I was pleased with that pun, but Simon didn't get it all when I used it earlier, not even when I shouted 'HARK!' at him) a barrage of emails from our families, demanding present suggestions and wittering about Christmas dinner and bastarding Christmas puddings, not to mention the Christmas cards from people I have not seen in years and didn't much like even back then, containing the miserable hell of the round robins detailing Jemima and Sebastian's latest astonishing achievements. *And*, instead of one dispiriting Christmas party for the whole company in a second-rate hotel, there are millions of the bastarding things to go to. There is a 'team' Christmas lunch (Ed might cry), a department party and then the full company party. They are all in jolly nice hotels or restaurants, though, but there will be a fateful combination of lots of booze and the need to keep up the façade of being a Proper Person and also the tiny fact of them jumping to the conclusion that I am single and childless, which is why you should never assume because it makes an ass out of you and me and FML, and who am I any more, using expressions like that. On the plus side, if I keep the HIIT classes, I might manage a semi-slinky dress for the parties, instead of seeking out something whose main plus point is 'forgiving' …

Oh God. So much to do.

Secondly – tonight was finally the hallowed Christmas Fair. I say 'finally', but it was actually pretty much a race against time to get ready for it. But we did it.

I had to take a precious afternoon off, having fibbed slightly and claimed I had a doctor's appointment, cunningly telling Alan and co. that it was for 'Women's Problems' in order to forestall any questions. Technically, I told myself, it *was* 'Women's Problems', as everyone seems to think children *are* women's problems rather than men's. I have blithely used the 'Women's Problems' excuse for years, but somehow it is slightly more embarrassing to have to trot it out to whippersnapper millennial sorts than the repressed middle-aged chaps at my old job.

Cara, Katie, Sam and I, with a handful of other stalwarts, turned up at the hall this afternoon and basically threw every single fairy light we owned at it. I had sneaked into the park early one morning before the dog walkers and pinched a bin-bag full of ivy, which possibly may or may not technically be stealing, but is probably OK as it is For the Children.

I also purchased a staple gun in a fit of enthusiasm, and I think it may now literally be the best thing I have ever owned. It's amazing! Anything you want attached to a wall – BAM! Staple-gun it! I may staple-gun Simon's bollocks to the wall, as he insisted he was far too busy to come along or pick up the kids today, saying that he had told me that it was a bad idea to take over the PTA. I stapled-gunned ivy all over the hall, ignoring the naysayers who were fretting about whether we were allowed to staple-gun things to the wall, and only slightly envisaging Simon's face (the other good thing about a staple gun is that when people annoy you when you are stapling, you can secretly pretend you are Robert de Niro in *Taxi Driver* and mutter 'You lookin' at me?' as you staple, which is remarkably satisfying). Kiki meanwhile floated about getting in everyone's way and draping herself becomingly in ivy, until I brandished the staple gun at her menacingly and told her to pull her weight.

The stallholders arrived, bearing their many wares. I had assumed they would be lovely, jolly, friendly, smiley ladies, but it turns out the crafting world is a cut-throat place, and I was forced to intervene in several spats as they attempted to encroach on each other's space/annex extra tables/block views of competitors with strategically placed scarf stands. I may have to do more research next year, as apparently putting 'Kooky Kandle Krafts' next to 'It's a Bomb' bath bombs (a truly unfortunate name) was a major faux pas, as they have been carrying on some sort of blood feud for years over Kooky Kandle Krafts mistaking one of It's a Bomb's lurid concoctions for a cupcake she had just bought and attempting to eat it. It seems it got very ugly, as Kooky Kandles foamed at the mouth, and in between spitting out glitter accused It's a Bomb of attempted murder (sort of understandable with that TRULY AWFUL NAME) and It's a Bomb counter-accused Kooky Kandles of shamelessly stealing her stock, and they have been sworn enemies ever since.

Other than that, it was relatively uneventful. To Sam's immense relief, no one pissed on him during his Santa turn, though he did complain afterwards that spending two hours in a polyester Santa suit had given him prickly heat on his bollocks ('I mean, there is a reason why I never wear man-made fibres, Ellen!'). He then grumbled that knowing his luck, this would be the week that all his lurking round Sainsbury's paid off and he finally met the love of his life beside the extra virgin olive oil, just as he was squirming about, trying to discreetly relieve the itching, so that the love of his life would probably run for the hills, thinking Sam had crabs.

Peter and Jane vanished into the melee of screaming, sugar-crazed children and old ladies (where do these flocks of old ladies come from that populate Christmas Fairs? You never see so many of them roaming in gangs at any other time. Do they have a special bus that they travel the country in, visiting every Christmas Fair they pass, and collecting more OAPs en route to swell their numbers, the better to block the aisles by standing around complaining about how disappointing the home baking stall is, and really, £3 for a sponge that looks like that, they would be *ashamed* to ask £3 for such a Sponge of Shame, and wasn't it a pity there was no nice fruit cake?), and reappeared periodically to demand more money. I discovered afterwards that Peter had spent most of his money on the tombola, gambling with a dogged enthusiasm that suggests we might have trouble keeping him out of the bookies in future. Or perhaps I should try to harvest his potential gambling addiction for good and encourage him to become a professional poker player like Victoria Coren Mitchell? Apparently she makes loads of money playing poker. He might have to work on his poker face, though, as currently you can tell at least ten minutes in advance when he is working up to a poo (actually, Simon does the same), and even if he has only managed a silent but deadly fart he still can't help but give a little snigger of joy at his latest achievement. I did once have high hopes that perhaps he could be destined for a career as an international gigolo playboy, as he is very good at charming old ladies, but that was before the farting showed no signs of abating. He could easily combine the international gigolo playboy thing with being a professional poker player, though, because as far as I am aware, they both involve spending a lot of time in casinos in places like Monte Carlo. Admittedly I have not put a lot of research into either career option.

Kiki had had to go home, apparently to get herself and her children changed into something even more photogenic, and returned clad in an eye-poppingly tight Christmas jumper dragging a mutinous Lalabelle and Trixierose dressed as elves, and a disgruntled-looking man in a suit and tie, who turned out to be her husband Keith, as he hissed repeatedly, 'For fuck's sake, Karen, can you just put that bloody phone down for a second and stop with the photos?' as Kiki hissed back, 'Stop calling me Karen. Everyone needs to call me Kiki for my fucking *brand*, OK? You've ruined that Insta Story now. I'm going to have to do another one. Don't you *want* that trip to the Maldives, Keith?'

Sunday, 4 December

After years of benign neglect by my father, he seems to have decided in his old age that he is ready to play the doting family man. Daddy and Natalia rang this morning to say they were 'just passing' again, and thought they might pop in for Sunday lunch. Up until that point I had delegated Sunday lunch to Simon, who had declared that we would just have cheese sandwiches. I was quite looking forward to Simon discovering that actually cheese sandwiches are not entirely the simple repast he had planned, because Jane will only eat cheese sandwiches if the cheese is grated, not sliced, and Simon will only eat cheese sandwiches if they have pickle in, but everyone else threatens to vomit on the spot if there is even a trace of pickle on *their* sandwiches and Peter doesn't like butter in his cheese sandwiches. By the time everybody has specified their cheese fucking sandwich preferences, I have lost the will to live and want to just tell them all to cock off and starve and feed the cheese to my lovely dog, who doesn't care if it's grated or sliced or even cut into manageable pieces, as he's perfectly capable of eating blocks of cheese whole. (As we discovered when he broke into the fridge and ate a chunk of cheddar, an unopened packet of taleggio, a good slab of brie and a whole camembert. He then projectile-vomited a fondue. Which was nice.) Anyway, the main reason I don't just feed him the cheese is because it gives him cheesy bum. He is hard to love when he has cheesy bum.

However, my allegedly 'just passing' father deciding to invite himself to Sunday lunch meant a mercy dash to Sainsbury's to grab provisions for a roast, where I may or may not have taken advantage of insisting that Peter and Jane stayed at home with Simon to also go to a very quick HIIT class while I was out, as I have got carried away with myself and bought a Christmas party dress that is not forgiving in the slightest, but is very definitely slinky. At Sainsbury's I also bought many amusing things as 'stocking fillers', which I will either put somewhere safe and find sometime around July, or I will forget about, or in the extremely unlikely event of them actually making it into anyone's stockings, everyone will be utterly underwhelmed by them and ignore them. I did get the last milk chocolate Chocolate Oranges, though, hurrah! I snatched them from under the nose of a scary-looking woman who I am sure I once had a run-in with at a soft-play – there can't be many people with 'Juztin Beebor 4ever' tattooed on their neck! She did look more than mildly threatening, though, so I beat a hasty retreat at that point, no doubt to Simon's relief, as he struggles to understand the necessity of Lovely Things for stockings and makes unhelpful comments like 'Why can't we just put their normal presents in the stockings? Why do we have to have all this bastarding tat for the stockings?' This is yet another sign that Simon has No Soul, for everyone knows that stockings are for small, trinkety things, and that the Big Presents (even if they are quite physically small, they are still the Big Presents) go under the tree, and one should not deviate from this or one will break The System and Christmas will be ruined FOREVER!

Lunch went off relatively well. Peter has developed a thumping great crush on Natalia and flirted with her most shamelessly before attempting to prove himself worthy of her love by eating his own weight in roast beef and Yorkshire puddings. Natalia seemed unimpressed by his feat, however, even when Peter informed her that he had just eaten twelve Yorkshire puddings, nine roast potatoes and four helpings of beef. I honestly don't know where he puts it – it is an astonishing thing. Since Natalia seemed disinclined to declare her undying love for him in recognition of his heroic digestive system, Peter announced that he could eat more Yorkshires than that, actually, and was all set for another helping, when I was forced to forbid it, for fear he might actually puke. I don't know where that child puts his food. He eats an obscene amount and never seems to put on an ounce, whereas if I had eaten as many Yorkshire puddings as he had, I wouldn't be able to do my skirt up tomorrow, HIIT class or no HIIT class.

Anyway, it was a tiny bit awkward when Daddy asked what we were doing for Christmas, and I had to say we were going to Mum's.

'Oh,' said Daddy. 'And Jessica too?'

'Err, yes. Jessica too.'

'Right,' said Daddy. 'That's a bit of a shame, because actually we had hoped to spend Christmas with you and your sister. You know, Natalia's first Christmas with the family. Couldn't you change your plans? And speak to Jessica too?' asked Daddy plaintively.

I choked on my wine. '*Change our plans?*' I spluttered. 'Daddy, are you seriously suggesting that you want me to tell *Mum* that we are not coming for Christmas because we are spending it with you and Natalia? Jesus *Christ*, Daddy! Have you forgotten what Mum is like? She will literally hire a hitman and have you killed, or have us kidnapped and driven to Yorkshire to make sure we spend Christmas with her. I don't want to have to go all the way to Yorkshire tied up in the back of a Transit van. I get travel sick! And not only that, Jessica does not change plans, you know that. I'm pretty sure Jessica bribed the hospital staff to keep Granny's life support switched on for an extra week so she didn't have to cancel her holiday to Antigua! She is not going to countenance the Christmas plans being changed.'

'Oh, you exaggerate, Ellen!' said Daddy. 'Jessica isn't that bad. Your mother, on the other hand … Well, I suppose I see your point. The woman is a stone-cold, batshit-mental bitch!'

'Even Grandpa gets to say batshit and bitch,' objected Peter. 'That's not fair. Why don't I?'

'Because I am not responsible for your grandfather's language and I am responsible for yours!' I snapped, wondering if I should be defending my mother against Daddy's description of her, especially talking about her like that in front of Natalia, but in truth I was struggling to come up with counter arguments against it, as it was a fairly accurate assessment of her character.

Christ, I will be glad to get back to work for a rest!

Thursday, 8 December

Spanxed to the hilt (I should perhaps have gone for a slightly more forgiving dress – the HIIT classes and lack of biscuits have not had *that* dramatic an effect), I tripped merrily off to the Big Christmas Party last night.

Oh, it was divine. I rather regretted the Spanx as I could not do justice to the lovely food and I *did* consider popping to the loo to take them off – but then what to do with them? They were too large to fit in my dinky clutch bag and too expensive to simply be abandoned. And what if someone found them and put two and two together and realised that I was looking rather more bulgy after my trip to the bogs, and they thought perhaps I had been shagging and had cast them aside in a moment of passion instead of merely wishing to restore the circulation to my nether regions? I kept the Spanx on.

The other downside to the Spanx was that I was somewhat lacking in blotting paper to absorb the lashing of free booze, so I may have ended up a little tipsy. Actually, I may have ended up a lot tipsy.

I have an unpleasant recollection of sitting next to Ed and asking him if the cock and balls on the wall at my interview was a new and cunning sort of psychometric test. He looked startled and said no, no, it most certainly wasn't. I expressed disappointment, and said I thought perhaps my handling of it had been the clincher that got me the job. Ed replied that no, what had got me the job was that I talked less hyperbolic bullshit management-speak than the other candidates, and therefore he chose me on the basis that I would be the least-annoying person to work with. I suppose there are worse reasons to be given a job.

There was dancing. If there is one thing I cannot resist when pissed, it is dancing. I danced with enthusiasm, but I fear without grace or elegance, although when considering the dancing, it is another reason to be glad I left the Spanx on, as however much I may have embarrassed myself with my moves'n'grooves, at least I did not inadvertently show my bits.

And then – oh then, the bliss! As the entertainment, there was a faded nineties boy band, who I had assumed had given up music years ago and were all working as insurance salesmen or something. But no, there they were, still touring. Admittedly, Christmas parties, however swanky, aren't quite the same as selling out the O2, but I was very excited.

'God, I love a bit of ironic kitsch!' said Alan when they came on.

I was indignant at this. 'Do not call the music of my youth "ironic kitsch", boy!' I declared. 'One day you will be thrilled to see that … um –' I struggled to think of a Cool Young Person's Band (I insist on Radio 2 in the car), so the closest I could come up with was Ed Sheeran, and even in my inebriated state I was pretty sure Alan did not think Ed Sheeran was 'cool' – 'a band you like is still touring and you get to see them live *for free* and almost close enough to lick!'

'Don't lick the band, Ellen,' said Alan, looking alarmed, 'I don't think that's allowed.'

I did not lick the band. I contented myself with singing along to each and every one of their Greatest Hits, even the ones that I didn't realise were theirs, nineties boy bands being fairly interchangeable even in the nineties. I think I may have bonded with Lydia over the singing, as she also proved to be a fan.

It was a splendid night. The only way it could be more splendid next year would be if they got Rick Astley or Chesney Hawkes along. I got a selfie with the band. I may frame it.

Friday, 9 December

Urgh! What stupid fucker came up with the idea of having a Christmas Party on a Thursday night? That was a very bloody stupid idea. I don't know why anyone bothered coming in today. No one got any work done and we all just shuffled around like zombies, desperately gulping tea, not entirely able to meet each other's eyes after last night's bonding and oversharing. I had to take some papers into Ed's office at one point and I thought he had gone out, until I heard a snore and realised he had gone to sleep under his desk! The perks of being the boss, I suppose, though it did occur to me that maybe he wasn't as hungover as us, he just spends most of his time asleep under his desk and that's why he doesn't like having to come out or go to meetings.

And then tonight I had the joy of the school Mums' (and Sam and Julian's) Night Out. Dear God, these nights were bad enough when you only had to attend, but it is amazing that I didn't kill anyone in the process of organising it, between everyone insisting that their various dietary requirements were catered for (Paleo, Slimming World, potential egg allergy because sometimes omelettes make her feel a bit dodgy, no foreign food, no sauce, no food touching other food – the only person who *didn't* make a fuss about the food was Helen O'Connor, who is genuinely coeliac) and getting the deposits (someone actually tried to pay in bitcoins, WTAF?).

But tonight it was finally the happy night! Despite my desperate manoeuvrings to try to sit between Sam and Cara, I ended up trapped at the other end of the table between Erica 'No Foreign Food' Mitchell and 'Totally Paleo' Julian. I tried to look polite while Erica held forth to me on what does and does not constitute a 'Foreign Food' (chicken tikka masala is all right, as are kebabs, because they're 'not really foreign', but sushi is the Devil's Work, because her grandpa was in the war), and Julian purring that he was getting together a group for Pilates in the Park on a Sunday morning, if I was interested, and had I ever thought about modelling, because I had a very interesting bone structure, and he could offer me an excellent deal on a one-on-one photo shoot, just me and him, if I was interested. I even managed to bite my tongue when I overheard Abigail 'The Wrong Kind of Gluten' Porter ordering the fish and chips for her main course, despite the glutoniumed batter, because apparently 'that's not actually gluten like the gluten in bread, it's *different!*', but I took some comfort that Sam was trapped too between Fiona Montague (who had once again kindly informed me that I looked 'tired' when I arrived and offered me the number for her 'magical little facials lady, honestly, you wouldn't *believe* how it perks the skin up') and Darcy 'Death by Eggs' Chisholm, who was asking if there were eggs in every single item on the menu, and describing to Sam in great detail how difficult it is for her to avoid eggs, and how her doctor simply won't take her seriously, just because her allergy test came back negative.

I had resolved not to drink, because clearly alcohol is evil and wrong and after last night I was Never Drinking Again, but within five minutes of sitting down I was knocking back the cheap Pinot with the best of them in a desperate attempt to numb the pain.

Finally, finally, the last cheap cracker had been pulled, the final flimsy paper crown had floated to the floor under the table, the last joke had been told while Erica snorted that she was so over all these politically correct jokes, and why shouldn't she say 'golliwog' if she wants to, and it was time for the bill. Which was presented to me, as everyone looked at me expectantly, waiting for me to work out what everyone owed and then collect the money in. After the best part of a bottle of house white.

'Are we just splitting it all equally?' shouted Francesca Shaw, who had insisted she couldn't drink the house wine, and so had ordered a £40 bottle of Rioja, which she had refused to share with anyone else, followed by three large Baileys, and who also happens to drive a top-of-the-range Lexus 4x4, lives in an even bigger house than Lucy Atkinson's Perfect Mummy, and whose husband is something terribly busy and important to do with investment banking.

I mildly pointed out that I didn't think that was *terribly* fair to all the people who *hadn't* ordered expensive bottles of wine, or liqueurs, and was particularly unfair for those people who were driving and had been on soft drinks or water. Apparently this was quite unreasonable of me, and Francesca was stunned that she was going to have to pay extra. I finally got it all worked out, and announced how much everyone owed, when Deborah Green said helpfully, 'Yes, but minus the deposit we already paid.'

'No,' I said. 'I paid the deposit last month, and that's been taken off the bill already.'

'Yes, but we paid a deposit, so it should be £10 less,' insisted Deborah.

I explained again, but Erica and Abigail had also chimed in, insisting that the deposit meant everyone should be paying £10 less than the total I had given them.

The final straw was when Diana Baker looked up from tapping away at her phone and announced, 'I've been working it out too, and it comes out as £2 a head *less* than you are charging us.'

Through gritted teeth I ground out, 'I did *say*, Diana, that I was rounding it up by £2 a person, as service isn't included, and so that will pay for the tip. As well as making it a round number, so it is easier for change.'

'But that's a £60 tip!' said Eleanor Blackstone in horror. 'Why are we leaving them a £60 tip?'

'Well,' I suggested, as calmly as I could, given that what I really wanted to do was to smack my head repeatedly against a brick wall while screaming WHAT THE FUCK IS WRONG WITH YOU ALL?, 'maybe we're leaving them a £60 tip because they have been really quite busy with us tonight, because we're a massive table, and they haven't stopped bringing us drinks and coffees and running around after us all night, and so maybe THEY HAVE BASTARDING WELL EARNED IT!'

'Yes, but £60! I mean, they are getting paid for serving us tonight!' argued Diana.

'Minimum wage!' I shrieked. 'They get the minimum wage! Do you even know how much that is?

'I just think that maybe £1 each would be enough!' said Eleanor. 'I mean, if the minimum wage isn't enough to live on, then that's really something for the government to deal with, it isn't actually our problem, is it? Or they should just get another job, or I don't know, maybe take in some ironing or something?'

'OH MY FUCKING GOD! It's £1, Eleanor! One FUCKING POUND! You are spending three weeks in the Bahamas over Christmas WITH YOUR FULL-TIME NANNY along, and you are quibbling about a £1 or £2 tip? And also, if we make it £1 each, then no one will have the exact change and everyone will be wanting £1 back and then it will all take FOR FUCKING EVER AND I WANT TO GO HOME! WE ARE LEAVING £2 EACH FOR THE TIP, OK?'

We left £2 each for the tip.

Sam said afterwards it reminded him of the opening scene of *Reservoir Dogs*, only instead of waiting for the heist to go wrong and people to start dying one by one throughout the film, he thought I was just going to murder everyone there at once. Possibly just with the power of my extremely withering glare.

I don't think anyone else will ask me to organise the Mums' Christmas Night Out again. Oh bollocks, and I still have to get the teacher present money off the tight bastards.

Monday, 12 December

I have been noticing something at work that I never really noticed before – whenever Lydia, who is the only woman in our office with children (or rather the only one *admitting* to having children), leaves early or comes in late due to something child-related, everyone chunters and mutters and grumbles about it. Lydia seems a nice person, she pulls her weight, she gets her part of projects completed on time, she doesn't seem to be a slacker, but there is somehow this implication that by taking a morning or afternoon off here and there, she is somehow not doing her bit, that she is shirking her workload in favour of parenting. And yet should one of the *men* in the office leave to go and do something child-related, far from people viewing him as a workshy bastard, he is positively lauded as Dad of the Year for going to a Nativity or an assembly.

I've never really noticed it before, I suppose because I was the one dashing out to the Christmas concerts and sports days and open afternoons and no one really says anything to Lydia's face about how they resent her taking time off to be there for her children, but there is a definite undercurrent of irritation about how dare she try to be a mother and work as well. And I now recognise some of the barbed comments that are flung Lydia's way, because I've been on the receiving end of them myself, but without the context of the remarks made behind Lydia's back, I hadn't really realised how much this annoyed people. And it's not even just the men. Gaby from HR made snide remarks when she 'popped in' to the office and found Lydia not there 'again' (I'm pretty sure Gaby is a Grade A bitch anyway, though).

And yet, Lydia isn't actually taking any more time off than she is due. She doesn't stay late, like Alan does, and she doesn't come in early like James does most days, so he can avoid the school run and leave it to his poor wife, but she isn't taking the piss. People just *assume* that now she is a mother, she can't properly combine working – and doing her job well – with parenting. When I announced that I wouldn't be here this Friday afternoon because I had a dentist appointment (school Christmas Concert), everyone said, 'Oh, you poor thing! I hate the dentist, I hope it's not too painful!' and didn't question it any further. Alan went so far as to say that if I hadn't finished the stuff I was working on for the new project by the time I had to leave on Friday, it could easily wait till next week.

By contrast, when Lydia came in to a 10.30 a.m. meeting this morning at exactly 10.30 a.m., having arranged to come in late so she could go to her children's Christmas Concert (I want to go to her school, where the concert must only last an hour! Ours drags on forever, with endless verses of 'Rudolph the Red-Nosed Sodding Reindeer'. I swear there are more verses each year. I think they just make up new ones and add them on to fuck with our minds), Alan remarked nastily, 'Good of you to join us, Lydia. Of course, it would have been helpful if you had been in earlier so you could have given me the figures I needed for the Hunter project *before* this meeting, but I suppose that can't be helped.'

Lydia, rather marvellously, simply shrugged and said, 'Oh, I'm sorry, Alan. I sent you those figures on Friday, but it must have been after you'd left. Didn't you leave at 2 p.m.? Anyway, if you check your inbox, they should be there.'

I felt terrible for Lydia, though, because even as she said that, and Alan muttered something that sounded rather like a grudging, 'Oh, yeah. There they are. Um, thanks,' I could see a slight flush on her cheeks and set to her jaw as she justified herself yet again, and I thought maybe I should just tell Alan to shut the fuck up and stop being a dick, but then I chickened out, because I haven't been there long enough to start telling people things like that, and also, because I am a coward as well as a liar and didn't want to overly draw attention to myself on the whole subject of women and children, I simply said nothing and settled for silently hating myself instead, while coming up with cutting ripostes to Alan in my head. I did try to give Lydia a sympathetic smile, but I think it might have come out wrong, because she just gave me a rather odd scared look in return.

Wednesday, 14 December

Oh, happy days! I had no sooner walked in the door from work – I hadn't even taken my shoes off – when Jane presented me with her Christmas list. I had been feeling smugly smug that she had stopped nagging me about having an Instagram account, and was pleased that clearly all my stern lectures about growing up too fast, enjoying what was left of her childhood, and of course, the dangers of STRANGERS ON THE INTERNET being able to see her photos and so find her, murder her and leave her dismembered body in a bin-bag in a skip (OK, I maybe glossed over a few of these details in my bijou Stranger Danger rant), had finally sunk in and she had decided to just wait until she is thirteen. However, her list read:

My own Instagram account
YouTube channel
GoPro HERO camera
GoPro Drone
Tripod
Laptop with video editing software

I took one look at it and handed it back, with a single word.

'No.'

'OMG, like WHY NOT?' said a furious Jane.

'OMG, like, for a start, because I've told you not to say "OMG" or use "like" for, like, every, like, second, like, word, because it's, like, really, like, annoying! And also because I have told you that you are not having an Instagram account until you are old enough, and since you don't seem to have included a time machine on your list, you are still NOT OLD ENOUGH! So, hence, NO to the social media accounts, and also NO to the several thousand pounds worth of electronics, for a similar reason, BECAUSE YOU ARE ELEVEN!'

'AAAARRRRRRGH!' raged Jane. 'Don't try to be funny. It's so pathetic when you try to be funny. And it's awful when you try and pretend to be talking like me. It just makes you sound like a sad freak. You are not impressing anyone. And it is SO UNFAIR that you won't let me on Instagram. I can't believe I am the ONLY PERSON IN MY CLASS WHO DOESN'T HAVE AN ACCOUNT!'

'That's not true, darling. Sophie doesn't have one either.'

'Only because you have *brainwashed* Sam into not letting her have one and convinced him that Insta is full of paedophiles.

That's like TWO lives you've ruined, Mother. I hope you're like pleased with yourself!'

'Oh, for God's sake, Jane. Stop exaggerating. Freddy Dawkins isn't on Instagram either, and nor is Daisy Cooper.'

'OMG! OMG! THAT is who you are making me be like! Freddy Dawkins has NO FRIENDS because he's probably going to be a serial killer and so no one would even like FOLLOW his Insta because it would only be weird shit like DEAD ANIMALS or something, and Daisy Cooper doesn't even like have a TV because her mum doesn't even like believe in electronics because she like thinks the rays will fry your brain, and so Daisy doesn't even have like any friends because she hasn't even HEARD of like Zoella, and like her mum makes her wear clothes out of DEAD PEOPLE'S SHOPS! IS THAT WHAT YOU ARE GOING TO DO TO ME NEXT? WILL YOU MAKE ME DRESS OUT OF DEAD PEOPLE'S SHOPS? PROBABLY IN CLOTHES THAT BELONGED TO PEOPLE FREDDY DAWKINS KILLED, BECAUSE YOU HATE ME?' screamed Jane. She has not had a good paddy for a while, and evidently had been saving the rage for one good blowout.

'Jane, I really wish you wouldn't swear.'

'YOU SWEAR! YOU ARE SUCH A HYPOCRITE! And you're never here anyway. You have abandoned me to be a latch-key child in favour of YOUR career and now you won't even let ME try to have a career of MY own!'

'Jane, you're eleven. You don't need to be thinking about pursuing a career yet. And what are these dead people's shops you are ranting about?' I enquired, attempting to gloss over my own hypocritically bad language and general bad examples.

'You know. The dead people's shops on the High Street that you always make us look in, so you can buy second-hand books. And they always smell funny, and have loads of dead people's clothes and DVDs, even though who even *buys* DVDs anymore?'

'Do you mean the charity shops?' I said, confused.

'Yes! The dead people's shops!'

'They're really not, you know. You can get some very good bargains in them. Well, I hear you can. There are urban myths of people who find vintage Chanel handbags in perfect condition for a fiver, but in truth I've never found anything that doesn't look a bit like ...'

'Someone has died in it?' supplied Jane.

'Well, yes.'

'Because they are dead people's shops! And you are trying to change the subject away from the fact that you ARE RUINING MY LIFE!!'

'Look, Jane, darling,' I said soothingly. 'Even if I were to allow you an Instagram account – which I'm absolutely not going to do, by the way – I would definitely not even be thinking about buying you £600 cameras, or £800 drones, OR a new laptop as you have a perfectly serviceable laptop, nor would I be shelling out for expensive editing software. BECAUSE YOU ARE ELEVEN!'

'That is just another way that you are ruining my life!' shrieked Jane. 'IF you had let me go on Instagram when I first wanted to, I would totally have like a MASSIVE following by now, and so GoPro would give me all that for free. It's YOUR FAULT you have to buy me ANYTHING! I could be getting sponsored for EVERYTHING by now AND making loads of money for my future from YouTube ads. There is a TODDLER who makes LIKE MILLIONS REVIEWING TOYS. But no! No, YOU like have to make a STUPID FUSS about like "internet safety" and RUIN MY LIFE! It's like you don't even want me to be like happy or like a multi-millionaire YouTuber, because you don't even like LIKE me!'

'Oh, FFS!' I shouted back. 'Come on, out of the people in your class whose parents HAVE allowed them Instagram and

YouTube accounts, HOW MANY OF THEM now have millions of followers and are living off their sponsored posts? Hmm?'

'I never said it was easy,' snarled Jane. 'But everyone else in my class is STUPID! It would be *different* for me. And what about Kiki?'

'But everyone thinks that, darling,' I reasoned. 'And only a tiny handful of people are successful at it. And Kiki can only do what she does because she has someone to pay the mortgage and the bills. She doesn't actually have to worry about money.'

'Yes, but *someone* gets to be the *really* successful ones. So why *shouldn't* it be me? If you would only let me have a chance at it. But you won't! BECAUSE YOU DON'T EVEN CARE ABOUT MY DREAM, OR MY JOURNEY!'

Oh, these bastarding journeys. Everyone is on a fucking 'journey' these days. People can't just 'do stuff'. It is all part of the 'journey'. I blame *The X Factor*. That is where all this bloody 'journey' nonsense seems to originate from, unfortunate souls not realising that they are being exploited for car-crash TV by having their failed auditions filmed and broadcasted and then tearfully talking afterwards about how having their humiliation shown to the nation has just been part of an 'amazing journey'.

'For goodness sake, Jane, you are being ridiculous.'

'And now you are mocking my dream. You are making fun of me. I *know* I am meant to be a famous YouTube star, I just know it!'

'Oh, get a grip,' I snapped. 'I've never heard anything so ridiculous in my life. And what are you going to be "famous" for? Opening boxes? Kinder eggs? Putting on make-up? Pouting into the camera while revealing your latest #sponsored #collab? These aren't realistic goals. These people aren't going to be able to do this forever, and what will they do then, when all they are qualified to do is duckface and open packaging? What happened to your plans to become a marine biologist or an archaeologist or palaeontologist? Why, all of a sudden, have you become so fixated on this vlogging bollocks that I actually caught you giving a running commentary to your phone on *walking down the stairs* the other day, only you were concentrating so hard on filming yourself that you fell down the stairs and were lucky you didn't break your neck. I know I told you that you could be whatever you wanted to be when you grew up, but I didn't mean for you to become some fanny on the internet. But look. If having a social media account really means that much to you, why don't we compromise, and even though you're a bit too young, you can have a Facebook account, as long as you add Daddy and me as friends so we can check no undesirables are trying to contact you? Hmmm? How does that sound, sweetheart?'

Jane once again stared at me as though I had just suggested she took a shit in her hands and clapped.

'*Facebook*!' she whispered aghast. '*FACEBOOK*! OMG, are you *serious*? Facebook is so *over*. It's for *old people*. Like *you*. I can't believe you would even suggest that to me. That is just cruel. It's child cruelty. I could call Childline. Do you *know* what people would like say if they knew I had a Facebook account? I don't know why you like even bothered *having* me, when you hate me so much.'

And with that, she finally flounced out the room, giving the door a good hard slam on the way out, which woke the dog up, to his immense disgust, and caused him to cast one of his very judgy looks at me.

'Don't you start,' I said.

Thankfully Jane had left before I got a chance to answer her final (hopefully rhetorical) question, but when she is like this, I do honestly wonder why I bothered having children. Surely it isn't meant to be this hard. Was it worth all that effort I put into bringing up a strong, brave, independent warrior girl, who would march to the beat of her own drum, just for her to put all that spirit I tried to instil in her to use in arguing with me about every damn thing under the sun? And what was the point anyway? Teaching her about feminism and the suffragettes and dressing her in jeans and hoodies (in fairness, that was as much an aesthetic decision as an ideological one, because if ever there was a child that did not suit pink it was Jane, and most of the pretty girly skirts and sparkly T-shirts were pink, which just looked dreadful on her), just for her to turn around and decide that, apparently just like almost every other child in the country, she wants to be an internet sensation and make millions pouting on Instagram or prancing around on YouTube. Did Emily Davison die under the hooves of the King's horse for the nation's pre-adolescent girls to have no greater ambition than opening boxes and applying lipstick? DID SHE?

I was musing and muttering all this to myself when Jane stormed back in.

'Since you are intent on RUINING MY LIFE by refusing me the chance to follow my dreams, can I get my ears pierced for Christmas instead?' she demanded.

'Jane, we have been over this as well. I said you could get them pierced when you are thirteen.'

'Yes, but that's not FOREVER!' argued Jane. 'Why can't I have them done now? All I want is my ears pierced. That's all!'

'I thought all you wanted was about £3,500 worth of electronic equipment to make a fool of yourself on the internet,' I countered. Jane glowered at me dangerously. My resolve was cracking. I did not have the strength for another showdown. Jane glowered harder.

'OK, OK, I'll compromise. You're not getting them pierced for Christmas because I can't stand the thought of Granny moaning the whole time that you look common, but you can get them pierced for your twelfth birthday, OK? One year early. And ONE piercing in each ear. That's all!'

'Thank you, Mummy,' said Jane sweetly, and skipped off looking so smugly pleased with herself that I couldn't help but wonder if the whole YouTube/GoPro row had been expressly engineered just so that I would be broken and weak when she actually went in for the kill and asked for what she really wanted. In fairness, it's not really that different to the time Daddy said he would buy me a dress for a university ball and we went shopping in London and I found the *perfect* dress straightaway in Selfridges, and Daddy looked at the price tag and turned pale and said he wasn't paying that for a skimpy frock, so I then tried on every single dress in every single shop on Oxford Street until he lost the will to live and agreed that he would pay anything, literally anything, to be allowed to go home and have a large gin and tonic, so we went back to Selfridges and bought The Dress. So I suppose Jane does come by it honestly.

Only now do I appreciate why poor Daddy was so in need of that stiff gin, though. Parenting is bloody hard work, and actually those early, sleep-deprived, tiny-baby days were only the start of it. I keep assuming that at some point it will get better, easier, but it never really seems to. The challenges change, of course, but it never really seems to get any less hard. And it is all mixed up as well by the fact that although sometimes you could cheerfully throw your precious moppets out of the window (or deny their existence at work), equally you would never give a second thought to literally tearing limb from limb anyone who dared to even think about causing them any sort of harm, or indeed was foolish enough to suggest that your cherubs were in any way not utterly perfect. For although they are monstrous hell beasts, they are YOUR monstrous hell beasts, and also the best thing that ever happened to you, and you love them so much that sometimes you think your heart will burst. Gina Ford never told us how to deal with all this!

Friday, 16 December

I have been meaning to organise a night out with Hannah and Sam and Katie for ages, and have never quite got around to it, and it is nearly Christmas and if we don't do it NOW, then it will be January and everyone will be poor and depressed and on a diet/drying out/both, and so today I decided to just throw caution to the winds and after the hellishly long and soul-destroying Christmas Concert (perhaps my punishment for lying to work about being in the dentist was being tormented by endless tuneless singing until I longed for root-canal surgery as the less painful option), I cornered Sam and Katie in the playground after school.

'Let's go out tonight!' I said brightly.

They both looked at me as if I had grown an extra head. 'Tonight,' they repeated blankly.

'Yes, tonight!' I chirped.

'But Ellen, we haven't *planned* it!' said Katie in astonishment.

'Where would we *go*?' grumbled Sam, looking frightened.

'The pub, of course, like we always do. We'd be being *spontaneous*! People do it all the time at work,' I cried.

'They are *young* people, though. And … and … the children?' they whimpered. 'Our precious moppets. What will become of them?'

'I am a single father, remember, Ellen,' pointed out Sam. 'Robin is as much use as a marzipan dildo when it comes to actually stepping up to the mark and taking any responsibility for our children. Actually, he was about as much use as a marzipan dildo in bed too, if it comes to that,' he added, with only a trace of bitterness.

'It's perfectly simple,' I said. 'Katie, Tim will be home tonight, won't he, because you already told me that he was making dinner this evening, so he can make dinner AND put his daughters to bed, and Sam, Sophie and Toby can come to mine for a sleepover, and Simon can look after them. To be honest, it's probably less work for him than his own children by themselves, as with Sophie and Toby there, the boys will just play mind-numbing computer games and the girls will do whatever it is eleven-year-old girls do that involves so much wittering like demented budgies, shrieking and glitter, rather than Peter and Jane just fighting like cat and dog like they will do with no distractions.'

'But what will I wear?' wailed Katie. 'I haven't planned. I'll need to put on proper make-up and straighten my hair and I have not mentally prepared myself for that! I can't just go out with no warning. What will I say to Tim?'

'Has Tim never rung you to say he's just popping out for a drink after work, or casually informed you that he's going for a pint on a Saturday night?' I demanded.

'Well, yes, but –'

'No buts! It's exactly the same. Just text him, and tell him he'll need to be home on time because you're going out for a drink, because you are a grown-up and a real person and NOT JUST A MUMMY! CAN YOU DO THAT, KATIE? CAN I GET A HELL, YEAH?!'

'Err, I suppose so. But I still don't know what I'll wear. I haven't told the girls I'm going out, so they aren't prepared. What if they're upset?'

'Katie, trust me. Stick them in front of a couple of extra episodes of *Paw Patrol* and they wouldn't notice if you were dancing naked around the living room with your tits on fire, let alone if you've just popped out. Their father will take perfectly good care of them, perhaps not to your standard, and they will wear the wrong jammies to bed, but they will survive mismatching pyjamas for one night without lasting psychological damage,' I barked.

'OK,' wavered Katie. 'This feels weird, though. I don't know if I like going on a night out without building up to it for at least two weeks. It's not *normal*!'

'It's perfectly normal,' I reminded her. 'It's what we did for years and years before we had children and convinced ourselves that we must slavishly devote every waking hour to their whims and needs. But actually we will be better people if we occasionally take some time for ourselves and do something *spontaneous* that reminds us that we are people too, not just parents.'

'Yes!' said Katie. 'Yes, all right, I'm in!'

'Hurray!' I said. 'Sam, what about you?'

'I don't know,' whined Sam. 'My favourite blue shirt is in the wash, and I feel a bit bloated and I still have last week's *Outlander* to watch, and it might rain and –'

'Sam!' I said sternly. 'Man the fuck up, wear a different shirt and come to the pub. I have never heard such feeble excuses in all my life!'

'I'm just saying. OK, fine then, I'll come, but you can buy the first round, for being such a bully and making us leave our comfort zone.'

'I'm encouraging you to be *spontaneous*, FFS! What if you do meet someone wandering around Sainsbury's and they ask you for a date and you're all, "Ooooh, well, I dunno, I don't like going out without any warning!" Consider this a practice run.'

'I don't think I'm going to meet anyone at Sainsbury's anyway,' said Sam gloomily. 'All the single-looking men are skipping round with baskets full of asparagus and mussels and dinky little pots of artichoke hearts and expensive wine. I think they are put off by my trolley full of Petits Filous and frozen peas.'

'Well, then. Maybe this is your chance to meet someone tonight. You're not going to meet anyone sitting at home in your onesie perving over Jamie Fraser, and anyway, he hardly takes his top off this week AT ALL, so there was really no point to that episode.'

'You're right,' said Sam. 'What is the point of *Outlander* if Jamie doesn't get naked at least once?'

I then had to ring Hannah and talk her through exactly the same thing, complete with the *Outlander* spoilers, and the reminder that as a doctor, Charlie was technically probably more qualified to look after her children than she was. But I talked her round in the end, and off to the pub we all went.

After the first half-hour, during which Katie texted Tim obsessively and Sam complained his shirt made him look fat and Hannah rang Charlie to make sure he had remembered to pay the wedding venue deposit, I suggested maybe a little round of Gibsons.

'S'fucking brillant, bein' nout!' slurred Katie an hour later.

'We'sh should do thish more!' shouted Hannah.

'I ashked for extra pickle nonions! No schnogging tonight!' cried Sam. 'Oooh, he looksh fit, hash anyone got Double Mint?'

Monday, 19 December

FML, FML, FML! Fuck my fucking life! I am hurtling with terrifying speed towards my Annual Christmas Meltdown, which usually takes place on Christmas Eve, but due to the summons from Yorkshire has had to be brought forward a little.

Simon is getting on my tits as I still haven't forgiven him for the massive row about whether or not we needed a Christmas tree if we weren't actually going to be here on Christmas Day, to which I replied in no uncertain terms that we most certainly fucking did, and he suggested that if we *had* to have a tree, maybe just a very small tree would do, and I shouted muchly about Scrooges and Grinches and WANTING A PROPER FUCKING TREE, while he muttered about mental wives and something about 'a bit much' and looked with suspicious longing at the trap door to the attic. We got the proper tree. Of course we got the proper tree, because I am a Tree Nazi, and is it even Christmas without a proper tree?

Simon is also being a smuggety smug smug fucker and reminding me every twenty minutes or so that *he* has already accomplished all the things on *his* Christmas To Do list, including wrapping the presents he was to buy. Twat. I bet he's wrapped them badly. He keeps smirking at me and saying, 'I don't know why you always make such a fuss, darling, it's really not that hard.'

In addition to this, I have had Jessica emailing me every twenty minutes, trying to persuade me that we should go halvers on a NutriBullet as a present for Mum and Geoffrey, by which she means she wants me to buy it, wrap it and then hand it to her to give to Mum while murmuring something about it being from both of us, but actually taking all the credit herself. I'm not sure why Jessica feels it so necessary to go halvers on this bastarding NutriBullet, as she earns approximately eleventy billion pounds a year, so could easily afford to buy Mum and Geoffrey a dozen NutriBullets without blinking, but she has a bee in her bonnet. I'm assuming it's either because she can't be arsed full stop and so wants me to do the work, or she just can't be arsed going into a shop and so wants me to use my Amazon

Prime account so she can smugly continue to tell people how she has never bought *anything* from Amazon and only supports small, local, artisanal businesses. I don't even know if Mum and Geoffrey WANT a NutriBullet – if I gave Mum one from me, I would almost certainly get a tart comment about did I realise that she did still have all her own teeth, but if St Jessica of Smugdom is involved then she will probably accept it graciously. I am also trying to buy thoughtful and meaningful gifts for people instead of just giving into temptation and throwing money at the problem now I am slightly more flush. That is Not the Point of Christmas.

Oh, and fuckety twatsticks! I have just realised while looking for NutriBullets on Amazon, that the few things I have managed to do, which is dispatching my mother-in-law's present, might be a bit of a faux pas, in that I have sent the pug-obsessed Sylvia the same pug cushion that I sent her a couple of years ago. I thought it might cheer her up as a tribute to her late and much-lamented pug Napoleon Bonapug, who after many years of terrorising soft toys with his voracious sexual appetites, was sadly found cold in his basket one morning. There was a shocked-looking teddy bear in the basket beside him, which did give Sylvia some comfort that he had probably passed away while indulging in his favourite pastime. I suspect that while she might have taken one pug cushion as well-meaning, a second might be rubbing salt in the wound. Also, ever since Sylvia had a Damascene moment over the wonders of eBay, she has been increasingly difficult to buy anything for, as every day is Christmas for Sylvia – a constant convoy of exhausted couriers wends its way to her French retirement villa, while Sylvia quaffs pink sunshine wine on the terrace and opens each box with cries of glee, exclaiming, 'I don't even remember bidding for this, such fun! Michael, darling, look! Another one of these. Where shall we put this one?' and Simon's poor father mutters, 'It's not *distressed*, Sylvia. It's a piece of tat is what is it is. *Distressed* is what I am over you wasting more money and no, you DIDN'T "win" it. YOU BOUGHT IT. How can I get it through to you that buying things on eBay costs MONEY? YOU HAVE NOT BEATEN THE SYSTEM NOR WON FUCK ALL. Oh, I don't know. Put it in the spare room.'

I have at least ticked Natalia and Daddy off the list, with thoughtful, personal gifts of a scarf and a bottle of whisky. What on earth did people give each other before scarves? They are the ultimate default gift. You can even give them to men! Maybe I'll get Mum a scarf as well, and tell Jessica where to shove her fucking NutriBullet.

What else do I need to do? Maybe I should make a list. OK:

Make List
Buy Presents
Wrap Presents
Clean House
Do All Laundry Ever So Children Do not Look Like Scruffy Urchins in Front of
    Parentals
Buy Christmas Jammies to Give Impression We Are a Functioning and Loving
    Family (Hmmm – would matching jammies for me and Simon make us look
    like twats or be utterly adorable? Could I even get Simon to wear Christmas
    jammies? Unlikely)
Sort Out Understairs Cupboard
Do Christmas Crafts with Children
Make Children Write Christmas Cards

I'm sure there's a lot more. But at least I can cross off 'Make List' so I have achieved something already. Yay me! That has clearly earned me a glass of wine, not because I am a lush, but because it is FESTIVE! Simon has just looked over my shoulder at the list and enquired about the need to sort out the cupboard, do Christmas crafts and make the children write cards. This is because Simon is a Grinch and does not understand the true meaning of Christmas, which is to feel stressed and angry and resentful at everyone around you.

Friday, 23 December

We are in Yorkshire. We were up bright and early this morning, the car was packed, there had only been a very minor row, which simply ended in me shouting at Simon that I wanted a divorce, rather than that I would stab him as he slept, which, let's face it, at Christmas time hardly even *counts* as a row. Peter and Jane were loaded into the car and plugged into their tablets, despite my cheery cries that we should play amusing car games all the way to Mum's, which were met with groans of horror from the children and pleas for mercy from Simon.

'But it will be FUN!' I said brightly (as I looked up from sending one last email before we set off).

'No, it won't, Mum,' said Jane. 'You'll make us play the Animal Game and then you'll choose that weird animal that you always choose that none of us can ever remember and crow and call us stupid when we can't get it.'

'A mongoose is not weird. It isn't MY fault if you can't remember what a mongoose is.'

'Or you'll cheat and choose a rabbit, and then trick us by saying no when we ask if it is native to Britain,' complained Peter.

'That was a valuable lesson in both history and biology,' I said indignantly. 'That is what makes a rabbit such a good a choice. It throws people off the scent, because not many people know that it is in fact indigenous to North Africa and was introduced to Britain by the Romans. You'd know that too if you watched *Horrible Histories*.'

'Muuuuuum! We KNOW you only watch *Horrible Histories* because you fancy that one from the Dick Turpin song. You are like sooooooo embarrassing!' moaned Jane.

'Mmmmm, Mathew Baynton ...' I murmured to myself, as Simon said, 'Who?' and I resolved I should probably delete my browsing history.

'Well,' I tried. 'What about the Minister's Cat?'

'Only if it is Rude Word Minister's Cat,' said Jane hopefully.

'Errr, no, not the Minister's Cat then,' I said hastily, as Jane is distressingly good at Rude Words Minister's Cat and getting better all the time as her vocabulary increases. Well, her Rude Word vocabulary is increasing; I fear her ordinary one is not. Not that we would ever know, given that each sentence takes so long to get out, what with every second word still being bastarding 'like'.

I gave up on the car games after that, as not even I had the strength for the fights over I-Spy that would result from Peter's idiosyncratic grasp of spelling and his insistence that it was not cheating to pick something we had passed five miles back as his object.

As we were leaving the end of my driveway, Jessica rang.

'Oh God, Ellen, I'm so glad I caught you!' she babbled. She sounded absolutely distraught.

'What's happened, Jess? Is it one of the children? Is everyone OK?'

Jessica poured out an incoherent torrent of words, the only one of which I could make out was 'Neil'.

'Is Neil all right, Jessica? Has something happened to him? I can't understand what you're saying. You need to calm down, take a deep breath and repeat that slowly. Can you do that for me, Jessica? Stay on the line now, just talk to me,' I said, feeling rather pleased with my cool head in a crisis and also how much I had learned about how to deal with emergencies over the telephone from watching medical and police dramas.

'NEIL HAS GIVEN THE FORTNUM'S CHRISTMAS PUDDING TO AGNIESZKA! MY STUPID FUCKING HUSBAND HAS GIVEN MY FORTNUM AND MASON CHRISTMAS PUDDING TO THE CLEANER AS A CHRISTMAS PRESENT AND SHE HAS FUCKED OFF BACK TO POLAND WITH IT! I TOLD him that the Aldi pudding was for her. I don't know how he could have mixed them up, but he has, and I PROMISED Mum that I would bring the Christmas pudding and NOW I HAVE NO FUCKING PUDDING!'

'Oh.'

'OH. Is that all you can say? OH. I NEED ANOTHER CHRISTMAS PUDDING, ELLEN! You are going to have to stop at a Waitrose and get a Heston one. It won't be the same, but it's the best I can do!'

'What? Why do *I* have stop at a Waitrose? Why can't you stop? And how is *me* buying a pudding the best *you* can do? Why can't you just bring the Aldi one?'

'Because I'm DELEGATING, ELLEN! How can I be expected to deal with a supermarket on the 23rd of December in the fragile emotional state I am in? And anyway, we don't pass any Waitroses, but I'm sure you do.'

'We are going to the same place, Jessica! For the last 150 miles we will be going the same route. You will pass what I will pass. Just bring the Aldi pudding, it will be fine.'

'I can't bring Mum an Aldi Christmas pudding! Not when St Sarah of Smugness will be there twatting around with her organic artisanal cheeses and crackers handmade by fucking

Hebridean magical DWARVES or something, I CAN'T bring a pudding from Aldi!'

'I'm not doing it, Jessica. I'm just not. I don't know why you just assume you can boss me around and act like you are somehow superior and everyone has to dance to your tune. There is no reason why you can't go to Waitrose yourself. Is that clear? I am NOT going for you!' I'm not sure I'd ever said no to Jessica before. It felt amazing!

'How can you do this to me?' whispered Jessica. 'My *own sister*, refusing to help me save Christmas! How can you be so *thoughtless*, Ellen?'

'I'm not being thoughtless. You are perfectly capable of going yourself.'

'AM I, Ellen? AM I? I'm just *trying* to save Christmas, and excuse me if I ask for a little bit of help!' Jessica paused to sniff bravely. 'I cannot BELIEVE Neil has done this to me. No, Neil, you HAVE ruined Christmas. I'm NOT overreacting. Now kindly shut up, I'm on the phone to Ellen, *trying* to sort out *your* mess! Well, if Persephone is crying, GO AND SORT IT OUT! Sorry, Ellen, where was I? Oh, yes, you are very kindly going to pop into Waitrose on the way and get me another pudding. Thank you *so* much, you're a star.'

'No, Jess, I didn't agree to that. I'm NOT stopping, I TOLD you –'

'Anyway, must go, we've got a long journey. Thanks again, byeeeee!' And with that, Jessica hung up. And that is why I don't say no to Jessica because THERE IS NO FUCKING POINT!

'What was that about?' asked Simon.

'Apparently, we have to go Waitrose on the way or Jessica is going to cut Neil's bollocks off and serve them up instead of Christmas pudding,' I informed him gloomily.

After five hours in the car, which was approximately twice as long as it should have taken and involved much sitting in traffic jams on the motorway while Simon shouted 'GO ON YOU PRICK, MOVE! JUST MOTHERFUCKING DRIVE, YOU COCKSUCKER!' at the car in front every time the car in front of *them* inched forward a couple of feet, and much 'manoeuvring' between lanes, as Simon is eternally convinced that all the other lanes are somehow 'better' than the lane he is currently in, and one stop at Waitrose, at which point I seriously considered not returning to the car at all but just keeping walking, and innumerable pleas to stop for a wee or complaints from my darling children that their sibling was looking at them, we were at Mum's.

Mum and Geoffrey came out to meet us, as I snatched the iPads from Peter and Jane, hissing, 'Stand up straight and for God's sake just give them a hug and say hello nicely and try to make eye contact. Jane, shut the fuck up about your body autonomy and not having to hug people if you don't want to, and just HUG THEM or I will never hear the bastarding end of it!'

'Hello, darling,' said Mum graciously, then, looking me up and down, added, 'Gosh! You actually *finally* lost some weight. You look tired, though, darling, I'm not sure it suits you. Do you think this new job might be too much for you? I don't know why you want to work full-time anyway.'

'Hello, Mum,' I said grimly, while thinking that this was a new record, even for Mum, to manage to get a dig in about my weight, my job and my general looks before I'd even set foot in the house. And I should have known that after years of nagging me to lose weight, she still wouldn't be able to say anything nice and instead would manage to come up with something suitably passive–aggressive. 'Is Jessica here yet?'

'No, not yet, but I'm sure she won't be long. Now, do my lovely grandchildren have a hug for me? Darlings?'

I reflected that at least she remembered that they *are* her grandchildren, after her slip-up about Smugfuck Sarah's Spawn being the first grandchild for her and Geoffrey.

Just as Geoffrey and Simon were briskly shaking hands in a manly yet suitably emotionally repressed way, Jessica and Neil's car pulled into the driveway, driven by Neil, who had the look of a man who if he heard the words 'Christmas Pudding' one more time would happily drive off a bridge. Poor Neil must have had a VERY long journey with an outraged Jessica yapping in his ear the whole time.

As more greetings were exchanged and bags unloaded, Jessica grabbed me and hissed, 'Did you get it? Did you get the pudding?'

I dutifully handed her a Waitrose bag and she peered inside. 'ELLEN! This isn't the Heston pudding! It's an *Essentials* pudding! How could you do this to me? I ask you to do one thing for me, ONE LITTLE THING, and you cock it up!'

'Jessica,' I said, quite calmly for someone who was entertaining violent fantasies about beating their only sister to death with a Waitrose Essentials Christmas Pudding. 'That was the only sodding pudding to be had. It was the last one on the shelf. I have literally shed blood, sweat and tears for that fucking pudding, Jessica. I ran a gauntlet of stressed middle-class women intent on filling the boots of their Range Rovers with enough provisions to see them through Armageddon, and I fought an elderly woman in a twinset for that pudding, literally fought her. We wrestled in the aisle and she was surprisingly strong, so that pudding WILL HAVE TO DO!'

'But what will Mum say?' wailed Jessica.

'Oh, FFS!' I snapped. 'Take it out of the box, wrap it in a hanky, tell Mum that you heard that the Fortnum's pudding wasn't any good this year, so you managed to get this *amazing* handmade artisanal pudding at a farmers' market instead.'

'Do you think that'll be acceptable to her?' quavered Jessica.

'Oh, bloody hellfire!' I said, at the end of my Christmas-pudding tether. 'Tell her it's the same pudding as Kirstie Allsopp gets, that'll shut her up. She may even have the first ever Christmas pudding-related orgasm at the thought of having the same pudding as Posh Kirstie!'

Saturday, 24 December – Christmas Eve

Ah, there is nothing like the magical anticipation of Christmas Eve. The magic was slightly dimmed at breakfast this morning (all are bidden to breakfast at 8.30 a.m. sharp at Mum's house. There is no hope of a lie-in, or slinging sugary cereal at hollow-eyed children sitting with glazed expressions in front of tablets – Mum even has a toast rack), when Persephone and Gulliver were happily babbling about how excited they were about Santa coming, and Jane, despite fervent entreaties from me to SAY NOTHING to Persephone and Gulliver about Santa, scornfully informed them that Santa didn't exist. Persephone burst into tears and implored Jane to admit she was lying, while I frantically waggled my eyebrows and kicked Jane under the table, only to have Peter join in too.

'Honestly, Persephone,' he said, shaking his head in sorrowful disbelief. 'You're eleven, like Jane! I'm only *nine* and I know that there is no Santa Claus!'

'It's not true, it's not true,' wept Persephone and Gulliver (Jessica was out of the room, doubtless having another Pudding Crisis and berating Neil about something).

'Honestly, Ellen,' sighed Mum. 'Can't you keep those children under control for one moment? It's Christmas Eve, hysterical children are not part of my plan for today!'

'I'm trying, Mum!' I said through gritted teeth, as Jessica swept back into the room, surveyed her weeping offspring in dismay and said, 'Oh, *poppets*! What on earth is wrong?'

'Peter and Jane say Santa doesn't exist!' sobbed Persephone.

'They say it's you and Daddy who bring the presents,' gulped Gulliver.

'Oh no, darlings, they're just pulling your leg,' said Jessica firmly.

'Auntie Jessica, it's wrong to lie,' said Jane firmly. 'We're going to church tomorrow, and if there *is* a God, then he could smite you for lying!'

'Except there isn't a God,' put in Peter. 'He's made up, just like Santa!'

Persephone and Gulliver howled harder.

Sarah tutted and stroked her bump smugly. 'Of course, *my* baby will be brought up to respect all faiths, and acknowledge people's beliefs,' she announced, glaring at my agnostic daughter and atheist son, who were still taunting their weeping cousins about the inexorable black void of nothing that exists after death, and also the lack of Santa, which the cousins seemed to be taking rather harder.

I'm somewhat concerned by Sarah's presence here, actually – when Mum told me Sarah was expecting, I hadn't realised she would be fit to pop. It was rather a shock when she waddled in last night and I asked her when she was due, and she said the 5th of January. When I said I hoped she had brought her hospital bag and notes with her, just in case, I was loftily informed that she didn't need a hospital bag, as she was having a home birth, and when I enquired about the wisdom therefore of being away from home so close to her due date, she gave me a patronising look and informed me that EVERYONE knows that first babies are ALWAYS late. I considered pointing out to her that Jane had in fact been three weeks early, to our surprise (we were at a wedding when my waters broke and Simon was hammered, so it took rather a while to impress the gravity of the situation upon him. I still haven't forgiven him for the epic hangover he suffered during the delivery, which led to the midwives spending more time fussing over him and bringing him coffee than they did looking after ME, the one who had an actual BABY coming out of her bits. AND he ate my toast afterwards because I was throwing up. Bastard), but by then Sarah had already moved on to explain hypnobirthing me, and to describe how she is totally against the overuse of episiotomies by the medical profession, and how she has been massaging organic coconut oil into her perineum to prepare for birth, but there won't be any danger of tearing anyway, as she will simply be 'breathing the baby out naturally'. She asked if I had had an episiotomy, and when I admitted that I had, said, 'Yes, I thought so. You probably had *drugs* too. I am planning on completely drug-free, 100 per cent organic birth, just as nature intends. It's quite usual for women to orgasm during labour, you know, if you do it right, and listen to your body.' Simon choked on a Brazil nut at the mention of Sarah's perineum and downed an entire glass of red at the talk of orgasmic births, and I decided that she would learn the hard way soon enough, and spent the rest of the evening muttering darkly to Jessica about how much we hate sodding Sarah. I will say this for her: she does provide something for Jessica and me to bond over. Sadly, however, after this morning's revelations, even chuntering together over Smug Sarah, the First Pregnant Person Ever, might not be enough to make Jessica forgive me for my precious moppets ruining the Magic of Christmas for her darlings.

The rest of Christmas Eve was mainly spent peeling potatoes (Sarah being excused such menial tasks due to The Baby, and Jessica being occupied by attempting to convince Persephone and Gulliver that their entire childhoods hadn't been a lie, and obviously in Mum's world no men could be capable of peeling spuds, and apparently I was just making a *scene* when I said I actually just needed to do a couple of hours work before I started on the potatoes – nothing is more important than the potatoes apparently), while Mum told me how I was doing it all wrong and taking off far too much potato with the skin, and didn't I know that was where all the goodness was ('Yes, Mum, because you've literally told me that every single time I have peeled a potato since I was twelve, yet somehow neither I nor my family has yet died from fucking malnutrition'). Why the fuck do we need so many potatoes at Christmas anyway?

Peter and Jane did not help matters with Persephone and Gulliver's emotional trauma when they discovered that every time their cousins had calmed down, the hysterics could be restarted by shouting, 'I DON'T BELIEVE IN FAIRIES! THAT'S ANOTHER ONE DEAD, HA!' Although this was obviously extremely cruel and unkind of my beloved children, there was a part of me that agreed with them that Persephone and Gulliver should really just man up and stop being such drips.

While Mum was having a meltdown over the parsnips, I abandoned the sacks of spuds to try to do a little bit of work, as the Big Deadline is looming and I don't want everything to be a last-minute rush. I was hiding in our bedroom (separate beds, obvs. Mum does not encourage *that* sort of thing in anyone), when Simon came in. I looked up in exasperation.

'I brought you a glass of wine,' he whispered conspiratorially. 'And I finished the potatoes for you. Your mum had moved on from the parsnip crisis and was busy insisting that Geoffrey go back out to the shops because she had just realised that she didn't have any shallots and apparently ordinary onions wouldn't do, so she didn't even notice. So you can claim all the glory!'

Sometimes, just sometimes, I remember why I married Simon. I put down my laptop and suggested we thwarted my mother's attempts at moral rectitude and put some of that practice we had of doing *that* sort of thing in single beds as students to good use.

'Christ,' said Simon. 'If I'd known all it took was peeling some spuds, I'd have bought shares in King Edwards years ago!'

Sunday, 25 December – Christmas Day

The Family Festive Fun rolls on apace. I had somehow forgotten that Mum had adopted Geoffrey's family's frankly hideous tradition of not opening presents until after Christmas morning church, which was a shock to my own consumerist fiends as they descended with shrieks of glee on the mountains of parcels under the tree, only to be shooed away with stern admonishments by Mum and Geoffrey.

Church was … reasonably uneventful. We are not a church-going family, apart from when we are at Mum's for Christmas, so there was much grumbling and 'But WHYing' from the children (and Simon), especially from Peter. Since he decided to be a full-on, card-carrying atheist, he feels it is his duty to bring enlightenment to the opiated masses and so had to be repeatedly kicked on the ankle to stop him from shouting, 'There is no God, you know!' during the service, as Causing a Scene in Church would, in Mum's eyes, be even worse than ruining his cousins' lives with the fairy-killing and Santa-denying, as the vicar might judge her and adversely affect her prime spot on the flower-arranging rota.

I quite like a Christmas church visit, though, especially when it is to a pretty little country church, like in Mum and Geoffrey's village, although I am puerile and childish and sniggered when Mary asked how she should have a child for she was a virgin and the angel replied that the Holy Ghost would come on her, but I do like belting out a carol or two. It was unfortunate that I was a little carried away by 'Angels from the Realms of Glory' and didn't notice Peter carving 'bum' into the pew in front with the penknife I had thought was such a splendid Boy's Own gift for his stocking (Jane got one too, because Equality, even though I am always dubious about the wisdom of allowing Jane free rein to run amok with sharp objects), but today's graffiti is tomorrow's archaeology (or something), and in years to come it will doubtless just add to the charm of the church.

All in all, everything was going relatively well, apart from Mum accusing me of adding too much goose fat to the roast potatoes and making them greasy (there is no such thing as 'too much goose fat' when it comes to roast potatoes) and Sarah poking every single dish suspiciously before asking with a pained expression if it was suitable for her to eat when pregnant.

As we approached the Christmas pudding, and Jessica began to twitch for fear her duplicity would be discovered, Sarah evidently decided that insufficient attention was being paid to her, and she clutched her belly with a dramatic moan.

'Oh God, darling!' wailed Piers. 'What is it?'

'Arrrrghhhhh!' groaned Sarah.

'I TOLD you there was too much goose fat on those potatoes, Ellen,' said Mum crossly. 'You've given her indigestion.'

'Oooohhh, owwwww! Oh, I think I'm having contractions!' gasped Sarah.

'Oh no, darling!' shrieked Piers. 'The baby can't be coming yet. I haven't downloaded your birth meditation podcasts! There's no birthing pool here!'

'OWWWWWWW!' howled Sarah. 'What are we going to do? WHAT ARE WE GOING TO DO? THE BABY IS COMING!'

'Well, you'll have to go to the hospital, obviously,' said Mum.

'But I want a home birth,' insisted Sarah.

'You can't have a home birth here,' said Mum in horror. 'Where would you have it?'

'I could give birth in the drawing room,' panted Sarah, who was now standing up and rocking back and forth while clutching the sideboard dramatically.

'You can't give birth in there. I've just had it decorated,' replied Mum indignantly. 'Oh God, and my Egyptian cotton sheets upstairs. You can't have the baby here, you must go to a hospital.'

'OOOOHHHHHHHHH! OHHHHHH! Piers! Piers, you are meant to be massaging my back and helping me BREATHE!' screamed Sarah, as she doubled up over the sideboard. Geoffrey stood up and gently led his daughter away from the sideboard and gave her a chair to hold on to instead, while murmuring, 'Do you mind, darling? Only it's Chippendale, you know ...'.

'I *said* she should have brought her hospital bag,' I announced smugly to no one in particular. 'I *knew* something like this would happen, I just knew it!'

Sarah gave one more violent scream and shrieked, 'It's coming! Oh God, it's coming!' and let out the most enormous fart I have ever heard in my life. The sonic boom seemed to echo around the ornate cornicing of the dining room for some time, while we all sat in a shocked silence.

'Oh!' said Sarah straightening up. 'Oh, that's better!'

Mum, who was going off the Sainted Sarah by the minute, did her very best impression of a cat's bum with her mouth. Persephone and Gulliver, who were by now so shocked by life that they could not have been any more wide-eyed or horrified if they tried, whimpered something to Jessica, who muttered that she would explain where babies came from later. Jane helpfully intervened, and said she had seen the DVD at school and could explain for Jessica, if she wanted. She was brandishing her new knife at this point, and added something about how when the baby is born, they cut bits off it, and Persephone and Gulliver whimpered further as Jessica hastily declined their offer.

'Did Aunty Sarah just FART the baby out?' asked Peter in fascination. 'There was no farting in the DVD I saw. It came out the lady's hairy vagina. Doesn't Aunty Sarah have a hairy vagina? Is that why she is farting the baby out?'

Geoffrey, a man who had clearly never had vaginas, hairy or otherwise, discussed at his dinner table before, looked like we might have exchanged one medical emergency for another as he teetered on the brink of a heart attack. He grabbed a bottle of whisky from the sideboard and suggested Simon joined him in the study. Simon didn't need asking twice.

'Shall I get the Christmas pudding?' I said brightly. 'Custard or brandy butter?'

Tuesday, 27 December

Today started quite well, with everyone being nice to each other in the blissful knowledge that the end was in sight. Jessica and Neil left this morning, having specifically told me they were staying until the 28th, which was the only reason I'd agreed to stay until the 28th too, so Mum couldn't emotionally blackmail me about how at least one of her children likes to spend time with her, but somehow the cow managed to renege and escaped this morning.

Despite the departure of Jessica and family, and the fact that we were leaving tomorrow, Mum decided to have a massive meltdown after lunch because she was down to her last six pints of milk, there were only four loaves left in the freezer and she only had a dozen eggs – and therefore STARVATION WAS IMMINENT! As it had started snowing last night, and had continued to snow all day, Mum declared that the village shop would be bare, as any deliveries they may have had today would have been stripped by locust-like marauding pensioners (Mum seems to overlook the fact that she is also a pensioner by insisting it is different because she and Geoffrey always spent their winter-fuel allowance on wine, until the government so cruelly took it away from them). Therefore, insisted Mum, nothing would do, but that someone should set forth to go to the nearest supermarket fifteen miles away to buy provisions.

Piers, who truth be told was looking rather drained by Sarah constantly barking commands at him, volunteered for this task, claiming that their supplies of coconut oil were running rather low (good God, what sort of acreage does Sarah's perineum cover if she has managed to go through an entire jar of it since arriving?), but I suspect he just fancied an hour's peace and quiet.

We duly waved him off, with Mum remarking anxiously that their lane was looking really rather difficult with all the snow and she did hope we would be able to get out tomorrow to go home. Icy dread seizing my heart at the thought of being snowed in with Mum and Geoffrey (and eleventy billion pints of milk, forty loaves, five dozen eggs and a vat of coconut oil, after Piers's Mercy Dash). I airily announced that we would be FINE, for I had a 4x4 and thus nothing could impede our escape.

Peter and Jane complained that they were BORED with snow, and there was nothing to do now that their new favourite pastime of tormenting their cousins had been taken from them, and Mum announced briskly that only boring people got bored and suggested a variety of mundane tasks to occupy them, before they sidled off muttering that they thought they could probably find something to do. Mum smirked at me smugly and said, 'It's just a matter of knowing how to *handle* them, darling!'

'Mum, you do know they will just have sneaked off to find some sort of screen to slump in front of, don't you?' I pointed out. 'They haven't gone to write imaginative stories or poetry or perform a play.'

'Well,' huffed Mum. 'They might have.'

It was actually rather a lovely afternoon. The snow continued to fall softly, the fire crackled and the house was quiet for the first time in days. I curled up on the window seat to indulge myself with my ancient, battered copy of *Ballet Shoes*, having decided that the children hadn't really had that much screen time in the last few days, so a little bit wouldn't hurt, while I dreamt of my marvellous career on the stage that never was (I know we are all supposed to want to be cool tomboy Petrova, but I always had a hankering to be spoilt brat Posy, prancing around *en pointe*). Simon was pottering around somewhere, Geoffrey had vanished to his study, and Sarah had beached herself in prime position on the sofa in front of the fire, while Mum flicked through *Tatler*, pretending she knew people in the Bystander section.

As dusk fell, Sarah lifted her head and plaintively suggested that it would be rather lovely if someone could bring her a cup of hot water and lemon juice. Mum, who still hadn't forgiven Sarah for destroying her elegant Christmas dinner tableau with the Fart of Doom, ignored her. Sarah whimpered again, and I rather unkindly said, 'You know, Sarah, it's not actually good for you to loll about this much at this stage in pregnancy. You could get a thrombosis. It's much more natural to move about and stay active! A gentle walk to the kitchen to make your own drink would be much better for you.'

'But I'm pregnant,' whined Sarah. 'I can't believe no one will fetch me a hot drink in *my condition*. Where is Piers? Where is Daddy?'

When no further sympathy or offers of help were forthcoming, Sarah heaved herself to her feet, grumbling all the while, and then, as she stood up, there was a loud splashing noise, as a great gout of liquid gushed over the rug.

Mum, who had steadfastly pretended not to hear any of this exchange, looked up at this point and shrieked, 'My AUBUSSON! WHAT THE FUCK HAS HAPPENED?'

Sarah, who was standing in the puddle looking quite horrified said, 'I didn't piss myself. Really I didn't.'

'Holy fuck, Sarah!' I said. 'Your waters have broken!'

'What?' said Sarah. 'But they can't have. I mean, there was no warning. Everyone *said*. They said I would know when the baby was coming, they said I had to listen to my body, and I have been listening and it NEVER FUCKING SAID ANYTHING. AND NOW THE BABY IS COMING, BUT IT IS MEANT TO BE LATE, AND THE BASTARDS SAID THAT TOO, THAT FIRST BABIES ARE ALWAYS LATE, AND PIERS ISN'T HERE, HE IS LOST IN THE SNOW, AND HE WILL PROBABLY DIE OUT THERE BEFORE HE EVEN GETS TO MEET HIS BABY AND I WILL BE A SINGLE MOTHER, OH MY GOD, OH MY GOD, THIS CAN'T BE HAPPENING!'

I reluctantly laid aside *Ballet Shoes*, abandoning Pauline and Petrova mid-audition for *A Midsummer's Night Dream*, and sprang into action. I have watched every episode of *Call the Midwife*, including the frankly terrifying Christmas Special where ex-nun Shelagh seduced Dr Turner in her drip-dry nylon negligee, and I felt confident I could deal with this situation.

'Don't worry, Sarah,' I said cheerfully (I knew from *Call the Midwife* that it was important to maintain a sunny façade to keep the mother calm – but then again, it was also important to administer an enema. I decided to stick with the cheerfulness and not think about the enema). 'Babies take ages to come. You'll be OK. Now, remember to breathe. Piers will be here soon, there were probably just queues to deal with. Or maybe it took a while to find the coconut oil. Don't worry, everything will be fine.' I patted her hand reassuringly.

'OH MY GOD, WHAT AM I GOING TO DOOOOOOO?' screamed Sarah. She was clearly hysterical. I wondered whether I should slap her. In fairness, I have been longing to slap Sarah for years, and I would probably never have a better opportunity, but I suspected slapping women in labour, however irritating and screechy they are, is frowned upon, so I reluctantly decided against it, and patted her hand again and made what I hoped were Soothing Noises.

Sarah collapsed heavily back onto the sofa, still wailing, at which point Mum decided to provide a Greek chorus as she howled, 'Oh GOD, NO, NO! Ellen, DO something! Get her off the sofa! OFF! I've just had it upholstered in Laura Ashley. The cushions are their Summer Palace fabric, it's discontinued now. She's already wrecked the Aubusson, she's not ruining my sofa as well!'

'Mum, she's in labour,' I protested. 'I really don't think that your sofa is the main thing we should be worrying about right now! She needs to be warm and comfortable and reassured. I don't think you're helping.'

'The Summer Palace was £36 a metre! What part of "*it's discontinued*" don't you understand, Ellen?' hissed Mum menacingly. I was a bit scared.

'Look, just call an ambulance or something, Mum!'

'But what are we going to do with her until it gets here?' fretted Mum.

'I AM here!' pointed out Sarah

'The garage?' tried Mum hopefully. 'I mean, Geoffrey's Jag's in there, but I've never much liked it anyway, so it doesn't really matter if she scratches the paintwork.'

'MUM!' I said, shocked by her devotion to home furnishings in the face of the Miracle of Life taking place in front of her. 'We can't put her in the garage!'

'Why not?' said Mum. 'I mean, really, a garage is a modern version of a stable. It would be rather apt. Quite festive, really.'

'OOOOHHHHHHH!' groaned Sarah. 'Could someone PLEASE just phone Piers and tell him he needs to get back here NOW?'

'Mum, GO and call an ambulance, and then go and call Piers.'

'Right,' I said briskly, turning to Sarah. 'It's all going to be all right, Sarah. You've absolutely nothing to worry about. The baby won't be here for ages, and I won't let Mum put you in the garage. The Summer Palace cushions will just have to take their chances, but the ambulance will be here shortly anyway. Mum, WHY are you still here? GO and ring an ambulance, and Piers. And let Sarah speak to Piers when you get hold of him. And … and … then put some water on to boil. And get towels! Lots of towels!'

'Not my White Company ones, though,' said Mum mutinously. 'Maybe the old ones I use to dry the cats after their bath.'

'Mum!' I snapped. 'She's having a fucking baby! GO and make the calls, and stop worrying about your fucking towels! You can't give her the cat towels. The longer you leave it before you call that ambulance, the more chance there is of her giving birth on your fucking cushions!'

Mum stomped out, still muttering darkly, and I turned my attention back to Sarah, who was howling that she was having another contraction.

'Maybe you should breathe through it?' I said brightly (I was really very impressed with how well I was coping with a Childbirth Crisis). 'Visualise something lovely. Like a tropical beach! And breathe yourself onto it. How's that orgasm coming on?'

'Shut the fuck up, Ellen!' spat Sarah. 'This hurts like a fucking BITCH! BREATHING ISN'T FUCKING HELPING! I WANT DRUGS!'

'No, you don't,' I said soothingly. 'Remember, you are having a natural birth, you have practised all your hypnobirthing, and you are very against drugs and medical intervention. You can just breathe instead. You said that childbirth only hurts because we are conditioned to think it hurts, and if we simply believe otherwise, we will have a positive and empowering birth experience. Would you like to hold my hand?'

'FUCK THAT SHIT!' was Sarah's response, as she gripped my hand really much harder than I was sure was necessary. 'I have a baby coming out my FUCKING FANNY! What fucking IDIOT said it WOULDN'T HURT?'

'Well, you did? Come on, Sarah, remember to breathe,' I said helpfully, as the contraction passed and Sarah thankfully let go of my hand. I wondered if it would be unsupportive if I didn't let her hold it again, as that had been really very painful. She has quite a grip – probably something to do with being captain of the tennis team at school. It rather makes one feel for Piers, though.

'AARRRRGHHHHHH!' wailed Sarah. 'Shut up about fucking breathing. Did breathing help when *you* were giving birth?'

'No, I don't think so,' I said. 'It's just what people say, when you're in labour. Like you'd *forget* to breathe! I do vaguely remember shouting that at a midwife, actually, yelling that I *was* fucking breathing, that I was hardly going to start holding my bastarding breath just to spite her, was I? She wasn't very impressed, as I recall, but then again I was smacked off my tits on all the drugs, so what do I know? Maybe people do forget to breathe. Maybe all the panting does help. It all gets a bit hazy afterwards, you sort of forget what happens, apparently it's nature's way –'

'Oh God, stop wittering, Ellen, I'M HAVING ANOTHER ONE AND DON'T FUCKING TELL ME TO BREATHE. I WANT THE DRUGS! I WANT ALL THE DRUGS LIKE YOU HAD, IT'S NOT FAIR!!'

It occurred to me that Sarah's contractions seemed to be quite close together. I was trying to remember how far apart contractions should be before things start getting serious when Mum came back in, followed by Geoffrey. She did not look terribly happy.

'Piers isn't answering his phone,' she said anxiously.

'OH GOD, HE IS DEAD IN A SNOWDRIFT!' wept Sarah. 'ARRRGHHHHH! AND I'M HAVING ANOTHER CONTRACTION!!'

'Darling, must you make that ghastly noise?' enquired Geoffrey disapprovingly.

'Ellen, why is she still on the sofa? I *told* you to get her off the sofa!' complained Mum.

'AAAAARRGGGGHHHHHHHH! I DON'T WANT TO BE A WIDOW, BRINGING UP MY ORPHAN CHILD ALONE!' panted Sarah.

'Snow will have affected the signal, probably,' said Geoffrey knowingly.

'Did you call the ambulance, Mum?' I said.

'Not yet, I was trying to get Piers!' said Mum indignantly.

'MUM, CALL THE AMBULANCE NOW. IT'S A BIT MORE IMPORTANT THAN PIERS!'

Mum wandered off again.

Jane chose that point to appear, and it occurred to me that I hadn't seen Simon since lunch.

'Is Aunty Sarah farting the baby out again?' said Jane with great interest. 'Can I stay and watch? We didn't do farting the baby out when we watched the DVD at school, only the hairy vagina way.'

I made a mental note to have an Important Conversation with Jane about the gaps in her sex education.

'Maybe you could go and find Daddy for me, darling?' I suggested, as Jane huffed out, muttering that it wasn't fair, she was never allowed to do anything good.

'ANOTHER ONE! ANOTHER ONE! WHERE'S THE AMBULANCE? OH FUCK, OH FUCK, I THINK I NEED TO PUSH!' screeched Sarah, who was now prone on Mum's precious sofa, with her legs akimbo.

'You can't possibly need to push yet, Sarah!' I said in a panic. 'You've hardly been in labour for any time at all! Oh God, just DON'T PUSH!'

'I don't think there's any need for such language, young lady!' said Geoffrey reprovingly to Sarah, who was still swearing like a trooper.

'GO FUCK YOURSELF, DADDY!' shouted Sarah. 'YOU PUSH A WATERMELON OUT YOUR FUCKING ARSEHOLE, AND THEN YOU CAN TELL ME THERE'S NO NEED FOR LANGUAGE LIKE THAT!'

Mum skidded back into the room in a panic. 'They don't know how long it will take to get an ambulance here as they're all out or are stuck in the snow. They've some 4x4s with paramedics but they're all at emergencies and they say that this isn't classified as an emergency yet. They want to know how far apart her contractions are.'

Fuck. Timing the contractions. I knew there was something I should have been doing.

'I don't know! I don't know!' wailed Mum into the phone. 'Oh GOD, Ellen, you talk to them!' and she thrust the phone at me.

'Right,' said the nice ambulance lady soothingly. 'So can I just check – first baby? And she's thirty-nine. And no previous complications, blood pressure all been all right, etc.? And the baby is just a few days early?'

I babbled hopelessly that I thought so, as far as I knew, and she had wanted a home birth anyway, so I assumed there were no problems with the pregnancy.

'OK, do you think you could bring her in yourself?'

'Me?' I said, slightly dumbstruck.

'At the moment, if you were able to bring her in, that would be the quickest way to get her to hospital. Right now, with the weather conditions, I can't say for sure how long it's going to take to get an ambulance out to you. Do you have a 4x4?'

'Yes,' I whispered.

'Right, then the best thing is probably to pop off to the hospital yourselves and get her checked over. If things start moving faster while you're on your way, ring us back and we'll reassess.'

I hung up the phone, and whimpered.

Mum was peering out the window. 'The snow's getting worse,' she said, 'and her contractions are very close together. WHAT ARE WE GOING TO DO?'

'FOR FUCK'S SAKE, I AM HAVING A BAAAAYBEEEEE!' screamed Sarah.

I took a deep breath and shouted, 'WILL EVERYBODY JUST CALM THE FUCK DOWN!'

'Is Aunty Sarah going to get her hairy vagina out?' said a fascinated Peter, having sneaked in without me noticing.

'No! Get out! GO AND FIND YOUR FATHER!' I shrieked.
'And Mum, go and ring the hospital and tell them we're bringing
Sarah in now.'

Simon wandered in, followed by Mum, who was wittering
away to someone on the phone and interjected to say, 'I didn't
know what hospital to ring, so I rang our health centre, but there
was no answer, so I rang Julie Carmichael, who used to be the
receptionist before she retired, and Julie says how many centimetres might she be dilated, before she can say whether it's time
to go to hospital.'

'WHAT?' I said in disbelief.

'How many centimetres dilated?' repeated Mum.

'Tell Julie Carmichael to FUCK OFF!' I yelled. 'It's nothing to
do with her. Just ring the nearest hospital with a FUCKING
MATERNITY UNIT!'

'But *I* don't know where *has* a maternity unit, darling. Why on
earth *would* I? No, Julie, I'm still here. They don't know how
many centimetres she's dilated. I know. Oh, absolutely.'

'Shall I google it, Mummy?' said Jane, who had sneaked back
in.

'Yes, Jane, that would be very helpful,' I said. *Finally*, someone
with a bit of common sense.

'Are you fit to drive?' I asked Simon.

'Me? Fuck no, I've been on the red since lunch!' he replied
jovially, waving his glass at me to demonstrate his point.

'Oh, Jesus,' I said despairingly, looking round at Mum, who
was still on the phone, wittering to Julie Carmichael about cat
towels and the Summer Palace sofa cushions, Geoffrey
hurrumphing disapprovingly about everyone making such a
scene, and a thoroughly pissed-up Simon. Peter and Jane were

peering hopefully round the drawing-room door, and Sarah was still panting about pushing.

'Right,' said Jane cheerfully. 'I've found the nearest maternity unit, Mummy, and the hospital has an A&E too. I've put the directions into your phone for you.'

'Jane, I love you!' I said, profoundly grateful that at least one person was able to keep their head in an emergency.

'OK,' I said, hoping I sounded more confident that I felt. 'Mum, get OFF the phone, you'll need to quickly make a hospital bag for her. Get some clean jammies, any pads you might have, Tena Ladies will do –'

'I do *not* wear Tena Ladies,' interrupted Mum with indignation.

'Whatever! Just get some jammies then, and some blankets and towels – NOT the fucking cat towels – and anything else that might look useful. Oh, and your gravy jug.'

'My *gravy* jug,' said Mum in confusion. 'What does she need my gravy jug for?'

'For pouring water over *down there* for when she has a wee afterwards!' I explained. 'It makes it much less painful!'

'But it's from *Lakeland*!' wailed Mum, while Geoffrey went so puce I did fear he might actually be having a heart attack. 'Can't she use something else? Maybe the little watering can I use for the house plants?'

'JUST GET THE GRAVY JUG!' I barked, fearing we did not have time to discuss the subject. 'Simon, you will have to come with me.'

'Me? Why me?' complained Simon.

'In case she gives birth on the way. Someone will need to, I dunno, *catch* the baby, while I'm driving. And believe it or not, out of the LIMITED choices currently available, you are probably the best person to do that!'

I did consider taking Jane with me instead of Simon, as I suspected she might be more use, but I also feared that having to deliver a baby at the tender age of eleven might scar her for life. Simon had already (somewhat unwillingly) witnessed the Miracle of Childbirth via my own fanny, and therefore the damage was done with regard to him.

Eventually, amid much huffing and puffing and screaming and wailing (actually that was just Mum about her gravy jug), we got poor Sarah loaded into the back of my car, sprawled inelegantly among the dog hair and discarded McDonald's wrappers and crisps packets. Simon was unceremoniously shoved in the back too, where he cowered pitifully in the furthest possible corner from Sarah, and we set off, Sarah wailing periodically that she *really* thought she might have to push now, and Simon and me bellowing back, 'DO NOT PUSH! WHATEVER YOU DO, DO NOT PUSH!' as I drove hell for leather down snowy lanes, shouting abuse at the Google Maps lady, who was being particularly sanctimonious.

Thankfully, Sarah managed to not give birth in the car, though it is very distracting trying to drive with someone screaming blue murder in your ear all the way, but fortunately this is a talent I mastered many years ago due to Peter and Jane also liking to screech like demented banshees during any journey, and we arrived at the hospital. I came to an impressive though extremely illegal *Dukes of Hazzard*-style stop in an ambulance bay and hastily unloaded Sarah and Simon, before parking somewhere less clampable.

Fortunately, the car park wasn't busy, so I was able to abandon the car and tear back into the hospital while Sarah and Simon were still at reception trying to explain what was going on – or rather, Sarah was clutching her stomach and sobbing something about her orphan child was coming, while Simon looked frightened and gestured vaguely in Sarah's direction while mumbling something about 'babies'.

'And are you her partner?' enquired the confused midwife on the desk.

'No!' said Simon vehemently.

'Oh. So … are you the partner?' she asked me.

'What?' I said.

'It's OK. We don't judge. We see lots of modern relationships here,' said the midwife kindly.

'No, I mean, it's not that I have a problem with same-sex relationships,' I gabbled. 'But she's my *stepsister*. And *he's* my husband. You see?'

'Mmmm,' said the midwife, looking rather more judgemental. 'Yes, that is a *little* more unusual. But like I said, we're not here to judge.'

'It's not his baby either! We just brought her in because her husband had to go and buy milk because my mother is a batshit-mental dairy Nazi, and so someone had to drive her here, and maybe we could just stop talking now and you know, get the baby out?'

'We don't condone the use of terms like "batshit-mental", actually,' said the midwife primly.

'Well, you haven't met my fucking mother!' I hissed, as Sarah gave another dramatic groan and heave, and the midwife remembered what she was actually supposed to be doing.

Ten minutes later, Sarah was in the labour suite with a lovely midwife, who announced that she was nine centimetres dilated and the baby would be crowning shortly. I had attempted to leave once Sarah was handed over to the midwives, but she had clutched at me anxiously and begged me to stay with her, and since all the midwives were looking at me, and given that she was on her own and having her first baby, it would have been churlish to say, 'But Sarah, we've never exactly got on before today. Why would I want to watch you push a baby out?' So there wasn't much else I could do apart from say, 'Of course I will stay. No problem!'

There was a small unfortunateness when the nice midwife asked if Mummy would like some gas and air, and I shouted, 'Oh God, yes PLEASE! I love gas and air. It is exactly like being pissed, and today has been very stressful, so that would be fabulous!' The midwife frostily informed me that she had been referring to Sarah as being the one in need of pain relief and not me.

Much pushing and groaning and swearing ensued, which led me to look much more kindly on Simon's preferred delivery-room position of cowering in a corner, as I did pretty much the same once it had been established that no one was going to let me have a go on the gas and air, and after what seemed like an eternity, but according to the clock was only about twenty minutes, Sarah popped out a bouncing baby girl, without the need for an episiotomy, so all that coconut oil was not in vain at least.

'Would you like to cut the cord?' the midwife asked me brightly. I recoiled further into my corner. I had no wish at all to go Down There. Blurry though my own memories of giving birth are, I do recall Simon reacting with similar horror when the midwife asked him if he wanted to cut the cord when Jane was born. Rather alarmingly, she had then asked me if I wanted to cut the cord myself. Apparently replying 'I's totally off my own face on the luffly druggies jus' now. I think sharp things iss bad idea!' was not good form, and I felt quite judged.

Sarah was sitting up and cuddling the baby, with that slightly stunned but glowing look that some women seem to get after giving birth (not me, I looked sweaty and knackered, but I did manage the stunned part at least), and I had been summonsed from my corner to inspect the new arrival, who I pronounced to be 'gorgeous' (she wasn't – she looked like an angry prune, much like all newborns, but you are not allowed to say that), and I was eying up Sarah's tea and toast, as she didn't seem very interested in them, when Piers finally burst into the room, having been delayed by going round three supermarkets to get organic skimmed milk for Mum, and then when Mum finally got hold of him, having to go the long way round due to an Audi skidding and blocking the road.

'Oh!' said the midwife, who was still slightly confused by the family set-up. 'Is *this* one the daddy?'

Piers only had eyes for Sarah and his baby, though.

'Yes!' I said with relief, glad at not having to launch into more complex explanations. But as I attempted to sidle out of the room, Sarah, still glowing (annoyingly), turned to Piers and said, 'Darling, Ellen was simply marvellous! I don't know what I'd have done without her! Do you think we could let her choose the name?'

What? What the fuck? No! Don't make me name your baby! Names are very subjective. Simon and I almost got divorced over choosing our own babies' names, and I couldn't possibly name someone else's child. I had had a hankering for an Isolde, which Simon had dismissed as being pretentiously wanky and not mysteriously romantic, as I insisted, but then again, one of his suggestions had been Deirdra, which I had coldly informed him may well be a classic name from Irish mythology, but would nonetheless only remind me of Deirdre Barlow for the duration of the baby's life, so NO! So this could be my opportunity for an Isolde! I thought for a moment, before nobly saying, 'Oh, thank you, Sarah, I'm terribly flattered, but I couldn't *possibly* accept. You choose the name yourself!'

'Well,' said Sarah, 'what if we call her Ellen, for her middle name?'

I thought that was rather nice, actually, and I warmed somewhat towards Sarah.

'Really, if you're sure, that would be lovely!' I said, slightly tearfully. 'But don't make any hasty decisions. Think about it.' (They'd better not change their minds, though.)

I reflected, as I finally left the delivery room, that it was just as well the baby had been a girl, as I would have been royally pissed off if it had been a boy and they had called it after Simon for its middle name, as he had been literally no help whatsoever in the entire drama.

Mum and Geoffrey were waiting anxiously when we got home.

'Well?' quavered Mum.

'A little girl!' I beamed. 'Eight pounds, three ounces! Name to be confirmed, though there is a good chance she will be named after ME for her middle name, and mother and baby are doing well. Piers is there with her now.'

'Yes, yes,' said Mum impatiently. 'You rang and told me that already. But *what about my good Lakeland Plastics gravy jug*?'

'Yes, Mum, she did use the gravy jug when she went for a wee. I'm sorry.'

Mum gave a wail of anguish. What price a new step-granddaughter when her Aubusson rug and her gravy jug had both been sullied on the same day?

'FML!' I said. 'I need a drink!'

Astonishingly, Geoffrey was extremely nice to me and thanked me for my part in the proceedings. I felt very noble and heroic, and also extremely smug about how annoyed Jessica would be when she found out that I'd saved the day and was now regarded by the family as a heroine on a par with Grace Darling. Ha!

Friday, 30 December

I popped into the office today because it is fucking impossible to get anything done at home with Simon and the kids there, wandering about wittering. It also means I can conserve that precious annual leave for fun things like fucking school concerts – deep joy. Actually, I wish I had come in much sooner. It was bliss. I was the only one there, and the peace was amazing. It's astonishing as well how much you can get done when there is nobody ringing you or emailing you, or just stopping by your desk to ask if you want a cup of tea and lingering to chat for a minute. This only serves to confirm my conviction that the world would be a much better place if only there were no Other People.

Of course, the downside to being there by myself was that empty office buildings can feel quite eerie, and I started worrying that maybe a serial killer or psychopath was stalking the corridors, à la *The Shining*, and then I was too scared to go to the toilet, because if I *was* murdered, I certainly didn't want my bloody lifeless corpse to be found on the pan with my knickers round my ankles (especially since they weren't very glamorous knickers to get murdered in). So you know, swings and roundabouts …

Saturday, 31 December/Sunday, 1 January

Long gone are the days when New Year's Eve used to mean getting dressed up, trowelling on the slap and going out to get disgracefully, obscenely drunk before kissing a plethora of strangers in the street. In our misspent student days, Simon,

Hannah, Charlie and I had several riotous and badly behaved Hogmanays in Edinburgh (well, mine were riotous and badly behaved, and I recall Simon also being fairly uproarious, including his decision to drop his trousers on the Royal Mile one year, which led to him complaining he thought he'd got frostbite on his balls. Hannah and Charlie pointed out that they tended to have been slightly better behaved than us), but over the years, the desire to bring in the New Year by mingling with others has waned somewhat. I did try having a proper New Year's Eve party a couple of years ago, but that only had the effect of making me hate pretty much everyone I knew until Easter.

This time, therefore, we decided it would be nice to just have a few carefully selected friends round, and we could all put on our pyjamas, plug our darling children into the electronic babysitters and stuff our faces to our elasticated waists' content on M&S canapés and get mildly puggled while setting the world to rights. Thus it was that Hannah and Charlie, Katie and her nice but dull husband Tim, and Sam came over, complete with assorted moppets and a selection of comfortable slippers and vol-au-vents, and we commenced on New Year's Eve for the Middle-Aged.

Sam, made bold by the knowledge that I had rashly offered to have all the children stay over (except Katie's two, as they are small enough to a) need taking to the toilet and I don't do wiping other people's children's bums and b) be scooped up and carried back over the road to bed when necessary), as well as put Hannah and Charlie in the spare room to save them the trouble of trying to get a taxi in the small hours of New Year's Day (Sam himself living within a reasonable stumbling distance when unencumbered by precious moppets to escort home like a responsible adult), appeared with a bottle of what can only be described as Darkness. It was, he informed me, coffee tequila.

'Are you sure that's a good idea?' I said dubiously. 'I mean, we are supposed to be being civilised tonight. I've done mini sausages in Nigel Slater's honey and mustard glaze. There are tiny hamburgers to be heated up. Are shots really advisable? The children might see!'

'The children will know nothing,' Sam assured me gleefully. 'They will be too busy twatting each other in between staring slackjawed at iPads to give a shit what we are doing.'

'Hmmm ...'

In the event, the children were more interested in bursting into the sitting room every twenty minutes to demand if it was midnight yet, despite being in possession of almost every bastarding electronic device known to mankind, all of them with clocks on, until I shouted that they would go to bed NOW and not be allowed to stay up, if they did not fuck off RIGHT THIS MINUTE (*obviously*, I didn't actually tell them to fuck off, but I fear they grasped the sentiment that was definitely there).

Nonetheless, we did manage to have a very pleasant and almost adult evening, despite the wretched glaze for the mini sausages welding itself onto a perfectly good Le Creuset pot for all eternity, and Simon's blatant disregard of me *telling* him that the sausages were hot and to let them cool down first, instead shoving a nugget of molten pork into his mouth and then screaming that it was burning, burning, and spitting it out, only for my poor dog to pounce and gobble it up and find the same thing. Apparently, being more concerned about my precious pupsicle's burnt tongue than my soulmate's was not the act of a kind and loving wife.

By midnight, all the children were at a fever pitch of excitement, except Katie's two – Ruby had fallen asleep behind the sofa and Lily had succumbed under Jane's desk. We dutifully counted down with Jools Holland, and then shouted, 'HAPPY NEW YEAR!!'

'Is that it?' said Jane, in disappointment. 'I thought it would feel *different*, the start of a whole new year. I thought *I* would feel different. Everything is exactly the same. This is rubbish!'

'Yes,' I said. 'That's pretty much how New Year goes, darling.'

'Hurrumph!' said Jane, then, brightening, 'But seeing as I'm a whole year older, Mummy, maybe you'll let me have an Instagram account now.'

'You're not a whole year older,' I pointed out. 'You're about five minutes older. And so no, still no Instagram account.'

'OMG! So much for "New Year, New You"!' whined Jane. 'You are just as mean as the Old You was. It's SO UNFAIR!'

'Jane,' I said firmly. 'It is a fresh new year, you are quite right. And so I don't want to begin it by having the SAME ARGUMENT WITH YOU ABOUT INSTAGRAM THAT I SPENT ALL *LAST* YEAR HAVING. Are we clear?'

'Yes,' said Jane indignantly. 'It is very clear that your main aim for this year is to RUIN MY LIFE! VERY, VERY CLEAR!'

The only consolation was that I could hear Hannah and Sam having exactly the same arguments with Emily and Sophie, which led me to suspect that the girls had planned this onslaught to catch us at a moment of emotional weakness. I could also hear some sort of row between Simon and Charlie, and Peter, Lucas and Toby about why they were not allowed a beer to toast the New Year. None of this boded well for the year ahead, I felt.

Once the children had been dispatched to some semblance of settling down to go to sleep, still grumbling over our unreasonable insistence on protecting them from paedophiles and underage alcoholism, and Tim and Katie had ruefully departed back across the road, small children bundled beneath their arms, and I had had a brief scroll through all the 'Happy

New Year' texts and a quick look at Facebook to confirm that everyone was at a better party than me, and squinted at a very random photo that Alan had sent that seemed to involve him trying to push a party popper up his nose, and wondered if I should text him back suggesting that that was probably a bad idea, Sam produced his Bottle of Doom.

'Let's just have a little shot to toast the New Year, eh?' he wheedled.

'Oh, go on then,' we said eventually. 'Just one!'

So. The thing with coffee tequila is that it doesn't actually taste like tequila. It tastes rather lovely, like a slightly turbocharged shot of Tia Maria, which as everyone knows barely even counts as alcohol, much like Baileys. And so really, you think, what's the harm in having another one? And another one. An' nuvver one. And the *other* thing with coffee tequila is that, much like the grim nineties' combo of vodka and Red Bull, although it gets you shitfaced, it also gives you a caffeine blast so that you stay awake and continue to make a tit of yourself long after a normal drink would just have caused you pass out while still in possession of some small amount of decorum … Thus it is best that a veil should probably be drawn over the rest of the night, sufficing it only to say that there was dancing and singing and possibly a heartrending, tearstained and emotional rendition of 'How Much Is That Doggy in the Window' from me, dramatically clutching my disgusted and horrified dog to my bosom as I wept in his ear at the thought of the poor, unloved Doggy in the Window.

JANUARY

Sunday, 1 January

Euuurrrgh. Today has been, to say the least, painful. I was woken up by the small boys thundering downstairs at 7 a.m., and realising that since I had other people's children in the house, someone should probably put in an appearance and pretend to be a responsible adult. I gave Simon a kick.

'Mmmophhhh!' mumbled Simon, rolling over and pulling a pillow over his head.

'The boys are up,' I hissed. 'You should go and make them breakfast.'

'Nophoff!' came the groan from his side of the bed, which I think meant, 'No, fuck off!'

As Simon is blessed with that male ability to sleep soundly even when his beloved offspring are roaming below, potentially stabbing themselves/each other/the postman, and I, being but a weak and feeble woman, am jolted into consciousness at every squeak, squawk or squeal that might possibly have come from said offspring, I sighed, and heaved myself out of bed.

Vertical was bad. Vertical was very, very bad. Coffee tequila was most certainly no longer my friend. I couldn't quite believe I had been insane enough to book myself into something hideous called a 'Boot Camp Fitness' class this morning, feeling that

I was now a grown-up and healthy person. There was no way I could go to such a thing. I could barely stand up straight without vomiting, let alone contemplate burpees! I tottered down the landing and met Hannah coming out of the spare room, looking nearly as bad as I felt. Behind her, a fully dressed Charlie snored loudly, sprawled on top of the bedcovers. We regarded ourselves in the mirror at the top of the stairs with some dismay.

'FML!' whispered Hannah. 'If I was a dog that felt this bad, someone would put me out of my misery!'

Downstairs, Sam was snoring equally loudly on the sofa. Someone had thoughtfully placed a blanket over him. I had a vague flashback that it might have been me, as I recalled being very confused by trying to entirely cover Sam with the blanket because when I pulled it up to his shoulder, his feet were sticking out, but if I pulled it over his feet, his shoulders were uncovered, and I had spent some time trying to work out a solution to this baffling problem, before hitting on the genius plan of if only I could whisk the blanket into place *fast enough*, then I would have solved the dilemma. I hadn't, obviously.

I prodded Sam. He made a very unattractive noise and stretched out a supplicating hand.

'Coffee!' he rasped. 'For the love of God, a cup of coffee!'

'Get up,' I said unsympathetically. 'This was your damn coffee tequila that did this in the first place!'

In the kitchen, the boys had distributed what looked like the best part of an entire packet of Coco Pops (family size) in equal quantities between three bowls, every worktop in the kitchen, and the floor, and were now engaged in carefully slopping milk onto any surface that had not received its full quota of Coco Pops.

I attempted to lift the kettle to make healing tea, while Hannah and Sam huddled at the table, whimpering in pain.

Jane and the other girls appeared in the kitchen and looked around in disgust.

'Why do you all look so *awful*?' Jane demanded.

'I think maybe I'm coming down with a bug,' I whispered bravely.

'*I* think you're hungover,' said Jane unkindly. 'Really, Mother! You are not a good example to us, you know.'

'No,' winced Sam. 'But hopefully we will at least stand as a terrible warning.'

Later, the pain still showing no sign of subsiding, but having managed to dispatch all my houseguests, both expected and unexpected, I rallied the remains of my strength to make a New Year's Day roast dinner for Daddy and Natalia, as I had invited them over in a fit of weakness and guilt about going to Mum's for Christmas and abandoning them.

I felt rather less guilty when they turned up both looking sickeningly tanned after spending Christmas in Antigua ('Well, darling, with both you and Jessica with your mother, there didn't seem much point in us sitting round here waiting for you to get back,' said Daddy. 'You should try it, Ellen. It's amazing the difference even just a few days of sun in the middle of winter can make,' purred Natalia. Bastards. Both of them. I wasn't at all envious of their sunshine break, as opposed to my own festive season attempting to catch the Spawn of Sarah while they quaffed cocktails by the pool, and now I was stuck trying not to puke in the Yorkshire puddings with the WORST HANGOVER OF MY LIFE, all because I had felt bad about not spending Christmas with them).

Never had I been so grateful for Peter's overriding dedication to food, as he busied himself with trying to see how much trifle he could fit in his mouth at once, while Natalia watched in fascinated horror.

'Is he always like this?' she breathed nervously.

'Yes,' I said despairingly.

'It's just one of the reasons why having a brother is RUBBISH,' said Jane. 'No one should have to have a brother. Brothers are disgusting. I wish I was an only child.'

Peter screamed, 'No one should have to have a sister. Sisters are horrible. I HATE having a sister! I want to SELL her but no one will let me. Sisters are much worse than brothers, and Jane is the meanest bumhead poopants I HAVE EVER MET!'

Simon, slumped at the end of the table, lost in his own world of coffee tequila-induced pain, opened one bloodshot eye and said, 'What? What's going on? Why is everyone *shouting*? Oh, my poor head!'

Finally, once Peter and Jane had been separated, still spitting and hissing at each other like angry cats, and the dog had quietly finished up the remains of the trifle when no one was looking and then vomited it over Natalia's suede boot, and I had apologised all over again (while wondering why the fuck she keeps wearing such swanky stuff here. Surely she has realised that my house is a living example of Why We Can't Have Nice Things), and some semblance of order had been restored, and I had hidden in the larder for a quiet lie down for five minutes, resting my head on the cool, soothing tiles of the floor, it was finally time to wave them off.

'Why *do* you think she married him?' I asked Simon afterwards. 'Jessica thinks she wants a baby.'

'Oh God, I feel ill. I wonder if a beer would help?' groaned Simon.

'But what about Natalia and a baby?'

'She doesn't want a baby.'

'Why not?'

'Oh fuck, this beer is not helping at all. I wonder if I'm going to be sick. Well, not everyone wants babies, do they? And she's not exactly a spring chicken, is she?'

'She could still have a baby. *I* could still have a baby, come to that!'

Simon turned pale, an impressive feat given he was already ashen with his hangover. 'You don't want another baby, do you?' he said in dismay. 'All that business with Sarah hasn't made you broody, has it? Is that why you're suddenly obsessed with Natalia having a baby? Because really, it's *you* who wants one?'

I turned equally pale. 'Oh dear God, NO! Christ on a fucking bike, even had I been broody, which I most certainly am not, witnessing Sarah giving birth would have been enough to put anyone off. Peter and Jane are almost becoming civilised (admittedly only by their own idiosyncratic standards). I can't think of anything *worse*! In fact, after all that with Sarah, I was going to suggest we book you in for the snip. We don't have time for each other or the children we have, let alone a baby!'

Simon, although breathing a sigh of relief, immediately looked mutinous and started muttering that no one was putting a knife anywhere near *his* knob.

Friday, 13 January

Despite failing to attend the New Year's Boot Camp, I have been attempting to stick to a healthy-eating kick. I wouldn't go so far as to say I LIKE kale and quinoa, but I have eaten worse things. At least, I'm sure I must have. There was an unfortunate episode when I was misguided enough to eat something appalling in the form of a Brussels sprout salad for lunch, which led to me farting like a dray horse all afternoon, and obviously denying it, to the point where Lydia was insisting that we needed to get the maintenance team in to check there wasn't a dead rat in the ventilation system, while I staunchly denied being able to smell anything and insisted they were all imagining it (it was pretty bad. Worse than some of Peter's, and his arse is septic).

The Big Project is finished, hurrah, and so we went out and got absolutely shitfaced last Friday, and at one point in the night Alan sidled up to me to ask if he had sent me any photos at New Year, as he had apparently sent some 'unfortunate ones' before dropping his phone down the bog and killing it. By 'unfortunate photos' I assume he meant dick pics, as he looked profoundly relieved when I showed him the photo of him trying to put a party popper up his nose. I am not sure if I am pleased Alan respects me enough not to send me dick pics, or cross that he thinks me too old and haggard to bother sending dick pics to. I'm convincing myself it is the former. As a reward for finishing the Big Project on time, we have been given an even Bigger and more Important Project, since we managed not to fuck the last one up. So, no pressure.

Talking of no pressure, I don't know how much longer I can keep working these hours. The last push to get things done was tough, and reduced Simon to a snarling weasel of fury at having to pick up the kids more than he perceived as 'his' share. Since he is already in a foul mood with me, I decided in for a penny, in for a pound, and announced I was going out with Hannah and Sam tonight, while he complained about babysitting, and I reminded him once again that you can't actually babysit your own children. It's called parenting.

'I think this is the first time you've ever managed to stick to a health-and-fitness kick, Ellen,' said Hannah in surprise. 'You've literally been doing this every year since you were fifteen and you've never lasted more than two days, EVER!'

'I just wish there was a diet where you could live on pies and get thin!' I said sadly, sipping unenthusiastically at my vodka, soda and fresh lime, instead of delicious wine. 'I mean, imagine the fortune the person who came up with that diet could make. The Pie Yourself Thin Diet! Maybe this is my calling. Maybe this is how I will become rich and famous. Fuck off, Joe Wicks! Ellen Russell and the Pie Diet is the latest hot new trend. I can just see my cookbooks in the supermarkets now. Me on the cover, show-ing off my abs, holding a big, delicious pork pie. Maybe Greggs would sponsor it.'

'Or maybe it's never actually going to happen,' scoffed Sam. 'What with a) you have no nutritional training at all and b) it not being possible to lose weight while stuffing your face with pies.'

'And chips …' I added dreamily. 'Anyway, I do know quite a lot about nutrition from when Peter and Jane were babies. I read ALL the books when trying to be the perfect mummy and feed-ing them properly.'

'And did any of them contain recommendations on how to Pie Yourself Thin?'

'Well, no, but that's the point, isn't it? That's why I would become rich and famous for my revolutionary pie diet, like Dr Atkins when he said you could get skinny by eating lard. Same principle!'

'It's not *quite* the same …' said Hannah dubiously.

'Oh, whatever!' I said crossly. 'Oh, ye of little faith. What were your resolutions, then?'

'I didn't make any,' said Hannah smugly. 'I'm more interested in planning my wedding to Charlie.'

'And have you decided to appoint me wedding-planner-in-chief yet?' I demanded.

'No!' said Hannah. 'Because it's *my* wedding, not yours, and I have already had to tell you I am not going to consider a French-themed wedding, a Jane Austen-themed wedding or a *Peaky Blinders*-themed wedding (which, by the way, was most inappropriate) –'

'I just thought the suits and caps would be quite dapper,' I interrupted.

'So I will be planning my *own* wedding!'

'Can I come to wedding shows?' I wheedled.

'No. Because I'm not going to any wedding shows. I keep telling you, I've *done* all of that. Charlie's done all of that. We both just want something really simple that's about us committing to each other, not about fucking vintage gramophones or any other 'quirky' props or flowers or frocks or fancy fucking furbelows.'

'You're no fun,' I grumbled. 'What is even the *point* of one's friends filling one's hearts with joy by having second marriages when all hope of weddings had been abandoned due to everyone being married off, if you won't even do it properly?'

'Sometimes, Ellen,' said Hannah severely, 'it's lucky I've known you as long as I have, and can't stop being friends with you because it will take me till I'm eighty-five now to have a friend I have known longer, because sometimes you're very annoying. I want a marriage, not a wedding. Ellen, are you even listening to me? Are you on Pinterest again, looking for wedding tat?'

'Sorry, sorry, I was checking my emails. I missed one on the way home – why does everything always go tits up at about 6 p.m. on a Friday? Anyway, I was just trying to *help* with the wedding. I won't make any more suggestions. What about you then, Sam? What are you hoping the New Year brings for you?'

Sam perked up and said, 'Well, actually, I have decided this is the year I am going to be *proactive* about meeting someone.'

'WHO?' we shrieked. 'OOOOOH, WHO? Tell all!'

'Well, I haven't met them yet, have I? That's the point. I've had an epiphany!'

'You're a week late!' I sniggered, very pleased with my own wit.

'Shut up, Ellen,' said Sam, 'I am having a *moment*, here. Where was I? Yes, an epiphany. I can't be the only normal, single man out there, looking for another normal, single man, can I? I mean, it's just not possible. But at my age, I fear the numbers of us are dwindling and the chances of me finding someone through chance or fate or serendipity or call it what you will are becoming increasingly slim, and *time is running out*. I want to meet someone while I still have a chance of making them at least slightly quiver with lust for me, before my arse sags and my paunch expands. There are *only so many squats a man can do*! So, I have decided to take matters into my own hands, and fuck the universe's plans for me and all the rest of it, and thus I have joined some dating sites. And Tinder.'

Hannah looked dubious. 'Are you sure about this? I mean, I tried some dating sites before I met Charlie, and I didn't find they were really for me.'

'No, sweetie, but you got freaked out because someone sent you a dick pic within the first week, and the second site you tried was that "Shag My Pal" website, and you got Ellen to write your advert for you and her copy wasn't exactly inspiring, was it? I am braced for dick pics. In fact, I may start rating them out of ten. I may even start a website for them – ratemycock.com, or something – where I share the worst ones. Or, you never know, I may even send some of my own! And I will write my own blurb for it all, and make myself sound much better than I really am. So I'll lure them in one way or another!'

'Are you really on Tinder?' I breathed. 'Is that the one that bings your phone when there's someone nearby who wants a bit of casual sex?'

'No, darling, that's Grindr,' said Sam kindly. 'Though I think some people use Tinder for similar purposes, but it's the one where you swipe left or right depending on whether you fancy them.'

'Oooh!' I said in excitement. 'I've always wanted to have a nosy at that. Aren't you worried someone will murder you?'

'Ellen, for someone who earns their living as a software developer, your fear of modern technology is quite remarkable,' said Sam loftily. 'The chances of being murdered by a Tinder date are very slim, no greater than being murdered by any other date. Even Beardy Coffee Man may have had his dark side lurking somewhere, though I doubt it. His murder weapon of choice would probably be boring people to death while he drones on about why Nespresso machines are ruining the true art of making coffee!'

'It's not the *technology* that scares me, it's the people that use it,' I pointed out indignantly.

'And what about *you*, Ellen?' said Hannah. 'What are your resolutions?'

'Oh God, I don't know! I'm constantly failing on everything. I was going to be a better mother, a better wife, a better employee, give everything 110 per cent, but there's just no time for anything. I keep being late to pick up the kids from After-School Club because I can't get out of work on time, and I don't think Simon and I have managed to hold a civil conversation since before Christmas. I don't know what to do. I love my job, I can't face going backwards, especially not with the kids getting older all the time, but all joking apart, I think I need a wife.'

'What about an au pair?' said Sam.

'An au pair? Aren't they for posh people with kids called Cressida and Jeremy?'

'Don't be ridiculous, Ellen. Look how many of the mums at school have nannies or au pairs,' pointed out Sam. 'Your kids are maybe too old for a nanny, but an au pair would take the pressure off in the mornings and evenings, and then maybe you and Simon wouldn't be so stressed, AND you might finally manage your lifelong ambition of learning another language.'

An au pair. What a thoroughly excellent idea.

'Do you think I could get an au pair to do the PTA stuff for me too?' I said wonderingly.

'Probably not,' said Sam. 'I think that might be frowned upon, unless you got a really crafty one. You could enquire of an agency if they had a very bossy, craft-obsessed au pair, but they might be suspicious of your motives.'

'You never know! Such people must exist. Anyway, enough about me. Give us a squizz at your Tinder, then,' I demanded. 'Inculcate us in the dark arts of internet sex!'

'Tinder isn't just about sex,' sighed Sam as we shrieked, 'Swipe left, swipe left, OMG, look at that one, oooh, he seems nice, nooooonoooo onooooo, swipe, swipe, he used "you're" instead of "your" AND "too" instead of "to"! What about him? God, no, swipe, SWIPE!'

It was tremendous fun but mildly addictive, and makes me think it is probably best that I am safely married and have been brainwashed by Simon into believing that everyone on the internet wants to kill me!

Thursday, 19 January

I appear to have become Sarah's Official Parenting Guru. After my (admittedly Very Fucking Splendid) performance during the arrival of little Orla Ellen (according to Simon, there is no need to use her full name every time I mention her, but then how will I remind people that she is named after me because of my Heroic

Mercy Dash through the blizzard? – also, on the subject of names, I still think Isolde would have been much better and am rather regretting my noble gesture in giving up the chance to name the baby), Sarah has clearly decided that I am some sort of Oracle of Motherhood and has taken to ringing me up at least once a day to consult me about my wisdom and knowledge. At first this was extremely flattering, but the fact remains that the baby is only three weeks old and already this is getting a bit stressful. What if I have to endure another eighteen years of it?

Today's enquiry was about whether or not I would advise co-sleeping. What should I do? Do I tell Sarah to be a cold-hearted bitch and put her baby in a cot so she can at least enjoy a brief moment each night without another person hanging off her, touching her, clawing her and pawing her (apart from Piers)? But what if that makes Sarah and Orla have attachment issues and Orla grows up feeling unloved and unwanted, all stemming from her perceived rejection by her own mother when she was only a few weeks old? Or do I tell Sarah that of course she should co-sleep, it will provide a most wonderful opportunity to bond with her baby, and the oxytocin or what-ever it is will make her feel marvellous and she will regret it forever if she doesn't – and then she rolls over and smothers the baby in her sleep?

I mean, what I am supposed to say? For me, co-sleeping sounded like the most hideous thing I'd ever heard of. In an ideal world I wouldn't share a bed with *anybody*, not even Simon – we would occupy separate bedrooms like respectable Victorians, and he could pay conjugal visits. I wouldn't even need him to warm my feet, as my dog does that quite effectively (obviously, my beloved terrier is exempt from my dislike of sharing my bed – when Simon snores, I want to stab him; when my ickle Woofingtons snores, it is adorable! But anyway, I digress). So the idea of having to give over yet more of my precious bed space to the snorting, snuffling, frequently malodorous and often damp Bundle of Joy that I had been hefting about with me all day filled me with nothing but cold, dark dread. Other people, however, absolutely swear by co-sleeping as the best thing they have ever done, so what do I know?

I mumbled something to that effect at Sarah, vaguely suggesting that she should just 'trust her instincts' and do 'what feels right'.

'But I don't know what my instincts are saying!' wailed Sarah. 'I mean, the Health Visitor says I mustn't co-sleep ever because Orla will be crushed like a grape beneath my whale-like bulk –'

'Did she really say that? That seems a little harsh.'

'Well, no, I'm paraphrasing, obviously, though I still feel vast. I thought my tummy would go once the baby was out, but I still look bloody pregnant. I had Orla strapped to me in a sling the other day and some fucking bitch still stopped me and asked when I was due! But the Health Visitor says co-sleeping is a Very Bad Thing, but everyone at my NCT classes told me it was the only way to go and I just don't know what I am meant to be doing.'

Poor Sarah. Do any of us really know what we are meant to be doing? I mean, obviously, yes, there are some terrifically maternal women out there who were literally born to be mothers and just seem to always know the right thing to do, but for most of us, especially with our first babies, that first year of motherhood seems largely to consist of just trying to keep the baby alive, while wondering what IDIOT thought you were a responsible enough person to have a WHOLE OTHER HUMAN BEING'S LIFE in your hands.

And everyone has an opinion. Get your tits out./Cover yourself up, love!/Get them in a routine. Feed them on demand./

Bathe them nightly, it's comforting and reminds them of the womb./Bathe them weekly or their skin will get too dry./Babble at them in baby talk, it stimulates their development./NEVER use baby talk, it stunts their development./Co-sleep every night./ Put them in the shed so they learn independence/Use a dummy./ Have children when you're young./OMG, why did you ruin your life? You have no prospects now! Wait till your career is established./Ha ha ha, good luck with procreating now, you selfish barren witch!/Annabel Karmel organic purees./Baby-led weaning. What car seat, what pram, what sling, what cot, what fucking sheets for the bastarding cot, does this toy over stimulate them, is this toy too boring, am I reading to them enough, am I spoiling them by pandering too much to their needs, what baby gym, what potty, am I creating a post-apocalyptic landscape for them to inherit because I just don't have the strength to use cloth nappies, am I off-setting that with their organic cotton baby-gros, what percentile is the best to be in, are they too big, are they too small, is that woman's baby's percentile better than mine, should they have more teeth, less teeth, more hair, less hair, should they shit that much, should they shit more, should their shit be FUCKING GREEN? SHOULD IT?

Everywhere you turn there is conflicting advice and some bastard who wants to tell you their views on the subject. From the moment your bump first starts showing and COMPLETE FUCKING STRANGERS think it is OK to come up and start TOUCHING you, and then telling you that you are having a boy or a girl because of how you are carrying it, or are you *sure* it isn't twins, dear, because you're very *big* for sixteen weeks, aren't you, or launching into unasked-for tales of their cousin's auntie's brother's wife whose *baby nearly died* because she did that, you know, to the people who feel obliged to come up to you when your baby cries in public and firmly inform you that clearly your child is in distress because they are too hot/too cold/ hungry/want a cuddle, because OBVIOUSLY some RANDOM STRANGER has a far better idea of what YOUR BABY needs than you do, there is always someone who feels it is OK to put their tuppence worth in and make you feel like shit, like you are doing it all wrong and that you have no fucking clue. Which you probably don't, but even so!

And that's before the vast rafts of 'professional' advice out there. Gina Ford, Supernanny, books on attachment parenting, websites on how to let your baby 'cry it out'. Advice from health visitors and GPs and NCT leaders and La Leche consultants, and JUST when you think that you might have got the hang of things, they decide that, actually, all that advice was wrong and they are going to change the guidelines. You would think that was enough, wouldn't you, for new mothers to be bombarded with, but as well as all that, every D-list celebrity who has ever squeezed a human head through their flaps is in on the act now as well, 'sharing' their 'tips' on how to be a perfect fucking mother, just like them, with a perfect fucking body and an all-white colour palette in their tastefully decorated homes.

In most ways we are incredibly lucky to become First World parents in this day and age, when we can choose how and when we become pregnant and give birth, when we can access excellent health care that means we are not expected to have ten children in the hope that a couple of them might live to grow up, when we don't watch our babies dying of entirely preventable diseases or starvation, and all the problems I listed are obviously First World problems. But undoubtedly, this whole parenting industry that has sprung up is a massive headfuck for parents, especially mothers.

Once upon a time we'd have had a village, a tribe, a community to help us bring up our children, and we would not have known of any other way to do it, other than how our mothers, sisters, cousins and aunts had done it (unless we wanted to be stoned as a witch), but now, with our fractured families and frenetic twenty-first-century lives, the village is gone, and in its place is Modern Parenting, with all its judgement and conflicting advice.

It doesn't even really get any easier as they get older, either. Obviously one worries less about breaking them, and agonises less over their poo (although Peter does seem to poo an exceptional amount for a child of his size – where does it come from? Where? How can such a small child produce such mountains of shit on a daily basis?), but there are new worries – about school, bullies, the internet, screen time, vegetables, boundaries, lack of boundaries. That's the really scary thing about children – every one is unique and you only get one go at getting it right. There are no second chances. If you get it wrong, that's it, that was your one shot, and there is no going back. There must come a point when you can stop worrying, surely, when can you sit back and take stock and say, 'I think I did OK' (either that or, 'Well, I fucked THAT up epically, didn't I?'). But when?

Anyway, *obviously* I didn't say any of this to Sarah, and just suggested that as long as Orla is fed, warm and loved, none of the other stuff really matters, but if she is that concerned, maybe she should do some more research and see which option she felt more comfortable with …

God, it is so much easier to give advice about other people's lives, especially when you can dispense it from a distance from a nice, clean office, far from sicky muslins and stickiness!

FEBRUARY

Wednesday, 1 February

I always feel I should like February better – after all, it marks the end of January, where the only really good thing is the sales (I might have got a bit carried away under the guise of 'bargains' – I'm pretty sure a 'capsule wardrobe' shouldn't spill over into the spare room …), and even better, the start of February means it is only two weeks until Simon's birthday, which means I only have to endure two more weeks of his Annual Grump, whereby he stomps around being a Miserable Bastard from New Year's Day until his birthday, which unfortunately falls on Valentine's Day. He is even grumpier this year, as he is still not entirely feeling the love for me working full-time, but he agreed that the au pair was a good idea. I am hoping that this is because he sees the practical benefits and not because he is hopeful of a nubile young sexpot walking round the house in her scanties. I wonder if, in addition to 'bossy, craft-obsessed, tidy, good at ironing and not too talkative', one could also ask the agency to ensure whoever they find is on the plain and slightly chubby side. Almost certainly not.

February should be such a romantic month too, with Valentine's Day (which Simon refuses to celebrate, since it is his birthday) and leap years and ladies being able to propose, except of course that it is the twenty-first century now, and women can propose whenever they want – though does that mean they have to buy their own ring? What is the etiquette for that? I should not like to have to put in the effort of proposing AND having to buy my own ring, but then again I am lazy, and had Simon not proposed to me, I definitely would not have done it myself. It wasn't the most romantic, or earth-shattering of proposals – we had just finished our finals, and it was a swelteringly hot early summer in Edinburgh, which took us somewhat by surprise as we had spent the last four years freezing our tits off in draughty tenement flats and shivering as the Haar blew in and obscured Arthur's Seat, so the sudden warmth made a blissful change – we could even have sex with our socks off. After a few days, though, the city was stifling and airless, and so Simon drove us to Yellowcraig Beach in East Lothian, a glorious golden sweep of sand, looking across to an old lighthouse on an island that allegedly was the inspiration for *Treasure Island*. Being mid-week, the beach was deserted, and we had some romantic notion of making love in the sand dunes. It became rapidly apparent that this was a very bad idea, as a) sand gets everywhere and b) the beach was not quite as deserted as we had first thought, and some very disapproving dog walkers got rather more of an eyeful than they had bargained for, so we gave it up as a bad job and just lay and basked in the sunshine instead.

I was just drifting off to sleep and so was slightly disgruntled when Simon woke me up by taking my hand and sitting up to block my sun as he said something.

'Wha'?' I mumbled sleepily.

'I said, I think we should get married. What do you think?'

I sat up so fast that I nearly headbutted Simon in the nose, the romantic moment only being saved by his quick reaction of flinging himself backward onto the sand.

'Oh my God! Yes! I think that's a fabulous idea! Yes, let's get married!'

And so, just like that, we were engaged. We drove back to the city in Simon's antiquated Fiesta, that he insisted he couldn't ever wash because the dirt was the only thing keeping it together, holding hands (which made changing gear tricky for him, but nonetheless, he didn't let go) and beaming with happiness. The next day, he bought me a ring, a small and inexpensive but gorgeous moonstone and silver ring, from one of the crafty hippy shops on the West Bow.

We had planned to get married straight away in some tiny romantic ceremony, possibly just the two of us, and two strangers dragged into the registry office as witnesses, but as soon as my mother and Simon's mother got wind of the engagement, that was the end of that, and a Proper Wedding was in the works, complete with florists and bridesmaids and canapés and yards and yards of taffeta and quarrels between Mum and Sylvia over who got to wear the biggest hat. So it was two years before we actually managed to get a suitable wedding arranged that the mothers deemed appropriate, and we had very little say in our actual day (apart from my insistence that I MUST have puffed sleeves on my wedding dress, my fashion choices having been influenced from an early age by Anne Shirley – a decision I rather regret now when looking back at the photos).

The tiny moonstone ring was replaced by a 'real' ring shortly before Jane was born, after a brief and heady period of financial security and two full-time incomes with no childcare to pay for, and then we were caught up in the whirlwind of babies and property ladders and mortgages and catchment areas and school applications and parents' nights and homework, and somehow, bit by bit, I feel like we're becoming strangers and those two besotted kids, lying on that beach, so happy to be spending the rest of their lives with each other, are people from a book or a film.

Why am I even thinking about those kids and that beach on a pissing-wet Wednesday morning in February, when I am supposed to be paying attention in a Very Important Meeting? Oh, yes. February and leap years and proposals. Anyway, I should like February, but I don't because it is just such a MEH month. It should be spring, the daffodils should be flowering, there should be hope and joy in our hearts, but instead February just squats there like a big miserable grey bastard, cockblocking the spring and the sun. Fucking February.

Friday, 10 February

Heigh-Ho, Heigh-Ho, it's off to the in-laws we go! In a fit of extraordinary organisation, I managed to remember the approach of half-term, and even more extraordinary, Simon had even announced he would be taking the week off as he wanted to go and see his parents.

Unfortunately, I wasn't able to take all of next week off, as Lydia has booked it off too, as she also appears to have a Busy and Important husband who believes childcare is a woman's issue. Simon is not entirely thrilled that I will therefore only be able to take Monday and Tuesday off next week, and will have to get an early flight back on Wednesday morning and go straight to the office (though there is something about going straight into the office from the airport that makes me feel really quite jet-setty and go-gettery – I will have to shoehorn it into conversation several times on Wednesday morning 'On my way here from the *airport* …'), leaving him to travel back alone with the children.

I felt quite bad, though, when poor Lydia remarked that she was surprised I wanted to be off the same week as the school holidays, because it's so much more expensive to go away then, but, she added wistfully, she supposed that was the thing about having no children, your life isn't ruled by term dates and I probably hadn't even *realised* it was half-term, had I? I felt even worse when Alan, who had been muttering darkly about Lydia's time off and how she *always* gets first dibs on booking holidays just because she has kids and it wasn't fair, wished me a lovely break as I tripped out of the office for our long-overdue visit to Simon's mental parentals at their 'bijou chateau' (as his mother likes to call it) in France. In truth, the aged in-laws themselves are not so bad. Michael and Sylvia can be a little wearing, but ultimately mean well, and although Sylvia used to be a bit of a nightmare, she has thawed of recent years, due to a combination of her being forced to realise that her precious daughter is a clusterfuck of epic proportions, said daughter only being bailed out from her shitty life decisions with the profits from my own cleverness in designing that very lucrative app, and me teaching Sylvia of the joys of internet shopping, all of which caused her to decide that my horrid and uncreative computing job wasn't quite so bad, even though deep down I suspect she would still rather that I was an interior designer like Sukey Poste's daughter. I don't actually know who Sukey Poste is, but I have been treated to every detail of her daughter's brilliant career in wallpaper and soft furnishings. I suspect my own mother would also rather I was more like Sukey Poste's daughter, if only so I could get her a trade discount at Laura Ashley.

My main reservation about visiting Michael and Sylvia is, of course, that we will also have to endure my fragrant and delightful sister-in-law Louisa – and I use the term 'fragrant' very loosely, since she has shown no signs of becoming any cleaner since abandoning her New Age Wanker husband Bardo, and the 'holistic retreat' they had run together that she sank every penny she had into along with a large chunk of her parents' savings. Post-Bardo and retreat, Louisa found herself somewhat high and dry with six children and no income, until I was persuaded to step in and use the remaining proceeds from my *Why Mummy Drinks* app to buy her a house next door to Michael and Sylvia, so she and her offspring were not rendered homeless, and her parents could attempt to keep her on the straight and narrow (and also French property prices were, thankfully, much more reasonable than prices round us).

Despite all this, Louisa has not become any less irritating, any less sanctimonious or any less of a massive fucking tit. Every time I see her, I am suffused with fury and outrage at all the other things I could have done with my lovely windfall app money instead of propping her up in her deadbeat life. Simon usually has to remove me from the room and encourage me to take deep breaths, while reminding me that we didn't do this for Louisa, but for her children. All six of them.

Anyway, we managed to journey to France with relatively little drama, apart from Simon swearing profusely while loading the car with the eleventy billion bags required for us to go away for a week, and demanding why we needed so much *stuff*, and also questioning the need for Peter and Jane to be quite so well furnished with so many snacks for travelling, while I pointed out that if they were eating and glued to their iPads, then there was at least a chance they would ignore each other instead of twatting the everlasting fuck out of each other for the next eight hours. We obviously arrived at the ferry port ridiculously early due to Simon's worries about Delays on the Road and his conviction that if he is not early, then somehow the ferry people will trick him and send the boat out early for no reason other than to spite him, and we had to stop several times as Jane thought she might be sick while Simon muttered that the only reason she felt sick was three packets of Pom-Bears and a vat of Percy Pigs.

Once in France, Simon went into his strange Racist British Driver Abroad incarnation, swearing and shouting at the innocent French people for driving on their side of the road (sometimes I wonder if Simon was some Important Official of the Raj in a former life, such is his conviction that Foreigners Do Things Wrong), but as I said, everything is relative, and for us that was a fairly uneventful journey.

The fun really started when we got to Michael and Sylvia's bijou chateau. Firstly, Sylvia had neglected to inform us that she had got herself a replacement for the late, lamented Napoleon Bonapug – a little pug bitch, called, unsurprisingly, Josephine. Apparently Sylvia had thought it would be a nice surprise for us and my beloved Judgy Dog, who had accompanied us, farting rancidly all the way due to Jane sharing her crisps with him. This would have been a nicer surprise had the unfortunate Josephine not been in the midst of her first season.

Despite my warnings of potential molestation, Sylvia insisted that the dogs would get on fine, just fine (having seemingly forgotten the bitter blood feud that had raged between my poor boy and Napoleon Bonapug), and so she popped Josephine down to 'say hello'.

Judgy is a Proud and Noble Terrier, and disinclined to let a little thing like having no balls get in the way if there is a bitch in season around. And, I have to say, Josephine lived up to her name and was an absolute trollop, waggling her little puggy bum in his face, as he tried nobly to resist, but eventually he succumbed and leapt aboard, to Sylvia's horror. Fortunately, Josephine (who perhaps should be renamed Lolita) had her virtue left intact (if not her dignity), due to Sylvia's having clad her in a dreadful device called a 'doggy diaper', which is basically a canine sanitary pad. Thus it was that we were at least able to separate them easily enough, while Sylvia screamed 'NOT TONIGHT, JOSEPHINE!', though I sighed as I looked forward to a long week of trying to keep them apart, as family relations may get strained if Sylvia accuses my dog of rapey tendencies and I respond that clearly Josephine was asking for it.

On the plus side, there is always lots of wine at Michael and Sylvia's, and one needn't even feel greedy for quaffing it in gargantuan quantities as one is *en Français* and so it is only about €0.50 a litre. On the downside, one bloody well needs it to cope with Louisa.

Talking of the unwashed one, Michael and Sylvia grimly updated us on her latest antics over dinner – Louisa herself had not deigned to appear and say hello, despite living at the end of the driveway. Apparently, for reasons known only to herself, Louisa has decided to turn her home into a 'Woman's Co-operative'. When I asked Michael what exactly that was, he replied that as far as he could tell she had filled the place with a load of females who didn't seem to own a single hairbrush between the lot of them.

'But where does she put them all?' I said in confusion. 'I mean, between her and the children, there's not exactly space for anyone else in the house.'

'No,' said Sylvia gloomily, 'I know. Some of them have brought camper vans, and the rest have put up yurts in the garden.'

'Place looks like a bloody gypsy encampment!' said Michael crossly. 'But apparently men are now barred from the premises, so we don't have to worry about the stupid girl sprogging again, like we did a few months ago when she was teaching "Life Drawing" and modelling for the classes at the same time, flashing her bits at every Tom, Dick and Harry who signed up. Not until she gets bored and finds her next hare-brained scheme to pursue, anyway!'

Saturday, 11 February

Louisa finally wafted in to say hello today, accompanied by her full complement of vagabond children, whom she announced she would be leaving at Michael and Sylvia's for the day as she had so much to do, and it would be nice for them to spend some time with their cousins. Michael and Sylvia paled at this prospect, and Louisa's poppets and Peter and Jane shot murderous looks at each other. The battle lines between them had been firmly drawn a few years ago, when the eldest, Cedric, had attempted to steal Jane's iPod and she had responded by trying to stab him in the eye, and relations were further soured when Oillell, the youngest girl, then a toddler, now five(ish), had done a shit in Peter's bed, which Louisa had brushed off as being a 'perfectly natural part of practising her elimination communication'!

Louisa's oldest daughter, Coventina, at least seemed to be continuing on her life mission to thwart Louisa's determination to make her poor children be as feckless and irresponsible as she is, by washing, brushing her hair and being normal. On closer inspection, she also seems to have turned the second girl, Idelisa, onto her path of rebellion, as they were both clean, had their hair in ponytails and were sporting Gap T-shirts, I assume provided as part of Sylvia's eBay bounty. The others (I *think* the order is Cedric, Coventina, Nissien, Idelisa, Oillell and Boreas, and they range now from around eleven to three) looked like they had been raised by wolves. Coventina and Idelisa confirmed their revolution by asking Sylvia if they could go and do their piano practice, while Louisa looked disapproving and sighed that she didn't know what was *wrong* with those two. The others, meanwhile, continued their wolf-children impressions.

Louisa then turned to me. 'I am sorry to be so busy when you've just arrived, Ellen, but I have rather an important evening planned. We're having a poetry reading to celebrate the publication of my book, and I'd like to invite you to come along tonight. You too, Mother!' she barked at Sylvia. 'But not you, Si. I'm sure Mum and Dad have explained that no men are allowed in the Commune. We are an all-female group, dedicating ourselves to overthrowing the patriarchy and freeing ourselves from the chains of male oppression, and so having men present is counterintuitive to all our work.'

'I didn't know you'd had a book published, Louisa,' I said, partly in astonishment that someone would publish Louisa's ramblings, and partly in the hope that she might actually start earning some money instead of living rent-free in *my* (I mean our) house and leeching off her parents each month when she's frittered away the child support from her ex-husband.

'Yes!' said Louisa smugly. 'I mean, *obviously* I've had to self-publish, because the patriarchy has such a stranglehold on the media that there was no way that they were ready for the *raw truths* contained in my poetry, but that's fine, because I was not going to submit to their censorship anyway. My work is too important to let The Man butcher it to satisfy the maw of commerce. But once my words are out there, in their full and uncompromised state, well, this book is going to really change things.'

'That's nice,' I said weakly.

'So, 7 p.m. Don't be late, the readings will be starting promptly. And Mother, can you bring some wine and snacks for everyone?'

'What?' said Sylvia, who had drifted off into a reverie, probably having heard Louisa's speeches on censorship and the patriarchy eleventy billion times now. 'Oh no, darling, no. I can't come tonight, sorry! Josephine is in season. I can't possibly leave her at such a delicate time.'

'What?' said Louisa in outrage. 'It's my special night and my own mother will not come and support me because her *dog* needs her more?'

'Well,' said Sylvia, 'I'd have thought you'd be more understanding, Louisa. This being an important feminine time for Josephine.'

'Oh, fine!' huffed Louisa.

'Um, maybe I should stay here with Sylvia, you know,' I suggested. 'Just in case my poor dog tries to do anything nasty to Josephine. Defend her honour!'

'Ellen! *Someone* from my family has to be there to represent me on my special night,' shrieked Louisa. 'And also someone needs to bring the food and drink that Mum promised me.'

'I did not!' said Sylvia.

'Well, it's the least you can do,' snapped Louisa. 'Since it seems you prefer that dog to me!'

'I wonder why …' murmured Simon.

'And also, if you're not bothering to come, you can keep the kids overnight, so I can concentrate on my readings.'

With that, Louisa stalked off, leaving Sylvia and Michael mouthing helpless objections to having six feral monsters dumped on them (well, four, and Coventina and Idelisa, who were playing 'Für Elise' rather nicely in the drawing room), as well as the four of us.

It is quite remarkable how often Louisa gets her own way, simply by refusing to listen to anyone's arguments against what she has announced will be happening. In some ways (though not in any that relate to hygiene issues), she is very like my sister. But given the option of spending the evening jammed in a corner while the children fought or going to Louisa's and possibly getting a chance to have a good judge, curiosity at seeing the Commune and hearing Louisa's poetry won out.

Michael gave me a lift down, as they had caved in and were providing four litres of red wine and some bags of crisps, which were about the only 'snacks' available in rural France that could fulfil Louisa's vegan and gluten-free requirements. Louisa came flapping out when we arrived, shouting that Michael should not even be on the property and forbidding him to get out of the car, and complaining about driving such a short distance while he remonstrated that I couldn't very well have carried everything down myself. Louisa swept back into the house dramatically, leaving me to lug in all the wine and crisps.

Inside was pretty much as I had expected – all was dim and dark, with fairy lights and candles burning in dangerous places and a strong smell of cheap incense (in truth I am not sure what expensive incense would smell like). I made a mental note to check with Simon about insurance for Louisa's house, as I'm pretty sure she would not have troubled herself with anything so patriarchally tedious.

A stern woman came through from the back of the house and looked me up and down disapprovingly. I felt I had cobbled together a remarkably effective outfit for a poetry reading, giving I had had no warning it was happening, and was rather pleased with my black polo neck, denim mini-skirt (I don't CARE if I'm forty-two and all the articles say you shouldn't wear a mini-skirt over the age of thirty-five, and anyway, it's not like it's a mini like I wore when I was fifteen. It comes to just above my knees instead of barely skimming my groin) and black boots. I thought I looked artistic and poetical, though Simon had made me

remove my fetching black beret on the basis that a) it was 'ridiculous' and b) the locals might think I was just taking the piss. I
had, however, compensated for that by simply applying extra
eyeliner.

'Can I help you?' she sniffed.

'Hello!' I said brightly. 'I'm Ellen, Louisa's sister-in-law. I've
brought some wine!'

'Oh,' said the stern woman unenthusiastically. 'Yes. Louisa has
told us about *you*, I should have guessed. I suppose you'd better
come through.'

In the sitting room the furniture ran mainly to beanbags and
floor cushions. Until recently, I would have cheerfully judged
Louisa for her stereotypical hippy décor, but it was disturbingly
reminiscent of the Thinking Space at work, and therefore
suggested that perhaps Louisa was in fact annoyingly cutting-
edge. The stern woman (who had grudgingly introduced herself
as Stella) attempted to relieve me of the wine, but a sixth sense
made me suggest that, actually, I would just get a glass and
help myself. Stella looked unimpressed by this, but there was
no bastarding way I was going to make it through the night
without a drink. Another, cleaner-looking woman came in as I
was pouring myself some wine, and Stella muttered to her
urgently, the only words I could catch being 'sister-in-law' and
'inappropriate'.

Fortunately, Louisa chose this moment to make her entrance,
clad (for Louisa is nothing if not predictable in her hippyshit
bollocks) in a swirly kaftan, with what appeared to be some antiquated tea towels wrapped around her head. Three other women
followed her.

'Welcome!' gushed Louisa. 'Welcome, friends! Ask the others
to come through, please, Stella. I'm ready to begin.'

'Err, that's everyone that's here,' said Stella.

'Oh,' said Louisa, looking momentarily deflated. 'You did put the flyers out around the village, Gypsy, letting all the women know about tonight and that they were all welcome?'

The cleaner woman turned out to be Gypsy, who insisted she had indeed done just that.

'Well,' said Louisa, 'I think perhaps it's better like this, actually. More *intimate*, because after all, these poems are very *personal*. I'd like first of all to read my particular favourite, "My Yoni" …'

Louisa stood in the centre of the room, arms raised, and stared round at us all. I think she was trying to look at us intently, but she looked like Peter trying (and failing) to hold in a fart. Suddenly she dropped her arms and bellowed:

MY YONI!
GAPING!
BLEEDING!
BEAUTIFUL!
MY YONI!
LIFE!
BLOOD!
DEATH!
MY YONI!
PLEASURE!
PAIN!
A BABY'S HEAD!
IT BLEEDS,
IT PULSES,
IT LIVES.
STRETCHES.
OPENS.
IT GIVES.
MY YONI.

The other women applauded rapturously.

'That was so powerful, Louisa!' called Stella. 'It spoke to me! It spoke to me here!' She pounded her heart. 'And here!' She smacked her hand off her temple. 'And HERE!' and to my alarm she grabbed her crotch. 'I think all our yonis felt the power of Louisa's words, didn't they?'

Everyone nodded assent. I didn't really know what to say, so I murmured something non-committal, which is every proper British person's default setting in an awkward social situation. Apparently that wasn't enough for Louisa, though, as she demanded, 'Come on, then, Ellen. What did you think?'

'Yes, it was very nice,' I muttered.

'Oh, come on, Ellen. You can do better than that,' laughed Louisa. 'Didn't your teachers tell you not to say "nice"? Tell me what you really thought, how it really made you feel. Tell me where you felt the *power* of it moving in you.'

I wasn't convinced that 'Well, Louisa, it made me feel mortified and also a bit sick, to be honest' was necessarily the most tactful answer, though, so I settled for, 'Mmmm, it was certainly *different*!' which seemed to satisfy her.

Her next poem, Louisa announced, was called 'Blood'.

As Louisa ranted, 'Blood, blood, blood, a flood, a flood, a flood', I sidled out of the room in search of more wine, as Stella had managed to wrest the bottle off me while I was knocking back my first glass.

The woman called Gypsy followed me through.

'Is this the first time you've heard Louisa's poems?' she asked sympathetically.

I said it was.

'I thought so,' said Gypsy. 'They take some getting used to, I'm afraid. She's been practising all week.'

'Oh God!' I said. 'You poor thing!'

Gypsy laughed. 'Oh, I don't live here. I think Stella is the only one living here at the moment. Between you and me, I'm slightly scared of Stella. There were about six other women living here when Louisa first came up with the idea, but I think people thought it was going to be more of an artists' co-operative type thing, and they moved on when it turned out to be mainly Louisa and Stella ranting about the patriarchy.'

'Which in Louisa's case is ironic, as she lives off her father and her ex-husband!' I said. 'So where do you live, then?'

'Just outside the village. I teach art, and I have a smallholding, so I try to grow or make as much of what I need as I can. Running art classes doesn't pay awfully well. I sometimes think that I should try to expand on the art business, start running residential courses or something, but the whole reason for moving here, trying to find a simpler life, was because I had a breakdown after being too obsessed with making as much money as possible in as short a time as possible and spending it all on consumerist crap that I didn't need.'

'I quite like consumerist crap,' I admitted.

'Oh, me too. I would be lying if I said I didn't covet your boots, but I'm trying to remember what's important, that it's not all about *stuff*. That taking the time to drink my coffee in the morning sitting on my veranda is actually worth far more than anything I could buy with the money I'd earn gulping a takeaway coffee on the tube on the way to work. Though your boots might *almost* be worth it!'

'You must think I'm an awful person, then, pursuing the capitalist dream,' I said.

'Not at all!' said Gypsy in surprise. 'Everyone just has to do what's right for them. If you're happy, and your life is working for you, then that's all that matters, not what I think or anyone else.'

There was a screech from the sitting room.

'ELLEN! GYPSY! WHERE ARE YOU? YOU ARE MISSING THE POETRY AND I AM ABOUT TO DO "MAMMARIES ARE NOT FOR MEN"!'

Somewhat reluctantly, Gypsy and I shuffled back through to hear Louisa's poem about her tits. I don't know what she had to say on the subject of her bosoms, as I was too busy cringing in the corner because she flung off her kaftan and recited her poem while prancing round the room naked and jiggling her boobs. I firmly believe that one's personal grooming is one's personal choice, and it is no business of society's whether a woman chooses to shave her legs or wax down there or not – however, I have to say that when one's lady garden has reached the verdant state of Louisa's, then leaping about nude in a room filled with candles is not advisable, not from a grooming point of view, but simply due to the fire hazards involved. Midway through the recitation, Louisa paused and throatily intoned, 'Join me, sisters,' and Stella jumped up and got her kit off too. Oh dear God, it was worse than the time I went to a German sauna and discovered I was expected to go in naked. Neither of them seemed to believe in underwear, which was doubly worrying given the dubious stains on all the beanbags, and I was now seriously concerned about the fire risks to be had with so much pubic hair around the naked flames. I wondered if I was unselfish enough to use my wine to douse a burning bush – probably not, I decided.

'Come on, Ellen. Join us in our liberation!' cried Louisa.

'No thank you very much, I am fine,' I muttered. I do not do nudity. I am not one of those merry souls who can prance around the house letting everything blow in the breeze. I am British and I am repressed and I am quite happy with that, if it's all the same to you. Also, I was afraid that if I *did* take my kit off, someone might nick my (almost matching – it was all black anyway, which counts) underwear.

When the horror show was finally over, and the last wobbling tit was tucked away out of sight, Louisa came over and enfolded me in a rather sweaty embrace.

'Thank you for coming, Ellen,' she said soulfully. 'I have a gift for you.'

I stiffened. Louisa's gifts are always a double-edged sword, and I braced myself for whatever her offering was. She handed me a slim booklet and beamed at me in delight.

'It's a copy of my book. All the poems I read tonight are in there, and some more. *And* I've personally inscribed it to you, and signed it. And dated it.'

'Oh, thank you, Louisa!' Actually, as gifts from Louisa go, it wasn't as bad as it could have been – for my birthday last year she had given me a list of all the ways she thought I should 'detox technology' from my life and make it more like hers. 'That's very thoughtful of you!'

Louisa looked at me expectantly. Obviously, my thanks had not been effusive enough. I tried again. 'I'll … err … I'll treasure it. Pride of place on the bookshelf!'

Louisa cleared her throat and continued to stare at me. 'I mean, I don't think I've ever had a book signed by the author AND personalised. I'll … err … I'll really look forward to reading it!'

'That's €20, Ellen,' she said.

'Sorry?'

'The book. It's €20, please.'

'But you said it was a gift.'

Louisa sighed and smiled at me pityingly. 'It *is* a gift, Ellen. My words are a gift to all women. The gift is the words, but the book costs €20. You can't expect me to just give you it for free? I have to *live*, Ellen. And I have to cover my costs so that I can continue to spread my message to the world.

Artists can't just give their work away, or that cheapens its meaning.'

Many, many thoughts sprang to my mind. Not least, that being asked to pay €20 for a book that appeared to be about fifteen pages long and printed and bound at home was a fucking iniquity, followed by indignation that Louisa seriously expected me to pay her for a book of shitty poems *that I didn't even want* while she was living rent-free in a house that I had paid for. But the other women were circling balefully and I was terrified that if I refused to cough up, they might make me sit in a circle with them and talk about my *feelings* and ask me where I thought the source of my rage came from (Louisa. The source of my rage was definitely Louisa), and frankly, given the option of forking out €20 or having to endure another second with Louisa and her acolytes, the €20 suddenly seemed cheap at the price, just to be able to escape.

Back at the bijou chateau, Simon looked at my face and handed me a brimming glass of wine. 'That bad?' he said anxiously.

I nodded. 'Do you have any fags?' I whispered feebly. Simon looked shifty – we are both supposed to have given up smoking but have a tendency to relapse in times of extremis. It is extraordinary how often these relapses coincide with spending time with his sister.

'I *might* have bought a packet of Gauloises when I popped down to the village this afternoon,' he admitted. 'But you left me alone with all those children all night, AND I have deal with the kids on my own for the rest of the week while you swan off back to work. It's no wonder I'm stressed enough to start smoking again!'

'I'm not *judging* you for it. Gimme one! I need to cleanse my soul with more than just booze. And I'd rather reek of Gauloises than –' I sniffed at my jumper – 'patchouli oil or whatever it is I've come home smelling of. And "all those children" are your nieces and nephews, and I'm sure you'll not be overwhelmed looking after your own children once I've gone. Your mother will step in, I'm sure. She has told me at least six times since we arrived how "tired" you are looking and how worried she is that me working full-time to is "too much" for you.'

Simon made a non-committal noise about this, but he dutifully handed over the cigarettes and we went onto the terrace, where I filled him in on the night's events, as he turned paler and paler.

'Oh, fuck my life!' he said. 'Can she get any worse?'

I assured him that Louisa most certainly could get worse, because as I'd fled out the door she had shouted after me that she would be holding a masturbation workshop the next afternoon that she thought might be beneficial for me, as she could tell that my yoni's chakras were very blocked. I had, of course, declined, and Gypsy and the other women also murmured that they thought they had something on.

'Thank fuck!' said Simon. 'I seriously can't think of anything more disturbing than my wife and my sister sitting in a circle and wanking.'

And they say romance is dead …

Saturday, 18 February

Hurrah and huzzah, the au pair arrived today! She is French and her name is Juliette, which was slightly disappointing, as I had hoped that her name would be Marie-Claire and she would *habite en* La Rochelle, like in my French book at school. She does not *habite en* La Rochelle, she *habites en* Limoges. I don't know anything about Limoges, apart from it is famous for china, whereas I knew quite a bit about La Rochelle.

Juliette is very quiet, and has spent most of her time in her room so far, though she has only been here a few hours. I am also starting to panic about what I am supposed to *do* with an au pair. The agency guidelines said she can do 'light housework'. What constitutes 'light' housework? Dusting? What about hoovering? My hoover is very heavy. Should I buy a new hoover so it counts as 'light housework'? Also, what about wine? If we're having a glass of wine, do I offer her one? I mean, she's French, so she probably pours wine on her cornflakes (not that she probably eats cornflakes, it'll be croissants or pains au chocolate), but I don't want to set a bad example. Is one even allowed to drink in front of an au pair? I DON'T KNOW! Also, is it OK to just leave her a list of the 'light housework' I want done, or is that rude? Should I simply let her decide what needs to be done?

She is also not being very helpful on the whole helping me to learn French front, because when I very politely asked her if she *voudrais allezing à la discothèque*, she sort of winced and asked if I wouldn't mind speaking to her in English, as she was hoping to improve her English while she is here. As her English is pretty perfect already, I suspect it was my *diabolique* French accent that was the issue. Or maybe she was just worried I might want to *allez à la discothèque* with her.

We have all been playing super-happy families today, and pretending we are perfectly normal and functional and *of course* we always spend our Saturday afternoons playing board games and having cheery singsongs (the board games were done grudgingly, but there was mutiny over the singsong). Juliette seemed unconvinced.

I really think this is going to make a massive difference, though. With Juliette able to pick up the kids every day, there will no longer be the fraught tag-teaming between Simon and me as we frantically race to After-School Club and Breakfast Club and snarl that it's not our turn and argue furiously over whose job is more important and thus who gets to stay late at work. We shall be calm and neither of us will feel that the other's job takes precedence over their own, and oh my God, Juliette might even babysit so we can go out together as a couple on a regular basis and we will fall in love all over again and it will be very romantic and wonderful!

Simon's only comment on Juliette so far is that she seems 'very French'.

Wednesday, 22 February

Juliette is a wonder! I love Juliette! I never want Juliette to leave! She cooks the children strange French food, complete with bits and with vegetables, *and they eat it*! It turns out Peter is quite capable of using a knife and fork, after a dismissive comment from Juliette about how uncivilised he is and how much she dislikes such nonsense. As Peter is quite hopelessly in love with Juliette, he immediately abandoned eating his potatoes with his fingers and began using cutlery. I have begged Peter for *years* to have some semblance of table manners, pleading with him that a fork is not to be used simply to scrape food directly off his plate and into his mouth, which he has lowered to plate level. He has even stopped farting and inviting you to guess what he's been eating.

And Jane! Jane has decided Juliette is the epitome of everything cool, and since Juliette wants to be a lawyer, not an Instagram influencer, Jane has decided to be a lawyer too. Juliette told Jane that Instagram was only fun for looking at photos and wasn't a viable career option, and Jane, Jane who a few months ago was screaming at me for ruining her life for saying exactly the same thing, nodded sagely and said she quite agreed.

Simon and I have not had a row in the last three days, which is possibly a world record, and actually watched a TV programme together tonight (admittedly with Juliette there too, so there was no romance, etc., but it was still very civilised).

The 'light housework' is proving *slightly* more problematic, as in I'm not actually sure Juliette has done any – even emptying the dishwasher seems beyond her, so I am having to clear up after her when I come in from work – but to be honest, that is a small price to pay for all her many excellent qualities. It's just a pain in the arse that she had already said before she started that she will be going home for a fortnight over our school holidays, but it's not an insurmountable problem because long before Juliette came into our lives and started persuading my precious moppets to eat lentils (LENTILS! They ate LENTILS! And said they enjoyed them!), I had already booked myself one of the weeks off work and asked Simon to book the other one off, so we are covered, even if the children may revert to their usual pursuit of scurvy in her absence.

MARCH

Wednesday, 1 March

It's Jane's birthday. I can't believe my baby girl is twelve! Twelve somehow seems so much more grown up than eleven. I know it's such a cliché, but in some ways it doesn't seem that long since we were celebrating her first birthday. In other ways it seems like forever. I was looking at photos of her first birthday last night, and Simon and I were so young (and so thin, in my case), it feels like a lifetime ago, not eleven years. Though I suppose technically it *was* Jane's lifetime ago.

It's true that Mother Nature somehow erases your memories of the worst parts of dealing with babies and toddlers. After yet more rows with Jane about her need for inappropriate clothes, over-priced make-up and ruinously expensive electronics for her birthday, I rather longed for those simpler days when one could just do a smash and grab round the Early Learning Centre, flinging anything that looked vaguely age-appropriate and quiet into your basket, safe in the knowledge that it didn't really matter what you bought anyway, as the birthday child would really only be interested in trying to eat the wrapping paper and playing with the boxes that the presents came in. One forgets, of course, the mind-crushing daily tedium of it all – the tantrums because their sandwich is too sandwichey and the crisps too crispy and the blue plate, the blue plate that they screamed for and could not consider eating off anything else. Well, the blue plate is now just too fucking blue. Those long, long days with *Peppa Pig* being your only hope of getting to go for a piss in peace, and where every cup of tea was a potential death trap, determined as your precious moppet was to hurl it over themselves, which basically meant you never got a hot cup of tea, ever.

Sarah is still struggling with Baby Orla and ringing me nightly in the misguided belief that I will be able to offer wisdom. What does one say? 'Well, Sarah, yes, this bit isn't much fun when they scream and scream and you don't know why they're screaming, because despite everyone telling you that you would know what all your baby's different cries meant, it turns out that most babies only have one cry, and that is screaming like a fucking banshee, so you have to run through the full list of potential problems – too hot/too cold/wanting a cuddle/wanting to be put down/hungry/wind/needing to be changed every bastarding time they squawk. So you *think* it will be better when they are a toddler and they can walk and talk a bit, but that's when the fun really starts because now you spend your days chasing around after Conan the Destroyer of Houses, and, oh, yes, it's *amazing* when they say their first words, especially when it's "Mama" or "Dada" (and by the way, Sarah, hopefully Orla will be more communicative with her first words than Jane, whose first word was "No" and whose second word was "Bugger", which was more than a little mortifying and I have no idea where she got it from). But the thing is, then they never fucking shut up, not ever, they babble and babble and really, although you want to be interested and fascinated and hang on their every word, the truth is that toddlers talk a load of bollocks, and very dull bollocks at that. But hey ho, you have to hang in there pretending to listen, because Important

Development, and then you think, well, when they start school, that will be easier, and then you end up spending every morning screaming yourself hoarse about SHOES, TEETH, PUT YOUR COAT ON, GET IN THE CAR, and arguing about long division and losing letters from the school, and then you have to deal with them being teenagers, which will probably be a whole new bundle of laughs, but luckily sometimes they do go to sleep so you can look at them lying there, all rosy-cheeked and innocent and pure and think, "Ahhhh! They're perfect! I wouldn't change anything!" Until they wake up and you just want to lock yourself in a cupboard with a bottle of gin. But the bits when they are asleep are pretty good.' Oh, Fuck My Life! I'm going to have a teenager next year! How did this happen? Never mind Sarah's wails about Orla, I am going to be the mother of a teenager. I'm not sure whether that made Sarah feel better or worse.

Anyway, I am not going to think about my last year before teenagerdom. I'm sure it will be fine. I was a teenager once, so I'm certain I'll cope. Oh God, I was an awful teenager. Please don't let Jane be a teenager like me!

Having been denied every single thing she wanted in the world, Jane did hold me to my promise of getting her ears pierced on her birthday. So after school (I claimed another dentist's appointment at work, after even Ed had suggested that perhaps I needed to see a specialist when I tried Women's Problems. Alan has offered me the number of his private dentist, who apparently will fix my dodgy crown in a jiffy, so I think I am going to have to have had a miraculous cure from all ailments), off we trotted to a ruinously expensive jewellers to have holes punched in my First Born's ears.

Juliette had been hopeful of coming along with us for the Great Piercing, I suspect planning on adding some bits of metal to herself, and was quite sulky when I told her that she needed to pick up Peter. Also, I was quite looking forward to a bit of time just with Jane, and was planning hot chocolate and cake extravaganzas for afterwards.

I reminded Jane all the way there that she was getting *one* hole in each ear and no more, while Jane scoffed and said she would definitely be getting more when she was older, and that she fancied a lip ring like Charlotte Baxter, who babysits for me sometimes, and maybe she would get a tattoo as well. I tried to persuade her that tattoos aren't something to be taken lightly as you have them for life and people quite often regret the stupid things they have tattooed on themselves as teenagers, and Jane scoffed more, for she is TWELVE now and thus knows EVERYTHING!

A nice lady in the jewellers made me fill in many forms absolving them of all blame should Jane get septicaemia or her ears fall off as a result of the piercings, and finally Jane was sitting in the chair ready for the momentous event. As the ladies approached her, piercing guns in hand, bearing down on her from either side, Jane turned pale.

'Mummy! I'm not sure I want to –'

THUD! It was done. Jane had turned green. 'Can we go home?' she whispered. 'I think I'm in shock!'

'Don't be silly, darling,' I said brightly. 'You can't possibly be in shock, you've only had your ears pierced. Don't you want to go for hot chocolate?'

'I need to lie down,' sniffed Jane. 'That was horrible. They put metal through my ears and I don't feel well.'

'How did you think they were going to pierce your ears?' I said in confusion.

'I don't know,' sniffed Jane. 'I thought it would be nicer. I think I'm going to be sick!'

'So how do you feel about that lip ring and tattoo now?' I asked. Jane retched.

'Please can you just take me home, Mummy, and give me a cuddle?' she whimpered.

Before we left the shop, in addition to the eleventy billion pounds I had already paid them to poke holes in my daughter's ears, the nice lady insisted I buy a special bottle of stuff for cleaning the piercings, as apparently TCP no longer is deemed good enough, despite it being fine when I had my ears pierced, and indeed being my preferred cure-all for most ailments. It was worth every penny, actually, to have Jane for once stop pretending that she was about twenty-seven and starring in an American soap opera, and instead go back to being the little girl that she was for a while. I made the most of her wanting to be cuddled, as I suspect it will be a long time before I get the chance again.

Jane spent the rest of the evening doing an excellent impression of a dying swan, though she did manage to rally to eat her birthday pizza. She definitely gets her hypochondria from Simon.

After the children went to bed, I finally managed to summon the strength to deal with the many, many emails for the PTA. I am at least spared organising a Mother's Day Pop-Up Shop, which apparently was very successful last year, as a mother took umbrage over this and made such a fuss about wanting a home-made gift, not marked-up Poundland tat, that I announced we would simply not fucking bother. But there was the usual barrage of messages from parents who *still* could not comprehend the difference between the PTA (fundraising) and the Parent Council (school policy), and felt the need to bombard me with emails complaining that they were very upset that Emilia's class had watched a DVD on Friday afternoon, and why was there not a police officer on permanent duty outside the school, patrolling for inconsiderate parkers and dog-shit offenders? It seems that it is frowned upon to reply to these messages with a simple 'Fuck off, I don't give a rat's arse.'

Friday, 3 March

I am starting to wonder if Juliette is the angel from above that I first thought her to be. She is very good with the children, of course, but the issue of her helping out a bit in the house is still ongoing. Not only does she not actually do anything all day, but she is now actively creating mess – tonight I came home to crisp packets and yoghurt pots strewn around the sitting room, and the load of laundry that I had put in the machine this morning and politely asked her to either hang out or pop in the tumble drier, depending on whether or not it was pissing down, had been removed from the washing machine and dumped sodden in a basket, while she washed her own stuff.

I gently attempted to raise this with her, and she gave a Gallic shrug and pretended she didn't understand, despite her excellent English at any other time.

She remembered her English in time to appear in an extraordinary lack of clothing and announce that she was going out 'with friends' tonight, and that she would be back late, and we were not to wait up for her. I assume she is *allezing à la disco-thèque*, but she just gave me a withering look when I asked that, and made vague noises when I asked how late was 'late'.

Should I have just let her go off into the night wearing hardly anything at all? We are responsible for her, after all, but then again, she isn't a child – technically she's an adult. And at what time do I decide it has gone past 'late' and she's now officially missing, and call the police to admit that I let an eighteen-year-old girl with a selective grasp of English go out to an unspecified location with unknown friends and no set time to return without looking like a very callous and uncaring person? Also, if she gets herself murdered, it will really fuck up my lovely new childcare arrangements. No, no, of course I'm not even thinking that. I'm just concerned for Juliette's welfare. The childcare is the least of it. Well, it's not *all* of it, anyway, although I found a banana skin under a sofa cushion just now and am feeling slightly less concerned for her welfare.

Saturday, 11 March

Oh God, oh God, oh FML. There is not enough booze in the world to numb the ringing in my ears or the aching of my head or the black void where my soul used to be. Today was Jane's birthday party. A birthday party should be a relatively simple thing to organise. Some balloons, a cake, a game of pass the parcel, a few rounds of musical chairs – jolly good, here's a party bag with a mini Mars Bar and one of those squawker things. Now fuck off home, kid!

Oh no. No. Firstly, Jane decreed it must be a disco party. Disco parties are the thing this term. You are no one if your party is not a disco party with Disco Dave the DJ on the decks. Despite my attempts at suggesting maybe it would be fun for Jane to do something different, nothing would do but Disco Dave in the Church Hall.

I was a good mummy. In fact, I was a bloody excellent mummy! I booked the hall, I booked Disco Dave, I nobly refrained from asking Disco Dave if he would also be bringing Black Bess when he told me the iniquitous price he charges for his services, I toyed with baking a cake, I ordered one from Asda

instead with 'Jane Is TWELVE' printed on it and some butter-
flies, I got cramp in my hand spending an entire evening writing
out invitations for the whole bastarding class on the basis I
might as well get my money's worth out of Disco Dave, and then
the texts started coming in in reply to my invitation:

Hi we always go swimming on Sat afternoons, could u have party on Sun? x

Hi Ellen, Tilly would love to come but can you pick her up and drop her off
because I'm busy? Xxx

Oscar can't come at 2.30 he will be there at 3.30 x

Hi, is it OK if I bring Milly's brothers too? They love parties! Xxx

Olivia doesn't like disco parties, what about getting a magician instead?x

And so on. And so on. And so on. WTAF? What is wrong with
these people? Either your child can come to the party or not!
When did it become acceptable to demand that the party is
changed to suit you, or to bring extra kids or make conditions
for your child coming? Do I not have enough to fucking do
trying to juggle my own life, doing a trolley dash round
Sainsbury's after work last night envying all the bastards with
their baskets of wine and artisanal bread as I hurled armloads of
frozen pizzas and chicken nuggets in the trolley, before getting
home in time to let Juliette go out before she had a massive
French hissy fit at me? Bah fucking humbug was my view on the
world by the time we actually got to the hall for the party itself.

Disco Dave, it turned out, in my opinion should be renamed
Deviant Dave. A most dubious-looking gentleman. I resolved to
make sure he was not left alone with any of the children. And

then the children started to arrive. There had been several rows with Jane about the amount of make-up she was allowed to wear for her party, and about the party outfit itself, as apparently my idea of a party frock was nothing short of ruining her life, whereas her idea of a party frock wouldn't have looked out of place on a Marseilles hooker. (I assume. I have never actually seen a Marseilles hooker and I may be unfairly maligning them, but it was my own mother's favourite accusation about some of my more daring clubbing outfits in my youth.) We eventually found a compromise (I said, 'You can wear this or I'll cancel the whole thing'), Jane muttering darkly that it was not fair and everyone else was allowed to wear stuff like that, while I poo-pooed her and told her not to be ridiculous.

As it turned out, Jane was right. The boys were fairly ordinary in chinos and shirts but the girls! Oh my God, the girls! Fake tan, heels, fake eyelashes, make-up put on with a trowel, hot pants and boob tubes. One eleven-year-old had stuffed the front of her boob tube with so many tissues she looked like a tiny Dolly Parton. Part of me felt very judgemental, but part of me also felt very sad that these little girls felt the need to smother their peaches-and-cream skin with fake tan and foundation and totter around in heels while they were still getting their feet measured at Clarks. What made it even sadder was that once the party got going, they were quite obviously still little girls, as they kicked off their heels and screamed over Musical Bumps. Milly Fortescue was sick after too many chicken nuggets, Olivia Johnson cried because she lost at Pass the Parcel, and Jack Williams got locked in the lavatory and had to be broken out. The noise levels were unbelievable, and Disco Dave's patter was distinctly dodgy. It is done for another year, though, and next year I am going to put my foot down and insist on something small and intimate.

Thursday, 16 March

I came home from work tonight to find Juliette had actually tidied up, including putting the hoover round, and as well as feeding the children, she had made a casserole for Simon and me. I had had a long and shit day at work, and I could have kissed her when I walked in to find a clean and tidy house, with delicious smells bubbling away in the kitchen, instead of the swamp of crisp packets that is her usual habitat.

'You look tired, Ellen!' she said. 'Sit down and I will get you a glass of wine! Simon got in about twenty minutes ago. He looked tired too. You both work so hard!'

'What an angel this girl is,' I thought dreamily. 'What are a few crisp packets and late nights?' (Having failed to be murdered thus far, I have stopped fretting quite so much when she disappears on a Friday night in a skirt up to her unmentionables, trying to remind myself that after all, we were all young once.)

We were tucking into a frankly delicious boeuf bourgignon, while Juliette hovered, asking if we wanted any more wine or bread or salad, when she suddenly announced that she would like her 'boyfriend' to stay over tomorrow night.

Simon choked on a chunk of beef, and I inhaled my wine.

'Err, I didn't know you had a boyfriend, Juliette,' I said. 'Is he a friend from Limoges?'

'Non!' said Juliette. 'I met him at a bar. His name is Harry!'

Harry. A terrible part of me thought it could be worse. Harry is quite a middle-class name.

'And what does he do?'

'He is at college.'

'And what is he studying?'

Juliette gave one of her shrugs. 'So it is OK, yes, Harry can stay tomorrow?'

'I'm really not sure, Juliette. I'll need to discuss it with Simon. And also, how would your parents feel about you having a boy to stay over?'

Juliette snarled something that sounded like a French version of 'OMG, you are RUINING MY LIFE!' and stomped out of the kitchen.

'Fucking hell, Simon. What are we going to *do*?' I wailed. 'We are supposed to be *in loco parentis*. Can we just condone her shagging some random in our house?'

'She's eighteen, though. Not a child.'

'I know, but even so. I'm not sure I want sweaty teenage sex going on in my spare room, those are 300-thread-count sheets.' (I could hear my bloody mother coming out of my mouth.) 'And who is he? What if he steals things? And if we let Juliette have this boy to stay, how are we going to refuse when Jane wants a boy to stay? Or Peter wants to bring a girl home? Or you know, vice versa!'

'I can't talk about this, Ellen. I can't discuss an eighteen-year-old girl's sex life, it's *wrong*. You're going to have to sort it out.'

'Me? Why me? Why do I have to sort everything out?'

'I just told you. It's not *appropriate* for me to get involved.'

'Oh, that's just such a fucking cop-out! What about if it was Jane? Would you leave me to sort it all out then, too? Oh, don't bloody answer, I know you would!'

I eventually plucked up the courage to go up to Juliette's room and explain that we weren't entirely sure about her having a house guest just yet (house guest. Ha! Like I didn't know he was a fuck buddy), but she was more than welcome to bring Harry round for dinner and to meet the family.

Juliette looked utterly appalled at this and muttered '*Merde*' to my suggestion, which I took to mean that she wasn't keen on the idea of Harry joining us for a delightful dinner *en famille* instead of the rampant shag fest she had planned.

She is sulking, and I fear there will be no more boeuf bourgignon forthcoming.

Monday, 27 March

I swear to God that right at this moment, I might fucking kill Simon. Literally kill him, possibly with my bare hands by tearing off his head in a Hulk-style fit of rage. The fury began with a casual email around lunchtime.

> Hi sweetheart,
> I've just found out I'm going to have to go to Singapore for three weeks, leaving on Thursday. We don't have anything planned, do we?
> See you later xxx

'We don't have anything planned?' WE DON'T HAVE ANYTHING FUCKING PLANNED? No, Simon, no, nothing planned, ONLY THE TWO FUCKING WEEKS THAT THE CHILDREN ARE OFF SCHOOL AND JULIETTE IS IN FRANCE AND THAT YOU PROMISED ME, THAT YOU ACTUALLY SWORE TO ME, THAT YOU WOULD BE TAKING THE FIRST WEEK OFF, TO COVER CHILDCARE! OTHER THAN THAT, HEE FUCKING HAW!

Anger pulsing through me so strongly that I could actually feel a vein in my temple throbbing, I almost broke my keyboard hammering out my reply, which nonetheless, I felt, was extremely restrained under the circumstances, if only because both our work email servers filter out obscenities.

You can't go to Singapore, the kids break up for the holidays on Friday, and
Juliette is going home to see her family. Two weeks, I was taking one week off,
and you were taking the other. They can't ask you to go away when you've got
annual leave booked.

He replied:

Hi Babe
Thing is, I didn't actually book the time off yet, because I thought Juliette would
be there. And I have to go. Steve Parker was meant to be going, but he's got
shingles and there's no one else to go and oversee this part of the project. Really
sorry, but I'm sure you'll cope. Maybe you could work something out with Sam?
    Xxx

FUCK OFF SIMON! He's 'sure I'll cope'? That's nice, isn't it? I'll
just magic a fucking childminder OUT OF MY ARSE, will I?
Because obviously it is super easy to just book last-minute childcare for the holidays, because it's not like any other fucker needs
holiday childcare, is it? And maybe I could 'work something out
with Sam'? Yes, Sam and I often help each other out with childcare, it's true, but it's still not Sam's responsibility to step into the
bastarding breach and save the day because my own twatting
husband is too fucking busy and important to look after his own
children! And anyway, Sam's taking Sophie and Toby to
Fuerteventura for the fortnight.

Since I couldn't express my true feelings in an email, I waited
till Simon got home and pointed all this out to him. Foolishly, he
didn't seem to think it was such a big deal.

'Well, can't you just take a few extra days off, or book them
into a sports camp or something?' he suggested.

'NO,' I shrieked. 'I can't "just book them into a sports camp"'
because all the places were filled weeks ago and I didn't think I

needed to book any slots due to us having a long conversation about how I would take one week and you would take the other. So now I can't get a childminder or a camp or any kind of cover at all. Because *you* were supposed to be looking after *your* children!'

'Why do you have to make everything such a drama?' complained Simon. 'Is it so impossible for you to take a few more days off? I really don't see what the big deal is. Other people's wives seem to cope with the holidays.'

'You don't see what the big deal is?' I hissed dangerously. 'Why don't you take the time off then, if it's not a "big deal"? For years I turned down promotions and sacrificed the chance of a proper career so I could be there for the children, because we *agreed*, we discussed and we agreed that if we could manage financially with one of us working part-time, then that's we should do. So that's what I did, and now the children are older and I am FINALLY able to work full-time in a job I actually QUITE ENJOY, and that gives me some small sense of FUCKING FULFILLMENT, you still expect me to drop everything and just cover for you because you still think YOUR job is SO MUCH MORE FUCKING IMPORTANT THAN MINE?'

'You're overreacting, darling. All I've asked you to do is take a few extra days off and all of a sudden you're ranting about how I've ruined your life!'

'Because you say it's "just a few days" but it's always me who has to take those few days. Like it's always me who has to arrange the childcare, keep track of the birthday parties, take time off for concerts and assemblies and sick days, while you blithely swan around like none of this is anything to do with you with you whatsoever, but THEY ARE YOUR CHILDREN TOO!'

'For fuck's sake, you are just ranting at me now. Just discuss things rationally.'

'Discuss things rationally? We agreed that when I went full-time that we would share the childcare, NOT that you could abdicate all responsibilities as a father and just fuck off to FUCKING SINGAPORE at the drop of a fucking hat whenever you felt like it. We're SUPPOSED to be a team, but you seem to think it's only about facilitating you, because do you know, not once in all these years have you EVER taken any time off in the holidays to cover childcare. Not once!'

'That's not true. You're twisting things to suit yourself. I took half-term off, remember? Half-term, so YOU could go back to work and leave me on my own to deal with the kids all week, and then I had to cope with getting the kids back from France by myself, which was a bundle of fucking laughs, let me tell you!'

'Oh, please! It's hardly the same. For a start, you didn't take half-term off to help me out. You took it off to visit your parents, and THEY looked after them all week. Much like you would probably have expected me to look after them if I'd been there. And they're not exactly toddlers that taking a car journey and ferry ride with them is such an insurmountable problem. But yes, I do know you found it very challenging because you whined like a bitch for weeks afterwards, and now you actually think your voluntary trip to see your parents, even knowing I couldn't take the whole week off, is somehow equivalent to you trying to land me with this whole shit-show?'

'Oh, it's always about you, isn't it? It's always about how hard done by you are, how difficult you find things, how much you have to juggle, isn't it? And what YOU want, and what YOU need? What about ME, Ellen? What about what I want?'

'NOTHING IS ABOUT ME!' I screamed. 'THAT'S THE WHOLE POINT! NOTHING IS EVER ABOUT ME, IT'S ALWAYS ABOUT SOMEONE ELSE. WHAT THE FUCK DO YOU JUGGLE? If I want to work late, I have to ask you if you could possibly pick up the children and you act like you're doing me a FUCKING FAVOUR, but if you want to work late, you just do it and assume someone will accommodate you! So are we only to think about what YOU want? And what DO you fucking want?'

'I want a wife who supports me! I want a wife who is FUCKING THERE FOR ME AND ACTUALLY PUTS HER FAMILY FIRST, NOT HER FUCKING JOB!'

'How DARE you say I don't put this family first! When do you put US first? Or do you not have to bother because you are a MAN? Is it only a woman who is supposed to be a good little wife, and stay at home in her pinny, making sure her lord and FUCKING MASTER'S dinner is piping hot on the table when he gets home? Lipstick freshly applied and welcoming smile in place? And no fucking matter what SHE wants, BECAUSE SHE'S ONLY A WOMAN! So I am not allowed to have any ambitions, then? Is being a wife and mother supposed to be ENOUGH? Is "supporting your career" meant to take the place of having a career of my own? And I DID support you. I still do. I have been supporting you in your chosen career for years, and what fucking thanks do I get in return?

'Maybe if you had ever been a bit more flexible, I could have got much further in my own career by now, instead of all those years of having everyone glaring at me because I'm leaving at lunchtime again because it's Sports Day or I've had to miss a meeting because one of the kids is ill, but it's never ever you who picks up the slack, is it? And maybe my whole career would've been fucked up anyway because I had kids because I wouldn't be paid as much and I would have missed promotions while I was on maternity leave, or been passed over for fear I might go off again, but isn't it bad enough that society is trying to fucking screw mothers over anyway, WITHOUT THEIR OWN

HUSBANDS DOING IT TOO?? JESUS FUCKING CHRIST, is it any wonder that I let my colleagues think I didn't have any children after all the years of seeing how mothers are treated in the workplace?'

'Ellen, I'm not sure how we've got from me going on a business trip that I really can't get out of, to society's oppression of women on maternity leave, but – hang on! You've LIED to your employers about having children? What the fuck? You can't do that! Why would you do that? HOW could you do that, why would you deny your own children? What if you get sacked?'

'Why would I "deny" my own children?' I said furiously. 'You pretty much do. You don't let them interfere with your working life, so why should I? You're every bit as much a parent as I am, but nobody judges you, do they? So why should they judge me? And I won't get sacked, because my boss knows I have children, but he doesn't like people so he mainly hides in his office and only communicates by email unless he is absolutely forced into a meeting, and then he goes back to hide again. He's actually literally the most perfect boss you could ever have. And HR know too, but they never come down to our floor. It's only my immediate colleagues I OMITTED to mention the children to, and I'm not FUCKING SORRY, because people treat you differently when you're a mother. They shouldn't, but they do!'

'And what about me?' yelped Simon. 'Have you airbrushed me out of the picture too? Are you some sexy single lady now?'

'THIS ISN'T FUCKING ABOUT YOU!' I yelled. 'This isn't even about whether or not people at work know about the children. This is about YOUR fucking attitude to OUR LIFE and your assumption that I will just MAKE EVERY FUCKING THING HAPPEN and all you have to think about is yourself! It's like the way I am still doing almost all the cleaning and laundry and housework, even though we were meant to share that too when I went full-time, but you still don't fucking bother!'

'So get Juliette to do it!'

'See? SEE? Why do *I* have to get Juliette to do it? Why can't YOU get Juliette to do it?'

'Well, if you don't want to ask Juliette, get a cleaner!' said Simon.

'I don't WANT a fucking cleaner!' I shrieked. 'Well, that's not true, I would quite like a cleaner, but I worry I'd feel guilty about exploiting someone, and anyway, I'd still have to clean before they came so they didn't judge me, but that's NOT THE POINT! The point is, if we got a cleaner, it should be because we'd both decided that there was just too much for us BOTH to do with looking after the children and the house and working full-time. We shouldn't have to get a cleaner just because YOU can't be arsed pulling YOUR weight. And you STILL assume that it is something that *I* will arrange because that's "my job", you fucking arrogant arsehole.'

'I really don't understand what your problem is. You complain about childcare, we get an au pair. You complain about cleaning the house, I say get a cleaner, but that's not good enough. What the fuck do you want, Ellen?'

'I WANT you to take an equal responsibility for this family!' I howled. 'I WANT you to take responsibility for your children and share the childcare, I want you to pick up your own festering pants instead of leaving them lying around for me, I WANT you stop acting like you are somehow above all the petty fucking little trials and tribulations of life, just because you're a fucking MAN. And I WANT you to stop assuming that you can just do what you like and I will just somehow cope. All you had to do was listen to me and book a bastarding week off work. But you fucking didn't!'

'No, I didn't, did I, so it's too late to complain about that now. If it was that fucking important, YOU should've made it clearer to me. I really don't know what else you want me to do. And if I'm such a terrible parent, how come YOU'RE the one going around LYING to people about whether you even have children!'

'Oh, go fuck yourself!' I snapped. 'Right now, I wish I didn't have children. OR A FUCKING HUSBAND!'

'Be careful what you wish for, Ellen,' he said coldly. 'It might just come true.'

Arrogant bastard.

It's a strange thing, marriage, isn't it? You meet someone, you fall in love with them, you realise you can't live without each other, you stand up in front of all your friends and family to vow to spend the rest of your lives together, and you know that on one level, a part of your heart and soul would be wrenched out if this person were no longer in your life, but on another level, you have seriously considered googling 'how to kill someone with a tube of toothpaste' should the inconsiderate TWAT continue to squeeze the toothpaste in the middle instead of rolling it up neatly from the bottom LIKE A NORMAL PERSON.

I once thought that the longer we lived together, the less Simon's 'little foibles' would annoy me, but if anything they have become more irritating over time. Not to mention that part of being married is knowing someone so well that you know exactly what buttons to push to wind them up, like when Simon tuts and rolls his eyes and makes his 'I am a saint to put up with this' face, when I ask him for the eleventy fucking billionth time to take the bins out and I contemplate where in the woods behind the park would be the best place to dig a shallow grave.

Maybe it's just that all the little things add up – all the unre-placed loo rolls, all the overflowing bins, all the pairs of pants left tangled up inside the legs of his jeans for me to remove, because I obviously have no other fucking things to do. So many little things, over the course of a lifetime, that mean the love of your life is also the most annoying fucker you have ever met. No one told me it would be this hard, skipping up that aisle, ready for a life of married bliss, completely unaware that most of marriage consists of trying to remember that prison is not very nice, and you are probably too middle class to ever make 'Top Dog' and be allowed the trouser press.

APRIL

Wednesday, 5 April

Well, after all the ranting and raving furiously about me YET AGAIN being the one who either has to call in favours or take yet more annual leave, along with outrage about why I am always the one who has to arrange the childcare, after frantic googling and phoning round, I managed to get the children booked into an all-day sports camp for the first week of the holidays – i.e., the week that BASTARDING SIMON was supposed to take off, and since he had fucked off to sunny Singapore, instead of entertaining my precious moppets for the second week of the holidays that I had so carefully booked off months ago, I decided that when it came to the rage and stress, I would simply chuck it in the fuck-it bucket and I have booked a last-minute trip to Lanzarote for the children and me, which to be honest costs about the same as a week's worth of cinema/Laser Quest/McDonald's trips to keep them happy.

Also, we are even staying in a hotel, which Simon will never countenance because People and also because he apparently 'has enough' of hotels because he stays in them for work all the time. Oh, to be given the chance to 'have enough' of hotels! I can but dream. Not only that, but I just booked the hotel because it looked nice and didn't even consult TripAdvisor. Simon worships obsessively at the Oracle that is TripAdvisor – we are not allowed to go anywhere with less than a five-star rating. And even if a place has five stars, and eleventy fucking billion good reviews, woe betide them if in 2013 one person left them a two-star review. That is the establishment immediately crossed off Simon's list as sub-par. It is very fucking annoying.

In the meantime, in his absence, we are happily living on pasta (not considered by Simon to be a Proper Dinner, unless it is bastarding lasagne) and my (never very high) standards have become somewhat lax – the children were quite delighted to be permitted to eat their pesto pasta (pesto carefully blitzed to within an inch of its life so there were no offending 'bits', because they will only eat bits in Juliette's cooking – my 'bits' taste funny, apparently) and bought-in garlic bread (Simon will only eat homemade garlic bread) in front of their tablets tonight, which is something they are NEVER allowed to do when Simon is at home. Although the main reason for this is that it meant if they were slumped in front of mind-numbing electronics, then I too could pleasantly pass the time with a glass of Pinot Noir and a spot of Facebook stalking, instead of refereeing World War III, explaining yet again to Peter that really, it would be nice if he could refrain from cramming his food into his mouth so fast that he managed to bite his own finger, and listening to Jane wittering like a demented budgie about how Tilly lent Milly her Smiggle ruler and Milly lost it, and then Milly said Tilly had never lent it to her anyway and so Tilly said Milly, etc., etc., etc. Also, in Simon's absence there are no rows about whether the dog can or cannot sleep on the bed.

I feel bad sometimes that life seems to be easier without Simon, and I know it's just a temporary sensation, and that if I were on my own with the children full-time it would be very, very different to coping without him for a week or two, or likewise if he were away doing something dangerous in Afghanistan or somewhere that he might not come back from, instead of titting around the world being bored with hotel rooms. And I will probably miss him eventually, of course I will, but we have been married for so long now that actually, other than the massive bastarding childcare issue, it's quite nice when he goes away and then when he comes back it's like things are a bit more exciting again, instead of him just lolling on the sofa in front of *Wheeler* Fucking *Dealers* (I swear to God that I thought he was going to cry when Edd China left, and now he refuses to watch any of the newer episodes that don't have Edd, which means I have now seen every single wretched episode at least five times, even though there are ELEVENTY FUCKING BILLION of them).

I wonder if I should tell Simon we are going on holiday while he is away?

Thursday, 6 April

Hmmmm. I have not entirely thought through this 'going on holiday' thing. Firstly, the children will need shorts and T-shirts and sandals and such like, all of which they have inconsiderately outgrown since last summer. Since I only just came to this real-isation today, and I have no time to visit actual shops, I have had to spend an absolute bastarding fortune panic-buying them stuff online, and paying through the nose to have next-day delivery, as we are leaving on Saturday morning, so my splendid bargain holiday is rapidly becoming somewhat less bargain-acious! Astonishingly, I have also had to buy myself a new and rather slinky swimming costume for the occasion, as it turns out that those HIIT classes and disgusting salads have made a difference and while I would not exactly call myself skinny, I am definitely less chunky. I still have hopes of one day inventing the Pie Yourself Thin diet, but in the meantime it is jolly nice not to feel like a beached whale in my swimming costume, anxiously scanning the horizon lest Greenpeace appear and try to refloat me.

All this obviously then led to a hissy fit from Jane because she had not been allowed to choose her own clothes, because there wasn't time if I wanted everything to arrive tomorrow, and also because shopping online with Jane is no less soul-destroying than shopping in shops with Jane (well, OK, it is *slightly* less infuriating because you can at least drink wine while you are doing it), as she spends hours deliberating over exactly which of what appear to be six identical T-shirts is the one that takes her fancy. In fairness, she gets this helpful trait from Simon, who is equally impossible to shop with, which means I am always astounded by women who remark that they buy all their husband's clothes. I do buy him socks sometimes. When he's not being annoying.

I still haven't actually told Simon that we are going away. This is definitely not a problem though, as he is not due back until after us. I could always leave a note, like Shirley Valentine, in case he comes home early: 'Gone to the Canaries – see you in a week!'

Sunday, 9 April

Well, this is actually jolly nice! I am sitting most happily by a pool in the sunshine with a lovely cocktail, reading my book, while my precious moppets put the obscene amount of money spent on their swimming lessons to good use by splashing and frolicking merrily, and I'm actually feeling really rather chilled out! I even cleared all my emails and, under orders from Ed, who said I was looking very stressed out (couldn't really tell him that was more to do with my twatbag husband than work), switched on my out of office before I left, as he insisted that there is nothing currently happening at work that was so crucial that it couldn't wait till I got back.

We arrived mid-afternoon yesterday, after an incident-free journey, largely because Simon wasn't with us to turn Checking-In and Finding the Gate into a piece of dramatic performance art. The children, who had never travelled without their father, were astonished to find how many things there are to do/look at/eat/buy in airports when they are not being hustled rapidly to the gate.

Freed from Simon's Gate Tyranny, we browsed Duty Free. Well, I say browsed, Jane and I browsed while I kept a firm grip on Peter and promised to buy him a giant bar of Toblerone if he refrained from trying to touch anything. This bribery worked for just long enough for me to purchase one of the magical make-up kits that you only get in the airports that contain everything you could ever need, yet are small enough to pop in your handbag, thus making me feel like a jet-setting cosmopolitan traveller. Perhaps next I will invest in one of those 'holiday capsule wardrobes' they always witter on about in magazines, where all you need to take on holiday is a bikini, two small scarves and a pair of sparkly flip-flops, and somehow you magically knit them together into a variety of cunning 'night and day' outfits. Possibly not. I suspected that the travel writers who recommend these 'packing essentials' might be talking bollocks when I saw one who recommended taking a nice sponge bag on holiday because it could 'easily double up as a glamorous evening clutch bag'. I am sorry, but I have never, EVER seen a sponge bag that you could pass off as an evening bag. It was telling that there was no photo of *her* magic sponge/clutch bag.

Against my better judgement, I also bought Jane some mascara, which she insisted on putting on at once, which led to me having to explain to the startled flight attendant as we were boarding that she wasn't sporting two black eyes, she'd just got a bit carried away!

In another fit of rebellion against Simon's holiday strictures, I'd gone mad and booked us all-inclusive. I've always fancied the idea of all-inclusive. Just the very name is joyous – all you can eat and drink, what's not to love? Simon contends that it means you are restricted to eating in the hotel, and that you should go out and enjoy the local culture and restaurants, and all-inclusive is for people who want to go to Spain and eat egg and chips. I would agree he has a small point about supporting the local businesses as well as the big hotels, but I must say I am also loving the bliss that is all-inclusive, though I fear Peter may burst before the week is out, as he is taking his commitment to getting my money's worth out of the all-inclusiveness extremely seriously. I have never seen such joy on his face as last night, faced with the dinner buffet, when he turned to me and whispered, quite overwhelmed, 'You mean, I can have as much of everything as I want? Every day? Anything? And I can keep going back? Even for pudding? And it doesn't finish at 3 p.m.?'

I don't think I have seen Peter this happy since the first time I took to him to a Pizza Hut buffet, whereby he proceeded to demolish everything in sight until a frosty-faced waitress declared the buffet now closed, as Peter reached for one last slice of deep-pan pepperoni.

I meanwhile have resolved to take my money's worth in a more liquid form. I dutifully waited till 6 p.m. last night, as my mother has always drummed into me that drinking before then

was Bad and Wrong (a rule I frequently break at home, but for
some reason I felt Standards must be maintained when Abroad,
perhaps feeling one should Set a Good Example to the Foreigners
instead of conforming to the stereotypes about Boozed-Up,
Broken Britain), only to discover this morning by the pool that
most people start on the gin about 11 a.m., and go for a steady
drip-feed throughout the day.

I had been slightly worried that going away on my own with
the children might lead to other holidaymakers taking pity on
me, *Shirley Valentine*-style (though with Peter and Jane in tow, it
was at least unlikely that I would be receiving any offers to make
fuck on anyone's brother's boat), but actually, there are lots of
women here on their own with kids, and I have already bonded
with a nice lady from Bolton called Joanna, when she asked if I
wanted to read her copy of *Heat* magazine because she had
finished with it, and we agreed that clearly it wasn't because we
were getting old that we didn't know who anyone was in it
anymore, and then we reminisced about *More* and the Position
of the Fortnight and realised that neither of us could remember
anything about *More* apart from the Position of the Fortnight,
and then we decided that 11.30 a.m. definitely wasn't too early
for one's second cocktail of the day!

Wednesday, 12 April

I have been being very childish, I must admit, and ignoring
Simon's calls and texts – mainly because his first text upon arriving in Singapore last week had read, 'Here safe. Went to great
restaurant tonight, I think you'd have loved it!' I received this
while I was refereeing a screaming match with Peter and Jane
over whether or not I had added celery to their shepherd's pie (I

had, chopped so finely that it was invisible to the naked eye, and I KNEW they couldn't taste it, because I always add it and they've never tasted it before. They had just suspected it was there because they saw me putting the rest of the celery back in the fridge), culminating in me screaming that they could both fucking starve if they wouldn't eat what I had cooked and them threatening to phone Childline, before Jane fed hers to the dog, who gobbled it down and then promptly puked it up again, leading to screams from Jane that I had poisoned the dog with my toxic celery slop, while I responded he had only been sick because he had eaten it so fast he had choked. So I wasn't exactly overjoyed by Simon's message, and decided that I was probably better off ignoring it rather than texting what I wanted to text, which was 'Fuck off you smug wanker.'

It turned out ignoring him was actually rather satisfying, and so I didn't tell him we were going away either, until I got a very irate text today demanding to know where I was as he hadn't been able to get me on my mobile or the house phone and so had called Tim across the road, who had said that he thought that Katie had said something about me going on holiday, and so where the fuck was I, because he was about to call the police if he didn't hear from me, and report me and the children as missing.

I texted back 'Lanzarote' and ten seconds later my phone rang.

'What the FUCK are you doing in Lanzarote?' he bellowed. 'It's fucking midnight here, and I'm going out of my mind trying to find my wife and kids, thinking they've been abducted and are dead in a FUCKING DITCH, and you're sitting on a beach in LANZAROTE.'

'By the pool, actually,' I said calmly. 'I don't like the beaches here. The sand is black, which is not very aesthetically pleasing. Because of the volcanoes, you know.'

'What? Why the hell have you taken my children and gone there? How dare you not tell me?'

'Why shouldn't I take MY children on holiday? You made it very clear before you went away that all responsibility for child-care falls on me and is nothing to do with you, because you have much more important things to concern yourself with than piddling little matters like how your children are looked after in the holidays, and that such things are beneath you. So, I am sorting the childcare once again, like I ALWAYS do, only I'm doing it in Lanzarote, because why the fuck not? Am I just supposed to sit at home, twiddling my thumbs, thinking up one hundred and one things to do with fucking mince for dinner while you send me photos of the fucking Michelin-starred meals you are dining on each night? Hmmm?'

'I am here for WORK, Ellen. WORK! WORK that I do to keep a roof over YOUR head, and food on YOUR table –'

'Fuck off, Simon,' I interrupted. 'Firstly, your work is not keeping a roof over my head, because MY app paid off our fucking mortgage, remember, so you can drop that shit. You're having a fucking ball in Singapore, a couple of meetings, a couple of hours on site, and then you're out at nice bars and restaurants every evening and you're just pissed off that I might be having some fun too. So fuck you! I'm not discussing this any further. We'll talk about it when you get home.'

'And that's the other reason I was trying to get hold of you,' yelled Simon. 'I've actually managed to get things wrapped up sooner than expected, since you made such a fuss about me not being there to provide childcare, and I'll be home on Friday, only you're in fucking Lanzarote, so what's the point in me coming home early so I can look after the children like you demanded?'

'Well, we'll be home on Saturday,' I snapped. 'Because they go back to school on Monday. So thank you for your grand gesture, but unfortunately it was pointless, because it was *last* week that I needed you to help out, not next week, but of course you can't possibly be expected to know your own children's term dates, can you? Now if you will excuse me, it's time for my next cocktail, and I'll see you on Saturday!'

Somehow pressing 'end call' just isn't as satisfying as slamming an actual receiver down, but I jabbed the screen as hard as I could anyway. I considered lobbing my phone into the pool to prove some sort of point, but then I wouldn't be able to post photos of my cocktails on Facebook, so I thought better of it. One must always consider what the priorities are.

'Man trouble?' said Joanna sympathetically from the next sun lounger. 'Could be worse. I had to kick mine out for shagging the au pair. It wasn't the cheating that was so upsetting, it was finding out he was such a fucking cliché! I thought he'd have had a bit more imagination than to go for the old midlife crisis, shag-the-au-pair chestnut!'

Simon better not shag Juliette. I'll do a damn sight more than chuck him out!

Thursday, 13 April

It is astonishing, really, all the things one can do on holiday when one doesn't have Simon sulking and twitching and moaning about 'People' beside you. We have gone to the hotel discos (Jane begged me to never dance publicly again, after my 'spirited' interpretation of 'Uptown Girl' after several gin and tonics), we went on a bus trip to the markets (oh my God, so much tat! Quite a lot of it too naff to even buy in an ironic or kitsch way. There was a slightly unfortunate moment when Peter had to be hastily steered away from the pornographic keyrings, and I actually quite missed Simon, if only because the look of horror on his face at All the People, and the Wares on offer, would have been absolutely priceless), and tonight we went to the karaoke session.

I love karaoke. I am not usually allowed to do karaoke, because apparently I am tone deaf and can't sing, but I have to say I think Joanna's and my duet of 'Eternal Flame' was extremely moving and will stay with those people fortunate enough to have watched it for some time. Jane said it most certainly would, at least until their ears stopped bleeding, and forbade me to ever sing again, either publicly or privately. I think Jane is biased, though. She has never liked my singing. When she was about ten months old I took her to a baby music class, where the nice lady who took the class solemnly told us all about the importance of singing to your 'little person' and insisted it didn't matter what your voice was like, because, to your baby, it was the most beautiful sound in the world. I didn't like to tell her that Jane already put her hands over her ears and screamed 'NONONONONO!' whenever I tried to sing to her.

It has been lovely having this week with the children, though, and actually spending time just with them, with no rushing here and there. Jane has not even mentioned getting an Instagram account once, and after the first day left her precious phone in the room and didn't look at it. Even the fighting has died down, apart from the odd attempted drowning incident, which I laughed off to casual observers as 'japes and frolics'. I'm almost sure they believed me.

I think I spend too much of the time thinking of the children as pieces on a board that need to be moved from A to B or of things to be ticked off on the endless list – feed them/make sure they eat some vegetables/take them to Cubs/Guides/jiu-jitsu/ piano lessons/keep them safe from internet predators/make sure they do their homework/try to get them to read a book/teach them their times tables/make them change their pants (that's mostly Peter)/try to make sure they grow up into well-rounded and decent individuals and not the sort of people who believe everything they read in the *Daily Mail*/stop them getting scurvy – that there is no time left over to just *be* with the children, and listen to what they are talking about, and actually talk back to them instead of chanting eat your broccoli/get in the car/what's 9 × 8?/what's the capital of Norway?/who did that?/no, find it yourself/why does no one else ever flush the fucking toilet?/put your shoes on/brush your teeth.

And while I'm doing all that, I'm also trying to read emails and think about what to make for dinner and keep up with Facebook and deal with Simon's moods, and I'm just never really actually there in the moment.

We have spent lots of time this week just telling each other jokes, terrible cracker-style jokes involving groan-worthy puns, and just chatting about, well, nothing very much really. I am full of good resolutions that when we get home I will carry on like this – I will slow down, I will stop hustling the children from place to place and barking instructions at them, and instead will try to be more in the present with them. I know this almost certainly won't happen, but fuck it, it's nice to dream, even if dreams seem more like reality when one is sitting on a Spanish balcony clutching a glass of local wine and staring at the stars.

Thursday, 20 April

Juliette has not returned. She reunited with her French boyfriend Pascal when she was at home in Limoges, and has decided she cannot be parted from him ever again (Harry is apparently forgotten). I was tempted to text her and tell her not to be so stupid as to plan her life round a bastarding man. Things are, to say the least, rather frosty between Simon and me. In Juliette's absence, and until the agency can find us another au pair who suits, he is sleeping in the spare room, which suits me fine, as it means Judgy can sleep on the bed with me. According to him, how can he trust me when I take the children out of the country without telling him? I have pointed out that taking them to Lanzarote for a week was hardly on a par with taking them to the Middle East forever. Also, apparently, going on holiday without telling him was irresponsible. Which possibly it was, but it was also irresponsible of him not to have booked his annual leave when I asked him to, leaving me high and dry. I am not sure what will happen when another au pair arrives. Maybe he will move into the shed, which would suit me even better. In the meantime, we are back to scrambling desperately to pick up the children from after-school clubs, etc., while communicating through terse texts and passive–aggressive snarlings.

I think extra salt was possibly rubbed in Simon's wounds by both Peter and Jane excitedly babbling that it was the best holiday they had ever been on, *much* better than the usual boring holidays, and talking about it non-stop ever since we got back.

I have taken to mainly ignoring Simon, who keeps asking if I have told my work colleagues about the children yet, and keep pointing out to him that it is none of his fucking business actually. The only thing anyone at work in fact said was to admire my tan (which is rather good, as it happens. I know we aren't supposed to tan anymore, and I am deeply irresponsible for doing so, but I can't help it! I feel so much better when I am brown. It's like the difference between a big lump of pallid, unbaked dough and a lovely golden, just-baked loaf. Of course, it is always problematic trying to explain to the children on holiday why I am slapping Factor 50 on them, and basting myself in sun oil like a rotisserie chicken, but luckily they are accustomed to my 'Do as I say, not as I do strictures').

Lydia did remark wistfully while we making coffee that she did envy my holiday, I had come back looking so brown and relaxed, whereas she had spent the best part of £2,000 on a week at Center Parcs with her family and felt anything but relaxed. I wished I could tell her that the reason I had had such an enjoyable holiday wasn't actually because I was the carefree childless career woman she thought I was, but rather because I had just gone without my bloody husband, so I was already one child down and didn't have to listen to him moaning and obsessively reading TripAdvisor while shouting at everybody not to drink the water. Actually, I was slightly disappointed that despite using the tap water to brush my teeth on several occasions when I forgot to use the bottled water, I had not come down with a fast-track weight-loss bout of the squits – though obviously, having the squits on holiday with two children would be less than ideal, though there was an unfortunate incident one night when I thought I was successfully working a rather chic little mono-chrome look, in a white shirt and black trousers, but when I left the children at the table to quickly pop up to the room because I had forgotten my phone, a rather angry German lady obviously mistook me for a waitress and starting shouting at me about something in German. All I could work out was that it was something to do with food, from the dramatic sign language she was forced to employ, because I did Latin at school, not Spanish, and so I was forced to fall back on my only German phrase of '*Ich habe durchfall!*' On being informed I had diarrhoea, she did at least lose interest in whatever she had wanted me to tell her, and shooed me away with an expression of disgust.

Obviously I couldn't tell Lydia about any of this, though. I wonder if maybe I could just suddenly announce I have adopted some children. People adopt children of all sorts of ages, don't they? Angelina Jolie seems to, anyway. Maybe that would be the solution to my lies. Or I could invent a tragically deceased family member and claim they were orphans that I had taken in, like Oliver Twist. I fear both of these scenarios would involve a lot of questions, though. It must have been much easier for people to undo lying about not having children back in Victorian times, when you could just acquire orphans willy-nilly and no one thought anything of it. Look at *Anne of Green Gables*! Marilla and Matthew just go off and get an orphan and no one says a word apart from Mrs Rachel Lynde, and only then because she likes to look on the dark side and thinks the orphan might murder them! Fuck it, I'm sure I will think of something. I could use all the time I currently spend Not Talking to Simon to come up with a solution.

Monday, 1 May

Oh, super-duper, excellent, marvellous (I am trying to be slightly less foul-mouthed, after a pained note home from Peter's teacher when he stubbed his toe and declared, 'ARGH, twatdiddling fucksticks, that bloody HURTS!' I am obviously replacing it with sarcasm. I don't know how long these good intentions will last, however. I don't feel myself when I'm not swearing). There is a new headmistress at the school, who is trying to introduce some new ways of doing things, and apparently, after consultation with the Pupil Council, everyone thinks it might be *rather lovely* if Sports Day involved a 'strawberries-and-cream stall'.

There is a part of me that thinks, yes, yes, that *would* be *rather lovely*, it would totally tie in my shady-hat, floaty-frock vision of what Sports Day *should* be like, and there is another part of me that just thinks, 'OH FUCK RIGHT OFF!' (see? I *tried*, I just can't do it. Swearing is a part of me!) because she thinks it will be a *super* fundraiser for the PTA, if I could just organise that and make it happen. Yes, because I've got fuck all else to do, haven't I? I mean, it's not like I've got a *job* or a *family* or a fuck-ing marriage going through some sort of midlife crisis or a complex web of lies to maintain to my colleagues, is it? Oh no, what a marvellous fucking idea, Mrs Compton. I'll just throw together a little strawberries-and-cream stall to further your vision, shall I? Also, I don't buy for one second that the Pupil Council came up with this idea on their own (in my opinion the Pupil Council wields far too much power at school. Why must the children be consulted? Why can't they just be told what to do, like in my day? Oh God, I'm showing my age again! 'In My Day!' I'll be demanding they bring back National Service soon), because what child, when asked for ideas to enhance Sports Day, would choose something involving *fruit*? If they wanted an ice-cream van or a Haribo stall, I might be convinced that the hand of the Pupil Council was in this, but a strawberries-and-cream stall is plainly the headmistress's idea, one she has somehow persuaded the Pupil Council to endorse.

I do not have time for this right now. Apart from anything else, with all the summer activities coming up, it struck me that I was going to need some plausible reason for taking a number of Friday afternoons off. Alan keeps asking if I went to see his dentist and got that crown sorted, so that excuse is out. Ditto the Women's Troubles. What do people do on Friday afternoons? My father quite often took Friday afternoons off to play golf. Maybe I could take up golf. Maybe not. Alan and James are both keen golfers but usually play on a Saturday morning, so as the world has moved on from the days when one could claim a Friday afternoon's golfing WAS working as you were 'networking' etc., that probably wouldn't work. Also, then they would expect me to talk about golf and possibly even go and play golf with them, and a) I know nothing about golf, b) I have no desire to play golf and c) I can't even imagine Simon's face if I announced I was off to play golf on a Saturday morning. Though I'm almost tempted to try it, just to see if his head finally explodes!

So all in all, throwing a strawberries-and-cream stall into the mix as well is not exactly filling me with joy. Maybe I could just delegate it. Katie would be good at something like that. Or Kiki with two Ks. Strawberries are very photogenic, though it might involve too much actual organising and not enough time standing round taking selfies for her Instagram Stories for Kiki. I will send them both an email, suggesting it would be just the job for them, and then I shall wash my hands of the entire affair.

Saturday, 13 May

For reasons known only to herself, Jessica decided that the best way to celebrate her forty-sixth birthday was to bid us all to a family lunch. Sometimes I suspect the only thing that Jessica and I have in common is our unshakeable conviction that one day my children will be able to behave normally in public. Personally, I would rather have spent the day putting pins in my eyes. I am knackered. The au pair agency has not yet sent anyone else, and Juliette's yoghurt pots are quite forgiven. In the six weeks she was with us I had forgotten how much harder it is when you feel like you are constantly running on the spot to catch up. I almost rang her yesterday and begged her to come back, and to just bring Pascal – and bugger the sheets, they could shag all they liked, as long as she could pick the kids up from school in between the bonk fests.

Simon has reverted to working completely to rule as far as housework and childcare are concerned, and we are still barely speaking. He was only dragged along today under sufferance because Jessica rang him and wittered at him until he agreed to come to make her shut up.

Jessica seems to have given up her idea that Natalia's sole purpose in life is to impregnate herself with our father's essence and bear him a child, and the two of them have apparently got quite pally, so the Family Lunch was for all of us (except Mum, obviously, who was in Yorkshire, probably still mourning her sullied gravy jug).

Things didn't go well. Peter was incensed at being removed from the house on a day when new *Ninjago* episodes were being released, and Jane apparently was having her human rights abused again by my thwarting her plans to spend the day Facetiming Sophie. Simon was just disgruntled at being removed from his shed and made to go into the World of People, but Simon is always disgruntled about that. He was unimpressed by being made to remove his hideous old fleece as well, and despite it being a gloriously sunny day, insisted on shivering theatrically at frequent intervals. I think it was because he had had to take his fleece off, but on the other hand it could have been because of the ongoing frosty atmosphere still festering between us, as we sat on opposite sides of the table and glared at each other.

Everyone else had already arrived when we got there, perhaps in a strategic move to try and bag a seat as far from my children as possible, but alas, despite their foresight, my precious moppets were not to allow them to get off that easily.

Unfortunately, the school had had another instalment of Living and Growing the previous week, and the children were keen to impart their new-found knowledge to the family.

'Grandpa, did you know about condoms?' enquired Peter in a clear and carrying voice as soon as he sat down.

'You should always use a condom!' Jane informed him. 'You should always use a condom because of *diseases*!'

'And babies!' chimed in Peter.

'Though, Grandpa, did you know that if you do it in a lady's bottom, you can't get a baby like that?' Peter added helpfully. 'Natalia, is that why you don't have any children?'

Natalia spluttered something in Russian that sounded unrepeatable.

'Sorry, Natalia, I didn't hear you. Is it because of condoms or doing sex in your bottom, Natalia?' asked Peter.

Persephone and Gulliver were agog and wide-eyed during this exchange.

'Some *diseases* make your willy fall off!' Jane announced. 'I hope Grandpa's willy hasn't fallen off,' she said to Natalia, anxiously. 'And that he uses a condom, because he has had lots of wives and probably had sex with them all. Have you had sex with lots of other men, Natalia?'

Natalia choked at this, as I hissed, 'Shut up, shut up, shut up! What *do* they teach you at that school of yours?'

'Gonorrhoea!' shouted Jane. 'That's a disease you can get. And syphilis! I looked them up on the internet.'

'What *is* gonorrhoea, Mummy?' asked Persephone. 'It's a pretty word. Gonorrhoea. It sounds like a place in *The Lord of the Rings*.'

'Oh God, oh God, oh God,' I moaned.

'*Darling*,' hissed Simon. 'Can't you control your children, *darling*?'

'Evidently not, *darling*!' I spat back. 'Perhaps *you* could try controlling *your* children, instead of just ignoring them and leaving them to me!'

Ah, there is nothing like a good passive–aggressive exchange of '*darlings*' to make it obvious that a middle-class couple is not getting on!

'Well!' said Daddy brightly. 'It's lovely to see you all again. I see the children are as *spirited* as ever.'

'Shall we order some wine?' said Natalia faintly.

'Excellent idea!' I gasped, as Jane continued to describe the symptoms of a syphilitic cock, which she had apparently discovered courtesy of Dr Google.

'HAPPY BIRTHDAY, JESSICA!' shouted Daddy over the babble of venereal diseases and broken dreams.

I wondered if anyone would notice if I went to sleep under the table for a bit.

Tuesday, 23 May

How have a few punnets of strawberries and a pot of cream become so complex? My attempts to delegate the organisation to Katie and Kiki was not entirely successful, as Kiki's idea of organising it was to bombard me with emails suggesting I got Cath Kidston or similar to sponsor it, and reminding me that when I got in touch with potential sponsors to tell them that although the school doesn't have an Instagram page, they would be guaranteed *great* exposure on @kikiloveandlife and also to say that she was open to any collaborations or sponsorships they might be interested in. I told her to fuck off. Well, I didn't actually, obviously. I said that if she wanted to pursue that, she could do it herself as I am very Busy and Important, and she took a huff about my refusal to consider her innovative ideas. Lydia snuck up behind me and peered over my shoulder when I was trying to answer one of these emails. (Kiki feels that as she doesn't work conventional hours, then it is perfectly fine to expect me to deal with this while I'm at work, and if you don't respond immediately she just keeps messaging until you do, and if you silence her on one channel of communication, she finds another. I assume this is why brands pay her to take photos with their stuff – it's just to make her shut up and leave them alone.) Lydia didn't say anything about why I was answering messages about Sports Days and PTAs, but I have a horrible feeling she suspects that something is going on.

Katie's attempts to organise the strawberries-and-cream stall for Sports Day had been somewhat more practical, but she had been met with a stunned wall of silence when she tried to drum up some volunteers to actually man it, and in despair she asked if I would send an email out to the parents instead, as asking nicely had got nowhere, and Katie has not spent enough years in the playground yet to have had all the milk of human kindness leached from her, and thus she was worried that sending a shirty email might be seen as rude. I, however, have no such qualms and thus I sent round a brusque message announcing that if there were no volunteers there would be no strawberries and cream, and thus there would be no money for the school and they could all fuck off and die for all I cared. Once again, obviously I deleted the last sentence before sending.

The plus side was that my email did elicit some responses, such as one of the more, shall we say, *eco* mums (could use some deodorant, has shades of Louisa) questioning the ethics of a strawberries-and-cream stall, because had I taken into account food miles and packaging and the cruelty of the dairy industry and the low wages paid to the fruit pickers, and would there be a vegan alternative, and had I considered children with strawberry allergies, and why didn't I arrange for someone to come in and do a workshop on sustainability with the children instead?

Oh, yes, that's a great idea. I mean, that doesn't defeat the purpose of the PTA at *all*, does it? Spending money instead of raising it, just to satisfy some social justice warrior urges.

Or sleazy Julian regretfully informing me that he couldn't possibly help, as he was offering a photography package to parents to have their budding Usain Bolt's moments of glory professionally captured, so the egg and spoon race would be immortalised forever, and actually, could I please forward this on to everyone on my PTA contact list and encourage them to sign up for it?

Marvellous idea, Julian, yes, fantastic. Of course I have nothing better to do than help you market your questionable photography skills. Oh, wait a minute, actually, FUCK OFF! Or why not ask Kiki with two fucking Ks if she is interested in a #collaboration on #instagram since you are both so #selfob-fucking-ssessed?

Or Amelia Whittaker saying that she couldn't help because it was Rachel's last year at primary school and so she needed to watch everything, but she hopes we find volunteers because she always really enjoys the strawberries and cream.

Oh, that's absolutely fine, Amelia! I mean, don't worry that it's also Jane's last year, and that I might want to watch some of her Sports Day too – the only thing that matters is that YOU have a good day.

And my personal favourite, Claudia Soames, who sent a shocked email complaining that she couldn't believe she had even been asked to consider helping at a PTA event, as she had *children* and therefore couldn't possibly be expected to spare the time to help.

No shit, Sherlock. Just *imagine* asking people with *children* to help with the *school fundraising*! I mean, it's almost like we've deliberately singled them out on purpose!

There were many more emails from people offering a variety of spurious excuses about why they couldn't help (but all expressing excitement at the prospect of someone else running the strawberries-and-cream stall for them to guzzle from while pretending that they were in a Merchant Ivory epic, instead of wandering round a rather municipal playing field), but not a single one from anybody willing to help.

Such was my rage and general disillusionment with humanity

that I sent emergency texts to Sam, Hannah and Katie convening a General Summit Against People on Friday night in the pub. We haven't been out in ages, as Hannah is deep in wedding plans, Sam is busy swiping left or right on Tinder (not sure which is good and which is bad), and Katie's children are small enough that maternal guilt does not allow her to escape that often and miss bedtime, though I have assured her that this does wear off eventually and you will grasp at any straw to avoid read-ing *Green Eggs and Ham* for the eleventy billionth time. Simon has sloped off for after-work drinks several times recently, leav-ing me to deal with the screaming matches over how wetting your toothbrush and quickly jabbing it into your mouth and out again does not constitute brushing one's teeth, along with the constant getting-ups to complain of imaginary aches and pains until I crack and administer a placebo dose of Calpol, so it is definitely his turn to babysit. Or rather not 'babysit', actually – parent *his* children.

Saturday, 27 May

Ugh. 'We're going to be sensible and pace ourselves and just have a couple of drinks,' we all insisted. 'We're going to drink a glass of water or maybe even a soft drink in between every alcoholic drink,' we vowed. 'We're out for company and chat and a catch-up, NOT to get shitfaced,' we claimed.

Our good intentions lasted right up until we were in the pub and actually at the bar, when Hannah pointed out the financial prudence of buying wine by the bottle rather than the glass, and thus we began our inexorable slide down that slippery slope.

Hannah was hacked off because she is stressing out about wedding plans, with only a month to go, and feels Charlie is not helping enough and her mother is trying to help too much (due to Mrs P discovering Pinterest, I was completely barred from offering any assistance whatsoever, as apparently Hannah could not cope with two people bombarding her with emails filled with adorable wedding favours and quirky table arrangements).

'I mean, I just asked him to choose which shade of pink he thought we should go for in the peonies and he said he didn't give a fuck,' wailed Hannah. 'And meantime, Mummy is on the phone saying she has ordered a glass cutter off Amazon and is going to make vases for the tables out of old wine bottles and candlesticks out of gin bottles, and also she's seen another thing to make lanterns out of those big catering tins of instant coffee and she's got Marjorie from the old folks home to save her all their coffee tins and she's having a bash at that. It's going to look like some sort of alcoholics' convention in a scrapyard if I let her have her way! How does she even know about Pinterest? Someone must have tipped her off. Usually she doesn't venture further into the internet than John Lewis and Lakeland.'

I murmured something non-committal, as it was possibly me who had suggested to Mrs P that she have a little browse on Pinterest for interesting ideas for the wedding.

Katie was in a huff with Tim because 'He's just such an insensitive bastard sometimes, he thinks because he goes out to work while I am at home with the girls that therefore I should be waiting on him hand and foot. He doesn't realise how much hard work two small children are, and how much time they take up, even with Lily at school. And it's not like I'm even asking him to do much. I just want a bit of fucking *respect*.'

'Bastard!' we shouted. 'Inconsiderate bastard!'

'Nuvver bottle!' bellowed Katie.

Unfortunately, I decided to switch to gin, so when Hannah asked how I was and what was going on with me, instead of a blasé, 'Oh, you know, not much!' brushing things under the carpet British comment, I burst into tears.

'Oh my God, Ellen! What's *wrong*?' wailed Sam, patting my shoulder ineffectually.

I sobbed it all out – Simon sleeping in the spare room, how angry he is at me, how angry I am at him. How I finally feel like I've got a job where I am seen as an actual person, instead of as a parent, where people listen to my opinions and no one makes jokes about 'baby brain', or insidiously puts me down for being a mother, but how many lies I have told, and how *hard* it is to keep up with everything, and how, generally, things seemed to have turned to shit and I had no idea how to put things right.

'And don't tell me just to talk to him,' I wept. 'He doesn't *listen*. And it's not that easy. And don't tell me to just tell everyone at work about the kids either. I don't *want* to tell them. Then they'll just snipe at me like they do with Lydia, and I just want to be a *person*!'

'You probably have to talk to someone at some point, though?' volunteered Katie. 'You can't just pretend none of this is happening.'

'Of course I can,' I sniffed. 'I'm *British*!'

'Even so,' said Hannah. 'This is all a bit fucked up, sweetie. You need to sort it out. Simon loves you, I know he does. You're just having a bit of a rough patch.'

'But there are so many rough patches. Marriage seems to be just trying to remind myself why I married him in the first place. It shouldn't be this *hard*!'

'It is, though,' said Hannah wisely. 'But do you remember why you married him? And do you still love him?'

'I think so. But I don't know if he loves me anymore!'

JUNE

Thursday, 1 June

Strawberries and cream-gate rumbles on. Or rather it doesn't, as exasperated by all the lazy fuckers with their pathetic excuses about why they couldn't possibly help, I sent a curt email round this morning announcing that it would be cancelled due to a lack of volunteers. I can't do everything, and something has to give, and in the grand scheme of things the PTA was the least of my worries. Also, I failed to see why Sam and I should miss Jane and Sophie's last Sports Day and Katie should miss Lily's first Sports Day while we slaved serving up strawberries and cream to a bunch of idle arseholes to raise money for their children. So I said, 'Enough! No more! Stick your strawberries and cream where the sun doesn't shine!' (Also, I must confess, given the whole PTA sex parties thing, I did wonder if any event that featured whipped cream so heavily was entirely sending the right message.)

As soon as I had sent the email, pingpingpingping went my inbox! A combination of handwringing regret from parents that had received the cancellation email, but apparently had not received the preceding eleven billion emails pleading for help, because *of course* they would have volunteered *had they only known*, and angry parents complaining that they felt I was very unreasonable not to simply run the whole thing myself, as they were looking forward to their strawberries and cream and now Sports Day was spoiled. I ignored the lot of them. It felt *marvellous*. I was beginning to suspect that Fiona Montague and Lucy Atkinson's Mummy had been so attached to their clipboard when they were PTAing because they could use them as potential weapons to beat people around the head with, and not because they were just über-efficient.

Friday, 2 June – Sports Day

After binning off the PTA, and making increasingly spurious excuses (a funeral – I must keep note of what aging relations I have killed off so I don't repeat myself) and fobbing off Lydia's increasingly suspicious questions (FUCKING Kiki, and her endless bombardment of messages) so I could be there to give Jane my full and undivided attention, cheering her on, making more of those #happymemories, I turned up at Sports Day and merrily cried, 'Hello, darling, I've come for your last Sports Day!'

Jane just grumbled, 'I dunno why. I hate Sports Day. Sports Day is stupid and boring! Don't do anything embarrassing now you're here. In fact, why don't you just go and watch Peter and pretend you're nothing to do with me? I wish Juliette was here, she was cool!'

FFS! And after all the trouble I went to be there for her. RUDE!

Saturday, 10 June

I was bidden to lunch with Jessica and Natalia today (one doesn't get *invited* to lunch by Jessica, one is simply told where and when you are expected. It never seems to occur to her that people might have other plans. As far as she is concerned, if she has decided she wants to see you, she will see you).

I realised over lunch that I'd never actually managed to hold an entire conversation with Natalia before, one or the other of my precious moppets always intervening to witter utter shite at the poor woman or hurl some or other sticky substance over expensive-looking items of her clothing. I remarked on this, and she smiled wryly.

'Yes, I know!' she said. 'That's why I thought it might be nice for us to have lunch without the children …'

'*My* children are perfectly civilised,' sniffed Jessica. 'In fact, did I tell you that Persephone has passed her Grade Eight piano with distinction and Gulliver is entering the National Poetry Competition? Not a *children's* competition, the actual National Poetry Competition, and everyone says he has a very good chance of winning!'

I did know all of this, because Mum likes to phone me once a week and tell me how much better everyone else's lives are than mine – 'And Cathy Evans's daughter has just got her second PhD, and *Tom*, you know, Tom Henderson, sweetie, yes, you do know Tom Henderson, Eleanor Henderson's younger boy, no, darling, I'm *sure* you are thinking of someone else, of *course* he didn't have sweaty palms or wandering hands, *anyway* Tom has just got a *marvellous* promotion and he's bought an Aston Martin, and Felicity Moore's granddaughter is off to *Oxford*! And what about dear Peter and Jane? Have they stopped *biting* yet? Of course, *Persephone* is doing awfully well, isn't she!'

We chatted politely about this and that, Jessica boasted some more about her perfect children, I contented myself with thinking that my darlings might not be child prodigies but at least they had the emotional resilience not to have a complete breakdown at the revelation that Santa Claus did not exist, and also they had a sense of humour (a fairly fucked-up, dark sense of humour), which was more than the sainted Persephone and Gulliver had, and Natalia made vaguely interested noises, but I suspected she was as bored as I was by Jessica's gushings, especially when she interrupted Jessica holding forth on Gulliver's *really* quite groundbreaking use of iambic pentameter to suggest another bottle of wine. I warmed to Natalia.

By the time Natalia ordered a third bottle of wine (why had I had reservations about this nice lady? Why? It was now astonishingly clear that she was a very kindred spirit) and even Jessica was looking a little glazed, having exceeded her usual two-glass limit, I found my tongue was somewhat loosened when Natalia asked me how work was going and I confessed I might have done a bit of a Bad Thing.

After a rather garbled explanation ('Who is Lydia? Why does Alan hate children? Which one is James?'), I finally managed to get through to them exactly the pickle I was now in.

Jessica was as sympathetic as one would expect. 'For God's sake, Ellen. Do you *purposely* go about trying to fuck things up and make your life more complicated? Why on earth would you do something like that?'

'I didn't mean to. I certainly didn't mean it to get so out of hand. I just wanted people to look at me as something more than a fucking mother, to see that I was still a *person*, that having children didn't mean that I could no longer function as an adult –'

'Well, you're not exactly selling your ability to "function as an adult", are you, embroiling yourself in a ridiculous web of lies,' said Jessica tartly.

'Shut up, Jessica! I just wanted them to see that I could do my job perfectly well, before they all started chuntering about me taking time off for the kids' stuff. They never stop moaning about poor Lydia, and she probably actually works harder than the rest of them, but because they see her as a mother first, they assume she is not pulling her weight and is putting her family first, and I was *tired* of that, I just wanted to be more than a mother. Is that so wrong?'

'But you *are* a mother,' objected Jessica.

'I know I'm a mother! I *know*! But why does that then have to impact on every single part of my life? As long as I get the job done, it shouldn't matter at work, but it *does*! And no one makes the same jibes about *fathers*, bloody James and Joe and Ed, and fucking Simon and Neil don't get treated differently because they're fathers, do they? It's only women who do, and I was sick of it, and I just wanted to get away from it all for a bit. And now it has all got a little out of hand.'

'She's right,' said Natalia. 'Mothers *are* treated differently to fathers. I see it all the time. It's part of the reason I decided I didn't want children. Women are passed over for promotion or managed out of the door – it's not right, I don't condone it, but there's no point pretending it doesn't happen.'

'It doesn't happen to *me*!' said Jessica indignantly.

'Then,' said Natalia, 'you are either one of the very lucky ones, or you choose not to see it happening to you. Because Ellen is quite right, it does happen. I'm not saying that lying about having children is the answer, obviously, but I can see why Ellen would feel like that. I mean, I didn't want children *anyway*. I am not maternal – they are sticky and often smell, and I don't like sticky, smelly things – but I also didn't want that change in how society would treat me, I didn't want to become that second-class citizen. I shouldn't have had to consider that, but I did, and it's still the case. Women are treated differently and men aren't when they become parents. It's shit. And unfortunately, it's not even just the men who perpetuate it. Women in senior positions are often as bad, and the media feeds it too – certain tabloids are very keen on publishing articles by female columnists ranting about how working mothers do nothing but order their food shopping online and go home early.'

'So what do I do?' I said plaintively.

'I think you will have to come clean,' said Natalia. 'You haven't technically done anything wrong, especially if, as you say, your boss knows you do have children. Really, it is no different to people pretending they had a marvellous weekend and shagged a supermodel when in reality they sat at home in their pants, masturbating.'

'Eurgh,' I said, at the image of my colleagues that that put in my head.

'Also,' said Natalia, who was annoyingly wise despite the three bottles of wine, 'it's not very fair on this Lydia, is it? You letting her take all the heat for being the only mother in the office, while you are doing exactly the same thing as her, only under the cover of a web of quite unnecessarily complex lies.'

'I know, I know. But what will I say? What about my idea that I have adopted some orphans?'

'I don't think more lies are going to be the answer,' said Natalia gently. 'Just tell them the truth.'

The truth. Can I tell them the truth after all the lies I have spun? Maybe I should just look for another job. But I *love* my job. I don't want another job. Oh fuck my life, what have I done?

I couldn't quite face telling them that I thought Simon might be on the point of leaving me as well, because Jessica might actually have spontaneously combusted with joy at yet another opportunity to tell me how I had fucked my life up, and how much better she would have managed it all.

Friday, 16 June

Today, I think it is safe to say, was one of those days when every time you think it can't get any worse, it docs.

It started as a fabulous day. We had completed another big project and had brought it in bang on deadline, to the client's delight. Everyone had that almost end of-term feeling, of a massive weight being lifted from our shoulders. Ed even attempted a high five with James, before coming to himself and retreating to his office. There were grand plans for a massive piss-up after work, which I was rather looking forward to as an opportunity to just forget all the shit at home for a few hours, and everything was quite, quite splendid, right up until about 4.30 p.m., when Lydia told us that she wouldn't be able to come for drinks because her nanny had just called to say she needed to go home early, because the nanny wasn't feeling well, and also that she wouldn't be in until lunchtime on Monday, because she was going to her children's Sports Day. James and Alan sighed rather, and tutted, and Alan made his usual martyred request for some piece of unimportant information from Lydia that he could not continue life without.

When Lydia said she had already emailed Alan everything he needed, he snarled, 'Well, thank you so much, Lydia. I suppose I should be grateful you can occasionally take the time to do your *job* in between all your little jaunts. It's really very kind of you. I hope it didn't distract you from the really important stuff, like making cupcakes for the bake sale.'

'What do you mean, Alan?' asked Lydia quietly.

'Oh, I just mean, we'd all *love* to play the motherhood card and swan off early and come in late because our *children* are so much more important than our little *job*.'

'Don't be a dick, Alan!' I said. 'It's hot, we're all wanting to bugger off to the pub, but we can't go yet. Don't take it out on Lydia!'

'I'm not being a dick,' said Alan crossly. 'I'm just pointing something out. We have to pick up Lydia's slack while she's playing happy families, that's all I'm saying. Doesn't it piss you off, Ellen?'

'What slack?' said Lydia furiously. 'Tell me, please, exactly what slack you have to pick up for me? I get everything done, and more, I have never once been late for a project deadline, which is more than you can say. Sometimes, yes, I don't get it all done in the office, sometimes I go home and put my kids to bed and then work to midnight so I can get it all done, because it is the twenty-first fucking century and technology lets us do that. We don't *have* to be chained to the office from nine to five to achieve things, and I am *sick* of you lot whispering behind my back and implying I am somehow not up to the job. I have not taken one single hour off more than I am entitled to, I allocate my fucking annual leave extremely carefully so I can still be there for my children, and Ellen is right, you *are* being a dick!'

'How am I being a dick?' said Alan in outrage. 'How? I was just pointing out that it must be nice to just piss off whenever you like. I don't see that that's being a dick. I'd *love* to do what you do, that's all I'm saying!'

'What I do?' said Lydia. 'What, basically work twenty-four hours a day?'

'Well,' said Alan primly, 'no one made you have children. Why did you bother if you find it so hard?'

'Oh, come on, Alan,' I said. 'Give her a break!'

'Give her a BREAK?' said Alan indignantly. 'And who gives *us* a break? People like Ellen and me?'

'I don't think we really need a break. I mean, Lydia works really hard!' I put in quickly.

'Well, I certainly don't think Ellen needs a break,' said Lydia nastily. 'She's had plenty of afternoons off at the "dentist" and for her "women's troubles", and you've never given her the same grief. And no one has said a word about the time she's spending in work on PTA emails and messages about Sports Days.'

'Eh?' said Alan. 'Why would you be doing that?' he said to me.

'It's for HER kids!' said Lydia triumphantly. 'I was talking to Gabrielle from HR, and she asked me how we were getting on, with both of us trying to juggle work and family. Ellen has two children and a husband.'

'But you said …' said James.

'No,' I said feebly. 'You all assumed for some reason.'

'But why would you …?' said Alan in confusion.

'I don't know!' I said miserably. 'I kept thinking I could just put you all right and then it had gone on too long and I couldn't, and I *liked* being this new version of me that you all thought I was, and then I really couldn't say anything!'

'Well,' said Alan, still looking baffled. 'Surely that proves it then. If Ellen can have children we know nothing about and get the job done, and if James can have children and not have to vanish every twenty minutes, why can't Lydia, without slacking off?'

'Oh, for God's sake!' said Lydia. 'Because all she did was lie about where she was, so you were more accepting of it than you are of me doing it. And James can do it because he just expects his wife to pick up the slack.'

'Is this true, Ellen?' said Alan.

'Well, sort of! I mean, I do have two children and I didn't tell you about them because I didn't want all the shit you give Lydia. So all those times I said I was at the dentist and you didn't turn a hair, I was at school events, but no one gave a SHIT, because that's OK!'

'And you *did* make me feel bad,' snapped Lydia. 'All these months you let them throw me to the lions, while you swanned around pretending to go and do fuck knows what and letting everyone be fine about that!'

'I know, Lydia,' I said. 'I know. It was a shitty thing to do, and I'm sorry, I really am. I don't know what else to say. Except that maybe if I hadn't, then they would still be bitching about us both, whereas now they might actually stop and look at how they treat us.'

'Seriously?' said Alan. 'You think that this will make us think *better* of you?'

'Well, maybe not me, but Lydia. Maybe you'll appreciate that Lydia isn't slacking and can get the job done. And maybe James will stop and think about how hard it is for his wife when he doesn't help out and expects her to do everything, and that maybe there is some arse in her office who takes the same attitude to her as you do to Lydia.

'Anyway, I'm going home now!' I announced. 'To pick up my children. Have a lovely weekend, everyone, I will see you all on Monday. Lydia, I would say enjoy Sports Day, but that's unlikely if it's anything like my kids' one. But, you know, feel good for being there for them!'

'Hang on!' said James. 'If you have two secret children, does that mean you have a husband too?'

'Now that,' I said sadly, 'I really don't know anymore.'

I picked up my bag and walked out, pausing briefly to curse the wonders of modern technology that mean you have to use your security badge to swipe in and out, as that is not nearly as effective as a good old-fashioned door slam.

By the time I had picked up the children and got home, the adrenaline from the scene in the office had abated, leaving me with a cold sense of dread about what I might have done. I was mindlessly grating the cheese for the children's pasta, and feeling rather sick, when I realised that Judgy was not underfoot, hopefully begging for a morsel. Normally if I so much as move the cheese in the fridge he appears, staring at me menacingly until I crack and give him some, even though I know I will have to live with the rancid farts emanating from his cheesy bum, as it really doesn't agree with him.

It occurred to me that I hadn't seen him since we got home, when he jumped all over us in his usual guilt-making welcome, pretending he had been quite abandoned and he hadn't been with the dog sitter all day. I looked in the garden, but there was no sign of him, and I shouted upstairs to the children to see if he was there. I looked in all his favourite spots, every bed, every sofa, but no dog. Jane eventually slouched downstairs to see what all the noise was about and said, 'Oh, I let him out.'

'And did you let him in?' I enquired.

'Um, no!'

'Jane! You know he can't be let out unsupervised. Despite vast sums of money, effort and fencing materials, we have still not managed to terrier-proof the garden. Oh Jesus, where has he gone?'

Having checked the back garden again in vain, hopefully calling, 'Judgy, cheese! Come on, boy, nice cheese' to no avail, I went to start searching the street, muttering darkly about fuckwit children who can't follow simple instructions and bastard dogs who insist on running off and embarrassing me. Previous escapes have led to him being discovered in neighbouring kitchens, having entered through the cat flap, and scoffing the furious cat's food, pooing on Mrs Jenkins's prize begonias and terrorising Amelia Watson's guinea pig. I wondered gloomily what antics he would be up to this time, and reflected that I could really do with sinking a large glass of wine right now to try to quell the worries about what I would be facing on Monday morning, not searching for a sodding ungrateful runaway bloody Border terrier.

As I stomped along, still thinking dark thoughts about wretched dogs and children, as I shouted and whistled and cajoled with more promises of cheese, a small black streak shot between two parked cars towards me. It seemed like the same instant that there was a hideous squeal of brakes and the little black shape was flung towards me and then lay still. I seemed to be running, I never run, someone was getting out of the car and saying something, but I couldn't hear them, all I could see was a little whiskery face staring up at me, his big brown eyes no longer looking judgemental, but full of pain and fear. He whimpered as I reached him, and he still tried to give a thump of his tail to say, 'Hello, it's you, I love you.'

'Oh, lie still, boy, please, lie still. I'm here, it's going to all right,' I whispered. Everything was strangely blurry, and I realised that there were tears pouring down my face. Judgy hates people crying. He thinks it quite unnecessary and it makes his fur wet. I mustn't cry, I thought, I mustn't get him wet, he will be so cross.

Someone was talking behind me again, an older lady, who kept saying, 'I'm so sorry, I'm sorry, I didn't see him, I'm sorry.'

She was holding out a blanket and saying something about the vet. Then Katie was there too. 'Ellen, Ellen, we need to get him to the vet, right now!'

Everything snapped back into focus, and the strange slow-motion underwater feeling stopped.

The vet. Of course. Why was I sitting holding him in the street when he needed to be at the vet?

'This lady will drive you there, Ellen, I'll take the children,' said Katie firmly. Jane was there too, sobbing hopelessly.

'I'm so sorry, Mummy, it's all my fault, I forgot about him, I'm so sorry, will he be OK?'

'Please, Mummy, the vet will make him OK, won't she?' pleaded Peter, who was white-faced and horrified. Peter, who doesn't even *like* Judgy.

'I don't know,' I said slowly. 'I don't know. Katie, can you phone Simon and tell him what's happened?'

'Of course,' said Katie. 'I'll ring the vet and let her know you're coming too.'

The lady who had hit Judgy kept apologising all the way to the vet, but I didn't really hear her. All I could think of was the first time I had seen Judgy at the dogs' home, and they had brought this bouncing little bundle of fur out, so hyperactive he was prancing on his back legs with excitement, and those bright, wicked little eyes had looked into mine and I knew I loved him. He was about eighteen months old then, and had been rehomed twice, by people who thought that Border terriers would make quiet lap dogs. He leapt onto my knee, and I promised him his forever home. And he came to live with us, and he was ruling the roost before we knew it. He is disobedient and obstreperous and frequently smelly, he considers all beds to belong to him and only lets us sleep in them grudgingly, he is the reason I have child locks on the fridge to stop him opening it and stealing cheese. I couldn't stand the thought of those eyes going dark, of that little head never again cocking to one side, to regard me in judgement or disapproval. We called him Judgy because he made it clear from the start that he had certain views and expectations that we were supposed to live up to, and made his feelings clear when we did not. I wasn't ready to say goodbye to him.

At the vet, we were rushed straight through. Susie the vet, who knew Judgy well from many previous mercy dashes after he'd consumed things that he shouldn't, looked as white and horrified as I felt, but stayed calm and professional.

'He's still conscious,' she said. 'That's something. We'll put him on a drip to treat him for shock and check him over.'

'Can I stay?' I asked.

'Of course,' she said.

Judgy looked so little, lying there on the table. Even when Susie put the needle in for the drip, he tried again to wag for her, recognising an old pal. I just wanted to pick him up and give him the most massive cuddle, the way he likes, when he can snuggle right in and put his paws around my neck.

I kept scratching his favourite spot behind his ears while Susie examined him, and he would try and push his head further into my hand, so I scratched harder, but every time he tried, he would stop and whimper again.

'OK,' said Susie after a while. 'I'm pretty sure he's got a fracture on his front leg –'

'Oh God! But you can fix that! Can't you? It's just a broken leg – he's a dog not a horse! Some dogs only have two legs! He'll be OK, won't he?'

'I really hope so, Ellen, but he's a very small dog who got hit by a large car. His leg isn't the big problem. You're right we can fix that, but there might be internal damage as well, and he'll need a chest X-ray too. I can't say for sure how bad it is until we do all that, but he's conscious, like I said, and he's stable. That's all good.'

Simon burst into the room just then.

'Oh Jesus, darling. I came as soon as I heard. How is he? Is he going to be all right?' he asked Susie anxiously.

Susie explained again, and Simon said, 'So what happens now? Do you put him in plaster?'

'No,' said Susie. 'We'll need to anaesthetise him, and then X-ray him to see how bad the break is and check him for any other internal damage. What happens next will depend on those results. If it's just his leg, we actually have an excellent new orthopaedic specialist here who can operate and pin his leg back together. If there's more damage, we'll have to consider what's best for Judgy.'

'Oh no,' I whispered. 'No, you don't mean put him to sleep? No, no, you can't. Look at him! He's been wagging his tail, you couldn't do that! No, you mustn't, I won't let you!'

'Ellen, I'm just saying that at this stage, I can't give you a definitive answer, but whatever happens, you have to think about what's best for him, and not you. I know you love him, and that's why you will let us do our best for *him*, whatever that is. I don't think there is severe internal damage but I can't say for sure right now. But there is a possibility, yes, that we might not be able to make him better. And *if* that's the case, the best thing to do would be not to let him suffer. But we will do everything we can to help him, and not let it come to that. The good news, if you want to call it that, is that you do have a fairly comprehensive insurance policy, thank goodness, so you don't have to worry about the cost of all this.'

'Fuck the cost!' said Simon fiercely. 'It doesn't matter anyway. Just do everything you can for him, won't you? And if it's …'

Simon swallowed very hard and then went on. 'If it's bad news, you'll let us say goodbye first, won't you?'

I cried harder and Simon put a tentative arm around me, and I threw myself into his arms, sobbing against his chest.

'Of course,' said Susie. 'I'm going to take him through for the anaesthetic and X-rays now. You're probably better going home. This will take a while, and whatever happens he'll be staying in tonight.'

'Can I stay with him?' I sniffed.

'Not really,' said Susie kindly. 'You could bring him a blanket or a toy if you wanted.'

'We'll do that,' said Simon firmly, while I dissolved into more hopeless tears.

'Look, stay in here as long as you need, and then like I said, you're probably best going home,' said Susie. 'I'll ring you as soon as there's news.'

I sobbed and sobbed while Simon held me and stroked my hair and reminded me how tough Border terriers are, and that Susie said he probably would be all right, she just had to prepare us for the worst too, just in case. But his voice was wobbling too much to be really reassuring.

'You don't even like him!' I wailed.

'Of course I like him,' mumbled Simon. 'He's the only one who's pleased to see me when I come home. I love him dearly.'

'You call him a buggering pig dog!'

'So do you!'

We finally got ourselves together and went into the waiting room. The lady who had hit Judgy was still there. She had obviously been crying too, and she burst into tears again when she saw us come out.

'Oh God, he's not with you! Is he –?'

'He's having X-rays,' said Simon. 'They hope it's just a broken leg, but they won't know for sure until they've done the X-rays.'

'I'm so sorry,' she said for about the millionth time.

'It wasn't your fault,' I said sadly. 'It was mine. I should have kept a better eye on him.'

'It was an accident,' said Simon firmly. 'It was no one's fault.'

'Look, this is my number,' said the lady. 'Would you please let me know how he is?'

'Of course,' said Simon.

We drove home in silence. There wasn't much to say. When we got back I collected Judgy's favourite blanket (a very expensive lambswool number he had claimed as his own when I put it on the sofa) and his lion, which had once belonged to Jane until he had stolen it and removed the stuffing, before treasuring it. He liked to cuddle it at night, but he glared at you if you laughed at him cuddling his lion.

'I'll take you back to the vet,' said Simon. 'You're still in shock, so you shouldn't be driving.'

At the vet the receptionist said, 'Oh, Susie said you might be back. I'll just get her, if you'd like to wait in there.'

The receptionist should consider a career in poker, because she gave nothing away. I didn't know if Susie was coming with good news or bad news, but Susie was smiling when she came into the room.

'It *was* just a broken leg!' she said in delight. 'Quite a nasty break, but Liam the orthopaedic man is operating now, and he should make a full recovery! My goodness, he's a lucky little dog. He must have been hit quite hard to sustain a break like that. I'm amazed there wasn't any more serious damage. He'll be pretty battered and bruised and feeling sorry for himself, but terriers are tough. He'll bounce back pretty fast!'

I started crying again. 'Sometimes he acts more like a cat than a dog,' I wept incoherently. 'He can be very stubborn and very huffy like a cat. Maybe he has nine lives too!'

'Well, hopefully we won't ever have to put that to the test again,' said Susie. 'I'll call you when he's out of surgery, and all going well, he should be able to go home tomorrow.'

Once everyone had been given the good news, and Jane had finally stopped crying and been assured that it was just an accident and no one was blaming her, and the children were in bed, Simon came and sat on the sofa next to me. It had been an awfully long time since he sat there.

'We've been so stupid, haven't we?' he said. 'Well, I've been so stupid. You're right, things need to change round here. We need to start being a team again. All I could think today was how much I needed to be there for you, how much I wanted to be there for you, what were we going to do without him if he didn't make it, what if it had been one of the kids, why had we been fighting about the bloody bins and childcare when it was us and our family that was important, why weren't we fighting for that?'

'I was so glad you were there. I was thinking the same things. I've hated these past weeks when we haven't been talking and have been fighting all the time. I've even wondered if we were going to make it through it, or if this was the end for us.'

'Me too,' said Simon quietly. 'Do you want it to be the end?'

'Do you?'

'I asked you first.'

'No. No, I don't, but if you do, then I get custody of Judgy.'

'I don't want this to be the end of us either,' said Simon. 'I can't imagine life without you and the kids, or even without that malodorous mutt. I just never thought marriage would be this hard, you know. I thought we'd just skip off into the sunset, hand in hand, but it's bloody difficult!'

'I know,' I said. 'All the books and films finish with that fairy-tale moment and everyone lives happily ever after and the fucking pixies empty the dishwasher and clean the bogs.'

'Well, we both just need to try harder then, don't we? I didn't think I'd find it so hard to adjust to you working full-time. I didn't think I'd feel so resentful about it, but that's not really fair, is it? I suppose I need to be less of a selfish prick and help you out more, and you need to not go on holiday without telling me, and maybe try to talk to me in a rational manner about things instead of shouting. In fact, we should probably talk to each other more, and maybe even do date nights and stuff.'

'Can we not call them date nights, though? What with us not being teenagers in an American high-school film? It's a bit creepy, people in their forties talking about date nights! Anyway, you might not need to worry about me working full-time anymore. There was a bit of a scene at work today.'

'Fuck, what happened?'

'Well, it all sort of came out about the kids. Having them, you know.'

'You must have known that would have happened in the end?'

'I know. I just … I dunno … I hoped it wouldn't.'

'So, do you still have a job?'

'I dunno about that either. They were all looking at me and I didn't know what else to say, so I just sort of left.'

'You just sort of left? Darling, for someone so good at shouting, you are extraordinarily good at running away from conflict and emotions!'

'Well, so are you!'

'Oh, well. I suppose, worst-case scenario, they sack you and you can have my dinner ready and my slippers warming when I come home!'

'Simon! That's not helping!'

'Sorry. I was just trying to lighten the mood. Look, whatever happens, we just have to remember we will get through it together. OK?'

'OK.'

'And you do know that I love you, don't you?'

'Yeah, you're not so bad yourself.'

'Is that really the best you can do, Ellen?'

'Oh, all right, I love you too! Happy now?'

'Fucking ecstatic!'

'Marvellous.'

'Shall we watch some *Wheeler Dealers*?'

'No. Fuck off!'

Monday, 19 June

Judgy came home on Saturday, outraged at having his leg in a sling, and utterly disgusted that he had to be carried outside to do his business, as like all males of the species he likes to do his business in private while enjoying a moment of quiet contemplation. Such was his outrage at his undignified treatment that it seems likely that he will make a full recovery.

After the life-and-death drama of the weekend, and the sheer relief that Simon and I seem to be getting back on track and that I feel a bit like a poisoned thorn has been pulled out of my side now we are not at loggerheads and are trying to work together, not against each other, I had almost forgotten about the showdown before I had left work on Friday. When I got into the office today, Ed, my boss, stuck his head out of his office and asked if he could 'have a word'. I slunk in, feeling like when I was summonsed to the headmistress's office at school. Nothing good ever happened then, either.

Ed, who hates talking to people, did not look thrilled at having to leave his comfort zone either.

'Er, I gather there's been a bit of a misunderstanding,' he began.

'You *could* say that,' I agreed gloomily.

'The rest of the team seemed to think you didn't have any children?'

'Yes.'

'But you do, don't you?'

'Yes.'

'That's what I thought. So just a misunderstanding, then. One of those things. Good. Glad we've cleared that up.'

'OK. Was that everything, Ed?'

'Well, they asked me to speak to you about the misunderstanding and I have, um … The thing is, Ellen, are you happy here?'

'Yes. I love working here. It's been tough making the adjustment to working full-time again, but I think we're on top of it now.'

'Right. No, I was just trying to understand how this misunderstanding arose, you see. Did you feel you couldn't say that you had children because you were afraid you would be treated differently? Because we do have a policy of encouraging women back into work and not discriminating. Gabrielle gave me sheaves of paper about it – why she can't send a bloody email, I don't know! Bangs on all the time about sustainability and recycling and eco this and that, and then uses half a rainforest to print every communication. I keep telling her, paperless offices are the future, but apparently not for her department. Anyway, you shouldn't have felt you couldn't say you were a mother. It really wouldn't have made any difference to anyone, you know.'

Bless Ed. I think that was the longest speech I have ever heard him make. And I know he means well, and hopefully by the time Jane is starting work it really *won't* matter, but only a man could insist that mothers in the workforce were not treated any differently or penalised. And they probably aren't by decent people like Ed, but sadly not everyone is like Ed. And what a hypocrite Gaby is too, making snarky comments about Lydia and then sweetly citing the company policies that she so blatantly disregards.

Evidently worn out by such a rush of words, Ed stared gloomily at his desk and Gabrielle's heaps of papers for a while.

'Um, was there anything else?' I finally ventured.

'Hmm? Yes, actually. We're getting busier. Expanding. Max called this morning to say they are bringing in two new teams, and they want me to head them all up, and appoint team leaders for each group. I wondered if you'd be interested in applying for one of the positions. Not a lot more money, I'm afraid, but looks good on the CV.'

'Oh. Do you mean as team leader for the current team?'

'Probably not. I find people get arsey if someone is promoted over them like that. No, I thought you might do well with one of the new teams. I'd like Lydia to apply for one of the positions too.'

'What about James and Alan and Joe?'

'They are welcome to apply, but you two are my preferred candidates.'

'Have you told Lydia?'

'I was going to tell her next, if you want to send her in after you.'

Ed slumped further in his seat at the prospect of a second face-to-face conversation in one day.

'OK. Well, thank you, Ed, I really appreciate this. But I'll need to talk it over with my husband first.'

'Of course, there's no rush. I'd just like you to consider it.'

So that seemed to be that as far as any officialdom over the children/no children issue, but there was still the rest of them to deal with.

James, in fairness, was a little sheepish.

'I still think it was a really weird thing to do, Ellen,' he announced. 'But actually my wife says there are people who are arses to her at work too, and she completely sees why someone wouldn't admit to having kids. So I was wrong to be narky at Lydia, and I'll try to do better.'

Alan was still sulking, but actually Lydia was the one who was the most angry. She cornered me while I was making a coffee.

'I still can't believe what you did!'

'I know,' I said wearily. 'I know, I am a bad person, and I have no excuses and clearly karma thinks so too, because my dog got run over on Friday and it's put things into perspective a bit for me. All I can do is say I am sorry, and I was wrong, and I'd like to just move past this.'

'Oh Jesus, I'm sorry!' said Lydia in horror.

'Oh no, he's fine. Broken leg, but should make a full recovery. Only it made me think a bit about stuff, and yes, I was shit and I'm sorry, and I don't know what else I can say, OK, but it's been a pretty full-on weekend and I really can't handle any more drama or emotion, so if you want to hate me, go ahead and hate me.'

'Oh, FFS!' said Lydia. 'I had a whole angry speech and now I can't do it, can I? Not when your dog was run over. Part of me is just jealous I didn't think of saying I didn't have kids, to be honest. It would make life much easier!'

'Anyway,' I said, 'Ed wants to see you.'

'WHY?' said Lydia indignantly. 'Ed never wants to see anyone!'

'I think it's good news, but I'll let him tell you. And I really am sorry, Lydia. I'd like it if we could get past this and be friends as well as working together.'

Lydia made a non-committal noise.

Another good thing happened on the way home, when the au pair agency texted to say that they had found us the perfect girl, called Sara, from Pisa, who could start immediately. I quite fancy learning Italian. I feel I am halfway there, anyway, with my Latin GCSE, though after the Judgy-car-interface incident, I will hopefully never have to use the phrase '*Canus est in via*'! I wonder if she will make homemade pizza. At the very least, she may convert Simon to pasta.

JULY

Saturday, 1 July

Hannah and Charlie's wedding. Hurrah! The day came at last! Even though I had been excluded from the planning, to the point where Hannah threatened to take my phone and delete my Pinterest account if I made one more suggestion about how old wellies made an unusual and stylish receptacle for a flower arrangement, I was still extraordinarily excited.

I had planned my outfit with care and precision. In fact, I had had it hanging in the cupboard for weeks, a glorious confection of floral silk, with a fabulous hat. I had suggested white gloves might be an adorable finishing touch, but Simon had brusquely informed me that I was not the Queen.

I had purchased a suit for Peter, and Jane had eventually found a dress that satisfied both her style credentials and mine – i.e. it was mildly slutty, but did not actually scream 'jailbait'. We had had lengthy arguments about how much make-up she was allowed to wear to the wedding, and I had finally given up the unequal struggle and agreed that Sophie could sleep over the night before and they could do each other's make-up, so that at least Jane wouldn't look like the only one doing an impression of the Joker.

All in all, I had been exceptionally organised, and so was not best pleased when at 9 a.m. this morning Simon took his 'wedding suit' out of the wardrobe and looked at it sadly.

'I don't think I can wear this,' he announced. 'I hadn't realised how dated it was, because we haven't been to a wedding in ages. I'll have to go and buy a new one.'

'What? No! You can't, we are leaving at 12.30 p.m. Wear one of your work suits.'

'I can't do that,' said Simon indignantly. 'I don't want to look like I've just come from the office. No, I'll just pop into town and pick up a suit, and I'll be back before you know it.'

'Simon, NO, I forbid this! Wear something else. Why the fuck have you waited till today? I was going to have a bath. I was going to get ready in a relaxed and chilled-out way. I was going to have time to put on different colours of eyeshadow because you're supposed to be here helping with the kids, not buggering off to buy a suit. It's Sara's day off, because we're going to this wedding. She's going for a picnic with her friends from the language school. (Sara is bliss. She has not yet made the hoped-for pizzas, but she is much less inclined towards *discothèques* – or rather *discotecas* – than the errant Juliette.)

'Chill out!' said Simon (nothing makes me more stressed than being told to chill out). 'I'll take the kids with me.'

'What? Into shops? You do know there are three of them?'

'Yes, darling, it'll be fine! I *can* cope, you know. What's the worst that can happen?'

'Famous last words …' I muttered darkly.

In the event, Jane and Sophie refused to go with Simon, insisting that they too needed all morning to get ready. As Jane and Sophie together tend to entertain each other, especially if Peter is removed from the equation (since the departure of the civilising if corrupting influence of Juliette he has taken to farting on people for comic value again), the girls staying with me while Peter went with Simon seemed a reasonable plan.

I issued Simon with instructions for Peter, including not letting Peter talk him into buying energy drinks as Bad Things Happen, or Haribos, or an excess of Greggs' sausage rolls (Peter views a Greggs counter as a challenge), and Simon reminded me that he was perfectly capable of dealing with his son for a morning AND buying a suit.

Off they went, and I suggested brightly to Jane and Sophie that we could have a nice girly morning, doing facepacks and hair and make-up. The girls were unenthusiastic, and announced they would prefer to do their own thing, so I took myself off for a bath, anxiously checking the time as there was no sign of Simon.

Finally, at 12 p.m. I got a cheery call from him on his mobile.

'So, it turns out the suit needs to be altered! Won't be long, you go on ahead and I'll just see you there.'

'YOU BASTARD! WHY ARE YOU DOING THIS TO ME?'

'Calm down, it'll be fine.'

'What about Peter, he still needs to get changed and his suit is here.'

'He doesn't want to wear the suit. He says he told you that. We've bought a shirt and some trousers for him – hopefully you can just return the suit.'

'But he would look adorable in the suit.'

'He says it's scratchy and he feels stupid in it.'

'FFS! Don't be late. And DON'T let him have energy drinks.'

The suit was lovely. Peter was a vision in it. What did Simon and Peter know about *fashion*?

I finally shooed Jane and Sophie, doing passable impressions of mini-Lolitas, into the car and drove to the wedding, muttering darkly all the while. I couldn't believe I had let a man who didn't even see why Peter should wear a suit to a wedding talk me out of white gloves with my dress.

'Mummy, you shouldn't say you're going to chop Daddy's cock off!' remonstrated Jane.

'Yes, Ellen, he can get that done in a hospital if he doesn't want any more babies!' piped up Sophie. Dear God, I really must have a word with the school about their sex ed programme!

We arrived, I parked, then hustled the fiends inside to sit down. It did look lovely actually. Mrs P wafted through (*wearing white gloves*!) and said, 'Hello, Ellen, darling! Isn't it gorgeous? Hannah has done a wonderful job, though I can't help but think some quirky little touches might have been nice. I suggested wellies full of flowers on the end of each aisle, but she was quite shirty about that, and she was downright rude about my lovely Moroccan-inspired coffee-tin lanterns. Marjorie will be so disappointed. She's been pouring gallons of coffee down the old folks so that I had enough, they're all gasping for a cup of tea. And look! Haven't the children grown. Although … what has happened to Jane's face? And her friend's?'

'Apparently, it's called contouring,' I sighed.

'Oh! I don't think Elizabeth Arden did that in my day. Do you want a gin, darling, the bar's not supposed to be open, but I'm the mother of the bride, so I can sneak you one if you want?'

As there was still no sign of Simon and the wedding was about to start imminently, I agreed that a bijou gin would be very nice.

Shortly afterwards Mrs P surreptitiously handed me a glass and sidled off, announcing that she might just pop a few coffee-tin lanterns along the aisle before Hannah made her entrance.

I felt calmer once I had downed my gin, although there was still no sign of Simon. I sat down with Sam, who looked aghast at the girls' faces.

'I know! I know!' I said. 'What can I say? That's the thing with girls and make-up. They have to make their own mistakes. Why else would Heather Shimmer lipstick have sold so well in the nineties?'

Sam looked unconvinced and whispered, 'Where's Simon? Is everything OK? You haven't had another row, have you?'

'No,' I said. 'We're pretty good, except the *bastard* went to buy a fucking *suit* THIS MORNING and is coming straight here from getting it altered.'

'Who buys a suit on the *morning* of a wedding?'

'I KNOW! Also, he has bought Peter new clothes for the wedding instead of the *lovely suit* I had for him.'

'In fairness, Ellen darling, Peter has been moaning about that suit since you bought it. You've just been ignoring him. Toby wouldn't be seen dead in a suit either!' Sam gestured to his son, who was looking rather stylish in a shirt and chinos.

Just as I was starting to get very twitchy and was about to send a furious text to Simon, he finally sauntered in, looking, it has to be said, rather good in the new suit (as he bloody well should after all that). I had been very worried about what sort of outfit he would have deemed suitable for Peter, but he was clad in a similar shirt and trousers to Toby and was rather dapper, if with a slightly maniacal look in his eye, which suggested that Simon had not heeded my frequent warnings about the dangers of energy drinks and Peter.

'I told you I'd be in plenty of time, darling,' smirked Simon. 'You always worry too much. You need to learn to let go and trust me!'

Whether he was right or not, I was loath to admit it, but Simon was spared my reply anyway because the music started and Hannah came in. Hannah was glowing – far more stunning than on her first wedding day, though her eyes narrowed when she saw Mrs P's coffee-tin lanterns dotted up the aisle.

The ceremony was beautiful, and Charlie and Hannah were literally the most in-love people I have ever seen. There was a brief hold-up when it was time for me to do my reading and I realised sitting in the middle of a row had been a bad idea. I had to clamber over Simon, Peter, Jane and Sophie to get out, but I managed not to say 'Fuck' while doing so.

Afterwards, there was champagne and photos and a small row between Hannah and Mrs P about the lanterns, and also the fact Mrs P had sneaked her gin-bottle candelabras onto the tables, but mostly it was all divine.

Later there was dancing. I waltzed dreamily round the floor with Simon. 'We danced to this at our wedding …' I whispered romantically.

'Did we?' said Simon in surprise.

'Simon!'

'Of course I remember!' he said.

'Do you really remember, or are you just pretending to remember because you're hoping to get lucky tonight?' I asked suspiciously.

'What do you think?' said Simon, twinkling at me wickedly.

'I think that you are very annoying.'

'But that's why you love me, darling!'

'You're lucky that I do.'

'I am. And you're lucky that I love you!'

'I suppose so,' I admitted grudgingly.

In the end, I suppose that's what a marriage comes down to – finding the one special person you want to annoy and be annoyed by for the rest of your life.

Thursday, 20 July

It was Jane's 'graduation' day from primary school today.

Simon, without being nagged, reminded, threatened or shouted at, had booked the day off to come with me to it. Both Simon and Jane regarded me with some anxiety on this morning.

'Daddy, you won't let her make a complete scene and cry everywhere, will you?' pleaded Jane.

'Why would I do that?' I protested. 'I didn't cry when you started school, why on earth would I cry now?'

'Apparently all the mums cry at it, but that's no reason for Mummy to cry. I don't want her to embarrass me, just because all the other mums are being silly!' insisted Jane.

'Jane, if Mummy cries it is only because she loves you,' said Sara kindly (I bet Juliette wouldn't have been so diplomatic).

Jane made an unattractive noise in response to Sara.

'Of course she will cry!' snorted Peter. 'Mummy cries at everything. She can't even read or watch *Charlotte's Web* because she gets into such a state. She is *sooooo* going to embarrass you today.'

'Peter, enough!' I snapped. 'This is Jane's big day. Please don't wind her up.'

'It'll be your turn soon enough, Bumface! Then we'll see how funny you think Mummy's crying is,' Jane spat at Peter, before beseeching Simon to make sure I behaved myself.

Sara had requested to come with us, and we all met Sam outside, who said, 'Don't worry, Ellen, I've got plenty of tissues for you,' before we went in and took our seats, at the back, obviously, for we know our place, and Perfect Lucy Atkinson's Mummy and Fiona Montague had been camping outside the door since May to ensure they and their husbands got front-row seats. They were huffing and puffing with outrage that they had been told to put their giant cameras away, as the school would be issuing an official photograph of each child. Sleazy Julian was particularly incensed by this, spluttering that he was a *professional* photographer, and as such should be exempted from the ban, while the headmistress firmly told him to go and sit down. I have a horrible feeling Julian probably rather enjoyed the headmistress ticking him off.

The graduation was lovely. The children all looked so grown up going up to shake the headmistress's hand and get another certificate. (So many certificates – I have literally dozens of certificates from the school, they are very keen on certificates, and I'm never sure which ones I'm supposed to keep and which can be binned, and I've always been afraid to ask anyone in case they judge me. I'm pretty sure we are meant to keep this one, though.)

Although the rational part of my mind knew it had been seven extremely long years of arguments about the right way to do long division, of inane reading books and competitive 'projects' involving building Viking longships and Roman forts, I found myself quite overcome with emotion as I sobbed hopelessly into a very inadequate tissue, while Sam pressed a large, clean ManSize tissue on me, because it really didn't seem like any time at all since all those big girls and boys up there on the stage had been tiny little tots in too-big blazers on their first day of school, looking far too small and vulnerable to possibly be old enough to go to Big School.

And now, just as I'm finally getting to grips with primary school, Jane is done with it, finished, and off to Proper Big School in a few weeks, where they will probably look tiny and small and vulnerable in their too-big blazers all over again, as they face all the challenges of secondary school. How will Jane cope? How will *I* cope?

I wish someone had told me when my children were babies that none of those things I spent so much time worrying about – the right purees, the right educational toys, the right sleeping bag and night light and blankets, too much tummy time, not enough tummy time, overstimulation, understimulation – that none of that really matters. All you can do is your best, and love them and hope they turn out all right. I may have sobbed this snottily into Simon's shoulder as he hissed at me to get a grip on myself, and Jane glared in horror from the stage. I also wished I'd had the foresight to wear waterproof mascara, like Fiona Montague and Perfect Lucy Atkinson's Mummy had.

Jane was unimpressed with me afterwards. 'I told you not to cry!' she said indignantly.

'But darling, all the mummies cried!' I protested. 'And Sara cried too!' (though Sara's crying was considerably prettier and less snotty than mine – she just sniffed something about '*Bella bambina*' while I howled).

'If all the mummies jumped off a cliff, would you jump off too?' said Jane loftily, and annoyingly, for that is my usual argument to all her insistences that EVERYONE else is doing/ getting/allowed something. 'Exactly. And your mascara has run! Honestly, Mummy, if you didn't cry when I started school, why are you crying now?'

'I don't know. It's the end of an era, I suppose. The start of a new chapter.'

'OMG, you are *sooooooo* embarrassing. Can we get fish and chips for tea?'

'Yes.'

'And can I get an Instagram account to celebrate me being grown-up and my new chapter?'

'No.'

'You're so unfair!'

'I know.'

'I hate you!'

'I know.'

'You're ruining my life!'

'I'm your mother, that's my job.'

'Can we get ice cream too?'

'Oh, all right.'

ACKNOWLEDGEMENTS

As ever, this book has been a team effort, and there are an enormous number of people who need thanks. Just a few of them are everyone at HarperCollins, but especially Katya Shipster, Polly Osborn, Jasmine Gordon, Jenny Hutton, Tom Dunstan, Anna Derkacz, Alice Gomer and the whole sales team. My long suffering agent, Paul Baker at Headway Talent also deserves huge thanks, mainly for putting up with me. A special thanks to Kearan Ramful and the team too. Carly P, thank you for the guidance on all things vet-related, and for answering my many random questions – any inaccuracies about veterinary procedures are entirely due to me, and not to Carly's sterling advice. And Grace Cheetham always and forever has my eternal thanks for taking that first punt on me.

Alison, Eileen, Linda, Lynn, Mairi and Tanya – for all the gin, Rioja, FIAFs and sanity you provided through the writing of this book – thank you! And thank you to the Dahlings, past and present also, for your unwavering support and belief in me. And thanks too, to all the Saddell Survivors, but especially Gav, for the elephants at Culloden – a moment too hilarious and surreal to incorporate into a book, however much I try.

Ellie, Aaron, Callum and Alice – thank you for the Café Patron, for reminding me that Café Patron is a bad idea, for the playing of the Killers on repeat, for the lifts home, and for all the laughs.

Finally, my family. My husband was nicknamed 'The Dream Crusher' many years ago, due to his unreasonable refusal to allow me to stake everything we owned on a particularly ramshackle (but picturesque) hovel, but in the one dream that really counted, he backed me to the hilt. Thank you, Dream Crusher. And my moppets – I fear you are slightly neglected when I'm trying to finish a book, so thank you for understanding and FYI I don't love Judgy Dog *more* than you, I just love him differently. Last, but most certainly not least, enormous thanks are due to my parents-in-law, who fed and watered my children while I wrote, sobbed and gnawed my fingers to the bone and I am forever grateful for everything you do for us.

If your Precious Moppets have driven you to drink, swear, or indeed both...

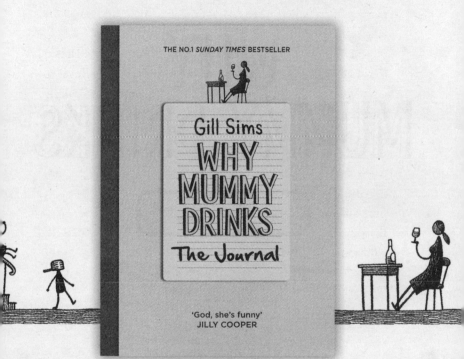

This journal probably won't make you a better, richer or thinner person, but hopefully will make you realise there is NOTHING WRONG with your life as it is, whether or not you're creating #happymemories...

Oh, and there's a drink recommendation at the end of each month... cheers to that!

Now you know
Why Mummy Swears...

Find out why her Precious Moppets
drive her to drink!

WHY MUMMY DRINKS

OUT NOW!

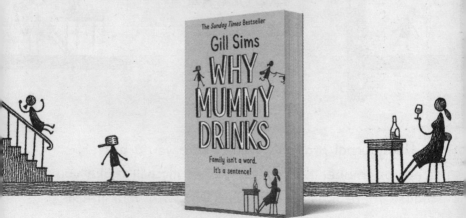

Keep up-to-date with Gill here:

#WhyMummyDrinks

🐦 @whymummydrinks   f @peterandjaneandmummytoo